WHEN
KINGDOM
COMES

WHEN KINGDOM COMES

D. S. CHURCHILL

Light Messages
Torchflame Books

Durham, NC

Copyright © 2022 D. S. Churchilll

When Kingdom Comes
D. S. Churchill
dschurchill1@outlook.com

Published 2022, by Torchflame Books
an Imprint of Light Messages Publishing
www.lightmessages.com
Durham, NC 27713 USA
SAN: 920-9298

Paperback ISBN: 978-1-61153-452-8
E-book ISBN: 978-1-61153-453-5
Library of Congress Control Number: 2022901624

For my sister,
my best friend.

WHEN KINGDOM COMES

Abright, white moon sat high in a black sky littered with silver stars. The clear, cloudless night went unnoticed due to the piercing grief of those down below, where flames from a massive funeral pyre sent shadows flickering into the darkness.

Elora had never known grief such as this. She watched the fire lick the white linen that she herself had wrapped around her parents' bodies. Tears fell in hot streams down her face. Her sun-streaked blonde hair was matted with gore and blood from the battle earlier that day—the battle that had killed her mother and father. The king and queen were dead, leaving her alone to rule, to lead her army, to persevere in the godless war that had raged on for eight long and bloody years.

Elora paid little attention to the wails of despair around her. Her people mourned the loss of her parents—the loss of the rulers who had defended and protected them.

Rian stood beside her and wrapped an arm around her shoulders. Leaning against him for support, she closed her eyes and pictured her parents' smiling faces, then startled when an image of Kristofer flashed through her mind. With a shaking hand, she wiped her face as Rian tightened his grip on her.

She cast him a glance. His eyes, so dark blue that they looked almost black, stared at her with concern from underneath long, black lashes. With a single nod, she acknowledged him and felt him tug her away from the towering flames. The next thing she knew, she was sitting on a high-backed chair in her tent, with no recollection of having walked there. Rian stood nearby, tall and dark, almost menacing. She watched him pinch the bridge of his nose between his thumb and forefinger, as was his way when he was troubled.

The flap to the tent flew open and Abignale walked in. His black robes billowed behind him, and his long, silver beard was tucked into the black belt around his waist. She felt him place a warm hand on her shoulder, and instantly felt comforted.

Abignale was old and wise, having seen more winters than even he could count. His ability to heal was renowned, and before the war, people had traveled from all four territories to seek out his medicines.

"Your brother's army has dealt us a devastating blow," Abignale said in a gentle tone. "Still, we are here, under the crest of these mountains. We are safe, and we will rise above this, Elora." He leaned down so only she could hear. "Be strong."

With a glance at Rian, he exited the tent.

Your brother's army...

The words lingered in her head.

"You are covered in blood, Elora."

Rian's deep voice startled her out of her dark thoughts, and she glanced at her hands, holding them up as if to see if he was telling the truth.

When she looked up again, Rian was gone, replaced by two handmaids who helped her climb into the tub of warm water that had been brought. She rinsed the blood and the dirt from her limbs. A clean white nightdress was laid out on the bed, and she dismissed the women with a wave of her hand.

Donning the white cotton, she sat on the edge of her bed. Rian came in again and eased her back against the pillow. He laid down beside her and pulled her into his arms.

"Sleep," he murmured. "Tomorrow is a new day."

She laid her head on his chest, and the steady rhythm of his heart beat lulled her into a restless sleep.

CHAPTER 1

E lora stood by the training fields, watching Rian as he trained with his men. The overcast skies added gloom to the day, and the lack of sun created a chill in the air that no one seemed to notice. Bare-chested and splattered with mud, Rian flung his arm out, hitting his general square in the chest, knocking him down. Breggen's usually blond hair and matching beard was brown with mud. Laughing, Rian reached down and pulled his general to his feet.

"One day, Lord, I will best you!" Breggen said, breathlessly.

Rian chuckled at this. "I look forward to the day." He ran an arm across his forehead, trying to clear the sweat and grime from his handsome face. "Is there no other?" he asked loudly.

Amused, Elora stepped forward. Sparring was something they had always done together, ever since her parents died and she had taken control of the Northern Army. The Westerners and the Northerners lived side-by-side, harmoniously, and while she and Rian were not joined by marriage, they ruled the two groups together, peacefully.

She smiled at Rian as she walked toward him wearing leather leggings and a black tunic that hung to her thighs. The black against the contrast of her light hair and fair skin added a titillating air around her that Rian always noticed.

"Me," she replied.

A loud cheer rang up from the crowd of men that came to watch.

Rian raised a dark brow in response, inclining his head. "Always an honor."

"Aye." She nodded. "That, it is."

Elora stood in front of him, barely reaching his chest. Although he was lethal in battle, she did not know anyone as kind or considerate as Rian. The people loved him, and once his home was restored from the clutches of the South, Elora had no doubt that his reign as king would be undiminished.

"What's it to be?" Rian said.

"The sticks. And I know you would not let me win so easily this time," Elora said, with an accusing gleam in her eye.

She often wondered if Rian held back when they fought.

Rian smiled. "I would do no such thing."

Although fully capable of handling herself in battle, Rian abhorred the thought of hurting her. Equally accomplished with a sword, both Elora and Rian practiced together often. He had height and strength on his side, but she was lighter and quicker. Often, their sparring brought forth an eager crowd of men, women, and children who enjoyed watching.

Bowing, a man with a long beard came forth with two thick sticks crudely shaped like swords and handed one to Elora and one to Rian. They took their stance, facing each other. Rian was the first to move. He brought his sword down hard, and she sidestepped quickly to avoid having to block the blow. Elora knew his height and strength were against her. She would tire much more quickly if she had to block all of his advances.

The mud was thick, it was hard to maneuver quickly. She lashed out, both hands on the pommel of her makeshift sword, but Rian expected this and defended himself with ease. The familiarity of fighting one another came from year after year of daily sparring.

Before long, Elora was filthy, and as usual, neither could best the other.

Panting, Elora paused and watched Rian, who stood statuesque in the morning light. A gentle rain was beginning to fall, which only added to the amount of muck surrounding them. Glancing at the crowd, Rian saw Abignale standing next to a group of children. His long silver beard hid the amused look on his ancient face as he watched the two duel. The black robe he wore was clean, free of mud and debris.

Rian returned his attention back to Elora. "We are at a standstill."

"Aye." Elora gripped her sword in her right hand.

Before he could blink, Elora raised her sword and attacked. Rian blocked her with ease, but his quick movement and the slick ground caused him to slip. Before he could right himself, Elora brought her sword to his throat.

"If I were your enemy, your head would be a foot from your body."

"In that case, I'm glad we're on the same side," Rian replied, his voice low.

Elora's smile faltered, and she withdrew her sword as Breggen came running over, laughing.

Tearing his gaze away from Elora, Rian accepted Breggen's outstretched hand.

"I believe you seem a little too exuberant at my misfortune."

Breggen's smile only widened. "How is it, Lord, that I cannot bring you down," he looked at Elora with admiration, "but you, my queen, can?"

Rian's deep laugh reverberated throughout Elora, and his good humor made her smile.

"It's all about footing, Breggen," she said. "Perhaps—"

"It was ill-luck," Rian said. "The weather conditions were against me."

Breggen and Elora exchanged a look.

"Of course, Lord," she said with feigned agreeability. "This has been most convivial." She smiled. "However, I take my leave."

Rian scanned Elora's face, surmising the apprehension and hesitancy she so carefully tried to conceal.

He nodded. "Aye. I'll escort you to your tent. Breggen, continue. Make a game of it. Training to die seems less daunting with laughter involved."

His comment sobered Breggen, who bowed before returning his attention to the soldiers around him.

Rian knew it was no game. He knew that Breggen understood the hardship they were under, and that he considered the well-being of the men to be above all else.

Rian and Elora walked side by side, away from the training fields. Rows of tan tents surrounded them. The women were starting small fires to feed hungry little mouths, while the men chopped wood.

Elora, seeming troubled, caught Rian's attention.

"What ails you?" he said.

Pausing in her tracks, Elora looked up to meet his gaze.

"Were it not me you were fighting against, you would be dead." Her brows were creased together with anxiousness.

Surprised at her response, Rian raised a dark brow. "Elora, my reflexes are not so dampened that I could not block that blow. I knew it was coming."

Her mouth fell open in shock, and with it, her accusation. "You do let me win!"

His answering grin knocked all traces of trepidation from her face.

"I suppose you would not have your reputation for being the most accomplished swordsman in the nation, otherwise," she said.

Making no response, for none was needed, Rian fell into step beside her. They passed the horse pen, and Elora could not resist reaching out to stroke a mare's nose. Upon seeing her, a large white horse came over looking for a treat he knew she often carried.

"I have nothing for you!" Elora cried, but she hugged the horse.

It was her father's, and a fine war stallion. She remembered when her father brought him home, as a colt. They had admired him together on the beach.

Rian watched her, knowing where her thoughts headed, and gently placed a hand on her arm, drawing her out of her memories. Elora pulled her arm out of his grip and walked hastily toward her tent, eager to put some distance between herself and Rian.

Sighing, Rian watched her go before turning and heading toward his own tent. The rain was beginning to fall harder, and upon spotting Eret, he ordered a bath brought. The servants, those loyal enough to stay, came quickly and filled the wooden tub with hot water. Rian watched the two men as they hastened to accommodate their king. He knew that they, like himself, had lost much in the war. Many had deserted from fear or grief. But those that didn't, those that fought back, they were worthy of respect.

Rian stood by the flap of his tent as the servants bowed and left. His tent, though scarcely furnished, was home and he was comfortable with it. He saw no point in dwelling on the past. The feather bed was large and comfortable, and the red and gold furs that covered the mattress added warmth and color to the room. At the foot of the bed sat a wooden trunk that held all of his possessions. A few feet away, in the center of the tent was a small table with two wooden chairs. The trunk often substituted as a third seat when Elora and Abignale would frequent his tent.

Rian peeled off his muddy clothes and eased himself into the hot water, his thoughts on Elora. A marriage alliance between the two had been brought to light more than once, but Elora would hear none of it. Even Abignale cautiously broached the subject, but she made her excuses and escaped the confinement of the conversation before more could be said.

Pushing the matter from his mind, Rian scrubbed the mud from his body and stood up, reaching for clean clothes. After putting on a pair of black leggings, he sat on the edge of his bed.

Spring was here. The long, harsh winter was behind them, and it was time to make a move. There had been no attack since the cold season started, and Rian knew it was only a matter of time now. He would bring the matter up with Elora at the next opportune moment.

Moving the entire camp would be an arduous task. The women and children would slow them down greatly. As would the livestock. It would leave them vulnerable and open for attack. He contemplated this idea for a long while, until a knock sounded on the post outside his tent.

"Enter."

Elora came first, holding a folded piece of parchment, followed closely by Abignale. Rian stood, and Elora wordlessly handed him the letter. It was an update from their spies that patrolled the South-Eastern borders, King Rake's territory. The letter was vague, stating only that Kayne was assembling his army. It meant that an attack was imminent, which Rian already knew.

He glanced up, realizing the moment he had been waiting for was upon him. He gestured to the chairs at the table, and

Elora and Abignale sat while he re-read the letter. This gave Elora the opportunity to study him while his attention was focused elsewhere.

He was bare from the waist up, which was nothing Elora hadn't seen countless times before. Living in such close quarters left little room for privacy. A marriage alliance would strengthen the armies, if the armies were not already joined. The only thing it would strengthen now would be morale.

Of course, it would permanently join their two nations, but it would leave her to rule under the presence of a man. A king would always have more power. Have the final say. As a married queen, each decision would have to be vindicated by her king, and Elora was not ready to give up that power.

Rian cleared his throat, jerking Elora from her thoughts.

"I see only one course of action to take," he said.

Abignale watched Rian sit on the trunk at the foot of his bed, and Abignale nodded for him to continue.

"We are stationary now. This area has provided us well during the winter, but this North-Western atmosphere is no longer safe. I think we should leave. It has been on my mind for some time now, that we should seek sanctuary within the Eastern borders."

"I, too, have thought this," Elora said. "But moving all of these people would be dangerous. Nor do we know if Rake would even allow two armies within his territory. Also, the South could view the merging of three territories as a hostility, and we do not need the Southern Army marching upon us right now."

"It would be considerably more dangerous to stay," Rian said. "We are surrounded by mountains on three sides. If Kayne's army attacks from the river, we are boxed in. And if Kristofer himself should come..." He kept his eyes on Elora's face, watching her grimace at the mention of her brother.

"He is right, Elora," Abignale said.

She nodded. "I do not dispute this. We can send a letter to Rake. Once we receive his reply we'll at least have a destination. We can begin preparing for the journey, but should he refuse us, what then?"

"He will not refuse," Abignale said. "Kayne's army grows by the day. They are taking over everything. The North and the West are already under Kristofer's control. It is only a matter of time before he sets his sight on the East. Rake's walls may hold for now, but two more armies within his borders would greatly strengthen his territory. Furthermore, his castle is well-protected. We will no doubt lose people on this journey, but we will lose far more if we stay."

Dreading the prospect of losing even one person, Elora sighed, but she knew Rian and Abignale were right. Should Kristofer lead an army to attack them, she doubted even Rian would be able to hold his own against her brother.

She nodded her acquiescence. "We will prepare a letter asking Rake for sanctuary. And in return, we shall combine our armies. It is the only suitable prospect."

Relieved, Rian nodded. "A large hunting party went out this morning, led by Brilor and Ayden. When they return, we will talk to them about assembling the men."

Brilor was Elora's general. And before that, he was her father's general. He and Ayden were brothers and excellent soldiers. With the two of them gone at the same time, the large group assembled to bring back meat left the camp weakened. A fact not lost upon Rian.

It wasn't the journey he dreaded, but the feeling deep down that something bad was going to happen. He felt it in his bones.

CHAPTER 2

I t had been four weeks since Elora sent a messenger with a sealed letter to the Eastern territory. She knew it would be at least another few weeks before a reply was received.

Stepping out of her tent, she raised her face to greet the warmth of the sun. There were buds on the trees, and the land was turning green once again. The winter had been long and brutal. There was barely enough food to go around, but they had survived it with minimal grievances.

Staring up at the cloudless sky, she threw a thankful prayer to the heavens for getting them through the winter.

"It's a magnificent day, is it not?"

Rian's voice cut through the air, and she returned his question with a smile.

"Aye. I'm eager for the warmth of summer."

Rian stood close, and she felt the familiar fluttering in her stomach. The sensation instantly brought her hand to her belly, and she frowned, confused and uneasy.

Rian sensed her discomfort, but was unsure of what caused it. He feared it was he who made her uncomfortable, but he could not understand why. They had known each other since they were children. He and Kristofer were the closest of friends growing up, often playing pranks on Elora, as she was the youngest.

Rian was uncertain whether it was he or Elora who had been more debilitated by the blow of Kristofer's betrayal. So many years later, it was still a sore subject, and one rarely talked about.

Elora opened her eyes to see Rian watching her carefully.

"Rian, forgive me. My thoughts are elsewhere."

She took a step away from him and saw a muscle twitch in his jaw.

"What is it about me that causes you to feel this way?"

His frustrated tone startled her, and she stared at him wide-eyed for a moment, before answering.

"It is not you—"

"You lie. I would care to know why I frighten you."

Elora's breathing picked up and she swallowed nervously.

"I believe it is just the impending journey."

"Indeed," Rian muttered.

Baffled, he watched her turn and walk quickly away, with half a mind to go after her. Deciding against it, he turned angrily and headed outside of the camp, seeking some peace that could only be found beside the raging river and towering mountains. Rian walked a quarter-mile outside of the camp and stared at the mountains that surrounded him. He grew up in the mountains and found comfort in being near the massive peaks. The river, fed from a melting glacier, roared beside him.

Leaning against a large boulder, he thought of Elora and her strange behavior. He could not figure it out, and he wasn't certain he wanted to. As he stood there mulling it over, the sound of someone approaching made his hand instinctively go to the pommel of his sword.

"I would not draw that sword unless you wish me to defend myself."

Rian relaxed against the familiarity of Abignale's voice.

"How do you always find me?"

Laughing, Abignale took a seat at the base of the rock Rian was leaning against.

"I went looking for you in camp, and when I could not find you, I figured you came out here to brood."

"I do not brood," Rian said. "I'm merely trying to understand."

"Elora?"

"Her behavior lately unnerves me, and I don't understand the cause of it."

"I should think the cause is quite obvious."

Rian stared down at the old man. "Me? Why, all of a sudden, would I cause her such unease?"

Abignale smiled beneath his beard. "You care for her, do you not?"

Rian narrowed his eyes. "Aye?"

"Elora has..." Abignale took a breath, "misconceptions concerning love."

With his amber eyes, he searched Rian's face.

"If it is Kristofer and her parents you are referring to—"

"Only in part," Abignale said. "A marriage alliance between you and Elora has been whispered around the camp for years. It is the natural ramification of both your stations, and the notion terrifies her. She fears marriage because, overall, your word would overrule hers. And she fears love because she's already lost so much."

Rian listened with mute intensity. "I've never pushed marriage, nor have I even broached the subject."

"Do you not love her?"

Abignale's liquid gold eyes found the answer they were searching for, even before Rian responded.

Rian threw his hands up in frustration. "I've never denied it. She, however, is seemingly uninterested, and I have no wish to push her further away."

"She has not yet realized her affection toward you, but it is there, Rian. All you need to do is bide your time."

Abignale rose to his feet, meeting Rian's furrowed gaze

with an easy smile. He placed a hand on Rian's shoulder and gave a gentle squeeze before turning and heading back to the camp, leaving Rian alone with his thoughts.

It took him hours to sort through his emotions and finally come to peace with Abignale's words and Elora's behavior. To lose one's home, family, and kingdom was debilitating enough. But she had lost everything to Kristofer, the one man she trusted and loved above all else. And once he betrayed her, she lost her parents not long after.

Rian and Elora had both suffered at the hands of the same man. They had both lost their families and their kingdoms to the South, to Kristofer. Would Elora not find solace in their shared losses to the same man? He spent a long time mulling it over in his head.

After finally accepting that he would not fully understand all of it at that moment, Rian followed Abignale's footsteps a while later. By the time he reached his tent, he felt more at ease. Pushing aside the flap, he stepped inside and sat on one of the chairs that surrounded the table, still lost in thought.

The sound of faraway screams brought him quickly from his tent. In the distance, he could see soldiers in red uniforms attacking.

"Rian!"

He turned to find Elora running toward him, sword in hand.

"Elora!"

"They crossed the river in the night. Look out!" she screamed.

Rian raised his sword above his head and blocked a blow aimed at his back. Elora met her enemies' blades with vigor, and they fought side by side, downing two soldiers instantly.

Moving toward the river, Elora and Rian fought each soldier they met. In the distance, Elora saw Abignale dueling three men cloaked in red. He moved quickly and with ease, and the three red soldiers were barely able to lift their swords. In the end, three bodies lay at Abignale's feet.

After grabbing an arrow out of the quiver on her back, Elora took aim and killed an enemy before he set fire to a tent. Chaos surrounded her. The sounds of her dying and injured people filled her ears. The entire side of the camp was up in flames. Four soldiers rushed toward her, and she was relieved that Rian was by her side.

Elora and Rian raised their swords, ready to fight, but the soldiers in front of them stopped and lowered their weapons, their gazes locked on something behind her.

Elora wheeled around and gasped. A huge black stallion stood before her, but it wasn't the snorting horse that made her heart pound. Kristofer sat on the beast, tall and proud. His blond hair, the exact same color as hers, whipped across his face. Unlike the red uniforms of his men, Kristofer was cloaked completely in black. His piercing blue eyes bore into hers, and the look of disgust on his face made her cringe. He lifted his gaze from Elora's face to his men, who shrank back instantly.

Elora stood frozen, staring at her brother. Rian's voice beside her brought her back.

"Call off your men, Kristofer," he growled. "This is a slaughter."

Kristofer's deep laugh surrounded them. "This is war. Slaughter is inevitable."

Rian took a step toward Kristofer, who reached for the sword that hung from his shoulder.

Elora grabbed Rian's arm. "You cannot fight him," she whispered.

Kristofer kept his blue eyes fixed on Rian.

"Kristofer...please." Elora rushed forward and grabbed the reigns of his horse. "Please!"

Her brother's face was unreadable as he tore his gaze

from Rian to look upon her. He studied her, taking her in. She met the intensity of his stare with ardor.

"Please?" she whispered so that only he could hear.

The flames burned higher around them, and suddenly the heat became unbearable. Kristofer jerked the reins from her hands and turned his black horse.

"Pull back!" he barked to his men.

Elora watched them ride away, a knot forming in the pit of her stomach.

"He was here for a reason," Rian whispered.

Elora looked around at the devastation. Bodies littered the ground, and the raging inferno had taken down more than half of the tents.

Breggen came running toward them. Relieved, Rian clasped his forearm.

"This attack makes no sense," Breggen said, anguish on his face.

"It makes perfect sense," Abignale said from behind them. "Kristofer was looking for something."

Rian nodded in agreement.

Soot and ash fell in torrents around them, and the stench of burning canvas engulfed them. Most of the tents couldn't be saved, but what could needed attention immediately.

"Breggen, do what you can to control the inferno," Rian said, "but don't jeopardize yourself or any others for a few trivial belongings. Afterward, assemble a group of men to collect the bodies. It is still early. We can have a proper funeral this evening. Bring the injured to Abignale. I don't believe the soldiers will be back, but keep your eyes open and your attention sharp."

Nodding, Breggen bowed, then rushed off.

Elora glanced at Rian. His right hand was pressed against the left side of his stomach, and his breathing was labored. She reached forward and pulled his tunic aside. Blood seeped from a large, jagged gash on his side.

Elora gasped. "How did you fight with this?"

Rian raised a dark brow in response while Abignale inspected his wound.

"You will need stitches. Elora, I imagine you can handle this. Take him to your tent I'll send someone with supplies. Go, quickly. The last thing these people need right now is to see their king fall."

Abignale turned and hurried toward his tent. His trunks were loaded with every medicinal herb one could think of, from medicines to ease pain, to teas that caused hallucinations.

"Can you walk?" Elora said.

Rian nodded, and Elora placed a hand on his arm, guiding him to her tent. The tents further from the river did not burn, and for that Elora was grateful.

Reaching the entrance to her tent, she pushed aside the opening flap.

"Take your shirt off and lay down."

Elora walked over to the large hearth at the opposite end of her tent to stoke the red coals and add a few more pieces of wood. Her father had taught the people how to build safe fireplaces for the winter. He used stones and sealed them with mud, and it was done in such a manner that the stones went above the tent to let out the smoke. The fireplaces had to be built carefully, but it was the only means of surviving the long, harsh winters.

"Lady?" A maid stood at the entranceway.

On top of the pile, wrapped in parchment, were clean cloths, a vial of green herbs, a slightly curved needle, and horsetail thread which Abignale had boiled already. In her other arm she carried a large wooden bucket filled with clean water.

"Set everything on the table." Elora returned her attention

to the now blazing fire.

"Will ye be needing anything else, Lady?" The young woman wrung her hands together, completely traumatized over the events of the day.

Elora smiled and shook her head. The maid curtsied quickly and left.

After taking the water off the table, Elora poured it into the iron pot and set it over the flames. She turned and found Rian still standing.

"Lay down!" She reached up to help him out of his shirt.

"Did you see the blades they were fighting with?" he said.

"Aye, they were serrated. I've never seen the likes of them before."

Rian laid down gingerly. "Imagine the damage those swords will cause."

The pain from his wound was unlike anything he'd ever experienced, and the jagged edges of the cut would make stitching it harder.

Nodding, Elora examined his side. "How did this happen?"

"Kristofer's general. He came at me while I was fighting two other soldiers."

Elora brought the pot of boiling water over and set it down next to the bed. After dipping a clean cloth in it, she held it by the tip and waited for it to cool before cleaning the blood off of him. Aside from his labored breathing, Rian made no other indication that he was hurt.

Elora threaded the needle and began stitching the wound closed. Rian made a sharp sound and she cast him a sympathetic look.

"Kristofer's general? The man with the scars?" Elora said, trying to keep Rian's mind off the pain.

She knew perfectly well who Kristofer's general was. A horrible man with burn scars on his face. He was tall and strong, and he killed without remorse. Dagr, she believed his name was. He was incredible with a sword, and lethal in every sense of the word. Although she was sad to admit it, her brother was worse.

Rian grimaced as the needle went in again.

"Aye," he breathed, his voice weak.

Elora paused and reached for a cup of wine that she had poured while the water was boiling.

"Drink. It'll help with the pain."

But, as she knew he would, Rian shook his head. He hated wine, for it dulled his senses.

"A little." She raised the drink to his lips.

Much to her surprise, he leaned forward and took several gulps before pushing the cup away. *The wound must be agonizing.*

While waiting a few minutes for the wine to take effect, Elora gently squeezed Rian's hand. She felt his grip tighten slightly, but he didn't look at her, and she knew all he was seeing was Kristofer.

Biting her lip, Elora picked up the needle and finished sewing the wound. She took the vial of herbs, mixed some with hot water to form a paste, and covered Rian's side in it. After tearing the white cloth into strips, she wrapped the linen around his waist. That being done, she leaned back on her heels and stared at his face. Sweat dotted his brow. Elora dipped another cloth in the water and patted his forehead. He shot her a grateful look.

Worried, and curious about what he was thinking, Elora said, "You are so distracted."

"I'm concerned. What was Kristofer looking for?"

It took Elora a long moment to answer.

"I do not know. But we can rest assured that he has found it."

CHAPTER 3

K ristofer stood at the edge of the woods. One long leg rested on a large stump while he surveyed his small, handpicked group of men. Each soldier, he'd chose specifically for this task—trained killers with no conscience, and every one of them answered to him.

"Lord?" A stocky, red-haired man came from the trees and walked over to Kristofer.

He waited to be addressed, but when there was no answer, he continued anyway.

"There is a congregation moving in from the East."

This caught Kristofer's attention. "Rake's men?"

Swallowing, the man nodded.

"Gaius, take a couple men and find out what Rake wants. Do not attack, and do not make your presence known."

Pleased at being given such a task, Gaius bowed low and turned.

Curling his lip at the man's back, Kristofer took out a long metal instrument, one of Kayne's inventions. It allowed the user to see miles away as if there was no distance in between.

Out of everything Kayne had invented, this was Kristofer's favorite. It was also one of the more pleasant instruments that had been placed in his hands.

Walking through the woods, he clutched the Seer, searching for a spot where he'd be able to see the marching army clearly. Kayne had been extremely specific with his orders. He didn't tell Kristofer what he wanted with Elora, only that he was to bring her to him.

Elora has caused Kayne his fair share of strife. She was an excellent fighter, but Kristofer suspected there was something more. Elora was the only woman within the four territories to lead her own army. And it seemed that men, women, and children came from all over to join her cause.

Kristofer's army had already taken over the West and the North, and he had every intention of invading the East. He suspected that was why Rake and his men were heading toward Elora's camp.

Kayne's thirst for blood was widely known, as were his brutal, merciless tactics. More than once, Kristofer wondered if Kayne was even human.

If the stories were true, Kayne would have to be older than Kristofer's grandfather, but he didn't look any older than Kristofer at twenty-six.

Holding the Seer up to his eye, Kristofer watched a congregation of men in green uniforms march up to the eastern side of Elora's camp. The color confirmed Kristofer's suspicions.

Deciding to keep watch for a while, he leaned against a large rock and made himself comfortable. It was going to be a long few weeks, and he didn't relish the thought of spending any more time with his men than he had to.

CHAPTER 4

E lora, Rian, Rake, and Abignale sat around a large table in Abignale's tent. Rake and his men had been with them for two weeks now, working out the finer details of moving the two armies across the territories.

"By my estimate," Rake said, "it will take more than two weeks, if all haste is made, to journey across the land as a single rider. With a mass behind you, it could take two months. By the time you reach my borders...your people will be safe, but the risk..."

He stood, fingering the tip of his dark goatee. His dark-brown eyes were shrewd but he was known as a just and fair man, although his temper often got the better of him. He stood several inches shorter than Rian, but his coloring was almost as dark. Although, he now had a touch of gray at the temples. He had a long, straight nose, high cheek bones, and his dark hair was shoulder-length. On his head rested a crown that rose to golden peaks.

"There is always a risk," Rian replied. "After Kristofer's attack, the morale in this camp is low. I believe these people are eager to get out. They view this area as a cemetery, and that alone will encourage speed. Rake, you and your men are heading out tomorrow. We can make an announcement tonight and begin the journey before the week is over."

"How will you make the journey, Rian? Your wound is slow to heal, and that will impede your riding."

Rian locked his gaze on Rake's. "It will not be as big of an issue as you think. Another week to mend will make a big difference, and the nature of this journey won't be as hasty as we would like. Even if an effort is put in to speed along the process, we won't move more than four, maybe five, leagues in a day. It is easily manageable."

Elora cast Rian a worried look. His wound was slow to heal, as were all the injuries inflicted by the serrated blades. Abignale told them that the jagged edges of the swords did more damage to the flesh than a regular blade. These wounds were extremely painful, too.

Elora took a deep breath and leaned forward. "If we stay here much longer, I fear Kristofer and his men will come back. We cannot handle another attack, even with Brilor and Ayden back. Too many lives have been lost. Our people know change is coming, and they've already begun preparing. Let us announce tonight. I agree with Rian. I think it's for the best."

Rake nodded. "As you wish, Elora."

Rian stood slowly, followed by Elora and Abignale. Rake swept from the tent, his red mantle billowing behind him.

"At least a plan has been set," Abignale said. "Now comes the hard part." He scanned Elora with his twinkling blue eyes. "I take my leave."

She inclined her head, but Abignale had already turned.

"For a moment, I thought Rake would refuse us," Rian said. "I think his relationship with your father is what inevitably tipped the scales."

"Perhaps you're right. But the constant attacks from the South have depleted his resources. Either way, he accepted our proposal. All I'm worried about is ensuring that these people have a safe place to go."

"Rake's people will open their homes," Rian said. "Most of our people are farmers. That alone will contribute much.

They know how to work the land. We will be able to provide food, which we know the East needs." He leaned against the center post that held up Abignale's tent. "It's also been on my mind to provide some type of festivity before we leave."

Elora sat down and watched Rian. His movements were ginger, and when he pulled out a chair to take a seat beside her, she saw him grimace.

"I fear Rake was right about your wound, Rian."

"I will not let my people suffer because I was too slow in raising my sword."

Elora raised a brow at his frustrated tone. "I'm surprised his blade touched you at all. I've never known you once to be wounded."

She stood, and without warning, pulled Rian's shirt aside. He made no move to stop her while she bent down to examine his side. The cut was healing, and perhaps he was right—another week might easily provide enough time for him to be able to ride. She knew he would do it either way.

"What kind of festivity are you referring to?" Elora's fingers grazed his skin as she pulled his shirt closed.

"We will not be able to bring a lot of the livestock that survived that last battle. A night or two before we depart, I think we should provide a feast. It'll solve the problem of what to do with the animals, and it'll give these people something to look forward to. Many of the women were left widows, and they grieve. Let them put their minds to something other than what they've lost."

Elora thought for a moment. "I think it is a good idea. We can announce that tonight also."

Rian smiled weakly at her. She felt a flutter in her stomach again and turned away. Before she was out of reach, Rian lashed his hand out and grabbed her arm. She stared at him in disbelief, and he noticed the play of emotions across her face, as he had so many times before.

Pulling her closer, Rian stood.

"Let go," she hissed.

But he only tightened his grip and pulled her along the length of him.

"Tell me," he whispered, with one arm wrapped around her waist while the other gripped her chin, forcing her gaze up.

Pushing against his chest, she tried to release his hold.

"What is on your mind?" he said.

Elora's breathing picked up. Rian had never so much as touched her, unless they were training. And to be trapped within the confinement his arms made her uncomfortable.

"Rian, please? Let go."

"Would it be so bad?" he said, in a whisper that sent a shiver down her spine.

Drawing back slightly, he searched her face.

"Marriage is a suitable prospect for us. Why do you detest the idea so much?"

Swallowing her nervousness, Elora pushed against him again, and he released his hold. She stepped back and stared at him before turning and heading toward the opening of the tent.

"We really need to have this conversation, Elora."

Elora spun around. "It is easy for you, Rian! If I marry you, my kingdom, my people, everything becomes yours! I lose my standing. You would rule me and—"

"Rule you? It is a partnership, Elora, not a game for control."

"I don't look at it like that," she hissed. "We rule the territories. Our decisions impact thousands of lives. I want to make my own decisions. I don't want to have to answer to a king."

Rian raised his eyebrows and stared at her for a long while, before sitting back down.

"You think I don't know that?" he said. "Your vision is clouded. You're not thinking clearly. Your parents ruled together peacefully, for years. As did mine."

"Our father's ruled peacefully. Our mothers—"

"Ruled peacefully beside them. This can't possibly be about control. What is it really over? Love?"

"Love?" Elora pushed an errant strand of blonde hair behind her ear and swallowed hard.

This was not a conversation she wanted to have. Nor did she understand why the thought of marriage caused her such anxiety. Rian would make an excellent husband, but he would always have the final word. How could she lay the lives of her people in someone else's hands?

Rian watched her carefully, ready to grab her again should she try to leave.

"I love you, Elora."

Shaking her head, Elora turned, but Rian moved so quickly that she had no time to react. Against the pain from his wound, Rian grabbed her arm and swung her around to face him. Furious, Elora tried to kick him, but he suspected the move and blocked it easily, pushing her backward until she fell onto the bed.

"Easy, Elora. I don't want to fight with you. I just want to talk this through."

Flushed from anger, Elora railed against him, but he pinned her on the bed.

"Get off," she snarled, trying to pull her wrists from his grasp.

"So you can run away before we resolve this? No."

Rian held her with ease until she gave up and stopped fighting. Accepting defeat, Elora turned her head away.

"Let me up. I won't leave."

Pushing himself off of her, Rian stood and folded his arms across his chest.

"You've known me since we were children," he said. "Why do you think I'd exert such control over you?"

Elora pushed herself into a sitting position. Unable to look at him, she kept her gaze fixed on the red furs underneath her.

"Would you not?" she replied. "Would you not overrule my word if you thought there was cause?"

Rian threw his hands up in frustration. "In what scenario, Elora? A concern for your safety? Yes, I would! Would you not step in to protect someone you loved? You are over-examining every detail. It's ridiculous."

"My own brother, Rian...look at the monster he has become. Imagine how he would rule? I would have had no say against him. As I would not with you."

"You dare to compare me to Kristofer?" Rian snarled.

Elora stood and faced him. "I did not mean it like that. I only meant that as a woman, I have no power over the men."

Reeling in his temper, Rian cupped her cheek, his long fingers wrapping around the back of her neck. He leaned forward and brought his lips to hers. Elora felt a warmth grow within her, and she nervously pushed at him. He wrapped his arm around her to bring her even closer.

"There is so much more between us, Elora," he whispered.

She let her head fall back so that she could stare at his face. His midnight hair and dark-blue eyes gave him such an allure that women often threw themselves at him. Elora had seen it herself countless times, but he never accepted their invitations. At least, not that she knew of.

He had a long, straight nose and full lips. He stood a few inches taller than most men, and the slightly darker complexion of his skin suggested that he wasn't from the Northern territory.

"I would never rule you," he said. "We would rule side by side. Together, we would strengthen our territories."

Elora rested her hands on his arms and leaned away. "I cannot."

Rian leaned down to kiss her again, and Elora tensed.

If Kristofer, of all people, could betray her, then anything was possible. Kristofer was her brother, the man she loved most in the world. And if he could leave her, so could Rian.

The thought was unbearable. She would never survive another betrayal. Seeing him so recently brought back the anguish of losing him all over again. She felt her eyes fill as she turned her head from Rian.

Holding her in place with one arm, Rian studied the emotional pools of her eyes. As he lifted a dark brow in concern, his arm tightened in response to what he saw.

"You have to let him go," he said.

It became too much for her. With a choked sob, she buried her face in her hands, and Rian's grip turned comforting. His loosened his hold but pulled her against him where she leaned her head on his chest. He felt the warmth of her tears slide down his skin, and he rubbed her back until she pulled away.

"You speak of love, but I see only loss," she said. "How did you put what he did behind you?"

She raised her head to look up at him. Her chest rose and fell rapidly as she tried to control her breathing.

Rian took a long while to answer. When he finally spoke, his voice was low and filled with anger.

"I did not put it behind me. I've accepted Kristofer's choices, but I hate him, and I hate seeing what he continuously does to you. Or rather, what you allow him to do."

"What do you mean?" Elora said.

"He was here, in this very camp this morning. In arms reach. Look at you now, Elora."

She lowered her head. "I miss him. Terribly."

"I am not without sympathy. Nor without understanding. I, too, think of him and the times together when we were children. But none of that can overcome his betrayal or murdering my family...my brothers."

"I know this," she whispered. "I loved the twins, and I miss them terribly. And yet..."

"You miss Kristofer more."

It was a statement she felt inclined not to respond to. It was obvious that her love for Kristofer was not returned, but still she thought of him daily and pined for the brother she once had.

Rian couldn't understand it. To love the man who had betrayed them—it was incomprehensible. The affection she held toward her bloodthirsty brother bothered him to no end. But every now and then, he, too, thought of Kristofer with something other than animosity.

"I know what you must think of me, Rian, and I wish I did not feel so toward him." She felt Rian shrug, and she looked up at him. "Do you ever think about what might have been had he not—"

"No."

She bit her lip, gaze cast downward, until he lifted her chin.

With a sigh, Rian said, "I don't think about him, because it still hurts..."

Elora looked up with wide eyes. She crossed her arms over herself and stared at him.

"Really?"

Rian gave a single nod.

"I always thought you were...I don't know...just angry..."

"Oh, I am angry, Elora. So angry..."

The sudden contempt in his voice lent some credibility to his statement. Something akin to fear rose upon her features, and Rian frowned.

"I am so afraid of him, Rian," she whispered. "I'm confused because I miss him and I love him still, but I fear him more than anything."

Or did she? Perhaps what she feared the most was that she loved him as much now as she did then.

Rian studied her pale face. The perfect arch of golden brows above light-blue eyes and a straight nose. Her full red lips sent a jolt of desire through him, but he suppressed it and reached to pull her into his arms. Her tension did not go unnoticed, but she did not fight him. Her cheek rested against the course black hair of his chest, her hand clenched to a fist in front of her face.

"I will not let him hurt you, Elora."

"Swear it."

"I give you my word."

He lowered his head and pressed his lips upon hers. She felt warm, but her stomach summersaulted and her nerves became raw. A cocoon of emotion wrapped her within an iron embrace. Thought after thought plagued her mind. Death, betrayal, destruction. And worst of all—loss.

She pulled away. "Please..."

She bit her lip hard, confused and afraid.

Rian pulled back slightly, but his hands remained on her. Elora jerked from his touch and ran from the tent.

CHAPTER 5

E lora paced the length of her tent angrily. It wasn't that she felt nothing for Rian. On the contrary, she felt a great deal. But it was a confusing mix of emotions, and she had no idea how to begin sorting through them. Up until the past few months, when marriage was suggested, she was fine around Rian. It never occurred to her that one day he would be what she was up against.

Tears slid down her cheeks, and she brushed them away. It was absurd to be so frightened by the prospect of marriage that she not only insulted Rian, but ran from him. More than anything, she wished for her mother. This would be the kind of a talk a mother and daughter should have. She missed her parents terribly, but she missed her brother even more.

There was a point when she and Kristofer could've talked about Rian. He would've listened and given excellent advice. He probably would have alleviated her fears. But his betrayal was like an icy blade through her. Still, there were times when her thoughts concerning Kristofer caused her such misery that she would become physically ill.

Wondering if she'd ever be able to put his betrayal behind her, she laid down on her bed and pulled white furs over her for warmth. She closed her eyes as images and thoughts of Kristofer plagued her mind.

Abignale shaking her awake a few hours later made her realize that she had fallen asleep.

"You need to dress. Rian is waiting for you so you both can announce your plans."

Wincing at the sound of Rian's name, Elora stood and moved to the trunk at the foot of her bed. An announcement such as this required finery that Elora no longer possessed, but she would make do with what she had.

After pulling a long red dress out of the trunk, she slipped off her black leggings and tunic, and pulled the dress over her head. Then she reached behind her back and pulled on the strings to tighten the bodice. It was more work than she remembered, and she couldn't quite make it tight enough. Sighing, she closed the lid on her trunk and sat down.

"Elora?" Rian's voice sounded from right outside her tent.

Her gaze darting around, Elora leapt to her feet and took a few steps back just as Rian emerged.

"What is it?" she asked sharply.

"We are waiting. I came to see what was delaying you." Rian crossed his arms over his chest and lifted a brow as he took her in.

He knew their conversation earlier was weighing heavily on her, but he wasn't bothered by it in the slightest. Having taken the entire incident to Abignale, Rian had sought out the old man's advice. He had agreed with Rian, perhaps not with the use of force, but that it was time Elora came to terms with the prospect of love.

Abignale didn't use the word *marriage* when he and Rian spoke. He said that it was love she ran from. The loss of control she felt when her parents died, and when Kristofer left, kept her from wanting to put more control in anyone else's hands. Should she love a man and something terrible happen, Abignale told Rian that Elora didn't think she could handle another loss.

Eventually, she would understand. Abignale's bigger concern, and Rian's too, was what Kristofer was doing so far from home. In the weeks that passed, there hadn't been any more attacks, or even a sighting of the Red Soldiers. And considering the vast expanse of forest on the other side of the river, he had ample space to hide himself and his men. But Rian knew that Kristofer had come for something. Both he and Abignale figured it was Elora, but they had no idea why. And if it was her that Kristofer was after, why hadn't he taken her?

So consumed by his thoughts on his earlier conversation with Abignale, that Rian momentarily forgot why he had come to Elora's tent in the first place. Her voice jolted him back to the present.

"The laces on this dress..." she said, her voice cold, "it appears that I've gotten too used to battle attire."

Undeterred by her tone, Rian strode over to her and swept her long blonde hair across her shoulder. With an expertise Elora didn't care to know about, Rian drew the laces tightly. The task completed, he placed a hand on her waist and turned her around to face him. He wore a clean white tunic, opened at the chest, tucked neatly into black leggings. His black boots came up to his calves, and with his red mantle Elora thought that he looked like a king.

They stared at each other until Rian's handsome face broke out in a grin. Laughing, he turned away.

"What could you possibly think is so amusing?" Elora said.

"It is nothing. Forgive me." He was still smiling. "Come. Everyone is waiting on us."

He held his hand out, and Elora stared at it for a moment. Her heart pounded furiously, and it wasn't the upcoming speech that had her so nervous.

Finally, Elora placed her hand in his. She knew their people would be greatly distressed if they knew a disagreement had gone on between the two of them.

The battle had left many women without their husbands, and the morale of the camp was low. There had been a collective funeral pyre for the bodies, but Elora found it extremely difficult to see her people suffer. For any reason.

Rake came out dressed completely in black except for the red mantle that blew gently behind him. His golden crown reflected the light from the flickering torches as he smiled at Elora and Rian.

"Elora, you are a sight." He leaned down to kiss her forehead.

Rian and Rake gripped each other's forearms. Elora smiled and inclined her head.

"Are we ready?" She looked first at Rake, and then at Rian, who still held her hand tight.

Both men nodded, and they made their way to the front of the crowd. It took a moment for everyone to quiet down. But when they did, Rian addressed them. Elora listened quietly beside him, remembering her father's decision to combine Rian's army with his own, so many years before. She was glad of it. His people became hers, and her people became his. And together, they ruled, trying to give them the best life possible despite the unconventional and trying times.

"My people, after the recent tragic events, and after careful consideration, your queen and I have decided to seek sanctuary within King Rake's borders at the end of the week."

All at once, the people began talking. There were cries of excitement and dismay.

Rian waited until the noise died down before continuing.

"It will be an arduous journey, but we feel it is our only course of action. We cannot stay, offering ourselves up like pigs for slaughter. We must move on. King Rake departs at first light to announce to his territory, and to discuss the accommodations that will be needed. We will be much more apt at defending ourselves there, and combining the three territories will greatly strengthen the armies. Furthermore, the queen and I have decided on a feast to be held in three days' time. I suggest making preparations for such a banquet, starting now."

Rian stepped back and released Elora's hand. She didn't even realize he was still holding her until the absence of his hand made hers feel cold. The crowd of people were dissipating, and Elora glanced at Rian.

"I hope they accept it easily enough," she said.

"They haven't a choice," Rake said. "They know they won't survive if they stay. And we still have no idea where Kristofer and his men have gone?"

"Not a word," Elora said. "Makes me uneasy."

Rake shook his head. "The man is lethal. He makes all of us uneasy."

He still remembered visiting the Northern Kingdom. Elora and Kristofer's father was a close friend, and his death, along with his wife's, was a devastating blow.

An image of Kristofer as the little blond boy who would run around tormenting his beloved younger sister with snakes, flashed through his mind. As the Northern castle sat on a cliff overlooking a vast ocean, there was no end to the critters he would find hidden along the rocks or buried in the sand. The thought almost brought a smile to Rake's face.

Several times a year, the kings would meet, alternating territories. Rake, and Rian and Elora's fathers, and Thanos, who was king of the South before Kayne killed him, would congregate. And through these meetings, Rake came to know the children, and he loved them dearly. His gaze came to rest on Elora's face, and he watched her internal struggle. Her fear and unhappiness tugged at him.

Feeling Rake's attention on her, Elora smiled and tried pushing her brother from her mind as she followed Rake and Rian to Rake's tent. Food had already been placed on the table, and the wine had been poured into three goblets. Rake held out a chair for Elora, and he and Rian sat down on either side of her.

The meal consisted of roasted duck in an apple sauce, potatoes with onions, carrots with cream, and bread. Elora picked at her food, her mind still on her brother.

"Elora!"

Rake's voice jerked her from her thoughts. She looked up to find both men staring at her.

"What?" she said, wide-eyed.

Realizing they had said her name more than once, she flushed with embarrassment.

"Forgive me. I…"

"Are you not well?" Rake said.

"I am quite well. My thoughts were on Kristofer. I apologize."

"My thoughts, too, have been on your brother," Rake said. "I was remembering when he would chase you with those snakes he'd always find."

She laughed, and even Rian smiled.

"I believe he had quite a bit of help." Elora glanced at Rian.

Rian flashed her a sheepish grin. "I never played a part with the snakes. I always found the spiders."

Elora shuddered. "I still despise those horrible things. I remember, Kristofer and I were waiting on the beach for your ship to arrive one summer. He was so excited to have you stay, and the second you were on dry land, the first thing you both did was find things to torment me with."

"Your fathers were beside themselves with you boys," Rake said. "Especially you, Rian."

"Aye, father took a hand to my backside more than once." Rian laughed.

"He raised a fine man," Rake said.

"Aye, he did," said Elora.

Rian inclined his head at their praise. "Do you remember the apple orchard?"

Elora nodded. "When you and Kristofer would pelt each other with apples rather than gather them. And I would go home, having to explain to my parents why there was only one basket of apples."

Rian's deep laugh reverberated throughout the tent.

"Do you remember when I missed him and the apple hit you?" he said.

She smiled. "I had forgotten about that. I thought you broke my nose. And Kristofer was so angry."

"He was furious with me for hurting you. He held you until you stopped crying, trying to convince you that your nose was indeed not broken."

The smile faded from Rian and Elora's faces as they stared at each other.

"I remember." She bit her lip as she glanced at Rake, who was smiling at them both. "Rake, you must think us so rude."

"On the contrary. It's pleasant to see some happiness on your faces. You've both lost so much."

He placed a hand on Elora's arm, and she smiled at him.

"I am glad you're here, Rake. I believe we will all be better for the decision to combine our territories. Now, let us reminisce no more."

Rian pulled a map out from behind his chair and laid it flat on the table after moving the dishes aside. It was an old, crude map, hand-drawn, but it outlined the territories in their colors. The North was blue, with a grey castle sitting on top of brown cliffs. To the East stood Rake's territory, in green, to indicate the vast forests that surrounded one side of his kingdom. The other side was completely encompassed by blue ocean. His territory was cut in half by the Manat River, which provided an excellent measure of protection against threats, as the water raged for most of the year. There were only a few safe places to cross year round.

The two-hundred-foot stone wall that surrounded his castle was painted in gray that had faded over time. The colors were smudged together.

The South was colored in pale yellow that gave the impression of endless deserts covered in hot sand, and prairies turned brown from the endless beat of the sun. The White Castle stood in the center, built to keep armies out.

Rian's gaze rested on the West, his home. White-capped, pale-blue mountains surrounded his gray, stone castle. The uniqueness of his home was that it was built into the mountainside. It protected its inhabitants from the elements, insulating them against the snow.

He allowed himself a moment to miss what was, before saying, "Let us figure out the most suitable route."

Leaning forward, Elora and Rake nodded their agreement, and the three of them stayed up late into the night, finalizing their plans.

CHAPTER 6

Kristofer listened intently to Gaius's report. So Elora and Rian have decided to combine their territories with Rake's. Smart move, and it's exactly what Kristofer would have done if he were in their shoes.

"You are absolutely certain of this?" Kristofer said.

"Yes, Lord," Gaius replied. "They are planning a big feast tonight, a celebration of sorts, and they'll leave three days after. Two, if everything runs accordingly."

He beamed at his own brilliance of infiltrating Rian and Elora's camp and learning of their plans so that he could report back to Kristofer. It made him feel important.

"Get me a map," Kristofer said to no one in particular.

One of the men closest to the horses stood quickly and brought forth a roll of parchment from a saddlebag. Kristofer took it without acknowledgement and laid it flat on the ground, using rocks on all four corners to keep it down.

After staring at it for a few moments, he deduced that Elora and Rian would follow the river, which flowed East and ran into the Manat River. There would be too many women and children to take any other route. Plus, having access to fresh water would eliminate the need to cart it.

"Dagr, Gaius, find out exactly what they plan to do."

Dagr stood slowly and threw an irritated look at Kristofer. They had been stationary for weeks, waiting and watching. Kristofer had yet to fail at any task Kayne had assigned to him, but Dagr was determined to see it happen. How he would love to be the one to slide a sword through Kristofer's heart. Although, he had serious doubts as to how close he would come. Kristofer was strong, and there were rumors in the Southern territory that he could not be killed.

Kayne had methods, and all sorts of concoctions in that White Castle of his. Dagr had his suspicions that Kayne had enhanced Kristofer's abilities in some way. But there was no way to prove it—short of asking Kristofer—and Dagr knew he'd lose his head.

Sighing, he swallowed his animosity and followed Gaius through the trees.

Kristofer watched their retreating backs with disgust, well-aware of Dagr's antipathy toward him.

He returned to his map and marked a couple locations where he thought an attack would be ideal. The bigger problem would be separating his sister from Rian and Abignale. Certain that Rian figured out what he was after, Kristofer would have to make sure he was preoccupied.

When Dagr and Gaius returned, Kristofer would move out. By his calculations, it would take three weeks to reach the Southern Territory if he rode hard. He wondered how much of a fight Elora would put up. That would slow him down, too.

It was dark by the time Dagr and Gaius returned. Kristofer was sitting near a small fire, a large rabbit roasting on a spit that he turned occasionally. Upon seeing his men, he leaned back and crossed his ankles.

Gaius bowed. "Lord, they are leaving the day after tomorrow, before the sun is highest in the sky."

His red hair was illuminated by the flames, making it look as if his head was on fire.

Kristofer nodded. "Bring the rest of the men here."

Gaius ran off to collect the soldiers while Dagr stood near Kristofer, watching him with disdain.

"What is your plan, *Lord*?" Dagr spat out the title slowly, as if it were painful for him to address Kristofer respectfully.

Kristofer ignored him and turned the spit that the rabbit roasted on. When the rest of his group was situated around the fire, he pulled the rabbit away from the flames and stood the spit upright, gripping it at the base. While the meat cooled, he turned to survey his men.

"Elora and Rian are moving out in two days' time. They'll travel East, toward Rake's kingdom. We will follow the river tomorrow and find a safe place to cross. Once they get settled for the night, we'll attack. Dagr, you and Theon separate Elora from Rian. Dagr, keep him occupied. The old man who travels with them is well-versed with a sword. Do not underestimate him. Once I have Elora, retreat. It'll take weeks, if not months, for us to get back to the South. Rian is injured, and the chaos from our attack will hinder any immediate following, so we must put as much distance between us and them in the short time following. Is this clear?"

Kristofer looked around at the men, who nodded.

He stood and pulled the rabbit off of the stick. Kristofer wanted this task done and over with, and he wanted to go home. Nor was he looking forward to his sister's accusing tears.

Kristofer walked away from the fire and sat down to eat. When he was through, he laid down. It was going to be many long weeks traveling with his sister. Rian and Elora's current location was incredibly convenient for them, as they were much closer to the East. But to get to the South, it would take months, and he didn't relish the idea of spending a moment longer away from his home than he had to.

CHAPTER 7

E lora made her way through the camp. Or what was left of it. Some families had already departed, eager to be out of the mountains and away from the battle that had taken place. While others were unsure if they should leave at all.

Tonight was the feast, and in all directions, her people were working diligently. Yesterday, a good portion of the livestock was butchered. A pig was already roasting in an underground coal pit, where it would cook slowly until this evening. The rest of the livestock would travel with them, which in itself would be a task. The animals would no doubt make noise, and they were easy game for larger predators.

Coming to the outskirts of the camp, Elora found Rian playing with a group of small children. He was kicking a makeshift ball to a little boy who squealed with excitement. Smiling, she watched him sweep the child up in his arms while a little girl kicked the ball as hard as she could. A few more children joined in, and Elora laughed when they decided to band against Rian and try to win the game.

After losing miserably to them, Rian made his way toward Elora.

Still smiling, Elora said, "I fear you are becoming inept in these games of yours."

Rian laughed. "Aye, it seems the more children that play, the worse I lose."

"It means a great deal to them that you do so. They love you."

"There is nothing like a child to take the edge off of a trying day. Shall we walk?"

Rian offered his arm, and they walked in silence until they came to the horse pen.

"I'm greatly looking forward to getting back on my horse." Elora nuzzled a dark-brown mare that came over.

Years ago, her father had presented her and Rian with two colts he found wondering in the woods. The mother was nowhere to be found. He gave Elora the mare, whom she named Ferox. And Rian received the stallion, Aethon.

Kristofer already had a horse, and it was he who came to show Rian and Elora how to break them so the animals could be ridden. Ferox and Aethon had been quick to learn, and both turned into excellent war horses.

Leaning over the pen, Rian stroked Ferox's head.

"I am as well," he replied.

Elora watched Rian. He had been withdrawn the past few days, and she didn't know if it was because they had kissed, or of the impending journey.

Elora hesitated, but turned toward him. "Rian, what is on your mind? Is it what happened between us? Is it me?"

Surprised, Rian faced her. They had not spoken of the kiss, and she pretended it had never happened.

"It is not you, Elora. It is on my mind that something will go wrong."

"Nothing will go wrong," Elora said, although she didn't believe it herself.

Rian met her gaze. "I apologize about what happened in Abignale's tent. I shouldn't have forced you the way that I did. It was a topic that was on my mind often, and I wanted it out in the open."

Elora took a deep breath. "It matters little now. Do not worry yourself over it. Let us focus on getting these people to safety."

"I don't regret what was said, for it was the truth. Although, perhaps I could have handled the situation better." Rian sighed. "I think your brother and his soldiers are still nearby. I haven't any proof, nor have I seen anything, but be advised. Keep your attention sharp."

With that, he turned and headed for his tent.

Elora paled at the mention of Kristofer. She often wondered where he was, and if he had left the area. She didn't think he had, either. If he had attacked Rian and killed him, it would not have been hard to establish his rule. He is her brother, and by law, her guardian. But all he did was wreak havoc amongst the camp. It made no sense.

Regardless of what was said about him, Elora had to believe that somewhere deep inside of him, the boy she grew up with was still in there. Rian was convinced otherwise, and even Abignale told her there was no hope. But Elora saw no other way to get through her days if she believed he was the monster he claimed to be. There had to be something else going on. But what it was, she could not imagine.

Elora opened the pen and hugged Ferox tight.

"Soon we will travel together, as we once did," she told the horse.

Feeling her human's distress, Ferox neighed softly and tossed her head.

"Easy girl. Everything will be all right."

Elora stayed with her horse for a long while. The sun moved across the sky, and as night fell, the excitement of the feast was soon upon her.

Elora kissed the animal before locking the pen, and made her way back to her tent. Exhausted, she plopped down on her bed.

She had already packed most of her possessions, and was eager to begin the journey. It seemed that the anticipation of impending change brought more distress than the actual task.

"Lady?" Brilor's voice sounded from outside.

She bid him in. He bowed low, and she acknowledged him with a warm smile.

"The feast is about to begin," he said.

Elora raised her eyebrows in surprise. The day had disappeared in the blink of an eye.

"Do you require anything?" he said.

"No, Brilor. I simply cannot figure out where the day went."

He smiled. "All days seem to pass with haste lately. With your permission, I take my leave?"

Brilor bowed after her answering nod, and Elora watched him go.

After changing into a simple blue dress unadorned with any embellishments, Elora exited her tent and walked to the clearing where the feast was to be held. Fifty or so makeshift tables that would each seat a hundred were laid out, and everyone brought chairs, or large logs that would be used as a bench. The men were bringing out whole sides of beef, four slow-roasted pigs, duck, chicken, carrots and potatoes, steamed apples, mashed turnips, bread with huge bowls of butter, and casks of wine. There were pies and cakes, custards and tarts.

Seeing Abignale, Elora smiled. "Have you ever seen so much food?"

He shook his head. "Not in such a long time."

He took two goblets of wine off of a wooden tray and handed one to her. Then he drank deeply.

Rian came up from behind them, and Elora offered him her drink. He declined by raising a hand. A servant brought him a goblet of water, which he accepted gratefully.

"Look how happy they are, Elora," said Rian.

She looked around at the smiling faces, at the children who were stealing bits of food off the table and giggling as they hid underneath to eat. It warmed her to know they could provide this at least.

A shy little girl came forward and held out a flower crown. Squatting, Elora let the girl put the crown on her head.

"What is your name, child?"

"Gaia."

"I do believe, Gaia, that this is the prettiest crown I have ever seen."

Beaming, Gaia threw her arms around Elora's neck, much to the dismay and shock of her frantic mother. The woman came running forward, but Rian held his hand up to stop her. Elora smiled at the little girl and handed her back to her mother, who bowed.

"Let us sit." Rian gestured to the two chairs at the head of the table.

Abignale sat on Elora's right, while Breggen and Brilor stationed themselves beside one another, next to Rian. In a few moments, everyone was seated quietly.

Elora looked down the length of the table and smiled. The mingling of two territories brought with it, at first, anger and hesitancy. Now, everyone came together as one.

Her people and Rian's people anticipated a few words from their king and queen. Some small tribute, perhaps, to those who died in the last attack.

Without hesitation, Elora said, "It is true that we begin a new chapter in our lives. But we have this night to remember and rejoice. Let us raise our cups in honor of those we have lost. They may not be here, but they are not forgotten."

A choir of, "Aye, aye," ran through the crowd, and everyone lifted their drinks to their lips.

"Let us begin," Elora called.

Food was offered to her and Rian first, and Elora watched

the people with interest. Rian had always said that a high morale was the most imperative part of ruling. She could not have agreed more.

Rian and Abignale were engaged in a conversation with Brilor and Breggen. Drinking deeply from her goblet, Elora enjoyed the taste of the wine. The food was delicious. Every indulgence had been made, for much of what they ate would be hard to travel with.

She ate more than she thought she would, and deciding that she would enjoy herself, Elora raised a hand, and a servant came forth to refill her goblet. Laughter coursed through the people, and for the time being, they forgot their miseries and heartily enjoyed themselves.

Rian's deep laughter caught her attention, and she turned toward him.

"Breggen insists on reminding me of what a scoundrel I was years ago," Rian said, through his mirth.

Her eyes twinkled. "I verify the reality of the statement, Breggen."

"I was not so bad. I just enjoyed pranks. And I still do." Rian shrugged a broad shoulder, but his face held every trace of humor.

"I can remember, less than a year ago," Breggen said, "when you rigged a bucket of water to fall on my head when I least expected it! And it was winter!"

Elora laughed until her sides hurt. "That was you?"

"Aye, but it was for a good cause!" Rian said. "Two children had just lost their father. I found them crying near the cow pen. There is nothing like the glory of a good prank to raise spirits. My method worked well. They went home much happier."

"At my expense!" Breggen said. "I would dare to say that almost every prank that goes on in this camp has Rian behind it." He looked at Rian with affection.

Rian took a bite of cake and chuckled. "I daresay you are right."

"Rian has been this way since he was a child," Abignale said. "Although, I have never been the victim of any of your antics."

"And I can assure you, you won't be!" Rian laughed again. "I imagine the consequences of pranking you would be most unpleasant, Abignale!"

Abignale's face broke out in a grin, confirming what Rian said.

The old man glanced at Elora, then leaned toward her and whispered, "Laughter is the very best medicine."

She had to agree.

They sat there for hours, talking and enjoying one another's company. Elora watched Rian with fascination. For a king, there was no one better. The people were fiercely loyal to him, and they adored him. She often noticed that Rian didn't treat his subjects as though they were beneath him. He accepted everyone, and even when punishment was required, he was fair and just. He would never tolerate conflict amongst his people, and he was always ready to settle even the smallest argument.

Rian caught her staring at him, and he grinned, causing her to flush. Thankful it was dark out, even with the light of the torches, Elora leaned toward him and whispered so that only he would hear.

"I will retire now. I fear the wine has gone to my head."

"Allow me to walk with you?"

Inhaling sharply, Elora shook her head. "It is not necessary, Rian. Stay and enjoy yourself."

He shook his head and stood up. The table fell silent immediately.

"We retire," Rian said to the people. "I expect the festivities to go on all night."

They cheered, and when Elora stood, so did everyone else. They bowed, and Elora smiled and turned toward her tent. The cacophony of voices filled her ears and made her happy.

"That was very successful," she said to Rian, as he fell into step beside her.

"Aye, parties often are."

Avoiding his gaze, Elora kept her eyes cast downward. She felt flushed and warm, and had to remind herself that it was just the wine. She hoped it was the wine.

Wanting to say something, anything to him, she was disappointed when they reached her tent before she could muster up the courage.

"Are you all right?" he said.

"Aye." She glanced at him, and the look he gave her made her heart pound. "Do you want to come in?" It was out of her mouth before she realized she had said it.

Rian nodded. "If only to make sure you drink some water."

"I admit, I may have indulged."

After stepping into her tent, Elora placed the iron pot over the hot coals.

"Abignale found rose petals in one of his trunks and made a tea," she said. "He told me he used to make it for my mother. Would you care for some?"

Rian sat on one of the two chairs at the table and nodded. He never cared for tea, but at least Elora wasn't running away from him. She took a seat beside him, lowering her lashes as Rian studied her face.

"You are flushed," Rian said. "Is it the wine?"

She pressed her palms against her cheeks. "I don't believe so. I am so confused, Rian."

"Over?"

"You." She rose from her seat, and with her back turned

to him, stared at the orange embers that hid underneath the wood. "I know I would not be saying this if not for the wine. I just...I don't know." She sighed.

"Your feelings are normal, Elora," he whispered into her ear.

She did not even hear him get up.

"You've lost more than most people have," he said. "I understand it, and I do not take offense."

"Do you not?" She turned to face him. "I would."

"We are not the same person, nor do we handle every situation identically." He raised his hand and let his fingers graze her cheek.

She pulled his hand down. "I do not want marriage."

Rian rested his hand on her waist. "I am not forcing you to marry me."

He leaned down and kissed her before withdrawing back to his chair.

She froze, a shaking hand coming up to cover her mouth. After a moment, she shook her head to clear it, and pulled the iron pot off of the coals, setting it down outside of the fire pit. Biting her lip, Elora turned suddenly.

"Rake will force me to marry. If not you, then someone else."

Rian threw her an amused look. "I've already thought of this, Elora. And I can assure you, you will not marry anyone else."

"I feel as if I'm losing control over my own life!"

"What you do not seem to realize is that I am the only other sane king in the nation. Rake would not dare alienate me over a woman. And yes, you are right. Your standing will always be below ours. But that doesn't mean you can't rule your people the way you see fit. As it is now, Elora, you've done more and proven yourself far beyond that of our mothers. You are not losing control. If anything, you gain it."

"Then why do I feel this way?"

She knelt next to his chair and looked at him for answers. Desperate for help. Desperate for him to shine some light into the darkest recess of her mind.

His eyes held sympathy. "Because change is coming. Because you lost Kristofer. Because you are worrying yourself over every small detail. Elora, you need to repose yourself."

"That is easy for you to say. Does anything worry you?" she snipped.

"A great many things worry me. But I'll be damned if I conjure up woe where none exists."

Sighing, Elora rested on her heels and stared absentmindedly at the leg of the chair she was kneeling in front of. Rian nudged her chin up and stared into the emotional pools of her eyes.

"We cannot fight the future. It isn't real."

Nodding, Elora gave him a weak smile. "I have been holding this in for a while."

"You should have come to me, rather than running away every time we were alone."

"I'm sorry, Rian," she whispered. "I can handle war strategies and ride into battle, but I can't handle my thoughts." She laughed. "We can always be grateful for wine."

"I was thinking the very same thing." Rian smiled. "You need to sleep. Sleep off the wine, and you'll feel better in the morning."

He stood and readied himself to leave, but the thought of being left alone right now was beyond Elora's comprehension.

"You're leaving?"

He frowned. "Aye..."

Biting her lip, Elora nodded. "All right."

Rian sat down and held a hand out, knowing she didn't want to be left alone.

"I'll stay until you fall asleep. Come."

He gestured to the bed, and Elora felt her pulse quicken. Too exhausted and emotional to care about what it meant, she laid down next to Rian, and he wrapped an arm around her shoulders. pulling her against him. She laid her head on his chest, and the dull thud of his heartbeat lulled her into a peaceful sleep.

When Elora woke up, she was alone. Rian was gone, but she couldn't remember the last time she had slept so peacefully.

She pulled herself out of bed and splashed cold water on her face. After grabbing her tooth powder out of the top of her trunk, she cleaned her teeth and rinsed her mouth.

Stepping out into the bright sunlight temporarily blinded her, but her head felt all right. It was the last day. They would begin their journey tomorrow, and everywhere she looked, people were running around frantically. They were trying to decide what to bring, what to leave, and then when their minds were made up, they changed it again.

Elora knew how they felt. But she realized, as she made her way to Abignale's tent, that she felt a sense of peace she had not felt in many months. The decision to leave the camp behind and join Rake in the East, along with her talk with Rian last night, lifted the weight of the world off of her shoulders.

Elora knocked on the post outside of the old man's tent and waited until she was admitted. Queen or not, Abignale deserved respect, and there were none more respectable than he.

"Enter!" Abignale said from the inside the tent, and she pushed aside the flap.

Rian and Abignale stood side by side, examining a map. The men looked up, and she smiled at Rian, who returned the warm gesture.

Abignale was pleased. Whatever happened last night was

exactly what Elora needed. He knew Rian would eventually get through to her.

Elora glanced at the map as she walked over to the table.

"What are you discussing?"

Rian placed a hand on the small of her back as she leaned over the table.

"The route we agreed upon," he replied.

"What of it?"

"It leaves us vulnerable and open."

Elora frowned. "It left us open and vulnerable when we agreed to it. Why worry over it now? We need the river, and there's no other course."

"That is our dilemma," Abignale said. "She is right, though."

Rian sighed, but he had to agree. With so many in tow, traveling alongside the river was the only logical course.

Turning her attention from the map to Abignale, she said, "Abignale, I'm mostly done with my packing. Do you need help?"

"No, Elora. My thanks, but I wish to finish myself."

"I've already asked him," Rian said. "He wants everything packed specifically."

Hiding her amusement, Elora stepped out of the tent and back into the sunshine.

Rian stood beside her. "How are you feeling this morning?"

"Much better. Thank you, Rian, for last night. I needed you, and you were there."

He smiled, unable to take his eyes off of her. "My pleasure."

Brilor and Ayden came up beside them and bowed.

"Almost everything is ready, my queen," Brilor said. "There is one thing..." He looked at Ayden.

"What is it?" Rian said.

"There is a woman waiting for you in your tent, Lady," Ayden whispered, so only they could hear. "She demands an audience with you at once."

Elora and Rian exchanged glances.

"Who is she?" Elora lowered her voice.

"She will speak with none but you," Brilor said. "How she even got into the camp is a mystery."

"I'll accompany you," Rian said, and Elora nodded. "Brilor, follow and stand guard. Ayden, have Eret maintain his post at the gate. Tell him to let no one in or out, and then station yourself outside of Elora's tent."

The men bowed again, and Ayden hurried off. Rian, Elora, and Brilor hurried to Elora's tent. Brilor stood by the entrance flap while Rian, hand on the pommel of his sword, entered first, followed closely by Elora.

A tall, thin woman with skin the color of the night sky, stood statuesque next to the table. She turned and bowed low. She wore black leggings and black boots. Her tunic was gold, and light from the fire danced off the shirt as she moved. Her long black hair was plaited into hundreds of tiny braids that fell down to the small of her back.

Awestruck by the woman's beauty, Elora stared for a moment.

"Who are you?" she said.

The woman pulled herself up and stared at Rian a moment, before answering.

"My name..." She placed a hand on her chest. "Zemirah."

Her rich voice held a thick, almost unintelligible accent. The golden bangles around her wrist clanked together as she moved.

"What is it you want?" Elora said, suddenly grateful that Rian stood beside her.

"I come to offer my army. I understand you...and he," she jerked her head at Rian, "fight Kayne."

"Aye..." Rian looked as confused as Elora felt.

Zemirah looked relieved. "A year ago, Kayne's army—his blood soldiers—raided my home across the endless water. He made war on my country and destroyed it. Too many of us have...died." She said the last so quietly, it was barely audible.

Sorrow crossed her ebony features as she was reminded of those she lost.

She cleared her throat. "It has taken us a long time, but my people and I are willing to fight with you. We are very good with our weapons."

Understanding her pain, Elora looked at Rian. "Did you know Kayne had invaded across the sea?"

"No." He looked at Elora a moment, before calling Brilor in. "Send for Abignale."

Brilor never took his gaze off Zemirah as he bowed his head and exited quickly.

"I understand you...um," she paused, struggling for the word, "...you move out tomorrow. My general and I, we've watched you for some weeks before approaching. I offer my sword, my allegiance to you...in return for accepting my army." She spoke slowly, cautiously, as if concerned she would use the wrong word.

"How do we know you speak the truth?" Rian said.

Zemirah shrugged with the obviousness of her reply. "You don't."

"Then why would we accept your proposal?" said Elora.

"My people...are most important to me. Some of us are nearby. Some are scattered throughout the land. Most of us are on war ships on the outskirts of the Eastern Ocean. Our home is gone, burned. The women raped, children and men slaughtered. Every day, Kayne grows in power. I cannot prove to you that I speak the truth. I can prove my skill with a sword, and my people are all trained in weaponry. We are not a large army, but we will fight to the death. We can provide for ourselves."

Abignale emerged and stared at Zemirah for a long time.

"What is this about?" he said.

Elora gave a quick recount of Zemirah's offer, and Abignale raised his eyebrows.

"We are headed East on the morrow," he told Zemirah. To Elora and Rian he said, "Rake will have to be informed of—"

"King Rake knows and has already accepted my proposal. My people are already within his kingdom."

The three turned and stared at Zemirah.

"He gave me this to give to you." She handed Elora a rolled-up parchment that she had pulled out of her breast.

Rake's crest was stamped on it.

After tearing it open, Elora, Rian, and Abignale read it silently.

> Elora, Rian,
>
> If you are reading this, then Zemirah has already told you of her plans to combine her army with ours. I knew her brother years ago, and I verify the truth of her words. More can be explained upon your arrival.
>
> Trust Zemirah. She will be an asset.
>
> I am yours,
>
> —Rake

"If Rake trusts you, then so do I." Abignale turned to Elora and Rian. "We need every able body we can get. We move out in less than twenty-four hours. I take my leave."

Abignale swept from the tent, his black robes billowing behind him.

"Zemirah, please wait here a moment." Elora gestured to a chair.

Looking at Rian, she turned and disappeared outside of her tent.

Rian hurried to follow, and held a hand out to keep Brilor and Ayden away.

He whispered in her ear, "I trust Abignale's intuition, and he is right. We need her help. Although, I'd like to test her skill with a blade."

"Tell her so," Elora whispered. "We cannot accept an entire army without announcing it to our people. Especially as we begin our journey. If she is indeed as skilled as she says, our people will have an easier time accepting her."

"So we are in agreement, then?" Rian said.

"Aye."

Upon returning to the tent, Elora found Zemirah exactly where they had left her.

"Rian is our finest swordsman. He wishes to test your skill with a blade."

Zemirah nodded in agreement and stood. She wasn't much shorter than Rian, which was remarkable for a woman.

"Where?" she said.

"There is a training field not far from here." Rian watched her every move.

Zemirah waited patiently for Rian and Elora to exit the tent. She followed them out, igniting stares and whispers from everyone they passed. Ayden and Brilor followed at a discreet distance. When they arrived at the field, Elora realized they had already drawn a large crowd.

Rian and Zemirah walked to the center of the enclosed pen and faced each other, each pulling their sword out of the scabbard on their hips. Without any indication, Rian attacked, and Zemirah deflected his blow with ease, causing a murmur to cycle through the crowd. Surprised, Rian advanced several more times, and Zemirah not only defended herself, but had Rian raising his sword in defense against her.

Pulling her sword out of its sheath, Elora entered the training field and attacked. Zemirah fought them both off. She was nimble, almost feline on her feet. She slashed at Zemirah's ribs, but the woman batted aside her sword, and Elora had to duck the razor-sharp edge of Zemirah's blade. Rian modified his poses, but no matter how innovative he was, Zemirah continued to stop his sword.

Elora drew back, leaving Rian and Zemirah to their duel. After a few more minutes, Rian lowered his sword.

"You spoke the truth." He panted. "I have never seen some of your tactics."

Zemirah smiled, sweat dotting her brow. "I will teach you. I have fought many men. Not one of them were as skilled as you are."

Rian inclined his head. Turning to Elora, he held his hand out and she accepted it wordlessly.

"Rake was right," he said. "This woman would be an asset in battle."

"Announce her now," Elora urged. "While these people are here. They will carry your words through the camp. There is no time for formality," she said, in regard to the look on his face.

Rian turned to face the crowd that had gathered, and sheathing his sword.

He boomed, "My people, I introduce to you, Zemirah. She and her army have come from across the sea to join our cause. Carry my words with you and continue your preparations. We still depart at first light."

"That was certainly to the point," Elora said.

Grinning, Rian gestured for the women to walk ahead of him. Brilor and Ayden followed closely behind him.

"Where is Breggen?" Rian turned to look at them.

"I'm uncertain, Lord." Ayden ran a hand through his platinum hair. "He will be furious he missed that fight, though. It will be talked about for months."

"Aye, the woman is indeed talented with her sword," Brilor said. "She didn't even flinch when Elora joined in."

Ever cautious, Rian said, "Aye, but she is still a stranger. Keep your eyes open."

With that, he followed Elora and Zemirah back to camp. When they reached the gate, Zemirah bowed again.

"I will take my leave. But before I go, I must tell you that there was a small group of blood soldiers hiding in the outskirts of the forest across the river. My general and I will meet you here at first light, and we'll keep an eye out for them, but we haven't seen them in several days."

Elora gasped. "Wait! Blood soldiers?"

A single nod from Zemirah made Elora's heart pound.

"Led by the Right Hand. Kristofer!" Elora turned to look at Rian.

"We already knew this, Elora," he said. To Zemirah, he said, "You were nearby when Kristofer attacked us. Yet you offered no assistance."

"They know nothing of our presence here. It was a difficult decision to make. I believe Kristofer's lack of knowledge concerning my army proves more beneficial to you."

After a moment, Rian conceded. "I agree."

Bidding her well, Elora and Rian watched her walk out of the gates.

Once Zemirah was out of earshot, Elora turned to Rian.

"We suspected Kristofer was nearby," she said, "but to have it confirmed!..."

"We must be all the more cautious. Zemirah said they were gone now. Perhaps they've retreated. Do not let it eat at you, Elora. Look at it like so: luck must be on our side. If her army fights half as well as she does, we can all but march into Kayne's region tomorrow."

Elora nodded, still uneasy. With a deep breath, she steadied her emotions.

"We still have much to do," she said, "and the morning will be upon us before we know it."

CHAPTER 8

E *lora was right.* Rian threw himself onto his bed late that night.

Exhausted, he fell into a deep sleep and woke up before the sun, feeling as though he hadn't slept at all. Deciding against lighting a fire, Rian looked around his tent. He pulled the furs off his bed, folded them, and placed them in his trunk, knowing they would be needed on the long journey ahead.

After glancing around the room a final time, he exited his tent and made his way to the front of the camp. Breggen would see to it that his belongings were brought.

Regardless of the early hour, people rushed about him frantically. Elora and Abignale were already waiting by the gates, directing people and livestock through.

"We are almost ready," Elora said, when Rian approached. "We should be on the road within the hour."

Rian nodded and took his place beside her. A deep sense of unease settled over him, and he couldn't shake the feeling. Glancing at Abignale, he realized the old man felt the same way.

It was more than an hour later when the horses were brought, and Rian and Elora climbed onto their steeds. The congregation of people followed, leaving the sanctuary of the mountains behind. The progression was slower than even Rian had anticipated, and as the sun rose higher in the sky, he was grateful for the river alongside them.

Pausing at midday for something to eat, Rian dismounted and found Abignale nearby, entertaining a group of children.

Rian sat beside him and turned to say something, just as Abignale said, "I feel it, too. Stay close to Elora. It is she I am concerned about."

Rian nodded. Worried his mood would affect the children, he smiled and pulled forth the ball they always played with. He tossed it high in the air, and the children squealed with delight, hopping up to chase after it.

Elora made her way over and handed Rian and Abignale several strips of dried beef, a slice of cheese and an apple.

"Have you eaten?" Rian asked Elora.

She shook her head. "Nay. I have no appetite."

"You must eat, Elora," Abignale said. "If only to keep up your strength."

He held out a strip of beef and the apple, and she took it.

Eating slowly, she turned to the men. "My nerves are raw."

"As are ours," Abignale replied. "We will keep our eyes open and our attention sharp."

Not feeling much better, Elora watched Zemirah make her way over, followed closely by a tall, muscular man. His skin was the same dark shade as hers, and the sunlight gleamed off his bald head. Large brown shaggy fur hung off of his shoulders, and when he reached forward to clasp arms with Rian, his arm was marked with blue symbols—something Elora and Rian had never seen before.

Zemirah bowed before them. "This is Kwame. He is my general."

Rian and Elora stood, and she gave him a warm smile.

"We are grateful to you for joining our cause," Elora said.

Zemirah translated, and Kwame said something back.

"He said he is honored."

Suddenly feeling like he was being watched, Rian looked around for the source of his unease. Seeing nothing made him all the more weary.

"Eret, bring our horses," Rian said. "We need to move out."

Elora frowned. "What is it, Rian?"

"If our progression today is any indication of the rest of this journey, it will set my estimate behind more than two weeks. We have to get back on the road."

Eret brought forward their horses and they mounted. Abignale let out a sharp whistle, and they waited for his snow-white stallion to trot up. Feher came and stood next to Abignale, waiting patiently for his master to mount.

"Move out!" Rian barked, and hundreds and hundreds of people clambered to put everything away and get back on their feet.

The horses trotted slowly, and as the day progressed, Rian became more and more agitated. He and Abignale stayed close to Elora in the front, while Brilor and Ayden followed the crowd in the back. It was daunting and tedious, and Rian pushed them further than Elora thought was necessary.

As the sun began to set, Elora looked at Rian with a questioning expression. He gave no indication of wanting to stop.

"Rian, we must make camp," she said. "These people are exhausted."

Rian shook his head. "Not yet."

"Yes! They cannot carry on. There are children to consider! What is this black mood of yours?"

Rian sighed, frustrated. "You are right. Let us make camp." Rian turned his horse to face the crowd of people behind him, and shouted, "We camp here tonight!"

Sighing in relief, Elora dismounted and handed Ferox's reigns to Eret. Most of the people sat down exactly where they were standing. Rian handed his horse to a young boy, who beamed at the task of unsaddling and brushing him.

After a meal of cold beans and bread, Elora laid down a blanket and sat on it. Rian, Abignale, Breggen, and Brilor followed suit, staying close to her. Their behavior grated on her nerves, but she ignored them and laid down. As the camp grew quieter, Elora dozed off, and eventually Rian fell into a restless sleep.

Far off, Elora was vaguely aware of a woman screaming. Rian was on his feet in an instant, reaching for his sword. He slept so close to her that his movement jarred her awake.

"What is it?" Elora grabbed her sword.

"Red soldiers…" Rian gasped. "Elora, stay by me."

Before long, everyone was awake and terrified. The sound of metal against metal reverberated throughout the camp, and Elora watched in horror as her people dropped.

"Get her out of here!" Abignale shouted to Rian. "Mount and ride!"

The chaos reached a feverish height, and Elora searched in vain for Ferox. Out of nowhere, three Red Soldiers surrounded her and Rian while two more confronted Abignale. Rian recognized Dagr instantly. It was his sword that had sliced Rian's side during the attack in the mountains.

"We meet again," Dagr drawled, the tip of his blade dripping red.

"Elora, get out of here." Rian kept his gaze fixed on the soldiers in front of him.

"I won't leave you!" she cried.

"It is you they want!" Rian snarled. "Run!"

Dagr's sword came down hard, and Rian blocked the blow. The other two soldiers surrounded Rian, and he killed one of them instantly. Abignale, having won his own fight against the two men that attacked him, joined Rian.

Knowing her brother was probably nearby, Elora bolted. She saw one of the Red Soldiers lifting his sword, ready to deal a death blow to an old man. She pulled a knife from her boot, took aim and threw it. It hit him in the chest, and he fell before he could take another life. The old man turned to look at her, and Elora saw his eyes grow wide. She turned slowly and came face to face with Kristofer.

"No," she gasped.

For a moment, nothing else existed.

"Kristofer, don't do this." She started to back away, hands held out in front of her as Kristofer advanced.

"Elora!" Breggen came running toward her, sword raised.

"Breggen! No! Get back!" she screamed, but it was too late.

A dagger sliced through the air, catching Breggen in the heart. He fell, clutching his chest where the knife had pierced his flesh. Tears blurred Elora's vision and she ran toward him, but Kristofer wrapped an arm around her waist and pulled her away. One hand gripped her while the other reached to disarm her. Her sword fell to the ground with a clang.

Fighting Kristofer with every ounce of her being, Elora struggled to get back to Breggen. He couldn't—wouldn't—die alone.

"Please! Kristofer!" Elora choked through her tears.

"Don't fight me, sister," he whispered.

He dragged her onto his snorting black horse and galloped away. As soon as Elora was captured, the Red Soldiers retreated as if they had never been there.

Rian watched Kristofer ride off. Sensing Rian's rage, Abignale grabbed his arm.

"You cannot go after her right now."

"He will kill her!"

"He will not," Abignale said. "He needs her alive. For how long, I don't know. You need to make arrangements for these people. We will head out for Elora at first light. We will get her back."

For the first time since the attack started, Rian heard the wails of his people. Looking around, he saw a screaming woman clutching the body of her lifeless child. Another one was draped over the body of her husband. All around him, agonizing cries filled his ears.

"Lord!"

Rian turned to see Eret running toward him.

"You must come! It is Breggen!"

Paling, Rian followed him and found Ayden and Brilor kneeling beside Breggen's body.

"No," Rian gasped, and pulled Breggen into his arms.

"I...tried...Kristofer..." Breggen said, his voice weak.

"I know," Rian said. "We will get her back."

Breggen managed a nod. "It has been an honor," he said between breaths.

"The honor is mine, Breggen." Rian held him tight as he took his last breath.

Abignale came forward and placed a hand on Rian's shoulder.

Brilor shoved himself away from Breggen's body. Unable to bear the sight anymore, he turned and stormed away. Abignale pulled Rian to his feet and guided him back to the center of the camp.

Zemirah came forward quickly, her sword gleamed red in the moonlight.

In her heavy lilt, she said, "You will go after her?"

Rian nodded. "I will not lose her."

"Allow me to accompany you. Kwame will stay here. He is fully capable. I have men working in Kayne's castle. They will help us."

Abignale nodded and hid his surprise.

"I will go, too." Brilor came forward. "Ayden will stay. He

can guide these people to the Eastern territory."

"Nay," Rian said. "We need you here, Brilor."

"Forgive me, Lord, but I cannot stay while Kristofer has Elora."

"Eret will stay also," Abignale told Rian. "Between he and Ayden, these people will arrive safely."

"All right," Rian said to Brilor. "Gather a few more men. Zemirah, you will ride with us. We leave as soon as the sun is up."

CHAPTER 9

Kristofer's arm was wrapped so tight around Elora's waist that she could barely breathe, let alone move. They rode long and hard into the night. The only sound was that of the horse's hooves beating frantically against the ground. Everywhere Elora looked, she saw Red Soldiers. Despair settled over her when she thought of Breggen and what Rian would go through when he found out that his general had fallen.

At first, Elora fought Kristofer for all she was worth, but he scarcely seemed to notice. He controlled the gigantic beast they rode on with ease.

It wasn't until her elbow collided with his stomach that he hissed, "If you don't stop, I will tie you."

Swallowing her panic, Elora ceased fighting. They were bound to stop sooner or later, and she would have a chance to escape then. But even as the sun rose into the sky, they rode on. The distance between Elora and her people grew. The sky darkened, and she realized they had ridden all night and all day.

Finally, Kristofer veered off the main road and urged his mount into the woods. He slowed his horse and dismounted, pulling her down with him. The second her feet touched the ground, her legs gave out and she buckled. Kristofer caught her and eased her onto the grass. They were in a small clearing in the woods. Soldiers circled them, and Elora was certain her pounding heart would explode.

Kristofer looked at his men. "I will return shortly. Keep an eye on her."

He walked away, leaving his horse, and disappeared into the trees. In his hand he held a long, thin metal instrument which Elora had never seen before. She jumped to her feet and watched him go before surveying the men around her. Their uniforms were the color of blood, and their eyes were cold and hard. A few of them stared at her with hunger in their eyes, and she felt her pulse quicken. She saw Dagr standing in the back with his arms folded across his chest. He eyed her with disdain, and she cringed underneath his stare.

One of the men—a brute with brown hair and small, dark eyes that were spaced too far apart—walked over to her, and she took a step away.

Alarm coursed through her when he muttered, "Pretty little thing."

He traced the outline of her face with his fingers, and she smacked his hand away. He retaliated with the back of his hand. She felt her lip split, and the bitter taste of blood filled her mouth.

In a mocking voice, "Why, Lady! Where are your manners?"

He grabbed her and grinned when she tried to push him away from her again. The men behind him chuckled.

Laughing, another soldier walked up to her and grabbed her hair, forcing her head back. She cried out, but the two of them shoved her down and pinned her arms over her head. One of them grabbed the neck of her tunic and tore it off her shoulders.

Panic crept into the whisper of her voice. "No...please!"

Trying desperately to twist free, she felt the soldiers hands tighten on her wrists. A maddening kind of terror seized her. She thought of Rian as rough, calloused hands slid over her. A helpless whimper escaped her throat, and the soldier laughed, enjoying the fear he instilled. It seemed her fate was hopeless, and she was so afraid that she bordered on absolute hysteria.

"Please," she begged in a whisper. "Don't!"

He laughed again, but the sound was cut short. He gurgled and something warm splashed her face. Looking up at the man who straddled her, she saw a sword sticking out of his chest and realized the warmth she felt on her face was blood. Kristofer stood behind him, murderously angry. The soldier toppled over, and the man holding her arms backed away slowly. Elora pulled the tattered remains of her tunic together and scrambled to her feet.

Kristofer stood with his sword drawn, glaring at his soldier.

"What would possess you?" he snarled.

"We only wanted a few minutes with her," the soldier croaked, his eyes wide with fear.

"She is not here for your entertainment." He grabbed the man's shoulder and shoved his sword through his belly.

Then he turned to the rest of the soldiers and hissed, "Does anyone else want time with her?"

No one said a word as Kristofer stared them down.

"Get out of my sight."

One by one, the soldiers got up and left. Wiping the blood off of his sword with the dead soldiers tunic, Kristofer sheathed his weapon and turned to Elora, who backed away from him in terror.

"Elora, I'm not going to hurt you."

She heard him, but she was still scared. The pounding of her heart was so loud, she wondered if he, too, could hear it. She didn't even realize she was crying until she felt the warmth of tears run down her face.

Clutching her tunic with one hand, she continued to back away from her brother.

Kristofer's expression was unreadable. He turned to a pack on his horse and pulled a clean black shirt from it, then walked over to her.

"It'll be too big, but it will cover you."

With a trembling hand, she took the tunic. Feeling desperate, violated, and helpless, Elora closed her eyes against the feel of the soldiers hands on her.

"It will not happen again." Kristofer's face was impassive, but his eyes were angry.

Feeling sick, she turned from him to slide her ruined shirt off her shoulders. He was right—the shirt, while too big, did cover her.

She crossed her arms over herself before turning to face him—the man she loved more than any other in the world. The man she loved and feared with equal measure. He gripped her chin, his thumb grazing the cut on her lip, and she winced.

For a moment, his touch felt like a memory, gentle and caring, but he dropped his hand and pulled himself onto his horse. With alarm, Elora backed away from him and the prancing beast. He whipped the horse around and leaned over to grab her arms before she could take off, lifting her with ease in front of him.

"Kristofer, I...please, you can't—"

He wrapped his arm around Elora and jerked her against him.

In a growling whisper right into her ear, "Do not fight me, Elora. Your fate is sealed. Accept it."

He nudged the horse out of the clearing as he felt Elora's head shake in denial against his chest.

"Please," she whispered.

Trying to turn to face him became impossible as he tightened his arm around her waist.

"What is it you want with me? I—"

"I do not want anything with you, sister. Kayne...*requests* an audience."

He felt her tense.

"You're bringing me to Kayne?" Her voice was barely audible. "Kristofer, please..."

She tugged at his grip to loosen his hold, and with a determination to escape, she twisted in his arms. She slammed her head back, trying to catch him unaware, but he suspected the move and avoided it with ease. After pulling his horse to a stop, he reached into his bag and took out a silver flask.

"Drink," he ordered.

She froze and shook her head, eyeing the flask with mistrust.

"No! Damn you!"

Managing to pull her arm out from underneath his, she knocked the flask from his hand. With a soft curse, he released her to retrieve what he had dropped. She leapt off the horse and ran, but barely made it a few feet before he tackled her from behind. She cried out as he flipped her over and pinned her down. With one hand holding her arms, he raised the flask to her lips and poured the sickly sweet liquid down her throat before letting her up.

Coughing, she jumped to her feet and wiped her mouth. Kristofer stood slowly, watching her. Her vision began to blur, and she raised a hand to her head. She felt foggy all of a sudden. Kristofer reached her just before she hit the ground, and swept her up. He mounted his horse and pulled her in front of him before easing out of the clearing.

He debated on the easiest, quickest way back to the South. If they stayed on the main road, which headed South, they would come across villages. They were still in the East, and the people that lived there would rebel if they saw Red

Soldiers. His men would destroy every village they came across. It could delay them.

He thought for a moment longer before deciding it would still be quicker to stay on the main road. The rocky river bed they would eventually come to would conceal their tracks before they took the mountain pass. It would be treacherous, but the pass alone would save an invaluable amount of time, as the ranges would lead them directly South. And once they were out of the mountains, it was an easy, flat ride home.

His men waited impatiently a mile ahead, and when he reached them, he turned to Dagr.

"Ride ahead. Keep to the main road until daybreak, then follow the river until the mountain pass. The less tracks we leave right now, the better."

Finding no reason to argue with him, Dagr nodded, and he and the men rode ahead. Kristofer watched them go, and glanced down at the top of Elora's head. Her weight alone would slow him down greatly, but the less attention his men had on her, the better.

They rode long into the night and finally paused when he'd exhausted his horse. Pulling off the main road, Kristofer entered the woods and found a place to make camp. He dismounted, then pulled Elora down and laid her on the ground. He knew she would sleep for hours more. Kayne's herbal medicines were potent, and Kristofer was relieved that he would not have to chase her again until morning.

After laying down next to her, he fell asleep quickly.

Elora awoke and momentarily forgot where she was. Thinking Rian would be right there, she opened her eyes and looked around. Kristofer's great black beast stood a few feet away, and the previous day's events crashed into her consciousness. Despair settled over her, but Kristofer was nowhere to be seen. Perhaps she could steal the horse and make a run for it.

Elora hurried to go pull herself onto the animal, but Kristofer's voice cut through the trees.

"Don't bother, Elora."

She glared at him. His wet hair hung to his neck, and she could see beads of water running from his hair to his chest. Ignoring her, he walked over to his horse and ran a hand over his side. Kristofer stood tall and strong, handsome and dangerous, unyielding, and endlessly angry.

Elora eyed him warily, wondering if he was as tall as Rian. Close, she decided, but not quite.

Rian was much darker, whereas Kristofer had her color. The blond hair and light-blue eyes came from their father. The more she studied her brother, the more she realized how much he resembled him. She felt like she was staring at a younger version of their father.

Kristofer was handsome and proud, strong and lethal. But somewhere within the passing of time, he had become cold and hard. Elora wondered if he was married. She seriously doubted it, but who knew what his life was like in the South.

Marriage. Rian. She closed her eyes against the pain of missing him. When he told her he loved her...she remembered his kisses and the games he would play with the children. She almost smiled when she thought about how he would let her win when they sparred.

As she stood there in front of her brother, she suddenly wondered why she thought marriage was such a poor idea. She would never have the chance now to tell Rian that. Kristofer was surely bringing her to her death, and her one regret was her behavior toward Rian. He would never know of her sudden realization. How she loved him...

Swallowing hard, Elora turned away from her brother and blinked back tears.

"There is a stream straight back. I'll give you a few

minutes. But if you run, Elora, I swear I will make you regret it."

His deep voice boomed through her thoughts and made her want to cover her ears. She turned to look at him, and saw him nod toward the stream. She followed his gaze with her own.

It was easy to find. She could hear the running water. Glancing around, nervous, Elora peeled her clothes off and rinsed the grime and blood from her body. Donning Kristofer's shirt again, she knelt by the water for a long time. Slowly, she got to her feet and crept further into the trees, away from him.

"My horse is that way." He stood leaning against a tree, with his arms folded across his chest.

Confusion colored her face as she tried to figure out where he had come from.

"Brother, please? I-I truly don't want to die. You could say you lost me in the woods—"

His laughter cut her off. "Who would believe you, Elora?"

His arrogance had her swallowing her panic, but he was right. She stood no chance of escaping him unless he chose to let her go.

Her eyes filled with fresh tears, and she cringed as he gripped her arm, forcing her in front of him. Once they were back in the clearing, he urged the horse out of the woods and inched through the trees. He worried his mount might trip, and he and the horse had been through much together.

Once they were out of the woods, Kristofer relaxed and they followed on the deserted main road. Elora found this odd. Where was everyone? Did they run and hide when they saw a band of Red Soldiers? She knew Kristofer was greatly feared, and maybe word had traveled that he was amongst the soldiers who were roaming the countryside.

As they climbed a hill, Elora saw smoke rising. Thinking

they would come to a village, she wondered if Kristofer would stop. She was hungry and felt weak.

They reached the top of the hill and rode down the other side. She could see houses in the distance, but it was Kristofer's sharp intake of breath that caused her to squint. The smoke she saw wasn't from chimneys, but from the remnants of a village that had burned to the ground.

Elora tensed, and even though Kristofer kept to the outskirts of the village, she could see the pile of mutilated bodies. Worst of all was the lifeless body of a baby with an arrow sticking out of its chest. Kanye's banner—a red flag with white flames, the crest of his territory—stood proudly beside the dead. Kristofer felt his sister go rigid. As he urged the horse faster, they passed the village, but Elora couldn't get the sight of the pillage out of her mind.

"Kristofer," she said, her voice weak.

He pulled on the reigns and let her down. Elora leaned over to vomit. Kristofer waited patiently for her as she wiped her mouth. He saw the look in her eyes, the defiant jut of her chin.

"You..." she said, accusation in her tone. "Did you...?"

"I did not give that order, if that's what you're asking. Get back on the horse."

Tears pooled in her eyes, and the image of the dead baby permanently branded itself in her mind.

"I will not," she replied. "That was Kayne's banner! You saw it." Whispering now, "There were children..."

"Aye, Elora. And it's not nearly as bad as some of the other things you will see."

His statement sobered her, and he leaned down and wrapped an arm around her waist. Elora was in such a state of shock, she didn't even notice. It wasn't until the horse began galloping underneath her that she felt Kristofer's arms around her.

Unable to bear it any longer, she slammed her head back, smashing Kristofer's nose. He jerked the reins at the same time Elora's heel connected with the horses side. The black beast took off running, and Elora elbowed her brother and jumped off the horse.

She landed on her shoulder, and waves of agony shot down her arm. Ignoring the pain, she took off. It took Kristofer a moment to get his animal under control, but he slid off the horse and raced after her. Instead of grabbing her, he blocked her path.

"All you're doing is delaying the inevitable."

Clutching her shoulder, Elora stepped away from him.

"Rian will come after me."

"I have no doubt," Kristofer said. "Pray he does not die for his efforts."

Elora winced as if she had been hit. If Rian should die trying to rescue her, she would never forgive herself.

"You would not kill him," she said.

"I would. Very easily."

"How can you?" she cried. "You were the closest of friends!"

"*Were*, sister. Rian would not hesitate to run a sword through me, any more than I would him."

His voice was so cold, and his eyes so hard, that Elora couldn't meet his gaze. She stared at the yellow grass of the plains and choked back tears.

Rian had always said Kristofer was lost to them, and she was beginning to think he was right.

"Why? Why did you do this?" She was desperate to know why he had betrayed her.

"My reasons are my own, Elora. Get back on the horse," he snarled.

"No!"

Kristofer grabbed her wrist and jerked her to him. Crying

out in pain, she pushed at him with her uninjured arm. With surprise, he looked at her and realized for the first time that she was hurt.

Furious at the delay, he hissed, "What did you do?"

"My shoulder."

Kristofer gave her a disgruntled look and pulled the arm of her tunic up so he could see. Already, the area surrounding her shoulder was bruised and swollen. He had seen it many times before.

"The bone moved. Lay down."

When she hesitated, Kristofer threw her a furious look and she cowered.

Once she laid down in the grass, he knelt next to her and placed one hand on her shoulder. With his other, he gently pulled her arm straight and then up. She felt the bone pop back into place, and relief washed over.

Kristofer helped her to her feet and let out a low whistle. His horse came galloping over and stopped right next to him. Silent tears spilled down Elora's cheeks as Kristofer lifted her into the saddle. After pulling himself up behind her, he turned his horse and headed for the Southern territory. Drained and exhausted, Elora leaned against Kristofer's front.

"Why did you never marry him?" Kristofer said.

"I...what?"

"Rian."

"I understand, brother. Why are you asking me?"

"I have no reason. Curiosity. I thought you would have."

"He wanted to," Elora said, with her mouth tight, uncertain why she would tell Kristofer this.

"You do not love him?"

Elora turned in the saddle and glared at her brother. "It's none of your concern."

At that moment, Elora remembered just a few weeks ago, when she was wishing for her mother or Kristofer to talk to about Rian. The irony made her smile.

"We have weeks of time to pass, little sister."

Frowning, Elora thought back to the castle on the ocean, where she and Kristofer grew up. They would spend hours talking. She adored him then, and clung to his every word. Kristofer had always been sharp, and he saw beneath the surface of things. To wake up one morning and learn that he had left in the night to join Kayne's army was beyond her. She was inconsolable.

When Rian learned of the betrayal, Elora feared that he was beyond repair. It was so out of place, but what tormented them further were the reports of Kristofer rising to become Kayne's right hand. Realizing that time was against her—for whatever Kayne thought to offer, she would refuse—Elora wanted this moment with Kristofer.

"A marriage alliance was brought up more than once," she replied. "I never saw the point. Our armies were already joined. Our families were both dead, and we already rule together peacefully. If I married him, I feared the control he would exert. My people's lives would be in his hands. I would no longer rule for myself, but under him."

"You think Rian would seek to control you?" Kristofer sounded surprised.

"You don't?"

"No, I don't. I think, out of all the men you could have married, Rian would allow you leniencies you would not find anywhere else." Kristofer looked at Elora and frowned. "What is the real reason you wouldn't marry him?"

"That is the reason."

"I don't think so. You have not changed so much over the years. There is more," he said in her ear.

"I suppose I fear losing him," Elora said, realizing it for the first time. "How ridiculous," she added, more to herself than him.

"We've spoken of it before," Kristofer said.

"You and Rian?" Elora asked, shocked. "When?"

"Aye. Years past. I came upon him watching you walk along the shore. Rian admitted then that he was in love with you. He would have been a fine match for you, Elora."

Kristofer's words sunk in like a heavy blow. How she never realized it before was shocking. It was the night he stayed with her and eased her worries. That was the night she fell in love with him. Or maybe...maybe she loved him long before and never realized it.

They rode for hours. Elora was too lost in her thoughts to notice the silence. She was terrified of what Kayne was going to do to her. She tried to keep her thoughts away from Rian. And Abignale. And Breggen. The less she thought of the people she loved, the less miserable she felt.

But her dark thoughts had a way of creeping into her mind. Elora's throat tightened at the thought of Breggen. Rian would, no doubt, be devastated. Breggen had been watching over Rian since he was a boy. When Kayne's army attacked the Western territory, Rian and Breggen were away. Rian's father thought it was time his oldest son took on matters of the state, so he sent Rian and Breggen East to negotiate terms with Rake and several wealthy lords that lined the North-Western and North-Eastern borders.

They returned to find their castle burned to the ground. Rian's parents and two younger brothers were inside. It was rumored that Kristofer was there, leading the attack, although it could not be proven. Rian never forgave himself.

Breggen talked him into leading his army North, and combining his soldiers with the Northern armies. Elora's father took Rian under his wing and guided him. He was young and inexperienced with ruling, although his father had taught him well. It soon became clear that Rian was a natural leader. His compassion for his people, and his fair and just way of guiding them, brought about a loyalty Elora and her father had never seen before. The people adored him, and he adored them.

Abruptly, Kristofer pulled off the road. He dismounted and helped Elora down.

"Why are we stopping?"

Without looking up Kristofer said, "Are you not hungry?"

He reached into his pack and pulled out several long strips of dried meat. Elora sat down and took the food he offered her. The last time she had eaten was with Rian and Abignale, and that was more than a day ago.

She ate the dried meat, but found it hard to keep down. Her nervousness made her stomach queasy, and she wished she hadn't eaten. The thought of getting back on Kristofer's beast of a horse was too much for her to bear.

Kristofer watched his sister in silence. His horse, so well-trained that he would not leave his side unless ordered to do so, waited patiently.

Kristofer made a clicking sound and the horse trotted off to graze. Elora eyed the stallion with appreciation. He was large and pure black, and at the base of his legs, covering his hooves, were long, black feathers.

"He is a magnificent animal," Elora said. "What is his name?"

"Asen."

Elora raised her eyebrows at the unique name. She stood and walked over to the grazing horse to stroke his head. Rubbing her hands together, Elora stayed by the horse, finding his presence less intimidating than Kristofer's.

As the sun set, Elora watched her brother make a fire, and walked over to sit next to the flames. Even though the air was warmer than it had been in months, she felt chilled.

Kristofer killed a rabbit, skinned, cleaned, and roasted it. When it was done, he used his knife and cut it up, and handed Elora several pieces.

She shook her head. "I'm not hungry, Kristofer."

He gave her a hard look. "Hungry or not, you will eat."

"I..." She took the meat, figuring the argument was pointless.

Elora began eating, and the hot food ignited her appetite. Famished, she finished what she had and looked up, wanting more. Kristofer handed her the meat he was eating, and she took it with saying a word. Once done, she felt much better.

Kristofer turned around and whistled for his horse. "Asen!"

Disappointed, Elora watched the horse approach her brother. She was too tired to argue with him about remounting, so she waited instead. Kristofer tied the reigns loosely to a nearby branch.

Elora said, "We're not riding?"

Kristofer left Asen saddled and took a seat near her.

"Are you so eager to meet Kayne?"

Elora swallowed, but ignored his question.

"I will leave you untied. Don't make me regret the decision."

Biting her lip, she turned to her brother and studied him. Maybe Kristofer was lost to her, but she still loved him. Even though he was taking her to Kayne, who inevitably would kill her, she loved him.

"There were so many times over the years that I yearned for you," she said, her voice roughened by unshed tears.

Kristofer met her gaze and held it.

"I'm not angry with you, brother. I have regrets, and I am frightened, but there is a part of me that is thankful to have you near."

She looked down at her hands and thought of Rian. If only she hadn't been so stubborn, so frightened. Rian would never know of her realization, and to die without telling him seemed too terrible to imagine.

Looking at Kristofer, she knew she could trust him to carry her words.

"Will you do something for me?" she said.

He did not move while he waited for her to speak.

"Will you tell Rian that I am sorry? Tell him...he was right, and that I love him." She brushed her cheeks with the palm of her hand.

Kristofer hesitated. "You could still survive this."

"We both know I will not. I am the only queen left in the Territories. The only guess I can make is that Kayne wishes an alliance between us, probably through marriage. It will give him control of the entire North, for the people will bow before me. Rian will die, and Kayne can move in on what's left of the Western region. With both of us out of the way, he'll be able to take down Rake's kingdom, probably within a week."

Kristofer said nothing. Although Kayne had not explained his plans, Kristofer could read between the lines. He also knew his sister would never consent to marriage with Kayne, which he suspected Kayne already knew. Therefore, he would kill Elora. And he would probably make a spectacle of her death.

Kayne's obsession with blood was widely known. The lifeline that flows through the veins...he found it fascinating. One of his more common methods was to drain a person of their blood. He loved watching their life flow out. This, Kristofer was certain, would be how Elora would die.

"I will carry your words, and see to it that they reach Rian."

Elora gave him a weak, but grateful smile. She laid down with her back turned her back to him and listened to the sound of the crackling fire until her exhaustion finally took over.

CHAPTER 10

Rian knelt in the clearing and picked up Elora's bloody, tattered tunic. Gripping it, he turned and held it out to Abignale. The old man took it and gave the two dead bodies a deplorable look.

"It may not be her blood," Rian said, his voice hopeful.

He followed Abignale's gaze to the bodies of the Red Soldiers.

Zemirah stepped forward and eyed the fabric. "It was torn from her shoulders."

Rian grimaced. He was grateful to have Zemirah with them, though. She proved herself to be an excellent tracker, although it was Rian who found the clearing.

"We should make haste," she said. "They are still more than a day ahead of us."

Rian nodded and climbed back onto his horse. Brilor and four men that he chose specifically for this task, veered into the woods on the right, while Rian, Zemirah, and Abignale went straight. They met a few miles later, on the road.

"No tracks," Brilor said angrily.

"We found the route they took," Rian said. "I think Kristofer sent his men ahead. He and Elora are riding alone."

Caidus, a short muscular man with red hair and an even redder beard, urged his horse forward. "It would be easier for Kristofer to traverse the countryside with just her. His men would draw entirely too much attention."

"Aye." Brilor nodded in agreement.

"What do you want to do, Rian?" Abignale said.

"Follow Kristofer."

"There is a way into Kayne's realm that not many know about," Zemirah said.

The men turned to look at her. Rian leaned forward on his horse, in eager anticipation.

"Once we reach a certain point," she continued, "I can lead us there. It will be far less dangerous than storming the gates. I've already sent word. My men will help us."

"Why have you said nothing of this before?" Rian growled, his voice colored by anger and suspicion. "Who have you sent word with?"

"With us, we brought a small group off the ships. After the battle, Kwame sent a woman ahead to warn my men in Kayne's palace that we are coming."

"A woman?" Brilor sneered.

"Aye, a woman. Our women are not raised as yours are. They are trained and will fight alongside our men. She is capable." Zemirah watched Rian carefully.

"So you lied to us," he said angrily.

"I spoke the truth. I came to join your army for the reasons I've said. However, should you have refused me, or turned against me, I needed to make sure my people escaped. As you are here for your woman and your people, I, too, am here for those I love."

Abignale smiled at Zemirah's boldness. He liked her and he believed her. He was far more concerned about Elora than Zemirah, anyway. Elora's time alone with Kristofer would torment her in ways he could only imagine. He knew she still hoped that Kristofer would come back to her, but Abignale took comfort in knowing that her brother would not hurt her. For the time being, Elora was safe. Abignale had told Rian this in an attempt to alleviate his fear over Elora's safety, but between Breggen's death and Elora's captivity, Rian was hard to reach.

However, Rian surprised them all by letting out a bark of laughter.

"Zemirah, I do understand," he said. "I can't say I would not have done the same. We have wasted too much time. Let us ride."

—∾∾—

Elora woke up before the sun. The fire, burning brightly, had been stoked and wood had been added to it recently. She sat up and looked around to find her brother a few feet away, leaning against a tree. His long legs were crossed at the ankles as he watched her.

Stiff and sore from both riding in the saddle and falling made her cross, and if possible, more frightened. She stood slowly, careful not to jar her shoulder, and walked into the trees without a word to her brother. There was no stream here, so she made do without water. Feeling like she could sleep for a month made her even more irritable. She felt drained and weak, and the pain from her shoulder only seemed to grow worse.

Once she was done with her toiletries, she headed back to Kristofer, who had already seated himself on top of his massive stallion. He turned his head, and she gasped as a wave of memories washed over her.

Elora was seated on the sand, the tips of her toes barely touching the waves that washed across the shore. Her maids were behind her, at a respectable distance, and she glanced longingly at the line where the sky met the sea. Kristofer and her father had been gone for almost two months, and she missed them both, but most of all her brother. Without his practical jokes, the castle seemed cold and uninviting. He did make her angry, and between him and Rian, sometimes they pushed her too far.

Ruining her gown moments before the party started was a perfect example. It was a few months past, and a ball was being held. Her gown was woven out of gold thread. Her hair had taken hours to do, and as soon as her hand had left the doorknob, Kristofer dumped a bucket of icy water over her head. Too stunned to say anything, she ran back into her chambers and slammed the door.

Mother had scolded him dearly. Not that he cared. But when he realized how upset Elora was, he went to her. A soft knock announced his arrival, which she ignored. Furious at him, she picked up the book that sat on her bed and flung it at him. He dodged it, and it hit the wall behind him with a dull thud.

"Elora, I'm sorry. In my defense, I did not realize you were fully dressed for the party. Don't cry."

She sniffed and wiped her cheeks as she made her way over to her armoire. Her dress, specially chosen for this night, was probably ruined and she had no idea what else to wear. Sorting angrily through her gowns, she shrieked with outrage when Kristofer leaned over her and closed the wooden doors. She hit him in the chest and pushed him away, but she was so angry that she burst into tears.

He chuckled. "All this over a dress? Elora, really?"

Or the time when Rian's ship arrived, and the entire family went to the shore to greet them. Their parents left the three of them alone to entertain themselves. Elora saw the boys whisper to one another, and immediately tried to run off. Rian had grabbed her and pinned her down while Kristofer delighted in dangling snakes over her...

"Remember, I love you, Elora," Kristofer whispered after dinner one night, weeks before he left.

Elora gasped as she felt her brother's hands wrap around her waist before lifting her into the saddle. As the horse started galloping, Elora tensed with pain. Her shoulder caused her a great deal of agony. Her eyes watered with every movement, and her vision began to flicker. His arm around her felt like a band, and she couldn't take a deep breath. She felt feverish. And then she knew no more.

Kristofer reigned his horse to a stop. His sister's limp body surprised him. After turning her in his arms, he noted her pale face, and when he raised a hand to her cheek, he could feel how warm she was. With a scowl at the delay, he lifted the arm of her shirt up and examined her shoulder, noting the bruising and the swelling. He could bind her arm, but he could not determine the extent of the damage.

After shifting her into a more comfortable position in front of him, he urged his horse forward.

Elora slept for a long time, but when she woke, she felt even worse than before and was trembling. Whether from fever or fear, she couldn't tell. She had no idea how many days had passed since he took her, but the sun was setting and it would be dark soon.

Kristofer could feel her shaking. Weak hands tried desperately to loosen his arm from around her waist. When that didn't work, she collapsed against him, trying to take deep breaths. She felt off, sick and sore, and his arm was so tight about her waist that she could scarcely breathe. Did he plan on squeezing the life out of her?

"Please, you're...you're hurting me."

Kristofer looked behind him, and nodding as if to confirm something only he knew, he slowed the horse to a trot and loosened his grip. He swung a long leg over the horse's backside and reached his arms up to help her down. She gripped the saddle horn and looked down, realizing she was seeing two of him. Pressing a hand against her forehead, she swayed on the horse and felt her brother grab her before she fell off.

He built a fire and left her sitting near it while he disappeared into the woods. Too weak to run, even if help were within an inch of her, she laid down beside the heat with her arm under her head, and closed her eyes. It was Kristofer sitting her up, one hand cupping the back of her neck while a warm cup was pressed against lips. She eyed the tea with mistrust, then turned her head.

"Drink it, Elora."

Finding it pointless to argue with him, she took a sip, but he poured the entire contents of the cup down her throat. It was spicy and delicious. Whatever he gave her warmed her, and after a few minutes, her shivering stopped and she felt a little better. After pulling her shirt off her injured shoulder, he swept her hair to the side and pressed his fingers against the joint.

She cried out in pain. "Don't!"

Ignoring her, he moved his hand to the back of her shoulder. She looked at him with wide, frightened eyes, fresh tears spilling over her lashes. He pressed his hand to the side of her shoulder and she gasped in pain.

Having no idea what he meant by all of this, she wanted more than anything to get away from him.

Grabbing his hand she whispered, "Please! Please…"

Kristofer leaned back on his heels and stared at her. "It's broken. I can't do anything for you until we're back home."

Home. The word crashed into her consciousness.

"Why do you even care?" she spat.

"My end goal was to deliver you to Kayne in the same state I found you in."

He saw the change his words had on her. At that moment, Elora finally understood what Rian had been saying.

"He is a monster, Elora. Not the brother you remember. Let him go."

With a choked sob, she sat up and buried her face in her

hand. She drew her knees up and hugged herself with one arm as he watched her dispassionately. A tearing sound had her glancing at him as she watched him destroy a shirt. Crouching beside her again, he took ahold of her wrist and brought it across her stomach and bound her shoulder. Once her arm was fully immobilized, he stood.

"Sleep. We still have many days of riding ahead of us."

Using the palm of her left hand, she wiped her eyes and turned from him. She knew they had covered more distance than was reasonable, and even if Rian had sent men after her, they would not catch up, even with the delays. If only there were some way to escape him. The problem, she foresaw, was that Kristofer still knew her. He anticipated her every move.

Elora closed her eyes and fell into a deep sleep while Kristofer kept watch.

Brilor kicked at the ashes, sending dust flying into the air.

"They've got to be at least two days ahead of us! How has he not exhausted his horse?"

Rian ran a hand over his face. His men were tired and hungry, and he knew they had to stop.

Kristofer was at least two days ahead of them, if not two and a half days. They had been following Kristofer and Elora for weeks now, and they were running low on supplies. Abignale estimated they were still a week away from the Southern Kingdom.

In a voice tight with control, Rian said, "We'll rest here."

He felt Abignale's hand on his shoulder.

"We won't do Elora any good, otherwise."

Rian turned to face the old man. "What if we're too late?"

"Do not despair. Nor should you conjure up woe. Kristofer will not harm her, and we know she is still with him."

"How can you be so sure?"

"If he wanted her dead, he would have struck her down when he attacked the camp. Now, rest!" Abignale turned from him, and with a firm voice, told Zemirah and the men to bunk down.

Thankful for the warmer region, Rian waited for sleep to overtake him, which did not come until many hours later.

―—∿∿—

Even with Kristofer as close as he was, Elora felt alone. She wished Rian was with her, and she wondered what he was doing. She was certain he would come after her, and she didn't know if that made her feel better or worse. How could he think to take on Kayne's army?

Wishing Kristofer would knock her out so she didn't have to think anymore, she leaned against him and absentmindedly rubbed her shoulder.

The day wore into the night, and they stopped to eat and rest. In the morning, they continued on. Elora still felt weak, but her fever was gone, and with her arm bound as tight as it was, the horse's movements weren't as painful as before.

―—∿∿—

After weeks of constant travel, Kayne's city came into view. At first, all Elora could see was the White Castle towers. Kristofer felt her tense in his arms, and could hear her rapid breathing. The closer they got, the more she pushed herself against him, as if pushing back would give her more time.

Every small village they passed was just as Elora remembered from before the war. Neat little cottages with gardens and wells reminded her of her home in the North. The villagers looked happy. They were not gaunt or frightened.

As they approached the gates, a cry went up.

"It is Kristofer! Open the gates!"

A loud grating sound filled Elora's ears as the gate was drawn up, allowing them access into the White City. Kristofer tightened his grip around her waist as he urged Asen forward. Elora gasped as they road through the city. It was beautiful, well-kept and clean. The people were happy and well-fed. Everyone who saw Kristofer bowed low in respect, and Elora's eyes widened in surprise. Small houses lined the well-traveled road, and all of them were neatly maintained. Children who played peacefully in front of their homes looked up at Kristofer with admiration. No one glanced at Elora or gave her any type of consideration, and for that she was grateful.

The castle loomed overhead. They passed over white brick roads that led to the drawbridge, which was lowered immediately. Once they entered the courtyard, Elora saw soldiers stationed at the parapets. The castle itself was magnificent, and the white stone it was built out of was clean, flawless, and menacing. The courtyard was bustling with happy faces. Women held the hands of their children while they browsed through the merchant's goods. It was as if the war had not touched the South.

Elora's castle had been similar. She remembered this. What surprised her was that they were now in Kayne's land. She had expected dismembered bodies lining the streets, starving children and poverty, burning homes and ashes...

Kristofer rode up to the great doors of the castle. After dismounting, he held his hand up to Elora. When she refused it, he reached around her waist and jerked her off the horse.

Taking a deep, uneven breath, she looked at her brother. Her plea was barely audible.

"Kristofer, please, I cannot do this."

He gave her a disgruntled look and gripped her arm, ushering her in front of him. Before they reached the doors, two soldiers opened them and bowed as Kristofer passed.

The snap of those same doors closing behind her made Elora jump.

He pulled her through a large white hall. The walls were covered with colorful rugs and tapestries. To the left was a massive entranceway where Elora could see flowers. When the breeze blew, she could smell their fragrance, and realized it was the castle gardens she was looking at. Servants wearing white robes bowed as they passed, and continued on their way. Three stairs that took up the entire length of the room led to another set of doors. Kristofer pushed them open and dragged Elora inside.

A large, rectangular table was in the middle of the large room where a man was hunched over several pieces of parchment. When he turned to see who had entered, Elora found herself staring at a tall, handsome man dressed not in the traditional red uniform, but in black, like Kristofer. His light-brown hair fell to his neck, and his brown eyes were large and gentle. Upon seeing Kristofer, he let out a bark of laughter.

"Four months is really pushing the limits, don't you think?" he said.

"Aye." Kristofer clasped the man's forearm. "We've had setbacks. Raum, my sister, Elora." He jerked her forward by her arm and then released her.

Raum studied her for a moment, his gaze going from her face to Kristofer's, as if noticing a resemblance.

"It is a pleasure, Lady. Although, I daresay, not for you."

The smile faded from his face, and Elora stepped back, suddenly afraid of him.

Kristofer ignored her and looked at Raum. "Has Kayne been informed of my return?"

"Aye. He is preoccupied and requests your presence in the morning."

"Are the men back?" Kristofer gripped Elora's arm again.

"As of two days ago. When you are, ah...situated, I'll update you. Since you are home, I'll take my leave?"

Kristofer nodded and Raum bowed before departing.

Pulling Elora alongside him, Kristofer exited the room on the opposite side from where they came in. To the right of these doors was a long staircase. They climbed up it, and at the top of the stairs was a circular balcony that overlooked the great hall. Doors aligned the entire perimeter and after walking over to one, Kristofer opened the door and pulled Elora inside.

"Everything in here is yours," Kristofer said, as Elora surveyed the room.

A massive four-poster bed with sheer curtains stood to the right. A table on the left had been set with covered dishes that let off a delicious smell. An intricately carved armoire stood across the room, and a wooden trunk sat by the foot of the bed. More than anything, Elora wished to be back in her tent, away from all the finery and richness.

With large eyes, she turned to Kristofer.

"I'll send servants." He turned to leave.

Her sharp intake of breath made him pause momentarily, before he walked out of the room and locked the door.

———

Kristofer sighed in relief, thankful to be away from her. Making his way to his own chambers, he stopped a servant and ordered a bath brought for his sister and one for him. He headed up another flight of stairs and opened the door to his chambers. Within a few moments, a large wooden tub was brought and filled with gallons of hot water. As soon as the servants left, Kristofer stripped and threw his clothes aside. He washed and dressed quickly before leaving his room and heading up another flight of stairs.

Without knocking, he opened a door, startling the

woman inside. Aelia sat on her bed, brushing her long blonde hair. Her large green eyes grew wide with shock and then softened when she saw who stood at her door.

"Did I startle you?" Kristofer closed the door behind him and sat next to her on the bed.

"Aye. I didn't know that you had returned. Did all go well?" She studied him, noticing the weary look he wore.

"Aye."

She cupped his face. "I'm happy you're home. I never feel truly at ease when you're gone."

He caught her hand and pulled her onto his lap. Aelia leaned forward to kiss him and wrap her arms around his shoulders, hugging him tight.

She could feel his tension, so she pulled back to look at him. Concern marred the flawless features of her face.

"What ails you? Did your sister cause you regrets?"

Kristofer grimaced. "I have no regrets, Aelia. You know this. Being in Elora's company for so long was trying."

"What is she like? I hear she is beautiful."

"She is."

"Is she—"

"Aelia, I have no desire to talk of my sister."

Raising her eyebrows, she gave him an amused grin. His tone would easily strike fear into the hearts of his men, but Aelia knew him better than they did.

Pulling herself off of him, she stood up and pulled her long hair over her shoulder to braid it.

"Perhaps you need a release for all that tension?" She threw the rope of hair over her shoulder, and it fell to her hips.

"Have you any suggestions?" Kristofer said.

"A few. None that I think would interest you. Perhaps you are hungry?"

"Not for food," he growled, reaching for her.

She stepped back, laughing, but he caught her around the waist and pulled her against him. Aelia barely came to his chest, and he towered over her.

Kristofer took her in. Her beauty was unparalleled. She was, by far, the most stunning creature he had ever seen. Her heart-shaped face and high cheek bones only added to her allure, and Kristofer was fiercely protective of her. She was his, and that would never change.

"I have questions!" she cried through her laughter.

"Your questions never cease. Ask me in a few hours."

Before she could respond, Kristofer kissed her. She wrapped her arms around his shoulders, relieved that he was here and that he was well.

—⁓—

They were less than a day's journey from the White Castle. Rian followed Kristofer's trail across the countryside, which was a task in itself. Kristofer knew how to keep his tracks inconspicuous, and just when Rian thought they had lost it, they would find some small trace of his trail.

"Rian, we will have to make camp soon," Abignale said. "We will reach Elora in time."

Rian turned to Zemirah. "Do you know of any place we can safely make camp?"

They were in Kayne's territory now, and they only traveled at night to avoid detection. It was Rian they all feared would be recognized, so care was taken and they avoided the roads during the day.

Zemirah shook her head. Caidus, Brilor, Afflen, and Rogan exchanged glances.

"We need to get off the road," Brilor said. "The sun is almost up, and people are out."

Not to mention, they were all exhausted.

"We have allies in this region," Rian said. "Are there any nearby?" he asked Brilor.

"Not for miles. And the closer we are to the city, I imagine it would be even harder to find friends."

Rian nodded, more determined than ever.

"There are trees up ahead," he said. "We'll camp there."

They road hard, making it to the trees just as the sun was streaking its first rays of light across the sky. They all got off the horses and led them by foot through the woods, keeping their eyes peeled for any holes that might trip their mounts.

After finding a small, secluded clearing, they tied their horses loosely, giving them room to graze. The animals were watered sparingly, and the group laid down on the hard ground, all asleep within minutes.

CHAPTER 11

Kristofer awoke, feeling refreshed and hungry. It was not quite light out yet, but the sun would soon illuminate the sky. Aelia slept peacefully, her head resting on his chest. They had stayed up late, and he doubted that she had slept well while he was away.

Her hair was spread out around her, covering her shoulders, and Kristofer ran his fingers through it, remembering the first time he saw her. He had been given reports of Rake's soldiers pillaging the countryside some leagues out of the city. He took Raum with him, and they split up to summarize the damage. There were three villages next to one another that had been destroyed and burned. Every living soul had been killed. The women raped and left for dead. Children slaughtered in their mother's arms. Men struck down trying to protect their loved ones.

It was in one of these villages that Kristofer had found Aelia. She was gathering apples for her family when her village was attacked. She returned a few hours later to find her mother and father slaughtered, their bodies left to burn with their home. Her little sister, she found behind the house, with her throat slit.

She had screamed, begging her sister to wake up, and she pulled the girl's body into her arms. Her screaming had alerted the two soldiers nearby and they found her. She was raped and left for dead.

When she was certain the soldiers were gone, she buried her little sister and took a seat beside the grave, waiting, praying that death would come for her. This was where Kristofer found her. At first, she was terrified of him. Even when he assured her that he would do nothing to hurt her, she cowered.

It wasn't her beauty so much that struck a chord within him, but finding her beside the grave. He brought her back to the castle with him and gave Aelia her own chambers. As the months went on and she came to know only kindness from him, she learned to trust again. They sought comfort from one another, and eventually Kristofer brought his problems to her. He found her advice sound and fair, and he came to respect her.

Aelia grew to love him deeply, and she knew she would never suffer at his hands. She had been with him for more than seven years now.

She stirred and glanced up at him, her cheeks flushing with thoughts of their night together. Now that she was awake, Kristofer untangled himself from her and stood up to dress.

"Are you leaving so soon?" Disappointment colored her voice, and he laughed.

"Why? Are you eager to be rid of me?"

"After last night, yes. I fear I shall never walk again."

Another laugh sounded throughout the room.

"You've worn me out, Aelia. I am hungry."

"I'll have food brought."

She reached over the bed for her gown before realizing he had torn it the day before. Holding up the remnants of her dress, she glared at him.

"If you seek to destroy any more of my wardrobe, I swear it, I will don a chastity belt and you can find your amusement elsewhere."

"Do so," he dared. "I enjoy challenges."

"Aye, you would probably destroy that, too." She got out of bed and stood on her tippy toes to kiss him.

After pulling open the doors to her armoire, Aelia reached in blindly and grabbed the first dress her fingers touched. That being done, she called for a servant and then sat down on the bed.

"There is a fair in the village today," she said, with eagerness. "Merchants are coming from all over the city."

"And you wish to go to it?" Kristofer said, already knowing her answer.

She looked hopeful. "Will you bring me? I haven't left the castle in months. Your order to keep me locked away when you're gone—"

"I've explained this to you. I will not yield." He took a seat next to her. "It is not safe."

"It is fine when you're gone for a short while. But you were away for four months this time." she argued.

"And I'm sure Raum was near tears. How often did you evade him?"

"Well, just the once."

Kristofer sighed in disbelief.

A knock sounded before he could respond, and two servants walked in carrying trays of hot food, which they set down on the table. Kristofer dismissed them with a wave of his hand, and once they were gone he turned to Aelia. He could feel his temper rising.

"I cannot keep you safe when I am not here."

"Safe?! Our city is fortified! There are soldiers everywhere. Even for just an hour—"

"Enough! You, above all, know the atrocities of war. We are in the midst of battle after battle. If I find out you've evaded Raum again, I will keep you confined to this room. Do not test me."

Aelia turned from him and plopped down at the table. Her fury amused him, but he wisely didn't say so.

After making himself a plate, Kristofer returned to the bed while her temper cooled. He knew his enemies were cunning, and he was certain that if they found out about Aelia, she would become a target.

He watched her anger color her cheeks as he ate peacefully. The servants brought the thinly cooked bread that was smothered in sugar syrup, knowing it was his favorite. Aelia eyed the food in front of her. Sighing, she picked up a hard-boiled egg and brought it to her mouth.

They've had this argument more than once in the past. He never gave in, and she fumed every time, finding it incomprehensible how any harm could come to her when she was surrounded by Kristofer's best men. She was often left in Raum's charge when Kristofer was away. If possible, Raum was even less lenient than Kristofer. She also knew that no one would stand against Kristofer concerning her. Actually, no one would stand against him at all.

Kristofer glanced out the window, judging the time. Since he had to meet with Kayne, he hurried to finish eating.

He rose and knelt down in front of Aelia. "I know it is frustrating, love, but this war cannot go on forever."

"You don't understand…"

"I understand clearly. Nor could I bear it should anything happen to you." He kissed her on her forehead and stood up. "I'll be back in a few hours."

Kristofer left her to her thoughts and walked down the endless flights of stairs to the Great Hall. Raum was already there, hunched over a parchment, his finger tracing a line.

He bowed his head. "Kayne requests that you bring Elora."

Kristofer grimaced. "Bring her to me."

Raum inclined his head before departing. They returned

a few minutes later, and Kristofer leaned forward and gripped Elora's arm, causing her to wince. Resigning himself to a morning of hell, he led his extremely nervous-looking sister through the great doors. Instead of turning right to go up the stairs, Kristofer led her straight, through a door that she hadn't noticed the day before.

After Kristofer had left her yesterday, she threw herself on the bed and cried herself to sleep. When she woke up, a bath was waiting for her. Finding it strange that she didn't hear anyone come in, she tested the door to find it locked. She bathed quickly, nervous that someone might come in. The armoire in her room had gowns of such finery, she was almost afraid to put them on. She chose a pale-pink dress and slipped it over her head, grateful that the light cotton had no laces. Even with all the fabric, she felt naked and vulnerable.

No one had come to see her. Not even the servants. Her bath sat in the center of her chamber up until Raum came for her. He was kind and gentle, telling her that her brother was waiting for her. She followed him out of her room and down the stairs, where Kristofer stood waiting for them.

"Where are we going?" she said, her voice shaking.

"To see Kayne."

Elora made a disgruntled sound in her throat and yanked her arm from her brother's grasp.

"Please, Kristofer." She gasped, backing away from him.

"Elora, I don't have the patience for this," he snapped, grabbing her again.

Jerking her beside him, he dragged her up to two huge doors. After pushing them open, Kristofer knelt, dragging Elora down with him.

"Come closer," a deep voice boomed.

Afraid to look, Elora forced her gaze up as Kristofer yanked her to her feet. Kayne stood next to a long table. He was tall and abnormally pale, with a mass of jet-black hair that hung below his shoulders. An aquiline nose sat below eyes, which were almost black.

Elora's breath caught in her chest, for he was not at all what she'd expected. There was an allure, an irresistibility about him that frightened and confused her.

Kristofer dragged Elora and threw her down in front of Kayne. She pulled herself to her feet and stood before him, unflinching. Kayne eyed her for a long while before turning his attention to Kristofer.

"I see the resemblance." His voice boomed throughout the room, even though he spoke quietly, which only added to his eeriness. "Was there any trouble?"

"No, sire. Everything went smoothly. It took a few more weeks than expected. The two armies are marching as we speak, to join the Eastern Territories."

"And I'm only just hearing of it now?" Kayne hissed.

Kristofer bowed his head. "I've only just learned of it. My men and I attacked the first night we left their camp. They will be on the road for at least two months, maybe more."

"Send men out immediately," Kayne said. "Dagr can ride in your place. I don't want those armies reaching Rake's kingdom."

Kristofer bowed. "Of course, sire."

Elora turned to her brother, full of anger. "You are a monster." She turned to Kayne and hissed, "What is it you want with me?"

"Insolent brat," Kayne snarled, and slapped her across the face.

She fell, but pushed herself back to her feet.

"Whatever you think to offer, I'll refuse it!"

Kayne looked at her, his frown turning into an evil grin.

"Even if it means peace amongst the territories?"

Frowning, Elora looked from Kayne to Kristofer.

"H-how is that possible?"

Kayne waved a hand in Kristofer's direction. "Leave us."

Without a look at Elora, Kristofer bowed and walked away. The door closed behind him.

"Sit," Kayne boomed.

His voice sent shivers down her spine.

Elora hesitated before sitting in a light wooden chair by the long table that could easily fit a hundred or more. Without looking at her, Kayne poured something thick and red into a goblet from a stone pitcher on the table. Elora had the sickening feeling that he was drinking blood. Disgusted, she looked down at her hands and realized they were shaking.

Turning suddenly, Kayne set his empty goblet down.

"You and Rian have caused me much strife," he said, his voice cold. "Yet the Northern Territory is under my control, and Kristofer has gained complete control of the West."

Elora closed her eyes against his announcement. It was nothing she didn't already know, but it still pained her to hear.

She took a deep breath. "If you have control of the North, what do you want with me?"

"An alliance." Kayne pulled out a chair and sat across from her.

"What kind of alliance?"

"I think you already know."

"If I refuse, you will kill me." Elora glanced at him.

His face sent chills up her spine. How could she marry him, knowing what he is? She thought of Rian, and her throat tightened.

"Why refuse?" Kayne replied. "Our marriage would unite the territories. You would be the most powerful woman in the world."

"At the expense of those I love!" Elora leapt to her feet. "I will never marry you!"

Kayne stood. "Then you'll die."

"So be it." Elora turned and ran from the room.

After throwing open the doors, she slammed into Kristofer. He grabbed her shoulders and stared at her tear-stained face. Sobbing, she jerked from his grasp and ran up the stairs. Kristofer froze before calling for Raum.

"Lord?" Raum stepped through the first set of doors and looked at him warily, cautious about being this close to Kayne's chambers.

"See to it that Elora makes it to her room and stays there," Kristofer growled, before turning and walking through Kayne's giant doors, which he closed silently.

Kayne glared at Kristofer as he stood before him, but Kristofer held his gaze, unblinking.

After a moment Kayne said, "That went exactly as I thought it would."

"Was it a marriage alliance?" Kristofer dared to ask.

"Aye. It appears your sister is more stubborn than you."

Kayne reached for his stone pitcher and poured himself another drink. After a few sips, he handed the goblet to Kristofer, who took it gratefully.

After drinking deeply, Kristofer set the cup down. He could feel his body grow warm and his hands started to shake. Balling them into fists, he gave himself a minute to recoup. Blood always had that effect on him. But it fueled him. Made him stronger, more lethal, and much more powerful.

Kayne traveled the world, finding herbs and plants that he brought back with him. He experimented for years, before he found a concoction that would enhance abilities. Only he and Kristofer knew of it. It was Kayne's greatest desire to defy death, and he was ever so close.

"Tomorrow at sunset, we will drain her," he said. "Make an announcement that we've captured the enemy queen. I'd have her death be a spectacle."

Kristofer bowed. "As you wish."

Kayne paused. "How is it you feel nothing for the girl? She is, after all, your sister." His black eyes studied Kristofer's face.

Kristofer didn't need to think. His loyalty, his life, was solely for Kayne.

"We've chosen our sides, sire. My loyalties lie with you."

Pleased with his response, Kayne turned around.

"Make sure the arrangements are made to my satisfaction."

Knowing he was being dismissed, Kristofer bowed and left the room. He made his way to his chambers and grabbed a small silver container before heading back down to Elora's room. Raum was standing outside her door, and Kristofer dismissed him without a word.

After pushing open the door, he found his sister sitting on her bed.

"You were stupid to refuse."

"I will not compromise my integrity and everything I stand for," she hissed through her tears. "What kind of message would that send to my people?"

"Then why are you crying?" Kristofer closed the door and leaned against it, crossing his arms over his chest.

"Do not patronize me, brother." Elora wiped her face.

She swept her blonde hair off her shoulder and turned away from him. Thinking of Rian and Abignale, she felt a fresh wave of anguish wash over her. At least she would soon see her parents, and Breggen.

She heard Kristofer make his way over to her, and she cried out when she felt his hand on her injured shoulder.

"Loosen your dress."

"What?!"

"Do not look at me like that, Elora," he snapped. "I can ease the pain in your shoulder."

She stared at him with mistrust. "How?"

Sitting beside her, he said, "Loosen the neck of your dress."

Eyeing him warily, Elora reached with her good arm to unlace the top of her dress, and pulled it down slightly over her injured shoulder.

"I don't understand you," she murmured.

Ignoring her, he dipped his fingers into the small silver container. The balm burned his fingers to the point of agony, but he ignored it as he rubbed the medicine into her shoulder.

Startled at the sudden burning sensation, Elora grabbed his hand, but he pushed against her shoulder harder, as if he was forcing the balm under her skin. Terrified, and in pain, Elora tried to stand, but Kristofer kept her still.

"Wait. It will ease," he said.

And so it did. After a minute, the burning lessened, and with it, the pain. Stunned, Elora reached across her chest and tentatively touched her shoulder. The pain was gone.

"Why? I don't understand you. Why heal me to kill me?"

"Again, Elora, my reasons are my own. You will die tomorrow at sunset. Let me console you by saying it will be quick and painless."

Elora bit her lip and nodded. *It could be worse.*

Keeping her gaze fixed on the furs underneath her, she said, "Remember my words to Rian."

"I have not forgotten." He stood and left the room.

The door closed with a snap.

Laying down, Elora closed her eyes as fresh tears spilled from underneath her lashes. At least she'd be able to rest better without the pain from her shoulder. Mentally exhausted, Elora fell into a restless sleep.

Aelia ran down the stairs to the main hall, in search of Kristofer. Raum watched her descend as if the demons from hell were chasing her, and he caught her before her slippered foot touched the last stair, looking at her with alarm.

"What is the matter?" he said.

Her eyes grew wide as she stared at him. "What do you mean? Kristofer said we would go to the festival!"

He shook his head in disbelief, certain something had been wrong, and with a chuckle, he released her and stepped back.

When Kristofer was away, he left Raum in charge of not only the army, but of Aelia. And Raum was certain Aelia was the more difficult of the two. Not only was she beautiful, but her independent spirit was nearly impossible to tame.

He replied, "Last time I saw him, he was with Elora…"

Raum and Aelia shared a look.

"He will not speak of her," Aelia said.

Raum shrugged. "He seems indifferent. He does not seem bothered or upset that she is here."

Behind them, the door snapped shut, and they both whirled around to see Kristofer standing behind them.

With his arms crossed, he growled, "I am more bothered to be the source of idle gossip. You would both do well to remember that."

Aelia had seen him angry on countless occasions. But his current demeanor frightened her, and even though he stood some feet away, she took a step back.

Raum bowed his head. "Forgive me, Lord. We meant no disrespect."

Kristofer jerked his head toward to the door in a clear dismissal, and Raum bowed and hurried off. He, too, had only seen Kristofer this angry on a few occasions, and he did not want to be the source of his anger.

Kristofer watched him leave, before returning his attention to Aelia. She wrung her hands together, and his expression softened somewhat.

"I went to your chambers," he said. "You were not there."

Suddenly fascinated with the tips of her slippers, Aelia

replied, "Well, 1...1 waited...1 thought you might be...well, finished with—"

She gasped as she felt his hand grip her chin, lifting her face so he could determine the source of her anxiety.

"What frightens you?" Kristofer whispered.

Aelia pulled his hand away. "You."

She stepped away from him again as she watched his face darken.

As if wounded, he sat down, his arms rested on his thighs, and he laced his fingers together.

In a voice tight with control, he said, "You think, after all these years, that I'd hurt you?"

His question surprised her. No, that was the furthest thought from her mind.

She shook her head. "I do not think that."

Kristofer lifted a brow. "Then what is it?"

Aelia kept her distance from him. But as she stood there watching him, she realized it was the absolute worst thing to do. He needed her, and even though he gave no indication of the sort, she knew.

She reached for him then, closing the gap between them with a few small steps. She wrapped her arms around his neck and sat down sideways on his lap. As his arms came around her, she rested her head on his shoulder.

"You are the one constant in my life, Aelia. I cannot have your fear me."

"It is your black mood 1 fear. Not you. What can 1 do to ease your tension?"

But even as she said this, she felt him relax beneath her. She was right. All he needed was comfort, which also surprised her.

She picked up his hand and kissed it. "Does Elora's presence here bother you so?"

"No. She will die tomorrow, anyway." His voice was casual, his body relaxed, and Aelia frowned.

"But she is still your sister. You were close once. You had to have been."

"Aye, as close as a brother and sister could be. But as I've said, we have chosen our sides, my love. Death, sacrifice—it is all an inevitable part of war. No, her death does not bother me. The merchants in the village you eagerly await to visit seem more daunting than my sister being in the castle."

It took her a moment to comprehend his statement.

"Oh!" With a smack to his shoulder, she stood up and took both of his hands to pull him to his feet.

She studied his face for a moment, and satisfied with the results, dragged him out the door.

The festival lined every street. Merchants came from all over the South with their goods, eager to sell. Excited to be out of the castle, Aelia dragged Kristofer from one tent to the next. He held her hand possessively, but her exuberance lightened his mood.

They passed a tent lined with masks and statues. Beside it, a makeshift table was covered with pies and pastries. There were cakes and tiny sweets wrapped in white cloth with twine sealing it shut. Apples cut and drizzled with honey sat next to tarts with diced fruit. Gingerbread and spiced plum purees were beside roasted pears. Aelia paused beside the table and glanced at Kristofer, who was already eyeing the sweets.

She laughed and pointed to the fruit tart. "That one."

Recognizing Kristofer, the young woman behind the table bowed.

"Lord." She smiled at them and handed Aelia the tart as Kristofer dropped silver into her outstretched hand.

As they walked away, Aelia took a bite and glanced up at Kristofer.

"Oh, this one is mine."

She grinned, but he snaked his hand out and took the pastry from her.

With an indignant scowl, Aelia returned her attention to the tents. There were shawls, brocades, jewelry, paintings, food, and toys. There were animals for sale, from magnificent horses to sheep and pigs. Beside one very ornate tent stood a massive elephant decorated in the colors of the South. In another tent, a large, brightly colored bird squawked at each passerby. Mesmerized by its beauty, Aelia stared at the bird for a long time, while Kristofer stopped to examine a weapon master's goods. Disinterested in swords and bows, Aelia moved on to then next tent—a doll maker. Overcome, she picked one up and smoothed out the floral dress it wore. Its black twine hair and button eyes caused a surge of emotion to shoot through her. As if the slightest touch could break the doll, Aelia grazed a finger over its hand-painted lips.

The merchant, a man whose enormous girth filled the chair he sat on, eyed her with caution. Obviously, with her being a noble, he had no wish to offend her, but he wondered at payment.

When Kristofer walked over, the merchant struggled to stand, but Kristofer held a hand up.

Aelia glanced at him. "Will you buy it for me?" she whispered.

"A doll?"

"Please?" Her voice was roughened by unshed tears.

Frowning, Kristofer handed the man a coin as he muttered his thanks.

Aelia held the doll against her chest. "I want to go home."

"You want to go home," Kristofer repeated, as if trying to make sense of her request.

She'd begged him to bring her to the fair, and they had barely walked a quarter of it. It was usually an event Kristofer resigned himself for, planning fully on spending the entire afternoon placating her.

"Please, I...I don't feel well," Aelia said.

He frowned, but placed a hand on her back and directed her through the crowds. Ignoring those that bowed, Kristofer took her hand, and before long they were back in the castle. Without a word, she left him at the main entrance and made her way up the stairs to her chambers, where she closed the door and leaned against it.

It had been so long since she felt this kind of anguish that she thought she had put the memories of her family to rest. But the doll brought back waves of emotion she had long since forgotten.

She felt the first warm stream of tears roll down her cheeks. Closing her eyes, she tried to shut out the memory of her sister's lifeless body. The doll that she had clung to in the final moments of life. Aelia remembered lifting her sister into her arms and finding the doll underneath her body. She recalled digging and digging, and as carefully as she could, placed her sister and the doll in the grave she'd made. She remembered pain that lasted long after her physical wounds had healed. And the agony of losing the people she loved most in the world. And she also remembered the first time she had seen Kristofer.

She sat on the bed, the doll resting on her lap, and thought of how Kristofer had lifted her onto his horse. The agony of riding on a horse after her ordeal...

Kristofer opened the door and closed it quietly. She felt his weight shift the bed, and his arms lifted her onto his lap, as if she were no more than a child.

"What is it, Aelia?" he whispered.

She clutched the doll tighter, bringing it to her chest. Unable to speak, she sat there with him in silence. The only sound was her occasional deep breath. Her tears fell in silent torrents as if years of pain had suddenly surfaced and needed a desperate release.

Kristofer's arm came around her back to rub her arm in gentle strokes. His other rested across her lap, his hand gripping her waist.

He gave her time and waited until her tears stopped. The hand on her waist came up to caress her cheek.

"Talk to me, my love."

When no response came forth, he said, "The doll brings back memories. You had one as a child?"

He felt her nod against his shoulder.

"Aelia, pain the likes of which you have experienced may lessen over the course of time, but it never fully fades. To lose loved ones is the most painful of all tragedies."

"I have not hurt in so long that I thought I had forgotten."

"I do not think you'll ever fully forget. Nor do I think harboring emotional distress internally is a good method of coping."

She raised her head to meet his gaze. "I am not harboring distressful feelings. Even so, when you were gone, I had not given a single thought to what happened. It is just that the doll brought forth a sea of anguish."

Kristofer took the doll from her and studied it.

"I do understand," he said, finally. "Do you wish to keep it?"

Aelia stared at the doll, which looked so much smaller in his hands.

"Yes... I...I want it." She reached forward and took it from him before leaning in to kiss him.

Her eyelashes were still damp, but she smiled up at him and he leaned forward to kiss her forehead.

"Come, read to me." He laid down on the bed.

She glanced toward the little table that stood beside her bed. On it was a thick green leather book with vines etched into its cover. A tall candle stood flameless next to it. Aelia reached for the book and laid her head upon his stomach before opening the cover. His fingers played idly with her hair, and the musical lilt of her voice gave him peace. They stayed together for the duration of the day, having meals brought so they would not have to leave her chambers, and it was there that they spoke as they had not in so many months. They reveled in one another's company—talking, laughing, reminiscing. Aelia spoke of her family as she had not in years. And whereas Kristofer did not speak of his past, he listened intently to her, happy to be able to hold her after being gone for so many months.

Later on that night, they laid beside one another. Aelia's fingers traced slow, erratic patterns on Kristofer's chest.

She whispered, "I miss days such as these. Where responsibilities have been put on hold, and we are able to do as we please."

Her head rose with his chest as he took a deep breath.

"The war will not go on forever, my love. When it is over, we'll have spent so much time idly that you'll tire of it."

"No. I do not think I could ever tire of you, Kristofer. You never cease to amaze me."

CHAPTER 12

Rian and Abignale crouched behind the thick shrubbery that lined the back of the castle. Zemirah had been right. One of her men stood waiting for them, and he led them through an underground tunnel that emerged near the kitchens. Ikeni was his name, and he informed them of Elora's execution scheduled for that very night. It would take place on the highest tower, just as the sun set. Kristofer and Kayne would be there, and probably a few soldiers.

"I can get you to the tower," Ikeni said in a heavy accent. "But from there, you will have to fight on your own. If they see me, I will not be able to help you escape. As long as you stay out of sight, you'll be safe here for now."

"Thank you," Rian said.

"You can rest in the tunnels just through that grate. I will bring you food." Ikeni turned around quickly and disappeared through a nearby servant door.

"Let us get out of here before we are seen." Rian removed the grate beneath his feet.

They climbed down the tunnel and positioned the grate exactly as it was. It was damp and cold, extremely narrow, and they all had to hunch so they wouldn't hit their heads. The walls were slimy and it was dark, but Ikeni had assured them the tunnels were safe and not used.

The eight of them laid down near each other and dozed off. The need to keep up their strength fueled their desire to sleep. When Rian awoke, it was much later in the day, and he found that Ikeni had brought them food. They ate ravenously and waited silently until he came for them.

The hours passed slowly, which grated on Rian's nerves. The tension was thick and nerves were raw. Caidus and Afflen sat next to each other, stone-faced. Abignale stood beside Rian, resting his hand on Rian's shoulder for reassurance. Zemirah and Ayden sat quietly. He clutched his dagger while she fingered the head of her arrows, reassuring herself that they were indeed sharp and deadly. The quiver rested on her thighs, and every time she returned one arrow, she grabbed another. Brilor and Rogan scouted the tunnels. And when they came back, they brought with them four Red Soldier uniforms.

Excited, Rian took one from Rogan and stared at the material in his hands.

"Where did you get these?"

"Four of these brainless idiots were patrolling right outside the tunnel," Rogan said. "It took us but a minute to kill them."

"And you were not seen?" Rian said.

"No, Lord. We were discreet."

"Afflen, Caidus, Rogan, don these." Rian threw them each a uniform, then looked at Abignale and pulled himself to his feet. "Brilor and I will be easily recognized, no matter what we wear. We will stay out of sight until the last minute. Abignale, Ikeni said he would bring us clothes. Even a cloak, and slouched posture, would hide you effectively. Now, all we have left to do is wait."

Each hour passed slowly. Just as Rian was certain that Ikeni would never come, he arrived carrying servant garbs and more food. Rian changed quickly, discarding the clothes he wore on the damp tunnel floor. As Ikeni explained what was happening in the castle, they ate.

"Elora is to be drained of her blood on the highest tower that overlooks the kingdom. An announcement has been made, and the entire city will be awaiting the execution. As far as I know, it is only Kayne and Kristofer, and perhaps a few soldiers, that will be in the tower with her. I do not know how you will fight Kayne. His body heals the moment blood falls from his skin. Kristofer alone could probably slaughter you all." Ikeni frowned.

"Leave Kayne to me," Abignale said. "Rian, you take on Kristofer. Out of all of us, only you might be able to hold him off. The rest of you," he eyed each man, "kill the soldiers. Zemirah, help them and free Elora. If necessary, join Rian and combine your blade with his against Kristofer."

Everyone nodded.

Rian said, "Is this clear?"

A chorus of, "Aye," sounded quietly in the tunnel.

Ikeni turned on his heel, beckoning them to follow. He led them out through the tunnels and paused at the other end of the grate, listening intently. They waited a few minutes for the nearby servants to make their way outdoors for the execution. As soon as Ikeni was certain the coast was clear, he removed the grate, and they climbed up the steep iron ladder that led to the kitchens.

Following the dark-skinned man through the corridors, Rian, the men, and Zemirah looked around at the wealth of the castle in awe. Tapestries of the most detailed designs hung in every room, which added color to the stark-white walls. But regardless of its beauty and richness, the castle made Rian's skin crawl.

Voices sounded nearby, and Ikeni ushered them behind a door.

"Quickly!"

They crept forward and leaned against the closed door, with their hands holding the pommel of their swords. Once the danger passed, Ikeni brought them up an endless twisted stairwell. Brilor leaned over and looked up, but all he could see was the rounding of each stair.

Ikeni paused and whispered, "They are on the top floor. Take these stairs all the way up, and Elora will be on the tower on the right. Move quickly. The sun is beginning to set!"

With that, he turned and disappeared behind a door at the foot of the stairs.

Rian looked at his group. "So it begins."

Elora waited, locked in her room as the sun flew across the sky. She had never known a day to pass so quickly. Terrified and shaking, she watched the handle of her door turn, announcing Kristofer's arrival.

"It is time, sister." He took ahold of her arm.

She stood and followed him out of her room.

"Let go of me," she whispered. "I will walk on my own."

Kristofer released her as they climbed the winding stairwell that led to the tower. Elora did not hesitate, nor did she cry. The only indicator of her fear was her pale face. They walked in silence, and finally reached the top. Kayne stood to the right. Red curtains had been drawn across the opening of the tower, and an angled stone slab was in the middle of the room.

Two soldiers came forth and grabbed Elora by the arms, dragging her to the stone. Holding her down, they chained her wrists, palm side up, to the slab. Her ankles were chained next, and the lack of mobility terrified her. Determined to keep her fear hidden from her brother and Kayne, she focused all of her mind's attention on Rian and those she loved.

Kayne glided over and leaned close to her, wearing a maniacal smile.

"I will kill everyone you love, and I'll do it slowly. You are just the first."

Against her determination, Elora let out a strangled cry. She turned her head away from him. His breath smelled like blood, and it curdled her insides.

"Draw the curtains," Kayne said.

The two soldiers came forth and stationed themselves on either side of the tower opening. They pulled on thin chains that parted the curtains in the middle. Kayne stood in the center and addressed the people. Elora didn't hear a word he said, for she lay there, staring at her brother. He returned her gaze evenly, and she gave him a disgusted look.

Kayne returned to her side, holding a long, hollow needle with a hollow rope of hand-sewn twine attached to the end of it. A heavy stone bowl was brought to Elora's side. His icy fingers gripped her upper arm painfully tight. Elora winced as she felt the needle penetrate her vein. Kayne dropped the twine into the bowl and began laughing.

Soon, Elora began to grow cold and unbearably tired. She struggled to stay awake, but her eyes were heavy. Somewhere in the distance, she thought she heard the sharp sound of sword against sword, but it was far away. Closing her eyes, Elora's final thoughts were of her brother.

—⁓—

They made it up the stairwell without incident. The first thing Rian saw was Elora tied down to a gray stone slab, with a needle in her arm.

"Get that needle out of her arm," Abignale whispered to Brilor.

Rian took a knife out of his boot and threw it at one of the soldiers who stood behind Elora. The blade slid into his neck, and he fell. The commotion alerted Kristofer, and he pulled his sword out of its sheath. Rian attacked him while

Abignale raised his sword, deflecting a blow from Kayne.

"You think to fight me, old man?" Kayne hissed.

"That is exactly what I plan," Abignale said, surprising Kayne with his speed and strength.

A furious fight raged on. Rogan killed the second soldier, with help from Afflen. Brilor reached for the needle, but before he could pull it from Elora's arm, a third solider drew his sword and Brilor had to defend himself.

Kristofer grinned at Rian and twirled his sword in his hand. They circled one another.

"How did you get in?" Kristofer said, with amusement arising from disdain.

As the two men continued to circle each other, Rian thought of everything Kristofer had taught him concerning sword fighting. Kristofer chanced a glance behind Rian, surveying the soldiers. Brilor was about to deal a fatal blow, and Kristofer pulled a knife from the belt on his hip and threw it. Another solider tackled Brilor as Kristofer's knife sailed passed him and landed with a thud against the slab that held Elora. Rian's sword met Kristofer's in a fury of blows.

"Brilor was your general," Rian hissed.

Clearly amused, Kristofer darted around Rian and aimed a blow to the back of his neck. Rian lifted his sword over his head and caught the blade on the edge of his own.

"You take things too personally, Rian."

His amusement infuriated Rian further. It was a personal battle for him.

Nearby, Kristofer's attention turned to Kayne.

"Sire!"

Abignale's sword sliced Kayne's arm, drawing a long gash down it. Kayne laughed, but his humor faded quickly when the wound would not heal. Kristofer's grin was replaced by a look of concern, and he grabbed Rian's sword out of the air with his bare hand. A steady stream of blood fell to the floor, but Kristofer seemed not to notice.

All at once, the stream stopped and Kristofer grinned.

Pulling Rian close to him using the sword, he leaned forward and whispered, "Next time we meet, one of us will die!"

He shoved Rian from him and leapt forward to grab Kayne, whose arm was bleeding profusely, then jumped off the balcony, using the curtains to make it to the terrace below. Rian and Abignale leaned over, but the two men were gone.

Rian turned to pull the needle from Elora's arm, but realized Brilor had already pulled it out. He brought his sword down hard on the chains binding Elora, and lifted her off the stone. She was cold and unresponsive. The irons clapped around her wrists dangled noisily.

"Run!" Rian said.

They flew down the stairs, Ayden and Rogan in the lead, and did not pass anyone until they reached the bottom. Abignale pushed his way to the front when a group of soldiers attacked them. It was a quick fight, and Ikeni appeared from behind the same door he entered earlier and aided them against the soldiers. In a matter of minutes, the Red Soldiers lay dead in a bloody pile.

Ushering them into the room, Ikeni pulled back a tapestry and pushed against a stone in the wall to reveal a hidden door.

"Quickly. In here," he whispered.

After following them through the dark tunnel, he led them through a series of turns.

Rian held Elora tight against himself. She was so cold and limp in his arms that he feared the worst. Abignale rested two fingers against her throat.

"She is still alive. Only barely. We don't have much time." He looked at Ikeni. "We need a safe place to bring her."

"There is a cottage not far from here, in the city. They are loyal to you, Rian. You can seek sanctuary there until the danger passes."

They moved as quickly as they dared, scarcely making a sound. When, at last, they came to the end of the tunnel, Ikeni stopped and listened intently for a few minutes.

"Help me," he said to the group, as he pushed against the grate that covered the way out.

Brilor, Afflen, Rogan, and Zemirah pushed as hard as they could. Finally, the grate gave out with a loud crunching sound. They froze and waited. When no one came to investigate the noise, they crawled out. Rian handed Elora to Brilor as he pulled himself out of the tunnel. Shouts could be heard from the courtyard. Rian recognized Kristofer's furious voice.

"Find them! They couldn't have gone far."

The drawbridge was lowered, and hoofbeats could be heard pounding against the ground. Grateful for the cover of darkness, they stayed close together, following Ikeni away from the castle and into the village. Rian's heart pounded.

They entered a maze of small houses. Each well-maintained little cottage looked just like the one next to it. Rian and his group found it confusing, but Ikeni seemed to know exactly where he was going.

The sounds of soldiers approaching had them backing up, leaning against one of the houses. Kristofer couldn't have been more than ten feet away.

"Lord, are you certain they escaped the walls of the castle?" a soldier dared to ask.

No reply came from Kristofer, but Rian and his brigade heard a gasping, choking sound. Kristofer had grabbed the man around his neck and was literally squeezing the life out of him.

"They are out here somewhere," he snarled. "Find them and kill them. But bring me Rian, alive."

As the horses galloped away, the group sighed in relief. Ikeni motioned with his hand and pointed to a small house across the road. After nodding that he understood, Rian clutched Elora to him and followed Ikeni into the house.

A woman stood by the door and ushered them in. Her dark hair had flecks of gray throughout it, and she wore it pulled back tight. It gave her a severe appearance, but her eyes were kind and gentle, and her voice soft.

She bowed respectfully to Rian and whispered, "Lord, I am Theda. You can rest here. It isn't much, but it will keep you safe."

"Thank you," Rian said.

Brilor sat down at a small table near the door and rested his head in his hands. Ikeni and Zemirah spoke rapidly in a language no one else understood, until he announced that he was returning to the castle.

Rian handed Elora to Rogan and clapped him on the shoulder.

"You have saved our lives. We are indebted to you."

"I wish you well, King." Ikeni eyed Elora's unconscious form before departing.

Theda bustled about. After grabbing a fur that was draped over a chair, she pushed open a door.

"There is a bed that you can lay her down on."

Rogan set Elora down on the bed and covered her with the fur Theda held out. Rian sat down next to her and squeezed her hand.

"She is freezing, Abignale," he said in a thick voice.

Abignale touched her forehead and then moved his hand to her throat, where he felt for a pulse.

"She is dying, Rian."

"But she is not yet dead!" After looking around desperately

for something that would help, his gaze came to rest on his own arm. "Give her my blood!"

Abignale gave him a hard look. "That is an extremely precocious art, and one that rarely works."

"We have nothing to lose, Abignale. Please!" Rian begged.

"I took this." Zemirah stepped forward.

She reached into a small pack she carried across her shoulders, and pulled out several needles and hollow twine— the very same Kayne used.

The men stared at her in awe.

"I saw it," she said. "The same thing that was in Elora's arm, and I thought it might be useful. I took what I saw."

Abignale smiled and shook his head. "You are an incredible woman, Zemirah." He looked at Rian. "This will weaken you."

"I will manage it."

Abignale took a needle and connected it to the other end of the hallowed twine. Using a candle, he held the needles over the flame for a minute. After inserting one end into Rian's arm and the other into Elora's, Abignale watched the twine darken as blood flowed from one end to the other.

"How long?" Rian watched Abignale work.

"It is difficult to say. You cannot do this all at once. If you lose too much blood, you will be in the same position Elora's in."

Rian looked at Elora's pale face. If she died, he didn't know what he would do. Knowing she didn't love him, Rian resigned himself, but he couldn't lose her altogether.

Zemirah and the men stood nearby and watched. Brilor was on his knees next to the bed, on the other side of Elora. He looked as worried as Rian felt.

After a few minutes, Abignale withdrew the needles.

Surprised, Brilor looked up. "That is all?"

"No, she will need more, but Rian cannot give it all at

once. It will help, though. Already her pulse is stronger."

Rian and Brilor exchanged looks. Rian managed a smile as he placed his hand on Elora's head.

Feeling exhausted but hopeful, he told his group, "Let us rest. The sun is almost up. We'll leave tonight, as soon as it grows dark."

They all bunkered down in the tiny bedroom and slept better than they had in days. After what only seemed like minutes, Rian was roughly awakened by Abignale.

"You need to give her more," he whispered. "She is failing again!"

Rian pulled himself up and gave the old man his arm. He felt the familiar sting of the needle as it slid into a vein.

Abignale left the room silently while Rian sat there, praying fervently that Elora would wake up. But her eyes remained closed.

A few minutes later, Abignale walked in and pulled the needle from Rian's arm.

"Don't stand," Abignale said. "Theda will bring you something to eat."

He stood beside Rian until Theda came in with a bowl of steaming stew. Rian took it gratefully, and when he was done, stood slowly.

"I feel fine," he said in response to Abignale's stern look.

After glancing at Elora, he left the room and went out to the table. Theda was leaning over a fire, where a large iron pot was bubbling.

"Can I bring you anything, Lord?" she said with eagerness.

"No, Theda."

Rian was lost in his thoughts. He worried that if Elora hadn't woken up already, she probably wouldn't.

Brilor came out and sat next to him. They exchanged worried looks, but said nothing.

The light seeping through the cracks in the shutters

wasn't enough to indicate the time, and as the day passed slowly, Zemirah, Afflen, Rogan, and Caidus joined them. Theda served stew and freshly baked bread, and everyone devoured it. Abignale stayed with Elora, never leaving her side, but Rian couldn't bear to see her laying there. He stayed in the main room with Zemirah and the men.

"Rian?" Abignale's voice came from the doorway. "Come."

He held his hand up to keep everyone else where they were while Rian walked over to him.

"What is it?" Rian was tired, but his pulse quickened with fear.

"Elora is asking for you." Abignale's laughter cut through the bands that had tightened around Rian's chest.

Rian was stunned, and it took him a moment to fully understand what Abignale was saying. Feeling weak with relief, he clasped the old man on the shoulder and entered the bedroom. Elora was laying slightly propped up, and when she saw him, she struggled to hold a hand out. Rian took her hand in his.

He knelt beside her. "I thought we'd lost you."

His hand felt so warm in hers, and she wondered if he was a figment of her imagination. Perhaps Kayne was playing tricks on her mind.

"Rest. There is time." Rian placed his hand on her shoulder and kissed her forehead.

She closed her eyes and drifted off. Rian stayed near her, even when Brilor came in.

"Abignale said she will be all right." Brilor sounded relieved.

"Aye." Rian nodded. "Once she wakes again, we can leave. Our horses aren't too far from here."

The front door opened and closed, and Rian leapt to his feet. Both men drew their swords, staring at the bedroom door, as if waiting for an imminent attack.

"It is all right! He is my son!" Theda's voice sounded into the bedroom, and Rian and Brilor hurried out.

A man stood by the doorway, hands raised, shielding himself from four swords. He was the spitting image of his mother, confirming her claim that he was indeed her son.

He swallowed hard. "Kristofer has led his men North."

"Lower your weapons," Rian said from behind his group. "Why would he go North?"

"When we heard the queen was captured, we figured something like this might happen. We laid a false trail leading Kristofer and his men away. Ikeni helped. It is infallible. At least until Kristofer realizes he was misled."

"Your name?" Rian asked sharply, cautious against their stroke of luck.

"Theyo, Lord."

"How much time do we have?"

"Hours, Lord."

Rian turned to Abignale. "If Kristofer is heading North, we must leave as soon as the sun sets, which will be soon."

"Wake Elora," said Abignale. "She needs to eat. Brilor and I will plan a route to get back East." He watched Theyo with curiosity. "And Rian?" he said, as he walked away. "Make sure Elora eats."

Theda handed Rian another bowl as he made his way back into Elora's room. Sitting on the edge of her bed, he let his knuckles graze her cheek. Her eyes fluttered open, and she jerked away from him before realizing who sat beside her.

"Forgive me," she managed. "I thought…"

"It's all right. Your brother is heading North, and we need to leave as soon as possible. Eat. I will explain everything to you once we are on our horses."

He helped her sit up, and she took the bowl from him eagerly. She ate only half, but the hot food made her feel better.

Zemirah came in just as Elora handed Rian the bowl.

"We are ready," she told Rian. To Elora, she said, "It is good to see you awake."

Too weak to respond, Elora gave Zemirah a light smile before returning her attention to Rian. She felt strange. Her limbs felt heavy, and she wondered if she would be able to walk.

"I'll carry you," Rian said, as if answering her thoughts.

He slid one arm underneath her shoulders, and the other under her legs, before lifting her. He cradled Elora as tenderly as a mother would a newborn babe.

Still unsure if she were dreaming, Elora rested her head against Rian's shoulder.

Rian thanked Theda as they departed. "Your generosity has saved our lives."

Theda bowed and smiled. "It is an honor, Lord. May the wind be at your back."

They crept through the streets, avoiding commotion. Instead of walking toward the gates of the city, they turned left and headed into the trees that surrounded the north side of the kingdom. This gave them cover and the opportunity to move swiftly.

Every branch that snapped, or any leaf that was stepped on gave them pause. They had left their horses a few miles outside of the city, and when they finally reached the animals, Rian handed Elora to Brilor so he could untether them. He mounted, and Brilor handed her back. Rian wrapped his arm around her waist, and panic filled her chest. Thinking of Kristofer and how he had dragged her across the country, holding her in place with one arm, she grabbed Rian's arm and pulled him away.

"You are safe, Elora." Rian's voice filled her ears, even as his arm came around her again, pulling her against his front.

He turned to his men and Zemirah, and gave them a hard look.

"Ride."

The moon gave them enough light as they rode through the night. Stopping only to water the horses, they continued northeast until the sun rose. Elora slept soundly cradled in Rian's arms. When at last they made camp, Rogan came forward to help Elora down while Rian tethered his horse near grass. He sat Elora down near the base of a huge tree while Abignale took a cloak out of his pack and draped it around Elora's shoulders. She looked up at him.

"How do you fare, Elora?"

His voice sounded far away, and she placed a hand to her head. Abignale took a seat beside her and placed a hand on her face.

"What ails you, Elora? Allow me to put your fears to rest."

Looking down at the grass between her fingers, Elora said, "I half-expect this to be in my head. I can feel your hand on mine. I smell the trees, the grass. I see Rian standing there. But will I wake to find myself back in Kayne's castle? Lastly, what I remember is Kayne pushing a needle into my arm. I was cold, and then I remember no more. Only to wake to find you and Rian standing over me. It cannot be."

Abignale nodded his understanding.

Elora shook her head. "I am so confused, Abignale. I love him. I love him so much. Yet I fear him terribly. And I hate him. He did not care! He didn't so much as flinch when they tried to kill me. He—"

"Easy, Elora. Kristofer is long gone. Sometimes it is hard even for me to accept."

"Really?" She looked up at him in surprise as tears flooded her eyes and cascaded down her cheeks. With a trembling hand, she brushed her face.

"I will be all right, with time. I never realized how

disturbing it would be to have Kristofer so near."

"Do not let your thoughts take control. You are safe, and you will recover. And you are so loved, Elora." Abignale smiled. "I will bring you food." He rose to his feet.

Elora nodded, then looked around for Rian and saw him say something to one of the soldiers. Two of them she didn't know, but they looked familiar. The soldier chuckled in response to Rian, and she watched Rian clap the man on the shoulder. He interacted with Zemirah, who handed him cheese and bread from a pack slung across her shoulder. Elora could not hear them, but Zemirah smiled warmly at Rian before turning away.

As she wondered if Rian still felt the same way he had before, her stomach summersaulted. Possibly, he had changed his mind, just as she had changed hers. It would be ironic, like everything else.

Rian made his way over to her, then sat down and handed her the food.

"Who are they?" Elora wanted to know.

Rian studied her for a moment. "Rogan, he is the tall dark-haired one. He is well-versed on traveling by the stars. It was he...well, and Zemirah, who got us safely to you in such a short time. Caidus, the red-haired man, is an accomplished archer. He can judge wind to hit the center of a target from three hundred feet away. I've never seen a bowman quite like him. Afflen is Rogan's brother. They are both excellent with a sword. And of course, you know Ayden. Brilor chose them specifically for this."

"He chose well." Elora turned to face Rian, and all that had been weighing on her concerning him came tumbling out in a pained whisper. "Rian, I am sorry."

Rian turned surprised eyes to her. "What for?"

Her head spun with emotion and weakness. For a second,

her vision flickered and she her squeezed her eyes shut against the sensation.

Rian reached for her. "Abignale!"

The old man hurried over, black cloak billowing behind him. He carried a cup and a wedge of cheese and handed them to Rian as he crouched before Elora. Abignale laid her down and waited for the dizziness to pass. After several long minutes, Elora's eyes met the old man's.

She tried to speak. "I feel..."

Abignale slid an arm underneath her shoulders and lifted her slightly.

"Drink this, Elora. It will help." He lifted the cup to her lips and helped her drink.

She coughed, surprised by the flavors of the tea. Spices she couldn't name left a tangy aftertaste on her tongue, and she thought she detected hints of wine.

With every sip, she felt warmth seep into her cold, stiff limbs. Her head began to clear, and the nauseousness that threatened to overwhelm her vanished.

Abignale pulled his arm out from underneath her shoulders and tucked a rolled up blanket under her head.

"Stay by her, Rian. She needs rest, but we shouldn't stay here too long. Kristofer may have already realized a false trail was laid."

Abignale walked away, leaving Rian and Elora alone. Desperately wanting comfort, Elora struggled again to sit up, only to have Rian place a hand on her, keeping her down. The feel of his hand on her once-broken shoulder had her remembering Kristofer coming to her room and healing her injury. The thought brought with it equal parts of fear and confusion, and she clung to Rian's hand. Too afraid to speak to him about her feelings, she turned again to watch the group that had risked their lives to rescue her. She knew there were not many swordsman whose blade could cross

Kristofer's and live to talk about it.

Rian's voice made her turn her head to look up at him.

"What is on your mind, Elora?"

He sat with his back against a tree. His long legs were stretched out in front of him, crossed at the ankles. She still clung to his hand, and at the sound of his voice, her fingers tightened in response.

"Um..." She forced a weak smile. "That there are not many who could cross swords with Kristofer and survive the ordeal."

Rian grinned as he grazed her cheek. "To protect what I love, it was but a small price to pay."

"Love..." she repeated, as his words brought with them a warmth and desire the likes of which she had never known.

"Aye. What? You mean to tell me you would not do the same for me?"

She laughed weakly, and Abignale, bent low over the fire, smiled to himself.

"Well, of course, Lord! With ease." Her smile died, and on the heels of a pause, she whispered, "Rian, I...I thought...I knew..." She sighed, frustrated with herself. "I was certain I would die, and that I would be with my parents and Breggen."

She saw him tense at the mention of his late general.

With a sympathetic look she continued. "I took such comfort in the fact that once I was gone, I would not be alone. To die because my own brother cared so little for me..." She bit her lip to keep the tears that threatened to spill at bay. "I agonized that I would not see you again, and I...well, I..."

Wondering why it was so hard for her to speak, she forced herself to sit up again. Rian's hand came to her back to help, and she smiled.

"What are you trying to say, Elora?"

She hesitated, then leaned forward and placed her hands on his arms to steady herself.

"You were right, Rian. You were right about all of it. I realized, after Kristofer captured me, that my concerns were misplaced. Even he thought so. And I thought you might have changed your mind. But...well, I don't think it's worth the risk of losing—"

"Elora?"

She drew back slightly.

"I have no idea what you're talking about."

"I love you!" she blurted out, startling them both.

Rian raised his brows in surprise, never expecting her to say those words. As if she had done something wrong, she clapped a hand over her mouth and refused to look at him. Her heart thumped against her chest.

"Have you?" she said.

"Have I what?"

"Have you changed your mind?"

His chuckle startled her, and she even glanced around to see what he found funny. Nothing seemed out of the ordinary, so she brought her gaze back to his face. She felt his hand wrap around her and pull her close. The hard length of him had her breath catching in her throat.

When his lips were but an inch from hers he whispered, "No."

His mouth covered hers hungrily, and she returned his kiss with ardor.

It was she who pulled away. Placing her hands on his chest, she pushed gently, and when his hand rose to cup her face, she leaned into it.

"I have loved you for a long time, Elora. I would not stop simply because your brother took you."

She raised a trembling hand to his before her tears finally spilled down her face. Pulling her even closer, he wrapped his arms around her and hugged her tight, whispering that she was all right, and that she was safe.

After Elora had exhausted her tears, she pulled away.

"I have not cried in years, and now I fear it's all I do." She flashed a watery smile.

"You will heal, Elora. I'll help you. I fear we must ride, though."

He stood and pulled her to her feet, but her legs would not support her and she buckled against him. He caught her easily and picked her up. With a jerk of his head, Rian summoned Brilor over, and he held Elora while Rian mounted his horse. Once Elora was safely in front of him, she leaned back.

Rian turned to address Zemirah and his men. "If Kristofer catches up with us, it will be a bloodbath. He'll be more lethal than ever. Ride hard."

He watched everyone nod. They took off, fleeing the South in hopes of escaping with their lives. As the rode, Elora closed her eyes against the memories of her time in the South. She thought of Kayne and gasped as she suddenly remembered something.

"Rian!" she cried, struggling to face him.

Being unable to move more than inch because of his arms, she leaned her head back and stared at him, in horror.

"Kayne had Kristofer send Dagr to prevent our people from reaching the Eastern Territory. Dagr will slaughter all of them. He—"

Rian held his hand up to stop her. "I figured Kristofer would report to Kayne, and I have made arrangements. Your rescue will delay Dagr's departure. And with the extra time, our people will safely reach Rake's Territory."

"But how? In so short a time."

"I've expressed the need for haste, and I told our people the truth, striking enough fear into them to get them safely across the countryside as quickly as possible. Eret was left in charge, and he is capable. Not to mention, the time it would take Dagr to traverse back to that part of the country. He would never make it in time to prevent our people from reaching Rake's borders."

"Oh, Rian."

"It was necessary. After the last two attacks, our congregation is smaller. It will be easier now for them to reach the East."

Rian's voice held a note of sadness, and Elora thought of Breggen.

"I'm sorry about Breggen." She placed her hand on his. "I tried to stop him, but Kristofer..." She remembered how quickly he had thrown the knife. "His reflexes are unlike anything I've ever seen. Maybe the rumors are true. Maybe Kayne has enhanced his abilities. He was unstoppable before, but now I fear he is beyond death."

"If that were true, Elora, I would not have wounded him on the tower," Rian said.

"I didn't know you had." She sighed, torn between the love she had for Kristofer, and her hatred of him.

"His attention was diverted to Kayne," said Rian, "who Abignale was engaged with. Somehow, Kayne was wounded by Abignale's blade, and when Kristofer turned, my sword managed to graze him. He deflected the blow before any serious damage occurred, but inevitably it was what got us out of there alive."

Elora let his words sink in. Absentmindedly, she touched her shoulder, remembering how Kristofer had taken her pain away. *Why would he do that?*

The conversation she shared with him concerning Rian weighed heavily on her mind, too. For a moment, she felt as if she had her brother back. Only for him to tear himself away again.

He had also protected her from his soldiers when they would have raped her. She could not understand why it mattered to him. Perhaps Kayne had ordered him to keep her safe. That was the only thing that made sense. If it was a marriage alliance he was seeking, he would not want a defiled bride.

Placing a hand on her forehead, she tried to stem the flow of thoughts.

"Be easy, Elora. You need to sleep."

"I am so cold, Rian. I fear I will never get warm."

She felt Rian tighten his arm around her.

"Abignale said you would recover with time."

In the jumbled confusion of her mind, time lost all meaning. Feeling secure within his arms, Elora fell into a deep sleep.

CHAPTER 13

K ristofer studied the tracks. Then he swore in anger as he mounted Asen.

"This was falsely laid," he snarled. "Turn back!"

"Why did it take us a day to follow them?" Dagr retorted.

He had been watching Kristofer the last few hours, and he realized that Kristofer wasn't himself. His movements were slower, and he seemed weary. It appeared that Dagr finally stood a chance, and he was prepared to take it.

Kayne had been furious when Kristofer returned with the news that Elora had somehow made it out of the city. He took his anger out on Kristofer and nearly killed him while torturing him for hours. Once he was calm, Kayne healed him. Mostly.

His encounter with Kayne left Kristofer weak. Knowing that Dagr sensed something was amiss, Kristofer was on guard.

Eyeing the man wearily, Kristofer hissed, "It is not your concern, Dagr. Turn back."

"No. I think it is time a new leader arose."

Dagr glowered at Kristofer, and the group of soldiers backed up.

"You seek to challenge me?" Kristofer said with an amusement bordering on disdain.

Dagr drew his sword and attacked. The men watched with interest. They, too, had noticed that something was off, but none would challenge Kristofer's leadership. Most of them adored him, and he commanded respect.

Kristofer lifted his sword and blocked Dagr's advances. Within a few moments, Dagr lay lifeless on the ground.

Annoyed, Kristofer left his body and turned back to his men. They would ride straight through to the East.

"We stop for nothing. Ride hard."

———※※———

Elora woke up and pulled herself away from Rian. He slept soundly. Beside herself, only Abignale was awake. He sat next to a fire, where a small pot hung over it. Smiling warmly at her, he stood and poured the contents of the pot into a steel cup and handed it to her. She took it gratefully. The first sip warmed her insides and took some of the chill from her bones.

She still did not feel well. Any quick movement caused her lightheadedness, and she knew she'd never be able to stand on her own.

She whispered to Abignale, "Will I ever return to my former strength?"

Abignale nodded slowly. "Kayne took your blood, Elora. He drained you. It is a miracle you are doing as well as you are."

"I still feel weak and cold."

"Your strength will return. I promise."

She wasn't sure how to ask what she wanted to know. Large blue eyes scanned Abignale's wise old face, searching for answers. "

What happened after I..."

Abignale shifted, trying to get comfortable. "After we reached the tower, you had already fallen unconscious. Rian took on Kristofer, and I attacked Kayne. I knew if I could nick him with my sword, he would panic. He does not bleed. Have you noticed? The second a wound is inflicted, his skin seals itself and he heals. I doused my sword with a poison that would delay his healing. I knew if a drop of his blood fell, he would panic. And that is exactly what happened. Kristofer saw his distress and paused, giving Rian an opportunity to wound him. Zemirah and the rest of the men killed the soldiers, and Rian carried you out of there. Zemirah has men working in the castle, and we were aided. He brought us to Theda's house, where Rian gave you his own blood. I still find it surprising that it worked. It is so rare..." He gestured for Elora to finish her tea.

She looked at Rian in shock. It was his blood that flowed through her veins. It was his blood that had saved her life.

She reached over and brushed an errant strand of dark hair off of his forehead. He moved and opened his eyes, causing her to grimace.

"I did not mean to wake you."

He pushed himself up, then pulled her into his arms and kissed the top of her head.

"Did you sleep?" he said.

"Well, actually. "Did you?"

He nodded, and she leaned against him, eager for his warmth. Sensing her discomfort, he tightened his arms around her.

"Are you still cold?"

"Aye. Abignale said it was the loss of blood." She turned her head and leaned back to get a closer look at Rian. "He also told me that it is your blood that flows through my veins."

He paused. "Does it bother you?"

"No, Rian. Not at all."

She smiled weakly at him, and he returned the gesture with a kiss to her forehead.

"I think it is fitting, actually," she said.

They watched Zemirah wake up, followed by the rest of the men.

She walked over to Elora. "I found a stream nearby. I will take you to it, if you wish."

"Yes..." Elora said with hesitation, wondering if she could walk.

Rian pulled her to her feet, but the second his hands left her, she collapsed. He caught her, then followed Zemirah and brought Elora to the water. After he left, Zemirah helped Elora out of her dress and helped her wash, surprising her with soap that she thought to bring on the journey.

"Only another woman would think to bring soap!" Elora said.

"Aye." Zemirah cringed. "Men do not mind their smell."

Elora laughed, grateful to have a woman nearby after all that she had been through. Her only qualm was the coldness of the water. By the time she was done bathing, she shivered and felt colder than she did before.

"Will you call Rian?" Elora said, her lips chattering.

Zemirah nodded, and when she returned, Rian followed her and swept Elora up into his arms.

"You should not have done that," he said disapprovingly.

Bringing her straight to Abignale, who told her the same thing, he made her eat and gave her the tea, which seemed to be the only thing that kept her warm.

While she drank, the men went to the water while Zemirah stayed by her side.

"Thank you, Zemirah, for everything you have done."

Zemirah bowed her head slightly. They sat in a comfortable silence until they heard Rian and Brilor returning.

Zemirah glanced at Elora. "Maybe I should have offered them my soap!"

Elora's laughter drew Rian's attention. He saw Zemirah

lean close to her, and then she, too, started laughing. Wondering at their humor, he walked over and crouched beside Elora.

"What is so funny?"

Zemirah took a deep breath and wrinkled her nose mockingly, and she and Elora burst out laughing again. Elora leaned over and pressed her hands to her side.

After catching her breath, she looked at Rian. "Nothing you would find amusing, my love."

"I would care to know," he said, curiously.

"As would I," Brilor chimed in.

"We speak of how badly men smell," Zemirah said.

Rian chuckled, as Brilor said, "We do not smell!"

"Of course not, Brilor." Elora smiled.

"This is what is holding us from departing?" Abignale said from behind them. "Of all unintelligent words to speak, this is..." He walked off, muttering to himself, and the four of them started laughing again.

Rian mounted his horse. Once Elora was comfortably nestled in front of him, he urged the animal forward while the rest of the group followed. They flew through the countryside. As the hours passed, Elora grew colder and she ached from head to toe. Trying to shift in Rian's arms was almost impossible, for there was no place to go. Her head pounded with every step the horse took, and she felt ill.

After what seemed like an eternity, they pulled off the main road and took to the rolling hills of the countryside. As a farm came into view, Rian gestured for them to stop.

"Rogan, discreetly find out if they have a place for wayward travelers to stay. Tell them your wife is ill."

Rogan nodded and rode ahead. As he disappeared out of sight, Rian pulled Elora off the horse and Abignale came over.

"Why did you not say anything?" Abignale said in disbelief. "Elora, you are spiking a fever." He looked so worried that

Elora grew nervous, but she didn't have the strength to move.

"Rian, hold her up." Abignale pulled his waterskin out of his pack.

He added an odd-smelling green herb to the water and raised it to her lips.

After a few sips, her headache vanished, and some of the cold faded. Clinging to Rian, she shivered against his chest.

"I cannot build a fire, Elora," he whispered. "It will give away our position."

She nodded her understanding.

After a while, the sound of an approaching rider made her jump.

"Easy, love," Rian said. "It is only Rogan."

Without getting off of his horse, Rogan told Rian, "It is safe, Lord. They are sympathetic to my pregnant, sickly wife."

Rian grinned. "Well-done. We need to get back on the horses, Elora." He stood and handed her to Rogan, then mounted his own horse and turned to his group. "We will seek accommodation at the farm over the hill."

They rode their horses into the barn while Rogan took Elora to the house. Nervous without Rian nearby, she clung to Rogan's shoulders.

"It's all right, Lady," he whispered.

The door opened, and an older man answered it. His eyes were soft and kind, which was the first thing Elora noticed. His hair was thinning, and what was left of it was gray. Hunched with age, he waved them inside while his wife came running over. She, too, had a kind face, eyebrows furrowed together with worry over Elora.

"Here," she said to Rogan, and pointed to a small cot in the main room. "I am Besda. This be my husband, Jaro."

Elora looked around. The house was scarcely furnished with a table and three chairs, the cot and a rocking chair off to the corner. Rogan set Elora down.

"We be seein' other riders with ye," the old man said, with cheerfulness in his voice. "Do they not wish to rest inside?"

Rogan hesitated a brief moment. "They are friends. My concern is for my wife. They will be all right outdoors."

"We best be inviting them, eh, Besda? You be heating warm food for them now."

Jaro left the house while his wife busied herself over the fire pit. He returned a few minutes later with Rian. After turning to greet her guests, Besda saw Rian and froze. The old man looked stricken, too, and Rogan's hand went to his sword. Holding his hand out toward Rogan, Rian looked at the older couple.

"Forgive our deception," Rian said. "We mean only to stay a few hours. She," he nodded at Elora, "needs rest and warm food."

The older couple looked at each other with unease as the rest of Rian's group came up behind him.

"We mean you no harm," Rian said.

Besda stared at Elora for a long time, before whispering frantically to her husband.

"She be our lord's sister."

Jaro turned with wide eyes and looked at Elora, who returned their gazes with unease in the pit of her stomach.

He looked at Rian. "All right. Be just for the night now."

Relieved, Rian crouched next to Elora while Besda offered her a plate of hot lamb and potatoes.

"There be plenty for all," she said.

Everyone ate warily, in awkward silence.

As soon as they finished, Rian said, "Go back to the barn." He turned to Abignale. "Will you stay?"

Abignale nodded while Rian's soldiers turned and left.

Jaro turned to Rian. "We be meanin' no disrespect, but are ye not Rian?"

"I am." He watched Abignale hand Elora something steaming to drink.

"I be remeberin' your father..." Jaro seemed to think better of dredging up the past. "We be losin' both our sons to this bloodthirsty war. I understand both sides be sufferin' heavy losses. Kristofer may have not a patience for discontent among his people, but he be just and kind. The same be said for you. We know what Kayne be, and we know what he do, but we be not wantin' to see any harm come to Kristofer."

Elora pushed herself up at hearing this. "Kristofer leads the city?"

"Aye, Lady," Besda said. "Kayne be preoccupying himself inside his castle. We be not knowin' anyone who has ever even seen him. It be Kristofer who takes care of us."

Rian, Abignale, and Elora exchanged a look. What Besda and Jaro said about Kristofer went against everything they knew of him. Elora could not understand why he would leave the North to govern the South.

"I do not wish any misfortune to befall my brother," Elora said. "It matters little to me what side we are on."

That was not entirely true. Though she missed him, she feared him. It was a mind-numbing terror that sunk its icy grip into her chest and clung on despite her best efforts to disengage herself from those emotions.

He had tried to kill her. He would have succeeded—and with no remorse. Yet there was a part of her that ached to know his reasons for abandoning her so many years before. Could there be a reason that held such value that she could forgive him?

Unlikely, but it captured her attention, nonetheless.

Rian glared at Elora. He would never forgive Kristofer for his betrayal, and he would never understand Elora's feelings toward him.

"We need to rest," Abignale said, sensing Rian's rising temper.

"Of course, me lord," Jaro said. "We retire. Should ye be needin' anything, we be right through this door."

He and Besda left the room. Rian and Abignale laid on the floor. Abignale fell asleep promptly, but Rian struggled with his thoughts. He worried Elora would end up more than just heartbroken over her brother. She had delusions concerning him. And no one, not even Rian, could get through to her.

Elora, too, had trouble sleeping. After pulling herself off the cot, she lowered herself to the floor slowly. Rian saw her and sat up.

"What are you doing?" he whispered.

She smiled at him. "Whatever Abignale gives me, it makes me feel better. I only wanted to be near you."

"You would choose a hard floor over a bed?"

"Aye. The cot will not support both of us."

Rian pulled her close, and she rested her head against his chest. After a few minutes in each other's embrace, they fell asleep.

—⁓—

Abignale woke up first, to sunlight streaming through the windows. Besda was up making food, while Jaro went outside to gather eggs. Elora and Rian woke up together.

"I feel better today," Elora said to Abignale, as he handed her the tea.

"You are still weak," he replied. "Do not strain yourself overly much."

"We need to go," Rian said. "We've tarried entirely too long."

"Will ye be eating?" Besda said.

Rian hesitated. Elora looked up at him. She was hungry and they still had several weeks journey ahead of them.

Reluctantly, he replied, "Yes."

Besda made enough eggs and salted pork to feed all of them, and they ate, talked, and laughed. The tension between Besda, Jaro, and the group seemed to have vanished overnight.

As they stood to leave, Jaro said, "I be gladdin' we met." To Elora, "Lady, I be hopin' ye strength returns soon."

He bowed, and Besda quickly followed suit.

"Your hospitality was ever gracious," Elora said. "We are most thankful."

Rian helped Elora to her feet, and she gave Besda and Jaro a last smile as Rian climbed onto his horse. Leaning over, he picked her up around the waist and situated her in front of him.

"Wait! Lord!" Besda called. "Be takin' this with ye, please."

She ran out of the house and handed him a cloth. Unfolding it, Elora saw cheese and dried fruit.

"I know it is not much, but it will give ye a break from meat."

Elora looked at Rian, wishing she had something to give in return. Rian leaned over and dug through the saddle bags to pull out a small bag of silver. Handing it to a speechless Besda, he smiled warmly at her.

"For your kindness," he said. "I know it will not replace the sons you have lost, but know that we are not your enemies."

A whistling sound jerked Rian's senses, and he shouted, "Take cover!"

But it was too late. An arrow pierced Besda straight through the heart and she fell, a smile still etched upon her face. Crying out, Jaro came running and pulled his dead wife into his arms. A moment later, he also took an arrow in the back.

Elora turned and saw Kristofer leading a group of Red

Soldiers right toward them. Terrified, she could only stare at Rian.

"He will not take you again," he said. "I swear it."

He urged his horse forward as Brilor and Ayden came out of the barn, followed by Rogan, Zemirah, Caidus, and Abignale.

"We cannot outrun them!" Abignale yelled. "Prepare to fight!"

They took cover from the arrows behind the barn. Rogan and Ayden dismounted and stood in front of the horses. Kristofer rounded the corner of the barn, followed by ten soldiers all on horseback.

Seeing her brother again made Elora's heart pound, and she pushed herself closer to Rian. He tightened his arm around her and controlled his horse with one hand.

"I'm here only for her." Kristofer nodded at Elora. "Give her to me, and the rest of you can go."

"No," Rian growled, then whispered in Elora's ear, "Stay on the horse."

He swung his leg over his horse and glowered at Kristofer.

"Attack," Kristofer said to his men, his gaze trained on Rian. "Do not harm her."

Kristofer's men attacked, and a fierce battle raged between the two small groups.

"I should have killed you a long time ago," Kristofer growled.

"We will finish this now," Rian hissed.

Their swords reverberated off each other with such force that sparks flew from the blades. Rian's strength was fueled by anger and hatred. Kristofer, not yet fully recovered from his encounter with Kayne, felt the shift in power. Their fight was brutal. Neither one realized that Rian's men and Zemirah had killed Kristofer's soldiers. It wasn't until Abignale lent his sword against Kristofer that the tides turned. Before long,

Kristofer was sweating, and he could barely lift his sword in time to ward off both of their blows. A final, powerful strike from Rian drove Kristofer to his knees.

Panting, he threw his sword down. "I cannot fight you both. Kill me and be done with it."

Rian brought his sword to Kristofer's throat. Breathing heavily, Kristofer stared at him.

"Rian?" Elora called softly.

Part of her was terrified that he would kill her brother, and the other part was terrified that he would not.

Rian stood, hands shaking as he looked down at Kristofer. He could end it now, save Elora the agony of having to deal with him again and again. But he remembered, and it gave him pause.

Abignale said, "He is defeated, Rian. Bring him back with us."

Elora gasped at the thought of bringing her brother back to the Eastern Territory. Rake would no doubt torture him and then kill him.

It took minutes, but finally Rian lowered his sword and nodded. Brilor and Zemirah grabbed Kristofer and tied his hands behind his back.

"You do not think he can get out of that?" Rian asked Abignale.

"Something is wrong with him, Rian. Can't you see that? He is not as strong as he usually is."

Rian glanced at Elora. She stared at the horse's mane, unable to watch her brother brought down. Rian was bothered that she would feel anything other than animosity toward Kristofer.

It wasn't until Kristofer was tied that Rian realized Afflen had fallen. Rogan and Ayden were both on their knees, next to him.

Kneeling beside Afflen's body, Rian closed his eyes. His

death brought on a fresh wave of anger, and he stalked over to Elora.

Kristofer watched Rian. He saw the anguish and the guilt on his face, but it was Elora who had captured his attention. She didn't look well. She was pale and thinner than he remembered. Half-expecting Rian to be bringing back a corpse, Kristofer was shocked that his sister was still alive.

Rian moved to Elora's side, where she leaned down to hear what Rian said. She shook her head and looked at Afflen's body. Kristofer could almost make out their words. He could have, before Kayne had tortured him.

"Rogan, we will bury him." Rian's voice shook with anger. "Along with Besda and Jaro. See to it."

Rogan pulled himself to his feet and glared at Kristofer. Devastated at Afflen's death, Rogan and Ayden picked up his body and rounded the barn. Kristofer's men were left where they had fallen, and Zemirah shoved Kristofer forward.

"He can ride Afflen's horse," Rian said. "I do not trust that black beast of his. Kill it."

Kristofer whistled, and his black horse turned and galloped away. Rian hit him hard. Completely unfazed, Kristofer pulled himself to his feet. Elora, feeling lightheaded, shook her head to try to clear it.

"She's going to faint," Kristofer told Rian.

With Zemirah's sword still at Kristofer's back, Rian turned to Elora and caught her just before she fell.

"Why does this keep happening?" Rian hissed at Abignale.

"There is too much going on for her. This," he gestured to Kristofer, "will torment her. We need to get her back so she can recover."

Overwhelmed, Rian shot Elora a worried look.

"I will stay with her," Abignale said. "Your men need you."

Without a word, Rian turned and walked away, leaving Brilor and Zemirah to guard Kristofer. He found Rogan,

Ayden, and Caidus digging, and took out his frustration with a shovel he found in the barn. They buried the three bodies before returning.

Elora was awake and looking grave. Her brother sat calmly a few feet away, which only added to her unease.

"Zemirah, keep watch over him." Rian jerked his head in Kristofer's direction. "He is cunning. Do not underestimate him."

Zemirah inclined her head just as Kristofer brought his arms under his legs so they were tied in front of him rather than behind him. Mounting Afflen's horse on his own, Kristofer seemed to accept his defeat with ease.

Rian climbed onto his horse, and Rogan handed Elora to him.

"We will not stop until dark," Rian said to them. "It does not matter if we are seen now. Prepare yourself for a long day."

CHAPTER 14

Rian had spoken the truth. The day seemed endless, and the sun took its time moving across the sky. The few times she glanced at her brother, Elora noticed that he seemed completely at ease, with not a care in the world.

When, at last, the sun set and it became dangerously dark, they found a deserted barn. At one time, it was probably used for storing hay and feed for livestock.

"Rogan, Caidus." Rian gestured to the barn.

The two men dismounted and drew their swords before entering. They came out a moment later.

"It is safe, Lord," Caidus said.

Rian climbed off his horse and held his arms out for Elora. Keeping an arm around her waist, he helped her walk into the barn. Rogan was already building a fire, and Rian sat her down near the soldier before going back outside, hand on his sword, to watch Zemirah order Kristofer off his horse. Even with his hands tied, his movements were graceful. He slid off his horse with ease, arching slightly, when Zemirah's sword jabbed him in the back.

"Are you even human anymore?" Rian murmured, shaking his head.

Kristofer grinned. Upon entering the barn, he saw his sister sitting close to a small fire. He studied her for a moment, wondering how she had survived. Elora looked up and met his gaze. They stared at one another until Zemirah shoved him forward. She took him to a beam, where she tied his hands behind him. When she was through, Kristofer stretched his long legs out in front of him, crossing them at the ankles. Aside from his hands behind him, he was the picture of ease. Even Abignale found it odd.

Rian walked over to Elora and handed her a piece of bread.

He kissed the top of her head. "I'm sorry, love. I should have killed him at the barn."

"Why didn't you?"

He raised a dark brow in response and crouched beside her.

With a sigh he said, "Because I, too, remember Kristofer as a child."

Elora reached up and let her thumb graze Rian's face.

"I forget how close you were," she said. "Sometimes it's hard for me to see beyond my own pain."

"It's of no consequence, Elora." He glanced at Kristofer. "I worry you will suffer more than he, at the fate that awaits him."

Elora grimaced and looked down. Rian nudged her chin up and saw her struggling to hold back tears.

"They will torture him, Rian." Biting her lip hard, she tasted blood. "Is there nothing you can do? I know he will be executed, but can you not approach Rake? Beg clemency? Anything? He will take your words into consideration. He will only dismiss mine. Please?"

Rian knew Elora would ask this. He doubted that Rake would show Kristofer any type of mercy, even if Rian were to say something. As they were entering the Eastern Territory, it would be entirely up to Rake to deal with Kristofer.

"I will try," Rian said.

Elora gave him a watery smile and nodded. Rian handed

her cheese and bread, encouraging her to eat, but she had no appetite.

"I did not suffer at all at his hands," she whispered to Rian. "I know that he took me, and I know that you think my affection toward him is foolish. But he protected me against his men and—"

Rian's face darkened. "What do you mean? Protected you against his men?"

Drawing her legs underneath her, Elora took a deep breath, wincing at the memory.

"The first night, we made camp at a clearing in the woods. Kristofer left me alone for a moment, and as soon as he was gone, two of his men tried...to rape me. He killed them both."

"Perhaps he was under orders to bring you back unharmed."

"I don't know, Rian. He was so angry."

"One good deed will not undo the years of brutality."

Rian knew there was no getting through to her concerning her brother, and Elora knew Rian would never understand. She thought about Kristofer coming to her room and healing her shoulder. Knowing the story would not make a difference to Rian, she kept it to herself.

Elora nodded and took a bite of her bread as Zemirah came over to sit beside her. Rian stood to join Rogan and Caidus, who were taking turns throwing a knife at a makeshift target.

Smiling at the other woman, Elora said, "Zemirah, have you a knife?"

"Aye." She pulled one out of her boot and handed it over.

Elora waited until Rogan handed the knife to Rian. She watched him draw his arm back before she threw her knife. It knocked Rian's out of the air, and he spun around, thinking it was Kristofer. After realizing it was Elora, he laughed.

A faint smile played on Elora's lips. "You've lost."

"You cheated." Rian bent down to retrieve both knives.

Elora flashed him a brilliant smile as Abignale handed her a steaming cup.

"Abignale, what is this?"

"An herbal concoction of my own invention. It warms you, does it not?"

She sipped it gratefully. "It is the only thing that does."

Abignale left the women alone and sat down to watch the men play their games. Elora turned around to look at Kristofer before rising slowly to her feet.

"I can manage, Zemirah," she said, in response to the look on the woman's face.

Once on her feet, Elora paused, cautious as a wave of dizziness washed over her. Taking her uneaten food, she inched over to Kristofer and knelt beside him. He ignored her as he watched the ongoings with intense fascination. She let her hand graze his shoulder but drew back quickly, as if she had burned herself, when he jerked from her touch. His blue eyes bore into hers with an intensity that had her lowering her gaze.

She held out the food. "Are you hungry?"

He continued to study her. "Not particularly."

She bit her bottom lip so hard that the bitter taste of blood filled her mouth. She felt her throat tighten, but blinked back tears and forced herself not to cry.

"I cannot bear this, Kristofer," she whispered.

"Let it be as it is, Elora. It's all part of war."

"It's barbaric! Are you not frightened?"

He chuckled. "Of torture? I would not say I look forward to it, but it does not frighten me."

"I cannot bear the thought of you suffering. Maybe I can appeal to Rake—"

"Don't waste your breath. Your pleas will fall on deaf ears." He watched Rian playfully shove one of the men, before returning his attention back to Elora. "Did you carry your words to Rian yourself, then?"

Startled by the change their conversation was taking, Elora nodded slowly.

"I did, yes," she replied.

"And I assume you will marry him?"

Frowning, she nodded again.

"You would have been there," she said, bitterness in her tone.

He turned to her. "Do not harp on the past, Elora. I find it infuriating."

The force of his anger was so great that she drew back and took a shaky breath that had him narrowing his eyes in annoyance. His shoulders were beginning to ache from being tied so long, and he shifted. It took him less than a minute to free his hands, and as he pulled his arms forward, Elora gasped in fright.

He grinned. "I have no desire to harm you, little sister."

His proclamation did nothing to reassure her. She was weak and pale, thin and unnaturally still. Her fear over what happened had taken a serious toll, and he had no doubt that the time she spent with him made it all the worse.

His tone changed then. The mocking undertone and the anger disappeared, replaced by the gentle voice she remembered so well.

"Easy, Elora."

After a moment, he saw her relax.

"I don't understand, brother. How is it that Rian defeated you?"

His laughter made Rian turn around. And seeing Elora beside him, Rian's hand flew to the hilt of his sword.

"Suffice it to say, little sister, that Kayne was not nearly as pleased with your departure as you were."

"Torture?! He *tortured* you? I don't understand. You look well enough."

He laughed again. "He has methods you cannot even imagine, Elora. You do not seem to realize what you are up against." His gaze darted behind her before resting once more on her face. "Go."

Rian was nearly upon them, and Elora turned to see him give her a dark look.

"Get away from him, Elora," Rian growled.

He held a hand down to her, and she took it with hesitation. He pulled her to her feet and moved aside so she could pass him. His meaning was clear, and with a last look at her brother, Elora walked back to the fire.

"Stay away from her," Rian snarled, looking down at Kristofer.

He raised a brow in response. "You act as if I summoned her over here. If you could control your woman, we would not have need of this conversation."

Rian drew back and punched Kristofer. It didn't seem to faze him much, which only made Rian angrier.

"How did you save her?" Kristofer said, ignoring the pain from Rian's fist.

With a look of disbelief, Rian crouched before Kristofer.

"I gave her my blood."

Kristofer raised his eyebrows in shock, but Rian had a question of his own.

"Elora told me that your men attacked her, and that you saved her. Is this true?"

With a grimace, as if Kristofer did not want anyone to know of any good deed he may have performed, he sighed.

"Aye."

"Why?"

It was Kristofer's turn to look confused. "I had orders from Kayne to bring her unharmed."

"And were those not your orders, would you have allowed it?"

"Are you asking if I would have allowed my men to rape her?"

Rian made no move to respond. He watched Kristofer, studying his face as he waited for an answer, which came after careful consideration.

"Unwilling women never interested me. So no, I don't suppose I would have."

With a quizzical look, Rian glanced at the rope sitting beside Kristofer and reached for it.

"I will only pull out of it again."

Rian ran a hand over his face, wondering why he hadn't killed Kristofer when he had the chance. He knew Kristofer would still be a formidable opponent, even in his weakened state, but to attack him now would be murder, and Rian knew Elora would never forgive him. He wasn't sure if he could deal the fatal blow, anyway.

He let out a harsh breath before crouching and pulling Kristofer's arms behind him to secure them to the beam. With that done, Rian turned and walked back to the fire, unnerved, as he always was when he had to face Kristofer.

"I do not want you near him," Rian said once Elora was in earshot. "If you are too close and he seeks to use you against me, he will kill you."

Exasperated, she flung her hands in the air.

"He won't!"

"He already has!" Rian crouched before her and used his hands to steady himself.

His dark-blue eyes were made even darker by the change in his mood.

"If you go near him again, Elora, I swear it, I will kill him."

"You cannot—"

"I can, and I will. He is not the child we grew up with.

He is a grown man, and he is deadly. I'd rather see his blood at the end of my sword than yours on his. Take my words seriously."

Furious, Elora turned away from him.

"I do not want to fight with you," Rian said. "You are in no position to defend yourself. I could not bear it were anything to happen to you."

His words tamed Elora's temper somewhat, but the ache at losing her brother to Kayne was stronger than ever.

Without responding, Elora laid down with her back to Rian. The argument with him made her feel dizzy, and she realized he was right. She could not defend herself. At the moment, she could not even lift a sword.

Sighing, she turned toward him. "You are right. I am weak, and were I not, I would still be no match for him. I do not want to fight with you either, but you cannot ask me—.

Rian held his hand up, putting a stop to their argument.

"Elora, please? Let us sleep. We will both feel better in the morning."

Knowing she would get nowhere with him, she nodded. She was exhausted and sore from the constant riding. Abignale agreed to keep watch, so Rian stretched out beside Elora. He pulling her close, he kissed her lightly, and wrapped in each other's arms, they soon fell asleep.

Kristofer watched them and his thoughts once again returned to Aelia. Knowing he could not take on Abignale and Rian just yet, he leaned back and waited for sleep to overcome him. He knew his horse would gallop directly back to the city. With Asen being riderless, Raum would no doubt send men after him. He could still survive if he played along. He knew Rake's torturer's would take their toll on him, but he very much doubted they could damage him the way Kayne had.

Resigning himself to a week of pain, Kristofer thought of Aelia and hoped Raum would have enough sense to keep his capture a secret from her.

Kristofer had not so much as even thought of another woman since Aelia came into his life. She made the war bearable, and life worth living. As long as he knew she was taken care of, he would not worry about what would happen to him.

With ease, he pulled his wrists apart until the rope tore. After shaking his wrists free, he situated himself comfortably and leaned back as sleep overcame him.

CHAPTER 15

Rian picked up the rope with a sigh and glared at Kristofer, who returned his gaze with an easy grin.

"Why not escape?" Rian said.

Kristofer stood up. "Why expend the energy when we both know I will lose?"

Pinching the bridge of his nose, Rian glanced at Elora, who watched, unblinking, from her place on the floor.

Rian turned back to Kristofer. "Even with what awaits you in the East?"

"We both know I will survive your torture chamber," Kristofer said.

Rian nodded in agreement. "It is Elora who will not."

"Undoubtably."

"You will not survive an execution." Rian looked Kristofer up and down. "Or will you?"

Shrugging, Kristofer studied Rian. Whereas his sister had not changed overly much, Rian had. He was harder and stronger. Unlike Elora, Rian distanced himself from Kristofer and fully expected the worst. Kristofer could feel the hatred pouring off of him, as Rian blamed him for the death of his twin brothers and his parents. Even though Kristofer had not led the attack on Rian's kingdom, he had no qualms with fueling the rumors. He smiled at the thought.

Grabbing Kristofer roughly, Rian meant only to retie his hands behind his back, but Kristofer doubled over. Rian's touch sent debilitating pain from his shoulder down the length of his body. Kristofer had felt this before. It was the same agony he suffered at Kayne's hands—almost as if his bones were on fire.

The pain left as quickly as it had come, and Kristofer slowly turned to look at Rian, just as Elora walked over.

"What did you do?" she gasped.

"Nothing," Rian said. "I swear it. I meant only to tie him again."

Elora bent down and placed a hand on Kristofer's shoulder. Expecting pain again, he jerked from her touch, which startled them all. But when nothing happened, he pulled himself to his feet with shaky legs. Kristofer grabbed Rian's arm to see if the touch would set off another wave of pain, and when it didn't, he released Rian but watched him with caution. Rian raised his arm to strike Kristofer, but the look on the other man's face gave him pause.

Seeing what happened, Abignale came over. Sad, liquid eyes studied the younger man.

"What did Kayne do to you?" he asked Kristofer.

Chest heaving, Kristofer glared at Abignale. He could easily survive anything Rake's men would do to him, but another incident at Kayne's hands would surely destroy him.

Feeling nauseous, Kristofer leaned against the beam and closed his eyes, trying to recollect himself.

Worried over her brother, and disconcerted over his weakness, Elora walked away. She wanted to leave the barn and get on with the journey.

"Look at me," Abignale ordered.

Kristofer obeyed, and Abignale stared into his eyes for a long time. Rather than pull his gaze away, Kristofer met him with an intensity that unnerved the old man. He had known Kristofer since he was born. Not as close to him as he was to Elora, Abignale still felt confident that he knew him well enough.

Without taking his gaze off Kristofer, Abignale said, "Give me a moment alone with him."

Rian stormed off. "Prepare to depart," he barked to no one in particular.

An hour passed before Abignale emerged with Kristofer. Both expressions were unreadable, and when Elora and Rian questioned Abignale, all he would say was that Kristofer was beyond repair.

Rian looked at the position of the sun, judging the day, and figured it would take at least another three weeks to reach Rake's territory.

By the time they reached the Eastern borders, the only one who didn't seem overly exuberant was Kristofer. The castle would take a few more hours to reach, but they would be there before nightfall.

"Let me talk to him," Elora begged, unable to bear it any longer.

Rian sighed. "It will do neither of you any good. You heard Abignale as we left that barn. Your brother is gone, Elora."

The sky was not yet dark as the castle towers came into view. Relieved beyond measure, Rian called to the soldiers stationed above, and silently, the drawbridge was lowered. As soon as they were inside the courtyard, Rian swung his leg over his horse and climbed down.

"We have a prisoner," Abignale said from behind him.

Elora watched as four heavily armed guards came and pulled Kristofer off his horse.

"He is extremely dangerous," Abignale said. "Do not let him near a weapon."

Entering the palace in a subdued manner, the first person

Elora saw was Rake.

"Oh, Elora!" he cried. "We were so worried about you."

He cupped her face and kissed her forehead. His wife, Olibia, not far behind him, hugged Rian tight.

"We thought for sure you were unsuccessful." She cringed. "We had reports that Elora was executed."

"It is a long story," Rian said, fatigue in his voice.

Frowning, Rake nodded. "Of course. But is it true you brought Kristofer back with you?"

Elora grimaced, and Rian nodded.

"Allow us a night to recover?" he said. "We will meet with you in the morning. Elora is weak."

As if on cue, Elora swayed as her vision went black. It was Abignale who caught her before she fell, and Rian picked her up.

Olibia gasped. "Follow me. We've had quarters made up for you. We just did not know when you would return."

Rian followed Olibia through a maze of corridors and stairwells.

"Did our people arrive safely?" he said.

"All have arrived." She paused in front of a door and pushed it opened. "This is Elora's room. Yours is down the hall, on the left. What can I do?"

Rian placed Elora on the elegant four-poster bed.

She stirred, and Rian said, "Have a warm bath and food sent up. Abignale makes a tea that seems to help her."

Olibia nodded and shut the door.

Rian sat down beside her and took her cold hand in his.

"It is all right, my love," he whispered. "Everything will sort itself out."

She nodded, but she felt sick to her stomach and ice cold. Rian drew a blanket over her and stayed with her until the servants brought the tub. He rose to his feet and acknowledged the group of servants.

"She will need assistance," he said.

Realizing he was about to leave, Elora held on tight to his hand.

"I'll come back." He kissed her cheek.

Once he was gone, an older woman approached her.

"Lady, I am Mayda. I will help you."

Elora studied her for a moment, before accepting her hand. Mayda helped her undress and eased her into the tub. As soon as Elora settled into the water, she could feel some of the warmth creep into her bones. Mayda washed her hair with a lilac-scented soap that Elora thought was wonderful. It had been years since she last had this kind of treatment. After her ordeal with Kristofer and Kayne, she enjoyed the kind, gentle hands Mayda used. Once clean, she dried herself with a towel Mayda had left near the fire, and afterward slipped on a white nightdress.

The older woman drew the blankets over Elora's legs and propped her up with pillows.

"I'll have food brought, your majesty." She waited for Elora to dismiss her.

Realizing why she stood there, Elora gave her a weak smile.

"My thanks for your help."

Surprised that a queen would thank her, Mayda bowed and smiled warmly at Elora. The gesture heartened her, and she returned Mayda's smile with ease.

No sooner had she left, did the food arrive. Plates of roasted lamb and warm bread, sweet potatoes with syrup, rice with dried fruit, and apples topped with honey.

Even though the food smelled incredible, nothing appealed to Elora except the apples. She bit into one, and before she knew it, she had eaten half of the sweetened fruit. Her appetite came back, and she tried some of everything. As she bit into a slice of bread, a knock startled her. She froze, staring at the door without saying anything, until it opened and Rian stepped in. She released her pent-up breath in a whoosh.

"Elora. When you did not answer, I grew worried." He took a seat beside her.

"It's been so long since I've had a door. I...well, I don't know..." She smiled at him. "Have you eaten? The apples are...they are quite appetizing."

Rian laughed. "There is more honey than apple. You've always had a fondness for sweets."

After taking another one off the plate, she cut it and leaned forward to place it in his mouth. He swallowed but shook his head.

"I do not share your love of honey."

"That is absurd. Eat the meat, then. I'll keep the apples to myself."

"You seem much better. So it was only a bath you needed?"

"Apparently. The water was so warm that I feel as though some of the heat sunk into my skin. And the soap! It was lilac. I had forgotten..."

He laughed again. "I, too, had the lilac soap. It must be something Olibia came up with. I doubt Rake is handing out floral-scented soap to his soldiers."

This brought forth a hearty laugh from Elora.

They ate together, enjoying one another's company. Rian noticed the change in her immediately. Abignale was right. She just needed proper care. It would still be some weeks before she was back to full strength, but Rian was relieved to see the improvement in the few hours they had been back.

Feeling full and clean, and better than she had in weeks, Elora pulled a pillow out from behind her and leaned back.

"I'll let you rest," he said, but she gasped.

"You cannot leave!"

"Elora, I'll be no more than a few feet away."

Wide-eyed, she shook her head. "I don't want to be alone."

Rian hesitated. "We are not on the road anymore, love."

"I don't care about propriety, Rian. Please?"

Surprised at how helpless she seemed, Rian sat back down next to her.

"All right."

She wasn't sure why she felt afraid to be left alone. Before Kristofer took her South, she enjoyed her alone time in her tent. Now, surrounded by people, she felt more alone than ever. Maybe her capture took more of a mental toll on her than she thought. Realizing Rian would probably think she was crazy, and maybe she was now, she shook her head.

"You are right, Rian. I'm just discombobulated. Go. I'm fine."

"You're not fine." He laid down next to her and pulled her into his arms.

Rian stayed with her until she fell asleep. After carefully getting up, he stared at her, watching her sleep for a moment, before returning to his own chamber.

CHAPTER 16

E lora pulled herself out of bed, noticing at once that she was alone. Peering out the window, she realized it must be late morning, if not early afternoon.

She opened her armoire and stared in alarm at gown after gown of silk and lace. It had been so long since she had worn anything other than war attire, with the exception of a few dresses here and there, that she thought them impractical. After fingering a rich-blue dress, she pulled it out and held it up to her front.

"Would you like help with that, Lady?"

A voice from the door made her jump, and she nearly dropped the dress.

"Mayda, you startled me! Yes I would." She smiled.

"Forgive me, Lady. I knocked, but I don't believe you heard."

"I didn't." Elora frowned.

Mayda helped her dress and sat her in front of the vanity, where she brushed Elora's long blonde hair and wrapped it in an elegant bun. Strands of hair curled around her face, and as she studied her reflection in the mirror, she marveled, not for the first time, that she and Kristofer had the same eyes, curtesy of their father.

With a sigh, she rose unsteadily to her feet and left her chambers. She made her way down the stairwell and tried to remember the way to Rake's meeting room, which is where she was sure everyone was.

Finally, she asked a guard to escort her. She followed him to a set of a thick oak doors, which he pushed open for her. Rian, Rake, Olibia, and Abignale sat near each other at a long table, similar to the one she noticed Kristofer and Raum leaning over. Rian smiled at her, and the intensity of his gaze made her flush. She took his offered hand and sat next to him.

"How are you feeling, Elora?" Rake said.

"Better."

The weight on her shoulders was still there, but she knew it would not lift as long as Kristofer was in the dungeon. Rian squeezed her hand gently, knowing her internal struggle.

"That is good to hear," Rake replied. "Abignale says it will be some weeks before you are fully recovered."

Nodding, Elora straightened her shoulders. "I fear he is right."

They paused as a guard entered and beckoned to a stout, mean-looking man with hard eyes and a heavy brow.

"Ye sent for me, Lord?"

"Aye, tell us what information you have received."

The man scratched his greasy head, and Elora felt a wave of nauseousness as she realized who he was. She was heartened slightly when she felt Rian's hands come to her shoulders.

"Well, I be tellin' ye, sire, the man has frightened half of the dungeon guards. He be bleedin', and a lot, so we thinks he be human, but he don't even cry out. Our methods be... forceful, and he seem not even to notice it."

Elora closed her eyes and pressed a knuckle to her mouth, even as Rian's hands tightened, almost painfully, on her shoulders.

Rake glanced at them out of the corner of his eye. "Are you telling me that Kristofer is impervious to pain?"

The man blinked at Rake. "Imper—"

"Are you telling me he cannot feel pain?" Rake sighed.

With a shake of his head, the torturer continued. "I be not sayin that, sire. He be broken, barely movin'. He just seem not carin' what we be doin'. It be not right. We be gettin' not a word from im'. We took a brandin' iron to im', and he laughed!"

At this, Elora let out a disgruntled cry. "Rake, please!"

Ignoring her, Rake turned back to the man. "You are to send word immediately if there is news of any sort. I want to know anything that Kayne has planned, no matter how small. You are dismissed."

The man bowed awkwardly and left.

Rake turned to Elora and shook his head. "The man is your enemy, Elora. He nearly killed you."

"I do not care, Rake. This is barbaric. Kristofer is still a king!"

She felt Rian shift from her, and she turned wide, emotional eyes to look upon him.

"Nay, Elora," he said. "Kristofer abdicated his right to the crown when he betrayed us and joined our enemy."

She shook her head weakly, denying what he said, even though there was truth behind his words.

"Still..." Rian glanced imploringly at Rake. "Can you not execute him and be done with it?"

Rake rose halfway out of his chair before Abignale said, "My suggestion is to allow Elora to speak with him."

Elora gasped, and in unison, she and Rian cried, "No!"

"Aye," Abignale said. "I believe Kristofer holds some small affection toward his sister. Allow Elora to speak with him. Torturing him will only shut him down further."

"I forbid it!" Rian growled. "He will kill her if he gets the chance."

Abignale and Elora both shook their heads.

Abignale said, "I've been to the dungeon, Rian. He is in

no position to harm anything. That brute spoke the truth. Kristofer is broken, and he is in a great deal of pain."

Elora covered her face in her hands as a rage of emotions coursed through her. Was it possible that Kristofer cared for her? Abignale would not speak of his time alone with Kristofer in the barn, no matter how much she begged. If she could ease his suffering in some small way, should she not take every advance to do so? How she missed the brother she once had.

"I will go." She rose unsteadily to her feet, and ignored Rian's protests. "I cannot help the way I feel about my brother, Rian. Nor could I live with myself should I lose any chance to ease his discomfort. Whatever he is, I love him still."

Olibia stood and called for a guard to escort her to the dungeons.

Elora cringed against the stench. Lifting her skirts, she followed the guard until he stopped in front of a thick iron door. He unlocked the door with a heavy key and pushed it open. He bowed as she sailed past him.

Tears sprang to her eyes at the sight of her brother.

"Oh, Kristofer..." She turned to the guard and hissed, "Unchain him!"

The guard's eyes grew wide. "My queen, this is—"

"I know who he is! Unchain him now, or I'll see that you take his place."

Swallowing hard, the guard entered the dungeon and reached over his prisoner's head to unchain his wrists. Kristofer collapsed into the pool of blood on the floor. After ordering the guard to leave, Elora knelt down next to him and laid his head on her lap. His body felt warm, feverish.

"I'm so sorry, brother," she whispered, tears pooling in the corner of her eyes.

"Get out, Elora," Kristofer said, his voice weak.

She took the hem of her dress and wiped the blood off of his face.

"What can I do?"

She wanted only to relieve him in some small way, but he jerked from her touch. The movement sent a wave of pain down his side, confirming his suspicion that several ribs were broken.

"As soon as I leave, they will come back," she said, in anguish. "I'm not here for information. I came only as your sister."

She brushed a strand of hair off of his forehead and placed her hand on his chest. He was bruised and bleeding. Burns from hot irons were oozing clear fluid, and every time he moved, blood seeped from a deep gash down his chest.

His breathing was labored, but he spoke with force.

"I don't want you here."

"I know. Part of me doesn't want to be here. Oh, Kristofer, why not just tell them what they want to know?"

"I will...not betray...my king."

Knowing he was in pain broke her heart.

"I don't expect you to," she said. "I only wish you didn't have to suffer for it. Rian will talk to Rake. Perhaps together, we can convince him—"

"For...an early execution?"

"This is barbaric."

"War...Elora. Accept it."

"Would you accept it if our situations were reversed? Were it me in a Southern torture chamber, would you allow it?"

He studied her face as his chest moved with shallow rapid breaths.

"No," he whispered.

Unsurprised, Elora moved him gently, then walked to the door and called for a guard. She told him to bring water, which he did so hastily. After heading back to her brother, she tried to sit him up. He lifted a hand to stop her. Feeling helpless, she held the cup for him while he drank.

"Rake will have...me killed. We both know it."

She nodded.

"I do not want...you watching." He turned his head and spat blood out. "Promise it..."

"I promise." She took his hand and held it for a long time.

She could not bring herself to leave, knowing that once she did, they would hurt him again.

"Any battle plans..." He grimaced.

Every word he spoke caused waves of pain to assail him.

When he found his breath again, he whispered, "...I would give them would be woefully inaccurate...by the time they would prepare. Kayne will...will not send out an army... without me to lead it. Rake knows this."

"Then what does he want from you?" Elora said.

It took him a long time to answer.

"Revenge. Any insight into Kayne's activities. Elora..." he reached up slowly, his hand cupping the side of her face. "... you cannot fight him. His strength surpasses...that of any mortal man. If Kayne should ever ride...into battle, you all will fall." He said the last line slowly, pointedly.

"I will still fight," she replied. "But never against you."

"That's treason." He tried to shift, causing a grunt of pain.

She raked her fingers through his hair. "It is, and so be it. At least I will die with a clear conscience."

"As will I."

Not understanding at all how he could, Elora knew he was done talking. The memories of them together as children in the apple orchards came back to her, and she let herself feel the pain of missing the past.

"Do you remember the apple orchards?" she whispered, and he nodded. "Do you remember when Rian threw the apple and it hit me? You were so angry at him then."

"I would still be...angry if he hurt you."

His words brought forth a sob from her throat. Confusion, fear, and exhaustion seemed to overwhelm her. Even she wondered how she could feel anything for him, other than hatred and betrayal.

She felt his hand cup her cheek again.

"Don't be frightened."

"I cannot bear to lose you!" she whispered. "Knowing you are well in the South, fighting against me, is better than this."

He shook his head slowly, and she leaned forward to rest her forehead against his. He could feel her hot tears on his face, and it occurred to him that he might not survive the night, let alone make it to an execution. Even if he wanted to, with his skill and his strength, he did not think he'd be able to fight off one soldier, let alone a platoon of guards, which he knew were stationed right outside his room.

He knew Raum would take care of Aelia, and for a moment his pain vanished as he pictured Aelia sitting on his bed, brushing her mane of hair.

He found it difficult to take a deep breath.

"Elora..."

She leaned back and sniffed, and he somehow found the strength to lift his hand again and brush away the never-ending stream of her tears.

"Go."

Elora leaned over and kissed his forehead. She stood, then turned and walked away without looking back. She raced up the stairs and to her room, eliciting some surprised stares from the servants. After flinging open the door to her room, she fell upon her bed in a heap and cried.

She laid there, head upon her arms, for a long time. All the stress and fear of the past weeks, Kristofer's inevitable death and her conflicting feelings toward her brother, became unbearable. Elora felt strong hands on her shoulders, pulling her up. She knew it was Rian, and she threw her arms around his neck.

"He suffers terribly, Rian! You have to do something."

"I tried, Elora. Rake will not cave." Pushing her away slightly, he looked at her tear-stained face and wiped away her tears. "Let us clean you up."

Elora looked down at her dress in confusion. It was covered in blood. Kristofer's blood. Her hands and her arms were red. Rian called for a servant and ordered a bath. He wrapped his arms around her, and Elora leaned against him for support.

When the bath arrived, Rian left, and Elora stayed in the water until it grew cold. After throwing the blue gown on top of the fire, Elora put on a simple yellow dress and headed out of her room. It was nearly supper time, and as she came to the stairs, she heard Olibia call her name.

Forcing a smile, Elora held out both her hands

"Olibia," she said warmly. "We've scarcely had a chance to talk."

Shaking her head, Olibia took hold of her outstretched hands.

"I'm sorry for what anguish my husband is causing you." She leaned forward and kissed Elora's cheek. "Rian and I have both tried, but he will not listen to reason."

Surprised, Elora looked at her gratefully.

"Thank you. But Kristofer is accepting of his fate, and at this point, I just want it over with." Even as she said it, her eyes filled with unshed tears.

Looping their arms together, the women descended the stairs and headed toward the dining hall that could sit nearly two hundred men. The sand-colored marble floors gleaned against the candlelight, and in some small way, reminded Elora of the beaches of her childhood. Rian and Rake stood next to each other, arms folded, deep in conversation. Noting the women, each man held their hand out.

Rake took Olibia's hand and kissed her lightly on the lips. To Elora, he said, "Rian tells me you are engaged?"

A happy gasp escaped from Olibia's lips. "Is it true? Such wonderful news in such dark times!"

"Aye." Elora feigned a smile.

"We must plan, then!" Olibia said. "A wedding would be just what these people need."

"Now?" Rian said, surprise registering on his face.

With Kristofer's execution near, he hardly thought marriage preparations were appropriate just yet.

"She is right," Elora said. "A celebration will boost morale. And endless flow of wine and food will no doubt help to ease their losses, if only for one night."

"It will do all of us some good," Rake said. "I'm sure my wife will happily take on such preparations."

Olibia nodded vigorously. "I had wondered of it. You took such a long time to propose," she told Rian.

"I did not!" he said. "It took me a long time to convince Elora to marry me."

Elora laughed. "It only took years."

She forgot, momentarily, about her brother and enjoyed Olibia's excited chatter about the wedding.

The servants brought food, and everyone ate a fine meal. Kristofer's name was not mentioned, and for that Elora was grateful. Afterward, Rian escorted Elora back to her room, and again stayed with her until she fell asleep.

And that became their routine. Elora was grateful that Rian was near. It helped eased the burden of her brother, which weighed endlessly on her mind.

Two weeks later, Rake announced that Kristofer would be executed in three days' time.

Elora was tense for the rest of the day, scarcely eating,

and retiring early. Rian went to comfort her, but he could do little.

The night before the execution, she fell into a restless sleep in his arms. At some point late into the night, she awoke with a start, thinking she heard a shout. After listening carefully, she realized she was dreaming, and closed her eyes.

Unable to sleep after that, and feeling quite alone, since Rian had retired to his chambers, she threw on her robe and walked down the corridor to his room. She knocked quietly and pushed open his door.

"Rian?"

"Elora?"

She was surprised to find him awake. Several candles burned bright in his room, and he was reading a thick book, which he closed promptly when he saw her. She crawled into his bed and laid her head on his chest.

"Why are you awake?" she said.

"For the same reasons you are, I imagine." He kissed her.

She curled up next to him, eager for his warmth. Closing her eyes, she half-expected him to return her to her room, but he pulled her close.

"I love you, Rian," she said into his chest. "I do."

He tightened his grip on her. "And I, you. Sleep, Elora. Tomorrow will come whether we will it to or not."

"I'm restless." She pushed her hair off her shoulder and sat up. "Do you think Kristofer will find redemption?"

Staring at her, Rian shrugged. "For his sake, I hope so."

"He told me he will die with a clear conscience..."

"How that is possible, I do not know. But like you, I hope he finds peace." Rian took ahold of her arm and pulled her back to him. "Lay down, love, and try to sleep."

"I don't want to be alone, Rian. Not tonight."

"You can stay. I'll be here in the morning, and we'll face this together."

He sounded so strong and comforting that Elora did find sleep not long after. While holding her, Rian, too, fell into a restless slumber. But they were violently woken up a few hours later.

Brilor came in and shook Rian awake. "Kristofer has escaped! Half the guards in the dungeon have been slaughtered. Rake wants the two of you downstairs!"

It took Rian and Elora a moment to register the news. He turned to look at her, shock on his face. He hopped up and got dressed.

"I'll change," she murmured, unsure if she was relieved or horrified that Kristofer would survive.

Rian waited for her, and they hurried down the stairs to meet Olibia and an outraged Rake. Abignale stood nearby, hands folded in front of him. His face was impassive.

"How did this happen?" Rake snarled.

"We don't know what happened." Rian gripped Rake's shoulders. "Only that he escaped."

Elora took a seat at the great table and placed her head in her hands.

Rake stared at her. "We don't know either. A guard said he went downstairs, only to find half of the dungeon guards slaughtered, and Kristofer's cell empty." He turned to Abignale and hissed, "You said he could do no more damage!"

Abignale raised a steady eye at his tone. "He clearly had help."

"He could barely move, Rake," said Elora. "He could not have done this alone."

"And did the help come from within these walls?" Rake glared at Elora.

Olibia gasped. "Rake!"

Rian leapt to his feet at the accusation, and Elora stared at him.

"How dare you," she hissed.

"It is no secret you hold an affection for Kristofer," Rake growled.

"He is my brother!"

"All the more reason." Rake slammed his fist down on the table. "Where were you last night?"

"Rake, you go too far," Rian growled. "She was with me."

Rake lifted a brow at the confession before settling down. He took a seat and placed his head in his hand.

Olibia looked at Elora. "You must forgive my husband, Elora. For Kristofer to escape the day of his execution will not bode well. This is truly a disaster."

"I understand this," Elora said. "And I may not agree with torturing him, but I would not commit treason. And at this point, I'm fed up with the accusations! Rake, I and my parents before me have fought alongside you. I will continue to do so. But should you accuse me of treason again, I will withdraw my army and leave here."

Knowing she meant it, and knowing Rian would follow her, Rake grimaced. His temper cooling, he leaned over the table and laced his fingers together.

"Elora, I find myself begging for your forgiveness more than once. My temper got the best of me, as it usually does. I'm sorry. I did not mean to insinuate treason. Only a sister's love for her brother."

Rian took a seat, wondering why Abignale remained so quiet.

"What is your opinion on the matter?" Rian asked him.

"I'm not sure why we're surprised," Abignale replied. "The loyalty Kristofer commands from his men is unlike anything I've ever seen."

"It never occurred to me that they could get through our defenses," Rake said. "Or lead a half-dead man out without anyone noticing!"

"For all we know," Rian said, "Kristofer walked out of here on his own."

"Why not send men after him?" Elora said. "Would that not be the best course of action?"

Without looking up, Rake muttered, "I already sent a brigade of men."

Rian shook his head. "Then all we can do is wait."

CHAPTER 17

K ristofer only remembered bits and pieces of the journey back to the South. After having fully accepted his fate, Raum appeared, followed by a dozen of his men, and unchained him. He had no idea how they made it out of the castle, nor could he remember the fierce battle that raged between his men and Rake's.

He remained in and out of consciousness, and the blood loss he suffered worried Raum to no end. After they made it safely out of the castle, Raum and two men slung Kristofer over Asen. Raum had insisted they bring his horse, knowing the loyalty the beast had for his master.

"As long as he stays unconscious, we needn't worry about his pain," Raum told one of the soldiers.

"An assumption that he will survive the trek back," the man muttered under his breath.

But he did survive, and when he awoke next, it was in his own chambers in Kayne's White Castle. Staring down at his bare chest, he was surprised to find no evidence of the brutal assault he had suffered in Rake's dungeon. He felt stronger than ever. Moving gingerly, he was even more shocked to find his ribs healed. Having no idea what had really transpired, he leaned back on the bed and tried to remember. There were bits and pieces, and he thought he could remember Raum's voice telling him that all would be well.

The door to his room opened, and Aelia walked in carrying a pitcher of water and clean rags.

"Kristofer! You're awake!" She set everything down, then rushed to his side and fell to her knees. "I thought surely you would die."

How did he get back home? Stunned that she was kneeling beside him, Kristofer reached his hand out, letting his knuckles graze her cheek.

"I remember nothing." Kristofer glanced down, once again, at his chest.

Aelia sat down beside him, her eyes large and filled with worry.

"I don't know much," she said. "Raum came to me weeks and weeks ago and said that you had been captured. He left that hour, with a brigade of men to rescue you. I heard nothing until three days ago, when they returned with you. Kayne came to this chamber himself. He tended to you for hours. When he left and I came in, your wounds were gone. It was strange."

Kayne.

Realizing Aelia sat by him, crying silently, he pulled her to him.

"It's all right, love."

"You were torn apart." She wiped her face. "So much blood..."

"I'm not. I feel quite well, actually."

"Kayne..." Aelia whispered. "He is terrifying."

Kristofer asked sharply. "Did you speak with him?"

Aelia shook her head. "Raum brought you here to me. I tended you as best I could, but I did not think there was any hope. An hour later, Kayne arrived and told me to get out, and so I did. Raum and I waited, and when he was finished with you, he said you would sleep while you recovered. That was all."

Kristofer was silent. Not only had Kayne healed him, but Kristofer had never felt better. He felt powerful. Indestructible.

"I must speak with him." Kristofer pushed himself up.

"But you've only just awoken," she said. "You should—"

"He'll be expecting me, Aelia. I'll return shortly."

Kristofer stood up, in a daze of power, and dressed. He hurried out of the room, leaving Aelia sitting in stunned silence.

He knocked on Kayne's white doors before pushing them open, and knelt, his head bowed low.

"So you have survived," Kayne drawled.

"Aye. I do not know how." Kristofer watched Kayne seat himself at a chair next to his long table.

Kayne looked at Kristofer for a long moment before replying. "I gave you my blood."

He said it with such ease that one would think he was no more than swatting a gnat.

"Your blood? I feel..." Kristofer raised his hands and looked at them, "...strong."

"I imagine so," Kayne replied. "How is it *you* came to be captured?"

Kristofer hesitated, trying to think of the best way to answer it. "I...was...not at my full potential after Elora escaped. We did track them, and we fought. Rian alone is an accomplished swordsman. He, I could have defeated. But Abignale joined the fight against me. I could not cross blades against them both."

Kayne listened silently, his black eyes never leaving Kristofer's face.

"We'll make sure that doesn't happen again," Kayne hissed. "Next time you face Rian, make sure he dies."

"With pleasure," Kristofer said.

Kayne raised a hand and waved him away. Kristofer bowed before going back to his room, where Aelia sat on the bed. She wore a light-blue dress that fanned out at the waist, with a slightly darker ribbon tied in the back. Her hair was pulled back, but wisps of blonde curled around her face. Kristofer was certain she had never looked more beautiful. Her large green eyes studied him as she searched his face.

Standing in front of her, Kristofer crossed his arms over his chest.

"There are some things about Kayne that cannot be explained. What you witnessed was one of them."

Her eyes widened. "It isn't normal," she whispered. "I'm relieved, Kristofer. So relieved that you are all right. But Kayne—"

"Saved my life." Kristofer kneeled in front of her and took her hands in his. "Do not underestimate the full scale of his achievement, Aelia. I would not have survived."

Wiping her eyes, Aelia stood and brought her arms around his shoulders and drew him close. To see him like that, with his chest covered in deep, bloody wounds, seeping burns, his back torn open from a whip, bruises from beatings...it tore at her, made her sick. Even Raum warned her to prepare herself, for he did not think Kristofer would survive.

He held her for a long time, but his body was humming with energy, and he leaned forward to kiss her.

Aelia pushed him away. "You nearly died three days ago. I don't think—"

"I've never felt better, Aelia." He ran his hands up and down her back.

"At least tell me what happened!" she cried, and grabbed his hands. "How did you come to be captured? How did Raum know? He mentioned Asen. Why did Rake..."

Her list of questions went on and on until Kristofer sighed and raised a hand to silence her.

"All right." He gave her a diluted story, leaving out Kayne's punishment and the actual horrors of Rake's torture chamber.

Insinuating that he was overpowered by both Rian and

Abignale, which was verifiable, he explained the trek from the South back to the East with minimal detail.

Aelia raised a skeptical brow. "I don't understand why you patronize me. I'm not ignorant of the barbarity of war. Contrariwise, I have firsthand insight into the atrocity of Rake's soldiers. I do not believe for a second that Rian merely overpowered you, even with Abignale's help. I've seen you fight, Kristofer. You are indestructible. Stop sheltering me," she said with vehemence.

"I do not shelter you, Aelia. But you saw the state I was returned to you in. What more needs to be said?"

He was calm. Too calm. Something was off, and Aelia could not quite put her finger on it.

"You are different," she said. "Was it the torture chamber? Or Kayne's revival of your good health?"

"I'd wager both."

"How did he bring you back? You were but an inch from death."

Kristofer shook his head. Now was not the time to delve into Kayne's medicinal practices. The less Aelia knew, the safer she would remain. It was what Kristofer lived by concerning her. He also knew his protective nature caused her grief a good portion of the time, but he would not see her end up in an enemy dungeon over her loyalty to him.

"I promise you, Aelia. I will, one day, tell you all. But it will not be this day."

She remained silent and did not stir. Her anger was plain. Or maybe it was fear. Her hands, still holding his, tightened, nails digging in, without any conceivable knowledge that she was doing it.

"Damn you," she hissed.

"Be angry." He returned her infuriated stare with a calm, even one. "It is for your own safety that I keep certain knowledges from you."

"So I am to live in the dark until you deem it an appropriate time to confide in me?"

She pushed his hands away and tried to stand up, but he took ahold of her shoulders and pushed her down on the mattress.

"Let go," she hissed.

"Do not look at me like that, Aelia."

She pushed against him, but he grabbed her wrists and held them to the bed. She glared at him, her cheeks flushing with emotion.

"If I didn't know any better," he said, "I'd say my rise in health has frightened you."

She tried to pull her wrists free, but he tightened his grip, upsetting her further.

"It has! What is he?" she shrieked.

Tears of frustration formed in the corner of her eyes and crept down her temples. Unable to move, confused, and frightened that the devil himself had healed Kristofer, she turned her head away.

It wasn't until she felt his lips brush her forehead, felt the warmth of his breath against her skin, that she brought her eyes to his. His whispered confession came on the heels of a pause.

"I can do this, Aelia. I can. But I cannot do it without you. I need you to trust me, and know only that I seek to keep you safe. Give me time."

His voice was suddenly filled with pain—something Aelia had never heard before. The anguish in his tone was clear, and sent a chill up her spine. She braced herself against the confusion that came with his plea.

She tensed again as an image of him broken and bleeding replayed in her mind, and Raum's voice sounded in her head: *"He will die, Aelia. No one can survive this..."*

Her sob cut Kristofer more deeply than any of the torture

he suffered in Rake's dungeon. She tugged her wrists again, and this time he released her. Walking toward the window, she crossed her arms over herself in some small protective measure, and studied the floor with rapt attention.

"Aelia—"

"Are you human?" She could not bring herself to look at him.

The silence stretched long between them before she repeated, "Are you?"

"I believe so."

The fear that showed so plainly on her face as she brought her emerald eyes up to study him, was unbearable for him. He strode to the table and leaned against it, his arms outstretched to support his weight.

Aelia leaned over the sill and peered out, shoving a pillow out of the way in her frustration. The bay window provided a large seating area and a respite from the heat when the breeze blew in. Wiping her face, she looked down below to the courtyard and then further out to the fields beyond the castle walls. She stiffened when she felt his hands gently upon her shoulders.

"I know I owe you an explanation, Aelia. And believe me, there is one. But I cannot...I need more time."

She turned to him. "Have you any idea what it is like to wait? To sit there and wait while you're gone? Always, I wonder when I will receive news that you have fallen. And then Raum comes to me to tell me that not only have you been captured, but that it was Rake—"

"Rian—"

"On Rake's orders!" she snapped.

Kristofer sighed. "Your distress is registered, my love. You ask me to imagine your scenario. Now imagine mine. You would not survive a torture chamber. Nor do I think would you wish to. I can protect you, and keeping you out of harms reach is, and always has been, my priority. I could not bear to see your blood on the edge of my enemy's sword. My life, I can quite assure you, would lose its meaning. It is unfortunate, but you, because of me, are a target, Aelia. The South bends to our will. My men know better, but do not think that my enemies won't maim you. It is my fear over your well-being that provokes me to take such drastic measures."

Large green eyes searched his imploringly.

"You're frightened?" she said.

"Beyond."

Her anger died away.

"I did not think anything could frighten you." She shook her head as if waiting for him to laugh and tell her he was joking.

It was hard to imagine Kristofer afraid of anything. Entire armies fell to their knees before him.

She sat down on the sill, which she so often did when he was away, and stared again at the endless dry, sand-colored fields. Greenery didn't last long because of the heat, and she found the color of the grass to be quite beautiful.

Aelia was silent for a long time while she thought about their conversation. He needed time. In the grand scheme of things, it was a small request. Time. It was also the one thing she didn't want to give. But she knew Kristofer. He would not ask were it not of paramount importance.

Glancing at him out of the corner of her eye, she found him staring back, unblinking.

Finally she said, "All right. But one day—"

"One day, you will have your answers. I only ask that you don't bring it up again."

She nodded and hesitated before holding her hand out for him, which he eagerly grasped in his before sitting beside her.

He took ahold of her chin. "All will be well, Aelia."

Again, she nodded.

Releasing her, he leaned back so that they sat opposite one another. It took Aelia a long while before she finally moved close and laid her head upon his chest. He put his hand on her back. His chuckle made her glance at him, and before she could say anything, he brought her up so he could kiss her. She put her hands on his chest and pushed herself up.

"You infuriate me," she said.

His laughter surrounded her, and she, too, began to laugh.

"If only you knew how mutual it was," he replied.

Kristofer hummed with energy. It came off of him in pulsating waves. She could feel it. But he seemed content to sit there with her. His unbuttoned tunic had her running her hands along his chest. She marveled at the smooth contour of his skin, which, not so long ago, was a bloody heap of torn skin. His arms were healed. She could feel the hard muscle under her hands. There were no broken bones or oozing burns. She felt a surge of unease in the pit of her stomach.

He cupped her face, and she pulled away, pausing as another memory washed over her.

"*Kristofer's been captured...*" Raum's words sounded throughout her head as she realized that her biggest fear had come true.

"Aelia."

His voice brought her back as no other sound could. She met his gaze with hesitation.

He survived, she told herself. He was safe. It was all that really mattered.

Kristofer cupped her face, drawing her down, and with lips just above her own, he whispered, "Trust me."

He kissed her before she could respond.

CHAPTER 18

"**R**ead these reports," Rake fumed, as he handed Rian a thick piece of parchment.

Rian sat down and unrolled the paper while Elora read over his shoulder.

"How is this possible?" He turned to look at her.

She shrugged. "Kristofer told me that Kayne can bring a person back to life, even when they are an inch from death. Perhaps he used those methods to heal Kristofer."

"There was more blood on the floor of the dungeon than on a battle field," Rake said. "You mean to say Kayne can improve his condition in a matter of weeks? There is also a report of a woman." He handed another rolled-up piece of parchment to them.

Surprised registered on both Rian and Elora's face.

"Kristofer's woman?" Rian turned again to look at Elora.

"I've seen no evidence to verify this," she said. "When we reached the castle, Kristofer took me directly to a room and locked me in there. I saw very little."

"There is an uprising in the deep South," Rian said, after moment's worth of reading. "I imagine Kristofer will tend to the matter himself. If this woman has any value to him and we take her, we could easily use her against him."

"If that is the case," Elora said, "we can assure ourselves that she is extremely well-protected."

"This may be the break we've been looking for." A grin spread across Rake's handsome face. "Let us plan."

———∿∿∿———

Aelia bent down to pull a flower from the earth. The summer brought a colorful bouquet of wildflowers with it, and she was delighted. Kristofer sat against a tree, watching her, smiling because she was happy. She bent down to pick a pale yellow flower, almost the same color as her dress, and smelled it. After scooping up a few more, she fingered them as she took a seat beside Kristofer.

"The berries will be out soon." She laid her bouquet in front of her and looked up at Kristofer.

"Why is it we spend the summer picking berries and flowers?" he said.

"You pick nothing. You sit there while I overly exert myself."

His deep laughter surrounded her, bringing an easy smile to her lips.

"I imagine gathering flowers is comparable only to leading a mass army into battle," he said.

She rolled her eyes, then sighed and rested against him.

"It has been so peaceful the last month," she said. "If only it would stay so."

Kristofer grimaced. "It will not," he ventured cautiously. "I've received word that there is an uprising in the deep South."

She turned around to face him, her smile fading fast.

"I will leave tomorrow."

She gasped. "For how long? Why did you wait so long to tell me?"

"We've only just received word, and I did not want you to worry until the last possible moment." He kissed her head. "I will not be gone long, love."

"You've said this many times! Last time, you were gone for over four months! Not to mention—"

"I will not be gone for four months, nor will I fall to Rake's men again."

Aelia looked around at the sky and the trees. Delighting in the warmth of the sun on her skin, she cringed at the thought of being locked up in the castle while he was away.

"Kristofer, please, please. Allow Raum to escort me out—"

"No—"

"I beg you! It is unbearable. We will not stray far from the walls. I promise."

"You are relentless." Kristofer sighed in exasperation.

"I do not care if you send the army with us. But it is entirely too beautiful out now to stay indoors. Even for a little while."

Her plea fell on deaf ears. Unsympathetic eyes turned to face her.

"No, Aelia. As I've said, I will not be gone long. A fortnight, at the most."

She stared at him in disbelief. "I will not stay inside for two weeks!"

With a warning growl, "You absolutely will."

As she shook her head, her long hair blew in the breeze, and Kristofer reached to pull it over her shoulder.

With a sigh, he said, "Why must this always be a fight?"

"Because you are so terribly unreasonable. Your horse has more freedom than I do. An hour! That is all I ask. Please?"

Kristofer glared at her, and against his better judgement, he sighed, defeated.

"You will promise to stay near the castle walls?"

"Yes!" Aelia flung her arms around his neck.

"I will speak to Raum before I leave. Aelia, I'm warning you—"

"I swear we won't leave the grounds! I'll obey Raum."

"Yes, you will." Kristofer sighed. "I daresay, he'll be devastated when he learns of this."

She smiled, happy at her newfound freedom.

—⁓—

Kristofer kept his promise, and each morning, Raum escorted Aelia outside. True to her word, she kept close to the walls and did not argue when Raum told her to go inside. One such morning, Aelia found a bowl of fresh berries on her table. After seeking out Raum, she insisted they go pick more of them.

When he hesitated, she said, "It is not far from the walls. There is a small patch on the other side of the castle."

"If Kristofer learns of it—"

"The other side of the castle is just as well-fortified, and the archers overlook the forest. He shan't be angry."

"Well, we'll find out when he returns, won't we?" Raum said, and Aelia ran to grab a basket.

The sun was bright in the cloudless blue sky. Even though the hour was early, heat waves danced along the surface of the ground. Aelia found the castle cold and unrelenting when Kristofer was gone, and happily faced the warmth of the outdoors.

They walked to the outskirts of the castle wall where trees lined the borders. Raum grimaced, uneasy that they were so far from the security of the castle. The archers stood high above them in the crenels of the parapet, but when the guards changed duty, there would be no one. Raum decided they would go in before the guard changed, and stood watch while she picked her berries.

It was no wonder to him why Kristofer kept her so well-protected. She was exquisite. And she had come so far since Kristofer had found her. Her cotton dress was the lightest shade of orange, and her incredibly long, thick hair was braided down the length of her back.

She turned toward him and beckoned him over.

"Look at this," she whispered.

Bending over, Raum glanced at the rabbit nest, where three small, brown babies were nestled inside.

"Are they not the sweetest things?" she said, eyeing the rabbits with affection. "Their eyes are not even opened yet."

"They are rabbits, Aelia," Raum said, and she rolled her eyes. "Let us go in now."

She nodded and inched back, not wishing to disturb the nest.

From within the trees, Raum thought he heard something and he froze, whipping his head around while he scanned the tree line. Aelia followed his gaze. She found the thick nest of trees that lined the outskirts of the castle walls suddenly ominous.

"What is it?"

Listening intently, Raum said, "Nothing. Go."

He took ahold of her arm and moved quickly, desperate to get away from the trees.

"Run, Aelia!" he hissed, knowing he heard a sword unsheathed.

Paling, she saw three men come out of the woods. The first was tall, and his hair was so dark it looked almost blue in the sunlight. Raum glanced at the towers. An exchange was being made between the archers, and the replacements would not be there for several minutes.

He pulled out his sword. "Aelia, get out of here!"

She turned and dropped her basket as she ran. She didn't get far before strong, unyielding hands grabbed her around the waist. Before she could cry out, a large hand clamped over her mouth and dragged her back to where Raum dueled.

Raum fought diligently against the soldier. He was older,

with flecks of gray throughout his dark hair. Brilor grunted in pain as Raum's sword sliced his arm, wounding him.

Aelia struggled against the man who held her, watching anxiously as the tall, dark-haired warrior drew his sword and stepped forward from the trees. The older soldier stepped back while Rian attacked Raum, bringing him to his knees in three blows.

Fighting against her assailant, Aelia watched helplessly as Rian lifted his arm to deal a fatal blow. But her muffled scream made him pause.

She pulled the soldier's hand off of her mouth and whispered, "Please don't kill him! Please! I'll go with you, but don't kill him."

Raum turned his head to look at her just as the hilt of Rian's sword connected with his temple, and he crumpled. Aelia let out a terrified sob as the soldier handed her over to Rian.

"The archers will be here any moment," he said. "Move his body out of their line of sight."

Rogan and Brilor grabbed Raum's limp form and dragged him into the woods just as the first archer made his appearance. After mounting a dark brown horse, Rian pulled Aelia in front of him and urged his horse forward. He stared at the tiny woman in front of him, surprised, as she was not at all what he expected. To be honest, he had no idea what to expect concerning Kristofer's woman. She was startlingly beautiful, and her cry to save the soldier she was with stunned him.

Hearing hoofbeats behind him, Rian turned his horse quickly, tightening his arm around Aelia's waist. Rogan and Brilor approached.

"We are not being followed, Lord." Brilor was focused on the woman.

"We will be when Kristofer finds out. Ride hard."

Kristofer's name brought an unprecedented cry from Aelia's lips. Three pairs of eyes turned toward her.

"Kristofer will come for me," Aelia said.

Her voice was firm, but Rian could feel her trembling.

"Let us hope." Brilor eyed her with disdain as he thought of Breggen. "Although, I have yet to know a man who will traverse the countryside in pursuit of a whore."

Aelia blanched. She had never once thought of herself as Kristofer's whore. Nor did he treat her as such.

Rian turned the horse around, and they flew across the countryside. Terrified, Aelia wondered who they were. The man holding her matched Rian's description. She had heard rumors that he was devastatingly handsome, tall and dark. He could be no other. But what would Rian want with her?

Thinking back, she remembered Kristofer had told her that Rian and Elora had joined forces with Rake. Was Rian bringing her to Rake's kingdom?

Shear panic rose within her. After what Rake's men had done, the East was the very last place Aelia would ever wish to go.

They rode until the sky darkened and they could no longer see, before pulling off into a dense cluster of trees. After dismounting, Rian yanked Aelia off the horse and sat her down. He handed her a waterskin and she gulped the liquid down.

"Are you taking me to the Eastern Kingdom?" she dared to ask.

Her clear green eyes met those of midnight blue.

"Yes." Rian crouched beside her, noting her fear at his confirmation, which overwhelmed everything else. "But we will not hurt you."

Turning from him with full eyes, she was determined to keep her tears hidden. Rian stood slowly, keeping his gaze fixed on the woman. Aelia, he believed the soldier had called her.

Handing her a slice of cheese and a strip of dried meat, Rian saw her hesitate before taking it. Thinking it best to keep up her strength, Aelia decided to eat.

Rian walked back to Brilor and Rogan and whispered something to them. Aelia saw an opportunity and took it. She leapt to her feet and took off, but Rian grabbed her and pinned her down.

"Get me a rope." He glared down at her.

The light from the fire illuminated her features, and he could see the hatred in her eyes.

After taking the rope Brilor handed him, Rian jerked her to feet and tied her hands in front of her.

"Kristofer will kill you," she hissed.

"Aelia, is it?" Rian lifted a dark brow.

Her silence confirmed her name.

"We've broken him once," a deep voice said from behind them. "Rian's defeated him. We can do it again."

She turned and saw the older soldier standing there. Having no idea who he was, Aelia turned to face Rian again, and decided upon a different approach.

"I have no war with you. Nor do I wish to see blood shed in my name. Please? Kristofer will ride out, and too many lives will be lost."

Her words took all three of them by surprise.

Seeing the confounded look on their faces, she added. "I just want to go home."

"She lies," Brilor snarled. "She is but a whore. Are we even certain we've taken the right woman? Kristofer is bound to have an endless supply of them."

Aelia's heart raced. Her fear blinded her to reason as her mind raced with unrealistic thoughts. She had never considered that Kristofer might have other women. Or that he may not hold her in the same light she held him. He enjoyed her, no doubt. He enjoyed her company, and they had fun together but he had never spoken of love, or marriage. She was quite fine with their arrangement, thinking that he cared for her. She thought he loved her, but maybe she was wrong. Would he leave her to face Rake and his men alone?

Rian saw the change come over her face. He saw the tears build and run down her cheeks. He could see the terror of Brilor's words pulsing through her. Perhaps she was the right woman. The thought gave him hope.

"We will continue riding," he said.

Aelia stared at the ground, but when she felt Rian's hands on her, she jerked.

"I will not go with you!" She backed away and tried to loosen the rope that bound her wrists.

Rian climbed onto his horse and stared down at her.

"You have no choice." He grabbed her arms and pulled her onto the horse.

She struggled, but he tightened his grip.

"Fight me if you want."

———⁓⁓⁓———

The weeks dragged. Even though no one actually hurt her, she learned a whole new level of fear. Rian never let her stray more than a few feet from him, and no matter how often she tried to run away, he always seemed to be one step ahead of her.

By the time they reached the Eastern borders, Aelia was truly beside herself with terror. Her dread at facing Rake left no room to fight. Her fear consumed every fiber of her being, made worse by the taunts that Kristofer would never ride out after a whore.

As the castle rose into view, Aelia gasped. Her anguish was clear as the drawbridge was lowered. Rian lifted her off the horse and brought her inside. The castle was beautiful, but it did not compare to the Southern Kingdom.

Aelia's fear was so great that her legs could scarcely hold her up. Rian's hand was wrapped around her upper arm as he dragged her through the castle. After pushing open a set of doors, he shoved her through them.

"Rian!"

Aelia saw a woman rise from a chair. Blonde and beautiful, she smiled warmly at Rian before turning her attention to Aelia.

Realizing right away that this must be Elora, Aelia bit her lip. She looked so much like her brother. An old man sat next to her, his beard nearly touching the floor, and he also eyed her. At the head of the long table sat Rake and Olibia. Breathing hard, Aelia raised her gaze to glare at Rake—the man who was responsible for her family's death.

Abignale was surprised to find the hatred he saw in her eyes as she stared at Rake, and he wondered what could have caused such animosity.

Rian pulled her closer, and she stopped beside Rake.

"This?" Rake looked at Rian. "This is she?"

"As far as we could tell, yes." Rian sat down next to Elora, and Aelia watched him kiss her cheek.

Feeling a pang at the affectionate gaze they shared, she returned her attention to Rake.

"What is it you want with me?" She forced her tone to stay even, praying she did not quaver in front of him.

Rake stared at her with disdain. He hated Kristofer, and by default, he hated her. Anything to do with Kristofer made his skin crawl.

He turned to Rian and mumbled, "After all this, Kristofer better come after her."

After assuming they wanted her for information, she now

realized they wanted to use her as bait, and her eyes grew wide.

"That is the other thing," Rian's said, from behind her. "Brilor is firmly convinced the woman is nothing more than a common whore.

"Have you any evidence to the contrary?" Rake said.

"None," Rian replied. "Only that she was well-guarded. And she never left the confinement of the archer's aim."

Rake shook his head in disbelief. "So your trek was for naught."

He turned once again to study Aelia. Pale and slender, almost delicate, she gave off a defiant air, almost of superiority. She leaned away from him, returning his gaze with a look of disgust.

"Will Kristofer come after you?" Rake said, his voice cold.

Aelia grimaced and tore her gaze away from his. If he didn't come, they would kill her. Or worse. Would he leave her to this fate?

Trembling at the prospect, Aelia didn't realize there were ten pairs of eyes watching her.

"Your king has asked you a question."

Aelia glanced at the old man who had spoken, before looking at Rake.

"He is not my king," she hissed.

Rian stood suddenly. "Not your king?" he barked. "Yet you would follow Kayne?"

"I've never indicated such," Aelia retorted. "Nor will I accommodate any of you. Do what you will with me."

"Throw her in the dungeon," Rake said. "A week in there, and she may yet talk. If not, hand her over to the men. I daresay some good will come of her being here."

Aelia paled and let out a startled gasp. Her hand flew her to her mouth, and she backed away from Rake. Her reaction, not missed by any of them, had Elora sympathizing.

Rake called for a guard and ordered him to bring Aelia below. Elora watched her leave before turning her attention to Rake.

"Allow her a guarded room, Rake. Look at her. The dungeon will kill her. Maybe a kind gesture will win her favor. She seems to harbor severe hostility toward you, and maybe it's just fear. But if Kristofer does want her back, a dead body will surely fuel his rage."

"She is right, Rake," Abignale said. "You yourself have read the reports. Kristofer is not only alive, but he thrives. He should not be able to walk, let alone lead a brigade of men into the deep South."

"It is truly beyond my realm of understanding." Rake leaned back in his chair. "Give the woman a couple nights in the dungeon. We'll bring her up after and see where it gets us."

The guard shoved Aelia into a small stone room and slammed the door shut. The chamber was dark and damp. The stone floor was strewn with decaying hay, and the smell made her stomach churn. Holding onto the wall for support, she lowered herself into a corner and drew her knees up. She laid her head against them and cried.

Terrified and cold, she could only pray that the soldiers would not kill her. Or worse, rape her. She prayed fervently that Kristofer would come, but she herself was not sure if he would. Looking back on the years spent with him, he had never given any indication that he wanted more from her than what he had. And he was gone so much. Maybe Rian's general was right. Maybe she was only a convenience to him when he was home. And if he did come, he certainly could not take down all the guards by himself. What if he was captured again?

Hysterical, she cried herself into a restless sleep. When she awoke, having no perception of time, she wondered if they would starve her. No one came, and as the hours passed, she terrified herself into believing they would not bring food or water.

Dazed at the turn of events, Aelia could do nothing but wait. Every minute seemed an eternity, and her thoughts made every one of them excruciating.

Hours later, her door opened and the same guard who brought her down to the dungeon left a tray of stale bread, cheese, and cup of water. Tearing into the bread, she watched the door close before drinking the water in one big gulp. Feeling slightly better, she ate the cheese and curled back up in her corner.

———

Over two weeks later, the door flung open and a short, stout guard with dark curly hair and a nose too large for his face, walked in and grabbed her. He dragged her from the room, and his fingers bit into her arm as he yanked her up the stairs. Once again, she found herself facing Rake and his wife, Elora, Rian, and Abignale.

"Come forward." Rake brandished a roll of parchment.

When she didn't move, Rake smiled at her.

"I want you to read this."

Curiosity had Aelia putting one foot in front of the other. She reached a hand out and took the parchment from Rake. Elora and Rian stared at her as she unrolled and read. It was from Rake's spies. They wrote that Kristofer had not left the Southern Territory. For the past several days, all that was noted was that he trained with his men.

Stunned, Aelia let the paper fall from her hands, and glanced at Rake in stunned disbelief.

"You wrote this," she whispered.

"I did no such thing," Rake said. "And you know it to be true. The problem herein lies with what to do with you now."

Aelia met Elora's gaze, which was filled with pity. Rian's face was unreadable.

"He would not leave me here," Aelia said, more to herself than them.

"You are his whore, Aelia," said Rake. "Nothing more. It would do you well to tell us what you know."

Shaking her head, Aelia stepped away from him. His words wounded her to the core.

Wanting desperately to get away from them, she turned and ran to the door, but Rian stood quickly and grabbed her. He held her in place as Rake leaned back in his chair.

"Kristofer held up well against our..." he gestured with his hand, "methods of extraction. You, however, I do not think would. Your options, little one, are plain. Tell us what we wish to know, or we will send what is left of you to Kristofer. Although, it does not appear that he would care."

Rian held her in front of him. He could feel her shaking, panic-stricken at Rake's threat.

"Whether he cares for me or not, I will not betray him. Nor do I care what you do to me. But whatever it will be, do it now. The wait is often worse than the bite." Jerking herself free of Rian's hands, she stepped away from him and looked at Rake. "I would rather be dead than have to look upon you. Whatever you think of Kristofer, it is not so."

Rake leapt to his feet. "How can you believe that!"

"Your people are starving. Your walls may hold for now, but an invasion from the South will be detrimental for you. My city is not like that. They know!" Aelia turned her head to look at Elora and Rian. "They've both been inside. Who do you think leads our people? Who do you think provides and defends them against your monstrosities?"

Olibia gasped. "Kristofer leads the people?"

"What do you think?" Aelia bit back.

"Watch your tongue," Rian said.

"I will not. It appears that I have nothing to lose. So allow me to make my stance clear. I despise you." She turned to Rake. "You can do no more damage to me than what you've already done. I would see you burn in hell."

Rake hit her so hard across that face that she was thrown back. From her spot on the floor, she turned to face him. She wiped the corner of her mouth with the back of her hand, and blood smeared across it. Pushing herself to her feet, she faced Rake again.

"Rake," Rian warned, then turned to Aelia. "To us, your hostility appears unwarranted. Why do you feel this way?"

"I owe you no explanation."

Taking a breath, Elora gave Aelia a curious look.

"How is it you hate us," she said, "but my brother leads the same raids and you hold nothing but affection toward him?"

"Kristofer does not pillage!"

Rake snorted, and Aelia raised an eyebrow at him.

She turned back to Elora. "He does not give orders for useless carnage. He fights against you, for good reason, but he deals an incredibly firm hand against any of his soldiers that rape or maim, even against his enemies." Aelia lowered her voice and spoke solely to Elora. "You do not know your brother."

"Evidently, that is so," Elora replied.

"You cannot possibly believe this!" Rian said. "He murdered Breggen. In front of you."

"I do not know this Breggen," Aelia said. "But unless he was attacking Kristofer with a weapon, I can't see him harming a soldier for no reason."

Elora looked at Aelia. Her memories of Breggen's final moments brought a pang to her chest, followed by the horrible recap of her brother grabbing her and forcing her onto his horse. However, Aelia was right. Elora had never seen him raise his sword against those who could not defend themselves. His men have attacked, but he never did.

Did Kristofer have such control over his men that they don't even attack unless ordered to do so? Confusion washed over her.

Aelia seemed to read her mind. "His men might attack or kill under his orders. But Kristofer himself will not raise his sword against those who cannot fight back."

"Enough of this!" Rake roared. "Rian, hand her to the men and be done with her."

His words struck her harder than any physical blow could.

Rian looked down at her. Icy dark blue met those of liquid green, and he saw the plea within her eyes.

"She will do more good to us alive than dead." Elora stepped forward. "I wish to speak with her," she told Rake. "Alone."

Rake glared at Elora, but consented after a moment's hesitation.

"Return her to the dungeon when you are through," he said, his red mantle billowing behind him as he stormed out of the room, followed by his wife and Abignale.

Rian leaned forward and whispered, "Be careful with her, Elora. We have no idea what she is capable of."

With that, he turned and closing the door quietly behind him.

After taking a seat at the long table, Elora turned her full attention to Aelia.

In a gentle tone, she said, "Will my brother come for you or not?"

Aelia wrung her hands together.

"I would not know," she finally replied.

"I am not your enemy, Aelia. Nor do I wish to see you suffer. Kristofer has made his choice in life, and the cruel rise of fate sets him and I apart." Elora gestured to the chair beside her. "Sit."

"If you are trying to extract information from me concerning Kristofer, I would not help you, even if I could."

"Sit," Elora repeated. "I have no desire to extract information. Whether or not you believe it to be true, I love my brother, and I can see it plainly that you do, too."

Aelia said nothing. She stared at the hem of her orange dress, made filthy by the trek to the East and her time in the dungeon. Elora watched her. Even with the dirt and grime that covered Aelia, Elora found her beauty to be undiminished.

"He is not evil," Aelia said. "It seems clear that the affection I hold for him is not returned. But regardless, he is a good leader and our people love him."

Elora remembered Jaro and Besda's words, but she wanted confirmation.

"It is Kristofer who leads the South?"

"Aye," Aelia said. "You did not know this? It is no secret."

"But Kayne..."

"Kayne is king, but we all know the South would not survive under his leadership. He leaves Kristofer to handle the affairs of the kingdom. You saw our city. Our people thrive."

"Where do you come from?" Elora said. "How did you end up in such close relations to Kristofer?"

Aelia raised a brow and shook her head. "My past is my own. I have no wish to share it."

"I know my brother better than you think. I believe he will come for you."

Aelia looked up. "So the reports were falsified?" she said, with a glimmer of hope.

"They were not."

Aelia felt despair take over once again, and her throat tightened.

"Then why do you say that?"

"A feeling," Elora said.

"A feeling..." Aelia murmured, in disbelief. "I can assure you, he knows I'm not there. I just never realized I was so easily replaceable to him," she said, more to herself than Elora.

Elora reached over and took Aelia's hand in hers.

"Have hope. I will not allow Rake to pawn you off on his men."

She saw some of the tension lift from Aelia's face, replaced by confusion.

"Thank you," she managed, brushing the tears that crept down her face.

"I do have one question," Elora said.

Aelia looked at her and nodded.

"How did he recover from his time here? I went to him in the dungeon. He could not move, let alone traverse the countryside and recover in a few weeks' time."

Aelia grimaced at the memory and looked down at the clean hand that held her filthy one.

"I do not rightly know. He was returned to me in a bloody heap. I was certain he would not survive. The blood loss, the open wounds, the broken bones, the burns—I do not understand how an infection did not set in. Nor do I understand how he was even captured."

She looked at Elora questioningly, and Elora nodded.

"I will answer that when you are finished."

"I had never met Kayne," Aelia said. "Kristofer's soldier brought him to me, and there was no alleviating his suffering. Kayne arrived himself, ordered me from the room, and hours later, he emerged, telling me only that Kristofer would sleep while he recovered. And he did. When Raum and I went back in, he looked...perfect. Not a trace of his wounds were left. He looked peaceful, but he slept for nigh on three days. When he finally did wake, the first thing he did was go to Kayne. He does not speak to me of his time with the king, and I do not know what happened or how he was revived."

Remembering Kristofer's words in the dungeon, Elora had guessed as much.

She stood and paced before she turned to Aelia.

"After Rian came for me, we barely escaped. We took sanctuary in a farm house, but Kristofer and his men found us. Our soldiers killed his, but Rian and Kristofer have personal vendettas against one another. Of this, I'm sure you know. Rian attacked Kristofer, and it was fierce. Abignale, my healer, lent Rian his sword, and together they brought my brother to his knees. I've seen Kristofer fight—it should not have been so. He told me later on that Kayne had weakened him through torture, angry over my escape."

Aelia gasped.

"Another reason why I do not understand why Kristofer would follow him," Elora said.

Aelia shrugged. She had her own theories, but she would not offer any to Elora.

The door opened, and Rian stood there, arms folded across his chest. The thought of returning to the dungeon was unbearable for Aelia, but she forced herself to her feet.

"I know my way," she hissed at him. "Do not touch me."

CHAPTER 19

Elora returned to her chambers and waited for Rian. Once he was seated next to her, she looked at him thoughtfully.

"Defiant, is she not?" Rian laid back on the bed.

"Strong and loyal," Elora corrected, in a gentle tone.

"Did she tell you anything of use?" Rian said, already knowing the answer.

Elora shook her head. "Nothing we haven't deduced on our own. She doesn't understand how Kayne heals, either. She said that much."

Rian threw his hands up in annoyance. "This was a waste. Kristofer will not come, and we are saddled now with a woman who hates us."

"She hates Rake," said Elora. "You, my love, she is just terrified of. If circumstances were different, she and I would get on all right."

"Regardless, Elora. Something must be done about her. She cannot stay in the dungeon forever. Petition Rake and see if you cannot get her a room in a more comfortable environment. She may be strong, but she will not last much longer down there."

—⁓—

It felt like weeks. Or maybe months. Aelia could not tell. Maybe it hadn't been that long, but hearing not a word from anyone gave her mind leniency to believe Kristofer would leave her. This, above all else, nearly drove her mad.

No one bothered with her, other than to bring her food and water twice a day. Then finally, one day, the heavy iron door opened and Elora walked in wearing a gown of the deepest red. The color reminded Aelia of blood.

Holding her skirts up, Elora inched over to her and knelt. "Come with me," she said.

Thinking that anywhere would be better than the dungeon, Aelia rose on unsteady legs and followed Elora out of the room. It was cold and dingy, and iron doors lined the gloomy stone corridor. A small window with an iron grill was cut into every door at eye level. Soldiers in green uniforms were stationed every few feet, and although they didn't move, their gazes flickered over Aelia as she passed. Torchers hung in sconces every twenty feet. So little light made everything that much more dreary.

Aelia wrapped her arms around herself as she followed Elora. Stone stairs ascended to the floor above, and as soon as Elora opened the heavy wooden door, light bathed Aelia in its warm embrace. Her eyes became sensitive, and she squeezed them shut, bringing a hand up to protect her face.

Elora felt a surge of sympathy as Aelia struggled to adjust. After a few minutes, she lowered her hand. Her head turned in every direction as she took in her new surroundings.

"This way," Elora said.

She guided Aelia through a huge open room with a stone fireplace against one wall. It was scarcely furnished except for a large red rug that sat some feet away from the fireplace. Elora continued up another flight of stairs, where Rian waited patiently, and Aelia eyed him warily. The rumors about him certainly seemed to be true. Aelia had never seen hair that dark or eyes so blue. He moved fluidly, the way Kristofer did. As if every step was premeditated. He was taller than most men, and more than a foot taller than she.

However, she was more entranced with Elora. She looked so much like her brother that Aelia had a hard time not comparing them. She was tall for a woman, and Aelia remembered Kristofer mentioning that she was uncommonly good with a sword. Aelia did not even know how to hold a sword, let alone fight with one.

They followed Rian down the length of a long balcony lined with massive arches. Aelia looked over the railing. A few servants scurried about several floors below. Upon reaching a door, Rian pushed it open and waited for Aelia to step inside. Nervously, she entered, and gasped when they followed her in and shut the door.

"She was left down there for too long." Elora sighed. "I will stay." She turned to Rian.

He nodded and leaned over to whisper something in her ear.

"Yes, and clothes," she replied, before he left.

Elora took a step toward Aelia, but she backed away.

"Easy," Elora said. "I tried to get you out of there sooner, but my request fell upon deaf ears. Rake is not fond of my brother...or his women."

"How long am I to stay here?" Aelia said.

"I cannot answer, for I don't know."

A knock on the door made Aelia jump, and Elora gave her a sympathetic look. Food and a bath were brought in, and Aelia stared at the food with hunger in her eyes.

"Eat," Elora said.

A servant handed Elora a folded pile of clean clothes, which Aelia scarcely noticed. She grabbed a leg of chicken and devoured it. Starving, she ate as much as she could.

"I will make sure food is brought regularly," Elora said.

Aelia eyed her with suspicion. "Why are you being so kind to me?"

"Because I remember the terror I felt when I was a prisoner. Kidnapped by my own brother and brought to my death was hardly a pleasant experience."

"He does not talk about it," Aelia said.

"I would not think he would." Elora hesitated. "Why do you hold such loyalty toward him?"

Aelia frowned at the question. "My reasons are my own."

With caution, Elora said, "We have received another report that he trains with his men. He has not noticed your absence."

Feeling as if the wind was knocked from her, Aelia sat down on the bed, afraid her legs would no longer support her.

"It's not true," she whispered.

"I fear it is. He is still within the White Castle walls. He is not coming, Aelia."

Despair crept over her. "How long have I been here?" she choked.

"Over a month. If he was coming, he would have been here by now."

Aelia closed her eyes and sobbed. With her face buried in her hands, Aelia's shoulders shook with the force of her pain. Elora walked over and put an arm around her, but Aelia pulled away and stood up.

"What will you do with me now?"

"I don't know. Rake has yet to decide. But I will not have you rotting in the dungeon. Do you need my help?" Elora eyed the bath, but Aelia shook her head. "I will leave you, then."

She closed the door behind her, and Aelia glanced around before taking her filthy dress off. After stepping into the warm water, she washed her hair and scrubbed herself clean. Once finished, she grabbed the silk dress Elora had brought and put it on quickly, afraid someone might come in.

Feeling no better, she looked out the window at the setting sun. It would be night soon, and Kristofer had left her to face the darkness alone. Her fear gave way to anger. How could he leave her? She raised a knuckle to her mouth to stifle a sob. If he didn't rescue her now, why then did he refuse to allow her out while he was away? He told her she meant everything to him, but in her dire moment of need, he just left her in the East.

As the light faded completely, Aelia laid down on the bed, which was a drastic improvement from her previous quarters. But her tears, her fear, and her anger deprived her of sleep.

Taking a seat by the window once more, she stared longingly outside, wishing for freedom.

Elora kissed Rian and wrapped her arms around him.

"My heart breaks for Aelia," she mumbled into his ear.

"What did we expect?" he said. "That Kristofer would rescue her? It was a good plan, but useless."

He ran his hands down her arms, which she planted on his waist to kiss him again.

"For her sake, I had hoped," Elora said. "You came for me."

"I love you," Rian said. "And even if I did not, I would not have left you in enemy territory."

Elora whispered, "Olibia has begun wedding preparations."

"Has she? I daresay her exuberance will provide a fine time."

"Aye, she is excited."

"Are you?" Rian lifted a dark brow.

Elora smiled at him and nodded. "I am."

She looked forward to marrying him, but at the same time, she felt a flutter of nerves in the pit of her stomach.

Gladdened at her response, Rian smiled. "Lay down. It's

getting late, and I'm tired."

The night prior, they had stayed up late with Rake and Olibia. Elora tried to convince Rake to set Aelia free. She knew Rake would never sanction the torture of a woman, even one Kristofer involved himself with. But to hand Aelia over to the soldiers was just as bad. Rake had finally agreed to bring her up from the dungeons.

Laying on her side, with her back to Rian's front, Elora slept peacefully. Rian stayed, comforted with her so near. He did not even hear the door open, or the footsteps over to the bed. It wasn't until he felt the cold sting of a blade against his throat that he jerked awake.

Kristofer stood at the side of the bed, holding Olibia in front of him. He brought the knife from Rian's throat to Olibia's.

"Where is she?" he snarled.

His voice woke Elora up, and she gasped.

"Sister, I will slit her throat, I swear it. Where is Aelia?"

"Upstairs," Elora whispered, unsurprised that he was here. "I will take you to her."

Keeping his gaze fixed on Rian, Kristofer stepped back, pulling a sobbing Olibia with him.

Rian rose slowly. "Kristofer, let her go. We will take you to Aelia."

"You will take me to her anyway, or I will kill the three of you."

As if to prove his point, he jerked Olibia and pressed the knife to her neck. She let out a cry, and Rian saw a drip of blood creep down her throat.

"All right," Rian replied.

He looked at Elora, and she nodded and stood up. Rian grabbed his boots and laced them quickly.

"If any of you alert the guards, I will kill her." Kristofer jerked his head, indicating for Rian and Elora to go first, and he followed them closely, dragging Olibia with him.

They crept up a flight of stairs, and down a long corridor. Aelia's chamber was just around the corner.

Upon hearing voices, Kristofer paused and told Elora, "Get rid of them."

Elora saw two guards stationed outside of Aelia's room. Seeing who stood before them, they both bowed.

"I wish a moment with our prisoner," she said. "Be gone with you."

"Yes, my queen!" They hastened off, glad for the few moments of precious freedom that they would have.

Once they were gone, she turned to the other three.

"She is here, Kristofer."

After pushing open the door, Elora saw Aelia sitting next to the window, with her arms wrapped around her legs. Aelia looked at the door and leapt to her feet in a defensive stance as Rian entered. She eyed them with suspicion until Rian moved and she saw Kristofer.

"Kristofer!"

Relief washed over him. He knew that Elora and Rian would not harm her, but he was concerned about Rake and Rake's hatred toward him. Would he take his animosity out on Aelia?

"Aelia."

The whisper of his voice left no room for misinterpretation. It was a declaration of his love for her. That he would come back to the one place that had nearly killed him...

Elora had a feeling he would come for Aelia, and she looked at her brother with admiration and no small amount of amusement.

Aelia hesitated, though, the words of Rake and his men reverberating through her.

"Aelia, now!" Kristofer said.

She moved and stood behind him, her heart pounding.

They stood in the doorway, and Kristofer jerked his head at Rian, wanting him to go first. Rian's hands shook with the force of his fury, and he glared at Kristofer, unable to move. A slight shake of his head was the only warning Kristofer gave him.

"You hide behind a woman," Rian growled.

Undeterred, Kristofer smiled. Olibia's fear had Kristofer holding her up so she did not collapse in a trembling heap.

"Obviously, a fight between us would no doubt rouse the entire castle," he said. "And as you can imagine, it was hard enough getting in here. Now, I haven't the time for idle conversation. As of this moment, Rake lies in a bloody pool in his chamber. The quicker you accommodate me, the quicker you might be able to accommodate him." He looked at the doorway again. "Up the stairs."

Elora gasped. To lose Rake now would be detrimental. Not only to his kingdom, but his part in the war could turn the tides. They needed him alive. Should he die, his territory would fall into turmoil. The people would lose their leader, and despite his flaws, Rake was a good man.

Elora could not bear the thought of losing anyone else.

She stared at Rian. "Please, Rian?" she whispered.

He hesitated no longer. His thoughts danced along the same line hers did.

"Quietly," Kristofer ordered from behind them.

As they walked the length of the long hall, the only sound was Olibia's soft cries and their muffled footsteps along the stone floor.

"Open the door," Kristofer said.

Rian quietly turned the knob to the only door they came to. It led them to a mostly empty room. A few pieces of unused furniture were strewn throughout. The cobwebs suggested that the room had not been touched in years.

"Behind the tapestry," Kristofer said.

Elora pulled back a faded tapestry against the far wall, but saw nothing. She then looked at him for further instruction.

"Pull the lever down."

Elora stared at the wall for a moment, before seeing a stone lever nestled in the space between the wall and what appeared to be a cleverly disguised door. Once inside, they made their way slowly and quietly up the stairs and when they reached the top, Kristofer paused. They could hear voices, and he swore.

After listening intently, Kristofer determined that there were three, and he glanced down at Aelia to see the terrified pools of her eyes. It was a look he fervently wished to never see again.

"Elora?" Kristofer turned to look at his sister.

His silent question remained unanswered as Elora pondered how best to get rid of the guards.

Kristofer glared at Elora with impatience, and she could feel the heat from his gaze. Behind him, a torch illuminated his features, and she stared at his face. His height, his strength, the menacing air he gave off, all coiled in her stomach and a wave of nauseousness passed over her. It was, she realized with no small amount of alarm, because he was well. He had survived Rake's torturers and come back more frightening than ever—and she was so glad of it.

She was glad he was all right. Relieved, beyond measure, that she did not have to witness his execution. Her love for him was as strong as ever, and she bit her lip as a wave of guilt washed over her. He was the enemy. Even if Kristofer came back to their side, Rian would never forgive him. He would never allow Elora near him.

All of the emotions coursing through her took only a few seconds, but Kristofer was impatient.

"If you don't do something about those guards, sister, I will kill them."

His voice jerked her from her thoughts, and with a start, she looked at Rian for help.

"I'll go," he said.

But Kristofer shook his head. "No. Elora, now."

A thought came to her, and she glanced around.

"Wait over there." She pointed to the bend in the stairwell, then waited until they were out of sight before flinging open the wooden door.

Eyes wide, she ran up to the guards, murmuring something about a frightening disturbance downstairs.

"It is on the second floor!" she cried. "There is an empty corridor, and I'm certain I saw something. See to it!"

It took the guards a moment to register her complaint, shocked as they were that the queen was roaming the castle alone at night.

"Right away, my queen! Allow one of us to escort you back to your chambers."

Elora shook her head. "No, I am fine. Just see to it. We do not want enemies roaming our corridors!"

After bowing at the order, the three guards turned and hurried down the stairs, eager to put their queen's fears to rest. Once they were gone, Elora peered around the stairwell.

Kristofer shoved Olibia, and she cried out, causing Rian to turn with anger.

"Keep moving," Kristofer snarled.

They walked down the corridor that overlooked the floor below, before climbing another stairwell that led them to a part of the castle that had not been used in decades. There was no light, and none of them could see, except Kristofer, who directed them.

"Keep going."

Elora found Rian's hand and clung to it in the never-ending darkness. She was disturbed with herself for feeling the way she did toward her brother.

Rian squeezed her hand gently and kept her near until they came to the end of the hallway. A grating noise sounded as Kristofer's hand moved a stone in the wall that swung open a door to a secret passageway.

"Rian, there is a torch on the right," he said. "Light it."

Rian felt along the wall until he found the torch. By striking together the flint and steel he'd discovered underneath the torch, they found themselves bathed in light. Rian carried the torch and they walked for over an hour. A grate, with a narrow ladder, finally came into view.

"Open it," he ordered Rian.

When he hesitated, Kristofer jerked Olibia against him and she cried out.

"Now!"

Rian climbed halfway up the ladder and pushed hard on the grate. It popped out with no noise, landing with a soft thud on the ground above. He climbed back down to stand beside Elora.

Aelia looked up at Kristofer as he said, "Aelia, climb through and see to it that no guards are visible."

As she walked past Rian, he grabbed her hair and jerked her against him. Wrapping an arm around her chest, he held her in place and tightened his hand around her throat. Kristofer tensed.

"I cannot let you do this," Rian said.

Choking, Aelia glanced at Kristofer.

"Rian, I warn you. Do not engage me. Take her from me, and I will personally see to it that Elora ends up back in the South."

"Rian, let her go," Olibia begged. "He's already attacked Rake."

"Did you kill him?" Elora whispered.

Keeping his gaze on Aelia, Kristofer watched her try to pull Rian's hand away from her throat.

"No. But I will go back."

"Damn you," Rian hissed, shoving Aelia toward the grate.

"Go," Kristofer said to her, and she climbed out of the grate using the rickety iron ladder.

She popped her head into the opening of the grate a moment later.

With a shake of her head she whispered, "I see no one."

After he shoved Olibia into Elora, the women fell in a heap. Kristofer drew his arm back and released the dagger with a flick of his wrist, and it sunk into Rian's shoulder. After grabbing ahold of the ladder, Kristofer used his feet to push off the third rung, and leapt through the opening above. Elora gaped at his movement.

She ran to Rian.

"I'm all right," he said. "A flesh wound. Let them go. Rake is injured," he said, as Olibia ran over.

"I'm not sure he'll survive." Olibia sobbed. "Kristofer stabbed him with his sword."

"Go quickly." Rian glancing again at the grate. "Kristofer is beyond any of us now."

CHAPTER 20

T he grate led Kristofer and Aelia underneath Rake's city, and they emerged on the city's outskirts. The hour was still late, and Kristofer relied heavily on that alone to avoid detection. With Rake injured, he knew his sister and Rian would be preoccupied, and it was unlikely that they'd send a brigade after them.

The grass underneath their feet muffled the sound of their movement. The problem was that the stone keep was extremely well-fortified. Crenels were on every corner of the wall, and four archers stood in every crenel. The arrow slits provided a large field of fire. The portcullis was closed until daybreak, and the drawbridge was raised to prevent anyone from entering during these hours, which also made it nearly impossible for anyone to get out. Kristofer needed the guards to exchange shifts so that he could scale the wall.

His grip tightened on Aelia's hand and pushed her flat against the cold stone. Still stunned that he was here, she squeezed in response to make sure he was real—that it had not been a dream.

"The guards will exchange shifts soon," he whispered.

They continued to walk, staying as close to the wall as they could. The moonless night aided them in their escape. The guards, he knew could not see him or Aelia, nor would they expect anyone to be inside the wall. Their attention was solely on what moved outside.

Thankful for the moonless night, Kristofer moved with caution, still holding Aelia's hand. They crept along, pausing from time to time when a guard moved above them.

When they reached the Southern side of the castle wall, Kristofer released Aelia and brushed aside bushes and bramble. She heard a faint click and felt Kristofer take her hand again.

"This leads to the fields on the other side of the wall," he said. "Crawl quietly. I will meet you."

"Alone?" Her voice quavered.

"I cannot fit, Aelia. Go quickly, and wait for me. The guards will exchange shortly, and I'll meet you. Keep quiet."

He watched her crawl under the wall, before returning his attention to the towers. Regardless of the dark night, he could see clearly. The guards, he was sure, could not see him, but he didn't want to draw attention to himself. After having watched the castle for almost a month, he had dressed commonly and hid inside, following servants, so as to learn the secret passageways of the castle. He knew he could not rescue Aelia from the dungeon, so once rumors circulated that she had been brought upstairs, he made his move.

After waiting until the guard at the tower directly above him left his post, Kristofer scaled the wall. Once he was on top, he heard the soldiers behind him talking gaily. He lowered himself over the other side and climbed down. When he was thirty feet from the ground, he leapt off the wall and landed on all fours.

—⁓⁓—

Aelia waited, terrified in the long grass on the outskirts of the wall. Her dress was damp from the tunnel she had crawled through.

While crawling, she realized that the tunnel was really

some kind of unused drain. Maybe for a mote that had not been there in years.

Crouching, she covered her mouth with her hand to stifle her erratic breathing. Unable to believe that Kristofer had really come for her, she felt her eyes fill. Surely he would not have journeyed all the way to the East for mere entertainment. She must mean something to him.

Aelia waited for what seemed like an eternity, every sound causing her to jump in fright. As an hour passed, she began to wonder if perhaps he could not find her.

"Aelia."

The unexpected whisper of Kristofer's voice caused her to cry out in fright.

"Hush, love. We must move quickly."

He took a hold of her hand and pulled her through the long grass that lined the castle walls. He was hunched over, using the grass to shelter their escape from any archers that might be on watch. Every now and then, Kristofer would pause and listen while Aelia caught her breath.

A small trickling stream made its way over a bed of rocks stood in front of them, so Kristofer stopped again, and they drank quickly.

With the creek behind them, they ran until the grass faded and a neat row of trees stood before them. Having no idea where they were, Aelia held tight to Kristofer's hand as he turned west. They followed the woods until a cluster of small houses dotted the valley. As quietly as they could, they darted behind the village and followed the path further out until they came to a barn. Kristofer whistled, then waited until Asen galloped toward them. After a grateful pat on the horse's neck, he swung a long leg over the saddle and pulled himself up. Using only his legs to hold himself in place, Kristofer leaned over and held his hands out for Aelia, but she hesitated and he drew back with a scowl of confusion.

"Aelia!" His sense of urgency came out in a harsh whisper. "Make haste!"

Without waiting for an answer, he grabbed her around the waist and lifted her in front of him before urging Asen into a gallop. She sat rigid, traumatized, and her anguish came out in a choked sob that reached Kristofer's ears.

"Be easy, Aelia." he whispered into her ear. "You are safe."

Using one hand to hold the reigns, he wrapped his other arm around her and drew her up against him. He could feel the sobs rack her, and with a glance over his shoulder to make sure they weren't being followed, he urged his mount faster. Without any way to reassure her, he kept his arm around her until he felt her settle and relax against him.

"Rest, my love."

Aelia's exhaustion finally took over, and with Kristofer's arms wrapped around her, she fell into a fitful slumber. Every so often, she would startle awake, which gave Kristofer's mind all sorts of leave to imagine the horrors she had endured. Although she looked all right, Kristofer could attest firsthand that it meant little.

They rode through the rest of the night and into the early morning hours. As she stirred in his arms, Kristofer began looking around for a safe place to dismount and rest. He pulled into the woods, scanning the surroundings for a clearing big enough for the three of them.

Aelia looked around, and her gaze came to rest on the arm that circled her waist. Wondering if she had imagined her rescue, she turned slowly to verify that it was Kristofer behind her, and not Rian.

After pulling on the reigns, he dismounted and held his arms up to help her down. She placed both hands on his shoulders to steady herself as he pulled her off the horse. Having no idea what to say, Aelia wrung her hands together as she felt his gaze scan her.

"Aelia?" Kristofer took a step toward her, but she backed away and he froze. "What has happened? What did they do to you?"

Unable to look at him, marveling at the fact that he had come for her, and then confused all over again, she brought a knuckle to her mouth to stifle a sob.

"Talk to me, love."

His endearment brought forth more confusion as angry tears sprang to her eyes.

"Love?" she whispered, after a brief pause. "Love..." she repeated, as if the word was a stinging bee. "How can you call me such when you left me in the hands of your enemies for weeks?"

"I could not—"

"You could not what?" she choked. "Did you only come for me because it was Rian who took me in the first place? Rake said it was purposely he, for what is between the two of you is personal. He wanted to hand me to his men..."

"How—"

"They said I was your whore." She turned from him as a fresh waterfall of tears cascaded down her face.

Kristofer stared at her back, dumbfounded.

"My whore?" he repeated slowly.

She felt his hands on her shoulders as he turned her around to face him. Her head bowed, he took a hold of her chin and forced her gaze up.

"You were never my whore, Aelia. How could you believe it?"

In an attempt to jerk her face from his touch, which ended futilely, she swallowed past the lump in her throat.

"Rake said that you trained with your men. That you were well—to which I could offer no excuses, as your rise in health is baffling to us all—and that you did not notice my absence. That I was your nightly source of entertainment, and that there are other...that you have other w-women." Barely able to utter the last word, she tried again, unsuccessfully, to pull away from him.

His light chuckle had her gaze flying to his face with indignation.

"Other women? Aelia, be reasonable, my love. I can barely handle you."

"How dare you make light of this! How could you leave me there? Why did you not come sooner? I don't understand any of it. If you knew I was missing, why did you play in the courtyards? I read the reports myself. You—"

"Aelia! It was a ploy."

"A-a ploy? What can you mean?"

All traces of amusement had vanished from his face, and he held her tight, his gaze searching hers.

"It was all I could come up with on such a short basis. Raum told me what happened the moment I returned, and I rode out scarcely an hour later. I would always come for you Aelia. How could you not know that?"

Surprise marred her lovely face.

"I don't understand," she whispered. "They said I was your—"

"My *whore*?" He shook his head in disbelief. "How could you believe it?"

"When you didn't come...I don't understand."

Kristofer released her, and she took a step back to study his face, questioning the sincerity she heard in his voice. Her mind raced, but her fear was beginning to diminish, replaced by an anxiousness to know the truth.

He said, "There is a man in the city who coincidentally looks quite a bit like me. He is tall. his hair is the same color. I figured, at the distance between the courtyards and where Rake's spies are stationed, they would not notice that it was not I who trained. And I was right. If the Easterners believed I was still in the South, they would eventually allow their guard down. I feared if they knew what you really meant to me, that you would be impossible to obtain. I could not get to you in the dungeon. Not without slaughtering the entire platoon of guards they have stationed down there. The noise alone would have brought forth more soldiers, and so on. I had to wait for my sister to bring you up. As soon as I heard that you had been released from the dungeon, I made my move."

"But they said—"

"What would you have them say? Rake could not, in good conscience, sanction the torture of a woman—even mine. Nor do I think Rian or Elora would have allowed it. They only weapon he had against you were words, which he clearly knew how to use." His tone softened as he watched her brush the tears away. "You have never been a whore to me. You are a beacon of light in my life, Aelia. You redeem me, and I love you."

In the eight years they had spent together, he had never once said those words. Nor was she bothered by their relationship. She was safe. She was in love, and she was happy with him. But to hear him confess his love for her brought tender satisfaction and warmth to her person.

"You love me?" she said.

His eyebrows shot up as he stared at her in mute disbelief.

"No man would ride into enemy territory for a concubine. Honestly, I'm more surprised that you would believe Rake's words. I have loved you, Aelia, from the moment I saw you sitting bedside that grave. I will always come for you."

They stared at each other in silence—her in shock, and him in disbelief.

Without taking her gaze off of him, she looked as if she might take a step toward him, but seemed to think better of it and stood where she was.

"Rake convinced me that you did not want me," she

whispered. "In the dungeon, I was alone for so long that I thought I might go mad. My thoughts were always for you, but when you didn't come right away..."

He closed the distance between them and placed his hands on her waist, bringing his forehead to hers. They stood wrapped in each other's embrace for a long time, before his hand came to her cheek. He leaned down and kissed her.

"I will always come for you," he whispered into her ear. "I cannot marry you in the midst of a civil war. You would be the target of so many, as you already are."

He felt her nod against his shoulder, and she hugged him tight.

When they finally broke apart, he studied her for a moment, and she shifted self-consciously.

"Did they not feed you?" He frowned.

"They did. The dungeon was nothing but bread and cheese."

"I'm aware," he muttered.

He turned and stared blankly at the ground while straining to hear something.

"What—"

"Hush," he said.

Aelia fell silent, and he drew his arm back to send the dagger he held, flying into a bush. A squeak and a grin from him had her smiling as he pulled a dead rabbit out of the brush.

Kristofer built a small fire, then skinned and cleaned the rabbit. As it roasted, he leaned against a tree. Crossing his long legs at the ankles, he held a hand out toward Aelia, which she took in hers as she sat beside him. She drew his arm over her shoulder, leaned against him, and laced her fingers with his. She then closed her eyes and tried to focus on all that had happened in the last few hours.

"Tell me about them." She turned her head to look up at him.

He had been waiting for it—the endless stream of her questions.

"About who?"

He felt her shrug.

"Rian, Rake, Elora...all of them. Who is the old man? Has Rian always been so terrifying? Does—"

His bark of laughter silenced her, and her eyes widened as she turned to look upon him.

"What amuses you?"

"Rian...terrifying..."

His laughter had him leaning forward, and she felt herself smile at his mirth.

"Well, he is!"

"Perhaps to some." Kristofer still chuckled. "He and my sister are well-matched in their compassion for humanity."

"Elora was very kind."

"Aye. Her compassion might yet win her this war."

"How can you say such a thing? If they win, you will die."

He shook his head with confidence. "Nay, Aelia. I certainly will not die at the hands of my sister. And at this point, I do not believe Rian would win a duel."

"Arrogance will not stop the flow of blood."

"It is hardly arrogance, Aelia. It is fact, and one Rian and I both know to be true. He's bested me before, yes. But he had help, and I was not at my peak that day."

"You were ill because of what Kayne did to you."

Kristofer glanced at her, a muscle twitching in his jaw. She felt her heart beat faster, but she held her ground.

"Elora mentioned—"

"She should not have told you that. But yes...his actions took a physical toll on me, and I was not able to ward Rian off. Rian's anger and his hatred, along with the desire to protect my sister, made him nearly invincible. Abignale—do not be fooled by the old man—is...he's unlike anything I've ever seen, Aelia. Needless to say, if I could barely hold my own against Rian, I stood not a chance when Abignale attacked."

Aelia, try as she might, could not fathom the old man being as lethal of a swordsman as Kristofer made him out to be. Then again, the world was a peculiar place.

A shrug was all she could manage. How he could feel certain about his enemies and their actions was baffling to her.

"Tell me about Rian," she said.

Kristofer was silent for a long time. After a deep breath, he looked down at her.

"What is it you wish to know? He is *the* most accomplished swordsman that I've ever crossed blades with. I'm fairly certain he was following Rake's orders concerning you. He would not have harmed you. I was worried that your insolence would anger Rake, and that he would hand you off to his men. Which, you've confirmed he almost did."

"Rian loathes you. I've never seen anger like that. What did you do to him?"

Kristofer gave Aelia a disgruntled look. He leaned forward and turned the rabbit on the spick to evenly roast the other side, before settling back against the tree.

"Rian...believes me responsible for the death of his twin brothers."

Aelia gasped. "Were you?"

"I was not."

"Why not just tell him the truth, then?"

Her eyes, so large and innocent, made him smile.

"That is a woman's perspective. Rian is lethal. He would not believe me, and crossing blades with him is something I would only do if necessary. Besides, all these years later, it makes not a shred of difference."

"But you knew him once. Before you joined the South."

"Aye."

"Tell me," she urged.

Reliving the past was something Kristofer avoided, but one glance at Aelia told him she would not let the matter rest.

Resigning himself, he said, "I did know Rian, once. Then he and I were...close. His family ruled the West, and mine ruled the North. Often, our father's would join together to discuss terms, maybe settle a dispute. If force were needed, they would combine their armies, and not once did they falter. Both territories thrived under their leadership. When Elora was born, it was a celebration unlike any other, for it was assumed that she and Rian would eventually marry. Blood would now join the territories. After I left, everything became hectic. Rian—rightfully so—felt that I had betrayed him. My choices, Aelia, are my own. Do not question me on it."

She nodded.

He continued. "Dagr—my late general—outranked me at the time that Rian's castle was stormed. He and his general, Breggen, were away. I do not know where. Dagr slaughtered his parents, and during the chaos, set fire to the upper part of the castle, where Rian's brother's bed chambers were. The boys were but twelve years old. I could hear them screaming from the balcony below, but by the time I got there, they were dead. Dagr found me with my hand on the knob of the door, and a rumor began that I held the door shut while the boys burned alive. I fueled the rumor, but it wasn't so. I had tried to save them."

Aelia covered her mouth in horror, her eyes wide. Kristofer pulled her hand away from her face and smiled at her.

She said, "Why would you fuel a rumor of such an atrocious nature?"

"It is best Rian believes the worst of me."

"Why?" Aelia was so engrossed in the story, she leaned forward with eagerness.

Amused, Kristofer nudged her away and pulled the rabbit away from the fire. He held the stick while waiting for it to cool.

"That is a question I cannot answer," he replied.

Aelia shuddered at the thought of Rian.

"He frightens me."

"For good reason. But you only know Rian as an enemy. As a king, there would be no one better."

"You speak as if you admire him."

"There is much to admire in both Rian and Elora. Again, Aelia, you only know them as enemies. As a king and queen, especially united, their reign would be undiminished. That is, if this war ever ends."

"I don't understand you." She scowled. "If they win, you and I, Raum, we will all perish."

He shook his head again. "Do not let that thought plague you. Again, I do not believe Rian would win a duel. Because I took you from him, it will tip the scales. The East will make the next move."

She pulled back to look at him, tucking her legs underneath her.

"Rian defeated you," she said. "They tortured you for weeks. They nearly killed you. Without Kayne's intervention, you would have died in my arms. I know this is something you will explain to me later on, right? But you would have been king, Kristofer. You would have ruled alongside the enemies that you speak so highly of. Instead, you betray them. My own theories as to why are formulating as we speak. Yet you sit here, speaking of them with the utmost respect. Do they do the same for you? Do you think credit is given to you on your leadership in the South, by those in the East?"

"Absolutely," he said.

She sat, stunned, staring at him in confusion. Her anger rose as a flush crept into her cheeks.

"Absolutely," he repeated, then sighed as he stared at the fire in front of him.

She, too, watched the embers burning, flickering orange and yellow, while she waited for him to speak.

"You must promise me something," he said.

She did not respond, but continued to stare at the flames until she felt his hand cup her cheek and turn her face to look upon him.

"There will come a time when this war takes a violent turn. When that time comes—and it will—I will not...I cannot be with you. I want you to go East."

"What!" She shook her head frantically. "Rian will kill me! I cannot—"

"He won't, and you will. I am not asking, Aelia. If I fall, Raum will find you. But until then, you will be safe and protected in the East. I cannot ride into battle with your well-being undecided. Promise me."

It was a monumental moment between them. Kristofer's decision to leave his home, his family, became cognizable to Aelia. She understood, even though no explanation was provided.

"Will you tell them?" she said.

"Aye. And you, when the time arises. Do I have your word?"

Her chest rose and fell rapidly. On the heels of a frightened pause, she nodded.

"My word," she replied.

Kristofer reached for her arms and pulled her to him. While holding her firm, his ice-blue eyes searched her emerald ones.

"Elora will keep you safe because you are mine, which I've

made abundantly clear. Rian would never harm a woman. And even if the thought crossed his mind, my sister would never allow it. This is important, Aelia. Do you understand? You cannot stay in the South. This war will turn. It's only a matter of time."

"I understand," she said.

Her words meant more than one thing, and he understood them both.

She wrapped her arms around his shoulders and kissed him.

"Thank you," she whispered into his ear.

"What for?"

"Your endeavor East, of course." She gave him a sly look and kissed his neck.

"Oh, that! Traversing the countryside in pursuit of...what was it...my *whore*?"

"Aye, I believe that was the term used."

They both laughed. The seriousness of the earlier conversation behind them, they delighted in each other's company.

Aelia leaned in again to kiss him. After pulling her hair over her shoulder, she let her hands graze across his chest, marveling that he was here, and she was safe.

"I would not do that," he warned.

"You would deny me your bed?" She looked around at the trees. "Or any accommodation."

"I did not say that. I only seek to warn you that we have a perilously long journey on top of a horse."

She groaned. "Perhaps you are right. I am hungry."

She reached for the rabbit. He handed it to her, and she tore into it.

"I've seen men at taverns eat in a more ladylike fashion." He grinned.

"Is Rake—"

"Aelia, please! Do your questions never cease?"

She raised a brow at him before taking another bite.

"Why did you never tell me Rian was so handsome?"

He raised his brows and turned to look at her grinning face.

"Unacceptable." But he, too, laughed.

She pulled off a piece of meat and fed it to him.

"Are they married? Rian and Elora?"

"No." Kristofer took a bite. "They will be soon."

"Do you know Rake and his wife well?"

Sighing, Kristofer reserved himself to a day of answering her endless stream of questions.

"At one point," he replied. "It is no secret that Olibia is barren. And without an heir, Rake's kingdom will fall into turmoil if he dies."

"Is that why you did not kill him?"

"I did not kill him because I had no need to. If he dies, I imagine Rian will take control of the East. His territory is under my control, so he has nothing holding him to the West."

"Then why will his kingdom fall into turmoil?

"Because it's not Rian's domain. His and Elora's people will accept it, especially because they are all housed in the East for now. But I imagine Rake's subjects will want to elect their own leader. The problem is that no one is suitable to lead an entire territory, except Rian. Elora will stand beside him, no doubt. But even together, they might have an uprising if Rian takes Rake's place as king."

Aelia frowned. "I don't understand why it matters who rules, as long as they are just and kind. You speak of Rian as if he is."

"He would make an excellent ruler. But it is difficult leading a territory that doesn't want you."

You would have been king, Aelia thought.

It was not the first time that had come to her mind. But now she had a better understanding of the impact of Kristofer's decision to leave the North. It wasn't just that he had betrayed his family. It was that he had given up the crown.

"I know what you are thinking, Aelia. But the North is no longer my home. If the South wins this war, Kayne might establish my rule there. You do understand the implication of this?"

His words hit her like an icy slap across the face.

"You would have to marry a queen," she said, her tone bitter.

He laughed. "Are you so uncertain of my affection toward you?"

She gave him a dark look. "You would have been king if you stayed. In any political aspect, you cannot marry a commoner, and I am such."

"You are no commoner, Aelia. Nay." He shook his head. "If I take on such a role, you would be beside me."

She lifted her head in surprise, eyes widening at his what he'd said.

He took the rabbit from her hands and set what was left of it at his side, then pulled her onto his lap. Her hair draped down her back and pooled in a heap on the ground. He ran his fingers through it and brought his mouth to hers.

His kiss left her breathless. Before he could kiss her again, she put her hands on his chest to hold him.

"What is it you want, Kristofer?"

It took him a long time to answer. He took so long, that for a moment, Aelia wondered if he had heard her.

Slowly, he lifted his gaze to meet hers.

"I don't want to rule." He shook his head.

"But it is your birthright."

"Even so. The crown comes at an incredibly high cost. I want freedom."

She nodded her understanding. "Whatever you choose, I will follow you."

CHAPTER 21

Abignale leaned over Rake's bedside. His wound was grievous, but he would survive. Abignale turned and told Elora, Rian, and Olibia that Rake would live, and sighs of relief filled the room.

"I've done all I can for him," Abignale said.

He rose to his feet and turned to Rian, who had a hand clamped against his own shoulder.

"Let me look at you." Abignale had Rian sit as he examined his shoulder. "At least it is your left arm. You can still draw your sword if need be.

"Does it need stitching?" Elora came over to look closer.

"It can be cauterized," Abignale said, and Rian grimaced at the prospect. "It still seeps blood, and my herbs are low. Cauterize it and prevent infection."

Olibia walked over to her husband and sat next to him on the bed. She dabbed at his forehead with a cool cloth.

"Rian, if you go to your chambers," Elora said, "I will be there shortly."

Her gaze flickered to Olibia, and catching her meaning, Rian and Abignale left the room.

She sat behind Olibia and wrapped her arms around the woman, bringing her chin to rest on Olibia's shoulder.

"Are you all right, Olibia? This night must have been terrifying for you."

"I will be fine. I worry for my husband," she whispered.

"He will be all right. Give him time."

Olibia turned to Elora and gave her a kiss on the cheek.

"Let us talk tomorrow. Rian needs you, and I wish to be alone with Rake."

Elora smiled at her and walked up the stairs to Rian's chambers. He sat on a chair near the fireplace, watching the embers glow red under a small pile of wood. In his hands, he twirled the jeweled dagger. Upon hearing the door open, he turned his ear toward the door, keeping his gaze on the fire.

Elora ran her fingers through his dark hair. She could feel the tension and anger radiating off of him. Gently, as if talking to a child, she crouched in front of him.

"There is nothing to be done about it now. Unless you wish to send a brigade after them?"

Rian shook his head. "Kristofer would kill them. And an army would take too long to assemble. It's regrettable, but true—he always seems to be one step ahead."

"One day, you will meet him in a fair fight, Rian. Until then, let go of your anger. It will do naught but destroy you."

Rian handed the knife Kristofer had thrown at him, to Elora. She placed the blade in the dancing orange embers, careful to keep the handle away from the heat. She then turned to Rian and unbuttoned his shirt and helped him out of it.

"Lie down, Rian."

He leaned back as she poured water into a bowl. After dipping a clean cloth in it, she wiped the blood off his shoulder. Returning to the fire, she pulled the red-hot blade from it, and in one swift movement, held it against Rian's shoulder. His swift intake of breath dulled the hiss of the blade against his skin. It was over in a moment, and Rian let his breath out in a whoosh.

"I will leave it open to the air for a while," Elora said.

She glanced at the knife in her hand, eyeing the

craftsmanship of the hilt with appreciation. She turned it over and noticed the large ruby for the first time. Running her thumb over the gem, she frowned. She knew this knife. It was her father's, given to Kristofer as a gift when he was much younger.

She placed the knife down, deciding to examine it later, and sat beside Rian.

"If this war does not end soon, we will most certainly lose." Rian sighed. "Kristofer grows stronger and more cunning. We had a weapon against him, and we let it slip through our fingers. Did you know he would come for her?"

"I had a feeling he would." Elora kept her gaze fixed on the blade.

"So did I." Rian pushed himself up and kissed Elora.

He hesitated before releasing her and standing to walk to the window, where he looked outside.

"I think it is time to end this war, Elora. Once and for all, either way."

"You want to plan an attack?" she said.

"I think it's time to prepare for a final battle." Turning to look at her, he was stunned to see her nod.

"I agree," she replied. "You think to march to the South?"

"Of that, I am not sure. Even combined, Kristofer has more men than we do. If Kayne rides into battle, we do not stand a chance. How do we fight an enemy who is beyond death?"

"We will meet with Rake and Abignale and our generals," she said. "We will figure something out. We can hold a meeting and invite Kristofer. Aelia told us, it is he who leads the South. He will come."

Rian lifted a dark brow and snarled, "There is no neutral territory. Where would a meeting take place? And who is to say he will not betray the law of non-hostile meeting grounds?"

"He will not," Elora said. "Each side has spies. I'm certain Kristofer has men within this castle. How else would he know the tunnels as he does? Zemirah's men are still in the South. We do have that one advantage. If we prepare for finality, Kayne and Kristofer would hear of it before we even march. Nothing else makes any sense."

"When Rake is well enough, we will put the idea on the table." Rian returned his gaze to the window.

———

Rake recovered slowly. It took weeks before he was able to leave his bed chambers. In that time, Olibia stayed with him, scarcely leaving his side. She tended to his every need, not even letting the servants in.

One morning, Rake emerged and Rian called for a meeting. Deciding it was time, he and Elora sent word to Zemirah and her general. Zemirah preferred to stay with a small group of her people in the village while Kwame headed back to the ships they had situated on the Eastern shore a few leagues out.

Zemirah arrived immediately and told them that she would send word to Kwame herself once they reached a decision. Abignale, Rake, Olibia, and Zemirah met Rian and Elora in Rake's massive stone meeting room.

When all were seated at the long table, Rian stood and took a deep breath as he faced them.

"I think it is time we march on the South."

Rake raised a brow, but said nothing. The silence in the room became deafening.

Finally, Zemirah leaned forward. "Agreed. Let us be done with this, once and for all."

"How and where?" Rake said.

Olibia squeezed his hand. He looked at her and smiled, before raising her hand to his lips and kissing it.

Elora replied, "I think it would be best to send a messenger to the South, requesting a meeting with Kristofer. If we sit still," she said, before Rake could intervene, "eventually he will make a move, and our walls will not hold. He knows this castle as well as his own. He obviously has men in here. Let us meet him head-on and finish this."

"We are all aware that there is no more neutral territory," Rian said. "I suggest telling Kristofer that we will meet him halfway between our territory and his."

He took a seat beside Elora.

"How can you be sure he'll come?" Olibia said. "Or not violate the non-hostile laws?"

"He will come," Elora said. "I imagine he wants the war over as much as we do."

"Dispatch a messenger," Rake said. "We will meet in three months' time. Make sure to encourage non-hostility."

"I do not think that is necessary," Abignale said, from across the table. "Kristofer is still a king. He knows we will not violate the terms of a meeting. And neither will he. I daresay, he could kill all of us, anyway."

"Then why does he not?" Rian looked at Rake. "Why are you still alive?"

Rake shrugged. "Kristofer is a mystery. One I do not intend on solving."

—◦◦◦—

Kristofer sat on his bed, leaning against a pillow, while Aelia rested her head on his lap and read out loud. Kayne's monumental library provided an unlimited amount of books, and with the intensity of the heat outdoors, Kristofer and Aelia contented themselves with story after story.

A knock on the door made Aelia pause, and Kristofer turned his attention from her to the sound.

"What is it?" he snapped, annoyed at the disturbance.

A guard opened the door and stepped inside.

"Forgive the intrusion, Lord, but a messenger from the East awaits in the great hall."

With a casual wave of his hand, Kristofer dismissed the guard, and he and Aelia exchanged a look.

"What do you suppose it is?" she said, wide-eyed.

Frowning, Kristofer shook his head, but he knew what the message contained.

"Come," he said. "Let us see what they want."

The pair rose and made their way to the great hall. Aelia eyed the messenger, fearful of anyone who came from the East. Kristofer stood in front of the man, who bowed nervously before reaching into his pack and withdrawing a roll of parchment with Rake's seal upon it. Kristofer broke the wax and unrolled the letter. At his sharp intake of breath, Aelia looked up.

"What is it?" she said.

"Aelia, send for Raum and have him meet me in the drawing room. I will be there shortly." To the messenger, he said, "You, boy, what is your name?"

"M-Melos, Lord."

The boy was visibly shaken to be within the walls of the White Castle, and Kristofer was surprised he did not faint.

"Melos, wait here. You have nothing to fear. My men will not attack a messenger."

Aelia looked at him with curiosity, but he shook his head.

"Get Raum." He left her at the foot of the stairs.

She watched him walk toward Kayne's wing, grimacing inwardly at the thought, before heading up the stairwell.

Kristofer raised a hand and knocked on the giant, white doors, then waited patiently to be admitted. When Kayne's voice boomed through the entranceway, Kristofer pushed open the doors and knelt.

"What is it, Kristofer?" Kayne said with disinterest.

He stood hunched over a thin blue flame, where a long glass tube was perched precariously over the heat. Something thick and green bubbled within, and the noxious fumes it gave off made Kristofer curl his lip.

"Sire, this has just arrived from the East." He handed Kayne the parchment.

Kayne read it and laughed. "They wish a meeting with you, do they?"

"A petition, sire, to end the war. They will, no doubt, request a final battle." Kristofer sneered.

Kayne's black eyes met Kristofer's. "Then a final battle we shall give them."

An evil smile spread across Kristofer's face. "Will you ride with us, my king?"

Kayne's eyes seemed to glow with excitement. "To meet the bloodiest battle this world will ever know? Aye. They do not stand a chance."

Smiling, Kristofer bowed low and returned to the messenger in the great hall.

"Tell my sister I will meet her at the halfway point of our territories, one month from now."

Melos bowed and nodded, then turned quickly and darted away from Kristofer, whose maniacal laughter followed him out the doors. Once Melos was out of sight, Kristofer turned and headed to the drawing room, where Aelia and Raum stood side by side, waiting for him.

"What is this?" Raum said, as Kristofer sat down on a chair and placed his feet on the table.

"This, Raum, signals the end of this godless war. You both will ride with me in a month. My sister requests a meeting at the halfway point. It is, with certainty I say this, a request for a final battle, to end it all."

Raum's brows flew up in surprise. "Your sister did not strike me as stupid. They cannot possibly think they can win this war."

Kristofer laughed again. "She's far from stupid. I think my taking Aelia back sent Rian over the edge." His smile faltered as he turned to Aelia. "Love, wait for me upstairs. I have much to discuss with Raum."

Aelia glared at him, annoyed at his request, furious that he could sit there and laugh when such dire times were upon them. His face hardened, and he withdrew his legs from the table and stood. Aelia met his gaze in defiance.

"Aelia, do not make me drag you upstairs."

She turned from him and stalked out of the room. Kristofer and Raum watched her leave.

Raum shook his head. "If she were a man..."

Amused at her behavior, Kristofer grinned. "If she were a man, I'd beat her within an inch of her life."

He gestured to a chair, and Raum took a seat opposite of him.

"Raum, this battle will be unlike anything you've ever seen. My primary concern is making sure Aelia stays out of the crossfire. I want you to escort her East after the meeting."

Raum gaped at him in disbelief. "You do not want me fighting alongside you?"

Before Kristofer could answer, Raum stood, knocking his chair over.

"Is this because she was taken from under my charge?"

"Raum!" Kristofer held a hand up to silence him. "It is not a punishment. I do not think any soldier here could cross blades with Rian and live to talk of it. Consider yourself fortunate. Nor am I upset with you. My fear is that Aelia will die, and I cannot ride into battle with that on my conscience. I want her far away from here. Am I clear? Once she is safe, return."

Raum nodded slowly, and Kristofer relaxed somewhat.

"Can 1 trust you to follow my orders? No matter what they are?" He stared at Raum.

"Kristofer, 1 would follow you into the depths of hell."

"*That* is good to hear. For hell is exactly where we are headed."

————ᴍ————

Aelia paced the length of her room until she was certain she would wear out the marble floors. She then stormed to the door and flung it open, gasping when she came face-to-face with Kristofer, whose hand was clearly reaching for the knob.

She stepped back so that he might come in.

"Do you ever do what 1 tell you?" he said.

"1 am here, am 1 not?"

He took a seat on the bed, pushing the book they were reading earlier out of his way.

"Aelia, do you remember what you promised me on the way back from the East?"

She froze, swallowing hard, and her face paled.

She gasped. "So soon?"

"Aye. One month." Kristofer held his hand out to her. "Don't be frightened."

Her large, liquid eyes stared at him with fear, from underneath long lashes.

"What if you fall?"

"I'll survive this." His eyes were more promising than his words. "And so will you."

CHAPTER 22

Aelia sat sideways on Asen, her head resting on Kristofer's chest as they journeyed forth to meet with the Easterners. Raum rode beside Kristofer, and much to his dismay, Kristofer would have no others come along.

A tent came into view as they crested the hill near the midway post.

Aelia, try as she might, could not control her mounting terror at facing Rake and Rian again, and Kristofer felt her tension.

"All will be well, my love."

She turned to look at him, and gave him, what she hoped, was a reassuring smile.

As they approached the tent, Elora emerged from it. Dressed in black leggings and a black tunic, she looked like a warrior—every bit as deadly as her brother. Her sword hung from her hip, and there was a dagger hooked to her belt. Slung across her back was a bow and a quiver of arrows.

"Kristofer, what is this?" she hissed, eyeing Aelia and Raum.

"I will explain inside." Kristofer got off his horse.

Elora watched him help Aelia down, and lifted her gaze to study Raum. He inclined his head as he passed her, but Elora felt a wave of unease. The last time she saw him, she almost died.

Aelia stood beside Kristofer and flashed an uneasy smile

at Elora, who returned the gesture with hesitation.

Elora went inside first, followed closely by Kristofer, Aelia, and Raum. It was a small tent, with nothing but a rectangular table in the center. Abignale, Rake, and Rian were already seated. Each side-eyed the other with disdain.

"Who is this?" Rake stared at Raum. "And why is she here?"

Kristofer raised a hand to silence him. "Before we begin, I must ask it. Are there any others you brought with you? If you have violated the terms of non-hostile grounds, tell me now. For if I find out otherwise, I will kill you all."

Aelia's eyes grew wide as she turned to look at him, and Rian snorted with anger. Raum's hand went to the hilt of his sword as Rake rose to his feet.

"Elora?" Kristofer said.

"There is no one else, brother. Sit and explain. I have waited long for this."

He walked toward his sister with his hand outstretched.

"So you have brought it?"

From her boot, Elora pulled out the ruby dagger that Kristofer had thrown at Rian, and handed it to her brother. Turning it over in his hand, he ran his fingers over the jewel before placing the knife down on the table.

Rian stood. "What is going on?" he snarled. "Have you had contact with him?"

"Easy, Rian. She has not," Kristofer said. "Aelia, Raum, sit. It is going to be a very long night."

"You cannot dictate here, Kristofer," Rake hissed. "We are here to discuss the—"

"I know what we're here to discuss, Rake," Kristofer snarled, and placed his fingertips on the table as he leaned toward the older man. "I am here to make sure none of you die in the process."

The room went silent, and Kristofer looked at Abignale.

The old man nodded, and Kristofer took a seat next to his sister.

"I'm here to explain why I left," he said.

The entire mood of the room shifted. Elora and Rian exchanged a look. Rake eyed Kristofer warily, as if expecting another sword through the belly. Kristofer stared at the dagger that sat on the table, before glancing at Abignale again. For the first time in ten years, Kristofer grew uneasy. The silence became deafening as everyone waited for him to speak.

"Kristofer," Abignale whispered. "It is time. You've carried this secret for too long. Let us help you now."

Elora sat up straighter. Her eyes grew hard as she stared at Kristofer.

"What is he talking about, brother?"

Kristofer stood and turned his back to the group for a moment, before meeting Elora's gaze.

"Elora." Her name felt like a prayer to him. "Can you ever forgive me for what I have done?"

Of all things for him to say, this was the least expected. Elora felt her throat tighten, and for a moment, nothing else mattered but her brother. At a loss for words, she held his gaze until the intensity between them grew unbearable.

"I have waited...so many years to hear you say these words," she replied. "For so long I imagined all sorts of reasonings. At first I thought that you were really trying to protect me. And then I figured that there had to be a reason. Any reason. And now I...I fear you. You frighten me as no one else does." She pushed her chair back and stood, facing him. "You tried to have me killed. You slaughtered Breggen. You cut down your own people. Rian's family. And yet you stand here, asking for my forgiveness. I must know why you did the things you did."

Kristofer stood unflinching before her. At the mention of

Rian's family, he turned to look at Rian, who glowered at him.

"I have my reasons, sister. And whereas you may not understand them fully, know that I never wished for this."

Kristofer glanced at Aelia, who watched him. He could feel her eyes on him, and he wondered if he would lose her after his confession. The thought made him ill.

He turned to his sister again as his story poured forth.

"After Kayne killed Thanos and declared himself king, father came to me. He asked me to do what he believed no one else could. To leave my home and my family behind, and rise among the ranks, doing whatever I needed to do to become Kayne's right hand."

Elora gasped and covered her mouth with her hand. Rian narrowed his eyes and stared at Kristofer.

"Kayne's reputation for the extraordinary preceded his reign. Father knew what he would become. He knew that as the years passed, we would no longer be dealing with a human, but with some type of soulless, immortal creature. He was right. Kayne cannot be killed. At least, not by any of you."

"And you are here to tell us that only *you* can kill him?" Rian snarled.

"I am the only one who has any chance. Your anger and your hatred are clouding your judgment."

"My *anger*? What about my brothers? My family?" Rian's blue eyes blazed with emotion. "You sacrificed your own sister!"

Kristofer turned back to Elora. "Father told me that you would never betray your kingdom, and he was right. He said the same of Rian. That his loyalty to the West and his love for you would prevent me from seeking his help. And that there was going to come a time when Kayne would seek you out, as the only available queen in the realm. Everything happened exactly as he said it would. He would take me away for months at a time—you must remember—and he trained me. I don't know how he knew the things that he knew. Believe me, Elora, it was excruciating. The scenarios he drilled into me were something else entirely different from living them. He knew you would have to die, and that it would most likely be at my hand. At the time you were captured, I could not betray my standing in the South. I was so close. The only thing I could do was ensure you did not die painfully."

Elora rubbed her shaking hands together. "In the dungeon, you said that you could not betray your king. You were talking about Father, not Kayne?"

"Aye."

Elora did not realize that a tear crept down her cheek, until Kristofer reached up and brushed it away.

"I cannot make excuses for my behavior, Elora. And I cannot explain all of it to you in a single night. Especially when there is so much more we need to discuss before I return—"

"You're going South again?" she cried, pulling away from his touch.

"These are lies!" Rian roared, and stood.

Raum reached for the hilt of his sword, but Kristofer placed a hand on his shoulder.

In a warning tone, Kristofer said, "Do not draw your weapon."

"He speaks the truth, Rian," Abignale boomed.

All eyes turned to him.

Elora's mouth fell open. "You knew of this?" Her voice was shaky, uneven.

"I suspected as much from the moment Kristofer left. He confirmed it at the barn after we captured him."

"You claim this, yet you've said nothing all these years?" Rake scowled.

Abignale looked calmly at the angry faces around him. His gaze came to rest on Kristofer, and he smiled.

"If there was such a need for secrecy, I did not wish to be the one to put ideas in anyone's heads. You have my trust, Kristofer, and I will help you in any way I can."

Kristofer returned Abignale's smile. He had spent years wondering what would happen when he finally told his sister the truth. Would she cry? Would she be angry? Would she forgive him? Would she hate him? He had no idea.

Emotion shined bright in Elora's eyes as she turned to Rian.

"I don't know what to do," she whispered.

Rian shook his head in disbelief and placed his head in his hands. Aelia stared at Rian, wondering why Kristofer didn't tell him the truth about his brothers.

"Kristofer," she whispered. "Tell Rian—"

He gave her a sharp look that silenced her.

"Tell me what?" Rian's voice was menacing and filled with pain.

A muscle twitched in Kristofer's jaw, but he remained silent.

Finally, Aelia said, "He did not kill your brothers, Rian."

A rage of emotions coursed through Rian as he leapt to his feet, his chair falling backwards with the force of his anger. He drew his sword and brought the edge of his blade to Kristofer's throat. Aelia gasped as Raum pulled his weapon from its sheath.

Kristofer stood still, unflinching as the edge of Rian's sword drew a trickle of blood that ran down his neck, but he held his hand up to stop Raum.

The cut on his neck healed. The only evidence a thin trail of red.

With a look of disgust, Rian lowered his weapon. "You have sold your soul, Kristofer."

"More than you'll ever know," Kristofer replied, with no emotion.

"We were like brothers once." Rian took a step back to study the man before him. "Ander and Arius were barely twelve years old..."

He paused at the mention of their names and the wave of pain it caused. In all these long years since their death, he had never once spoken their names.

Rian glanced at Aelia for a long moment, before settling on Kristofer's face.

"Does your woman speak the truth?"

Kristofer stood before Rian. In his head, he replayed the night the Southern Army raided the Western Kingdom.

In a voice filled with emotion, Kristofer whispered, "The twins were dead when I got there." He cleared his throat. "Dagr set fire to their room. I heard them screaming from the balcony below, but by the time I got to their chamber, they were both dead."

"They say you held their door shut so they could not escape." Rian's voice broke, and he swallowed hard.

"I always thought Elora would be my undoing," Kristofer said. "But she wasn't. You were."

Rian gave him a quizzical look.

"Of all that my father trained me for, to go up against your family—I was ill-prepared for it. I tried to save the boys, but I was too late. Dagr found me as I was closing the door. I told him they were dead, and somewhere a rumor started that I kept them confined to the flames. I fueled the rumor."

Rian was gripping the back of the chair so hard that his knuckles turned white.

"You are lying," he said.

Elora placed her hand on his back to comfort him.

Kristopher continued. "I am not. It was the only time I ever faltered, and I vowed to never do so again. I killed the man who led the raid, and set the room on fire. Your brothers, your family, are avenged, just not by your hand."

"What of my parents?"

"Your parents died defending their home. I never raised my sword against them. Dagr dealt the fatal blow." Kristofer gestured helplessly with his hands.

The pain in his voice was evident. Aelia had heard this tone once before.

She sat demurely, hands folded in her lap as she studied the pattern of her dress with feigned intensity. She knew Kristofer better than anyone, and she often suspected his true loyalties laid with his family.

He was never the same after Elora was captured and then escaped. Raum, too, had noticed a change in Kristofer, but he associated it with the stress of rulership and the impending battles.

His loyalties would always be with Kristofer. Kayne was a monster, and it was no secret that he did not care at all for his people, his subjects, or the well-being of his kingdom. Kristofer ruled in Kayne's name, aye, but he took care of those in his kingdom. And that, Raum decided, is what makes a true ruler. The South was his home, but were it not for Kristofer, Raum would have left years ago.

He swallowed hard. "For the last decade, I have followed you, Lord, into battle. I have done every service you've asked of me."

Kristofer turned clear blue eyes to Raum. If Raum should turn on him, declare his loyalty to Kayne, he would have to kill him. It was something Kristofer prayed fervently would not happen.

"Raum—"

"Kristofer, I only serve the South because of you. And I daresay, most of your men feel as I do. It would be my honor to continue serving you as I have been."

Kristofer's relief was evident in the light smile he gave. Raum's loyalty and friendship lifted some of the tension Kristofer was feeling, and he nodded at Raum, full of gratitude.

After turning to look down at Aelia, his smile faltered.

"I am not what you thought—"

"You are far better, my love," Aelia said. "You'll see no judgement from me."

Elora watched her brother raise a hand to cup Aelia's cheek before returning his attention to her and Rian. She closed her eyes, remembering him as a little boy, and as the brother she adored. She realized she believed him, and opened her eyes to look upon him.

"I always knew you were never lost to me," Elora said. "When you left, I...we," she took ahold of Rian's hand, "... were beside ourselves with anguish. Neither of us could understand how you, of all people, could betray us. My mind races with memories of you and Father leaving for so long, so often."

"It was never my intention to make you suffer," Kristofer said.

He and Elora forgot that there were others in the room, and for those moments, nothing else mattered to either of them. For the first time in ten years, the world fell away as brother and sister looked upon one another, not as enemies, but as family.

Elora stared at him with a mixture of confusion, fear, happiness, and hesitation. Since he had left the North, Kristofer had become hard and cruel. But she realized, not to the core. It was the game he played, the role he had taken on.

His eyes were soft, his touch gentle. But the silence stretched between them with growing intensity.

Elora lifted a shaking hand, then thought better of it and dropped it, clutching her hands together in front of her instead. Kristofer moved toward her, causing panic to well up within her and Rian to raise his weapon.

"I know you fear me, and I don't pretend not to know why. My actions were barbaric, but I had no choice, Elora. Father used you, dangled you in front of me like a worm on a hook."

She frowned quizzically.

"He would say, 'What do you think will happen to Elora if Kayne's reign reaches all four territories?' And then, sister, he would tell me in great detail, what Kayne would do to you if ever he got a hold of you."

"Yet you took her from us and nearly killed her," Rian hissed.

Kristofer did not move. Nor did he take his eyes off of Elora's tear-stained face.

"I can explain that, Elora."

With a sob, Elora turned and ran from the tent. Kristofer grimaced and tried to follow, but Rian's sword caught him at the throat again.

"Rian, I must speak with her, and we don't have much time," Kristofer pleaded.

"Let him go, Rian," Abignale said, his tone gentle.

Rian lowered his sword slowly and stepped back, watching Kristofer exit the tent. Aelia looked uncomfortably at Raum, who shared her unease and took a seat beside her. She was grateful to have him near. The silence in the tent was so consuming that Aelia was afraid to breathe loudly.

The minutes stretched, and she glanced at the flap of the tent, wondering when Kristofer would return, and if he would get through to his sister. She knew how hard this must be for him, and sent out a silent prayer that Elora would forgive him. For it seemed to her that the only thing Kristofer cared about was his sister.

With a sigh, Aelia turned her attention to Rian, for he

stood near her. Kristofer and Raum were the same height, and both men were considered tall, but Rian stood taller than both of them. He was unrelenting in his anger. Aelia could sense it. She studied the midnight color of his hair. The color so dark that it reminded her of Kayne's hair, and she shuddered.

Rian shifted, and she watched his hand tighten on the hilt of his sword.

Unable to bear the awkward silence anymore she said, "Kristofer tells me you are an excellent swordsman."

Her voice drew every pair of eyes in the tent, but she only noticed Rian's. The man who managed to steal her from the South. Her fear of him was plain, but with Kristofer so near, she felt safe.

Rian turned slowly to look down at her. The only word that would describe her was exquisite. She was a rare, delicate beauty with passionate green eyes. Her hair was braided, and she wore an emerald-green dress that matched the color of her eyes. Other than the finery of the material she wore, she adorned no other accessories. Simple, elegant, and fiercely loyal to Kristofer, Rian felt a surge of hatred toward her.

Finally, after a long pause, he said through clenched teeth, "Kristofer taught me everything I know."

Aelia continued to stare at him. She remembered the morning she was picking berries and Rian grabbed her. He fought Raum, and she had begged him to spare Raum's life, and he did.

She pulled her gaze away from Rian's face to look upon Raum.

"Why didn't you kill him, I wonder?"

Rian followed her gaze, skeptical at her question. He remembered the weeks spent with her in front of him while he dragged her East, away from her home and those she loved. He remembered the fear on her face and the endless stream of silent tears. And he remembered her begging him to spare Raum's life: *"Please don't kill him! Please! I'll go with you, but don't kill him."*

Rian's eyes softened as he looked at her. Loving Kristofer did not define her entire being. A woman who pleaded for the life of a soldier when her own was at stake was worthy of respect.

"You asked me not to," he replied.

"And I'm grateful," Raum said.

Aelia smiled, and Rian chuckled. The tension eased somewhat, and Abignale marveled at Aelia's courage to speak, especially to a man she feared so much.

The tent flap opened, and Kristofer came in, followed closely by Elora, who held his arm. Rian glared at him, and Elora had a hard time meeting his gaze.

"Might we continue?" Rake said, impatience in his voice.

Elora released Kristofer's arm and sat down. Rian sat beside her, and Kristofer took a seat next to Aelia.

Kristofer looked at Rian. "I will not ask for your forgiveness. But I need your sword, Rian. I cannot do this without you."

Rian took so long to answer that everyone at the table leaned forward to hear his response.

"I will fight alongside you, Kristofer. But nothing more."

With an understanding nod, Kristofer turned to Rake.

"I know that there is much you wish to ask of me. But it must wait. For us to win this war, Kayne must be brought down. You've seen me heal. In this aspect, I am unlike any of you. We have this one night to plan. I have come up with one that I believe will work. I've had years to perfect it. Raum, where is the map?"

Raum reached into his pack and laid on the table a detailed map of the nation. All four territories were outlined in the colors of their realm.

"This was Father's." Elora touched the edge of the parchment. "I've often wondered where it went."

Turning to face Rake, Kristofer drew a deep breath.

"Kayne will ride into this battle," he said. "But he is highly superstitious. He'll ride on the third hour of the third day. We need him as far away from the South as possible. Abignale, you wounded him when Elora was rescued. Will that method work again?"

"I don't know, Kristofer. Who's to say he has not found a remedy for that particular poison?"

"Describe the antidote."

"It would be a green, foul-smelling—"

"Thick? Over a blue flame?" Kristofer said, remembering Kayne's newest concoction.

"That is it." Abignale sighed, shaking his head. "I have others. At least one I'm sure he's never heard of."

"It is a start. If we can weaken him, I can attack."

Rake stood and walked to Kristofer's side, where he leaned over the table to get a better view of the map. Aelia tensed at his closeness, and she felt a strong, steady hand upon hers. Kristofer lent her comfort, and she tightened her grip on his hand.

Rake said, "If you are lying..."

Without looking up, Kristofer continued to study the map, but his response brought forth a smile from Raum.

"What an intricacy to come up with when we all know I could have killed you already," Kristofer replied. "You are standing before me because I need your army. I cannot allow the East to founder before Kayne is brought down. Neither Rian nor Elora can lead your territory. Think what you will. But give me your army."

"You ask a lot," Rake said in a gruff tone.

Rian said, "Rake, all he would have to do is slaughter us here and now. The territories would fall, and he would control them. A much easier solution if he was after our blood. Yet we all still stand, including you. He could have killed you."

"He almost did," Rake muttered, then with a sigh, turned to the map. "This," he pointed to a mountain pass, "would be an ideal location to attack the South from the East. You said you needed Kayne away from the South?"

Kristofer nodded. "If there are poisons that will slow him, then he cannot have access to his antidotes."

"Then this would be ideal," Rake said. "It'll give the East the upper hand, without seeming partial."

"How do you figure?" Kristofer said. "The mountains alone will provide cover. But to march an army through any mountain pass is dangerous."

"Because it'll give the South cover, too," Rake replied. "If you lead your army through the pass, we can surprise attack. Once the battle starts, it'll continue."

Kristofer studied the range and shook his head. "I do not want to lose men unnecessarily."

Aelia's gaze was fixed on the map. "What about the rolling hills of Dungar?"

Kristofer raised a surprise brow at her. "What of them?"

"Look." She pointed to the map. "It has to be close to a thousand acres of nothing but hills. If the East marches there first, you'll have no choice but to meet them. The hills will cover both sides. No matter where you fight, men will fall."

"It would work." Elora was impressed. "Is it far enough away from your castle?" she asked Kristofer.

He studied the map for a long time. Using a long finger, he traced a trail from the Southern castle to Dungar, calculating the distance in his mind.

"It will work," he said, finally.

"When?" Rian asked.

"Three months from this night." Kristofer leaned forward

to pick up the ruby knife, and turned it over in his hands.

"What is in the ruby?" Elora said. "Why did you want me to have it?"

"I knew you would recognize it. I couldn't hand it to you, so I threw it at Rian—"

"I appreciate it," Rian said, his voice coldly.

Kristofer grinned. "I could not risk it being on my person and Kayne finding it. This was extremely difficult to get."

"Why do you need it?" Rake glared at the stone.

The light reflected off of it, giving the dagger an eerie appearance.

"I can't quite explain that just now," Kristofer replied. "Elora, keep it safe and bring it with you on the day of the battle. Abignale, if you can find a way to bleed Kayne—even a small amount—it will devastate him. Any poison you can think of, coat your weapons in it. We must weaken him somewhat."

"What will happen to you?" Aelia said. "He is stronger and quicker."

"I do not know how long it will last, but I can handle his sword, even if he cuts me."

With that, Kristofer took the blade and sliced his hand. As he held it under the light of a candle, a gasp rose through the group as they watched his hand mend itself instantly.

Clenching his fist, Kristofer turned to Abignale.

"Have you any explanation? I know how I came to be this way, but do you know anything else? How long it will last? It has happened before. When Rian stabbed me on the tower, I healed. After Kayne was through with me, I bled. Not at first. I held up fine, but after so many stab wounds, they stopped healing. I was weak, and I lost entirely too much blood in Rake's dungeon. Since Kayne healed me again, I have been invincible. Can you offer me any explanation?"

"Possibly. Abignale stood and walked over to Kristofer to

take the knife from his hand. "Hold out your arm."

He took Kristofer by the wrist and drew a deep gash down the length of his arm. A slight grimace from Kristofer was the only sign of pain, and Abignale leaned forward, watching the wound heal itself.

"I think I know what causes this. Did you drink his blood?"

"I have before, but not when Raum brought me back from the East."

Elora cringed at the thought, remembering when Kayne had poured something thick and red into a goblet.

"Do not look at me like that, Elora," Kristofer said, then looked at Abignale. "Rian told me he saved Elora by giving her his blood. I assume it was through the same method Kayne used to drain her? I was unconscious when I returned. I don't know what happened, but is it possible he transfused his blood into my veins?"

"That is what I was going to say," Abignale replied. "Whether through transfusion or ingestion, I think Kayne's blood has healing properties." He grazed his fingers over the now fully healed gash he had just made in Kristofer's arm. "It is astounding," he said, more to himself than anyone else. "I believe," he released Kristofer's arm and rubbed a hand over his face, "that blood has tiny cells that regenerate. It explains healing. Normal healing. I think Kayne found a way to speed the process up. The cells in his blood are designed to heal instantly. If his blood flows through your veins—which, it is clear that it does—you hold the same power. However, when cells regenerate, the old ones die. If you are wounded too often, the cells he gave you will die off or bleed out, leaving only your own. Once they are gone, you can be killed, and once we poison Kayne's blood, it will do you no good."

"So I must take Kayne down without shedding much of my own blood?"

"Yes."

"Can it be done?" Aelia's voice quivered, and she swallowed hard, trying to hide her fear through a mask of passiveness.

"I don't know." Kristofer sighed.

"Then there has to be some other way," Elora said. "I won't lose you when I've only just gotten you back."

"There is no other way, little sister."

The room fell into a tense silence, each one of them lost in their own thoughts.

Raum cleared his throat. "Kayne trusts you. It is possible that the betrayal alone will shock him enough for you to—"

"He'll raise his sword before mine is out of its sheath," Kristofer said. "My betrayal of his trust will do nothing more than anger him. It is why I need Rian's sword and your bow. No other archer is as accurate with his weapon. Elora, your skill with a blade can only have improved in the last decade. I think it's imperative for the rulers of the territories to band together. There will be discord when the war is over, regardless of which side wins."

Surprise registered on Elora's face.

"I cannot hold my own against you. Obviously," she said, in regard to her capture. "I cannot hold Rian off for long, either."

Rian said, "We have height, weight, and strength on our side, Elora."

"And you were trained by both Kristofer and Rian," said Abignale. "It is rare for the student to defeat the master. Do not underestimate your ability with a weapon. You are lethal."

Elora said, "When Kristofer's men attacked me—"

"Circumstances, little sister. There's a big difference being attacked in the manner you were, and being on a battlefield. You also had no weapon. In any event, do not negate your strengths. If you question your abilities or doubt yourself, you will not last. Do not let the past affect the outcome of the future."

Kristofer waited for acknowledgment from his sister before turning his attention to Rake.

"Rake, can you lead your army to the South-Eastern border before crossing the Manat River?"

"Aye. Why make such a request?"

"Dungar may be leagues of hills, but it sits along the South-East coast. I'm under the impression that Zemirah's army is primarily stationed on concealed war ships. If—"

Rian raised his head as plain shock registered across his face.

"How in the fiery depths of hell do you know of Zemirah?"

Rake, Elora, and Abignale raised their eyebrows. Because everyone else was looking at Kristofer, Aelia and Raum turned to face him, too. Having no idea who Zemirah was, Aelia and Raum waited patiently, intrigued and a little concerned over the events of the night.

Kristofer looked from one face to the next before finally settling on Rian. He met his cold stare with a calm demeanor.

"The woman has men stationed within my walls, in my kingdom. How would I not know of her?"

Having no idea why they were surprised, Kristofer took a seat. He watched Elora and Rian share a look.

Rake finally broke the silence. "Zemirah said her men are well-disguised. If you knew of them, why let them remain within your walls?"

Not particularly wanting the conversation to turn in the direction it was, Kristofer sighed. He also knew it was a question he could not ignore—one that must be answered.

"For a number of reasons," he replied. "I figured it might, at some point, help you all out. It is always convenient to have spies in a castle, and I was able to feed them the information

I wanted you to have. Of course, it does not always go according to plan. But I figured it would be helpful at one turn or another, and I believe I was correct. Was it not Ikeni who led you out when you rescued Elora?"

Rian placed his head in his hands, and even Elora looked mildly disturbed. After a long, tense silence, Rian looked at Kristofer.

"I'm uncertain how you know these things, but I have a question. When you threw that blade at Brilor, when we fought on the tower, were you aiming for him?"

"No. My soldiers were preventing Brilor from removing the needle from Elora's arm. Throwing the dagger severed the connection. Kayne may have been occupied with Abignale, but I could not risk strolling over and yanking it out myself."

"So ironic," Elora muttered.

"What is he talking about?" Aelia said. "Who are Zemirah and Ikeni?"

Kristofer swore under his breath, causing Raum to look at him.

"This is not what we are here to discuss—"

"You had to have known certain questions would arise," Abignale said. "I understand your desire to plan, but you owe certain explanations. And if this is the least required expectation, answer them, Kristofer. A few moments of idle chatter will not add to the decade you've been away. Would anyone care for wine?"

Kristofer nodded, and Abignale poured several glasses from his pack and handed them out. Rian refused with a lift of his hand, but everyone else accepted. Leaning back in his chair, Kristofer swirled the wine before taking a sip.

"My aim was not for Brilor directly," he said. "There was no other way—"

"So you would sacrifice what would have been your general—"

"Yes, Rian, I would have!"

Kristofer slammed his hand down and stood, followed immediately by Rian. The men glared at each other from across the table. Elora started to speak, but Rake held up a hand to silence her, wanting to hear Kristofer's explanation.

"I knew you took the tunnel into the kitchens," he said, "aided by Zemirah's men. I also know where you took shelter following your escape of the castle walls. I knew the trail North was falsely laid. I did not lead my men leagues in the wrong direction for the sights!"

Elora's head began to pound, and she pressed her fingers to her temples in an attempt to alleviate her headache.

"I don't understand," she said. "You knew the trail was falsely laid, yet you followed it anyway?"

"For the same reason I allowed the delays on the way to the South. It was not to alleviate your physical discomfort so much, although your shoulder was an issue. It was so Rian and whatever brigade he assembled could catch up, in hopes of saving you. I did not wish for your death, and the orders to capture you were greatly disturbing to me. Rian, I do not expect reasoning or understanding on your part, but I did not want this. I did not want any of it! And I certainly had no desire to see my sister chained and murdered in front of me. You ask would I sacrifice Brilor? Yes! The same way I sacrificed Breggen. And even after I killed your general, you did not deal the fatal blow at that barn in the country. Why?"

The anger and the tension between him and Rian filled the whole tent and came off of them in pulsating waves. As the silence grew and became deafening, Elora finally answered.

"Because he remembered you as a child."

She looked at Rian, repeating the very words he spoke to her when she put the same question to him all those long weeks ago.

"And yet you can honestly forgive us for torturing you to the point of death?" Rian said.

"I survived it." Kristofer shrugged. "It doesn't matter now. My point is this: our history dictates our actions. Elora forgives me as easily as she does because of the years we had prior to this damn war. You could not kill me when the opportunity finally presented itself because somewhere within, you hold a small measurement of affection for me. It is an unfortunate flaw in human nature. I know you have more questions, and I will give you all the answers you are looking for. But as of this moment, we have more pressing matters which require our immediate attention."

It was true, and Rian acknowledged Kristofer's speech with a single nod.

"All right," he whispered. "Let us plan."

The tension faded somewhat as they all hunched over the map. The spoke for hours, long into the night. Finalizing, revamping, and regionalizing battle strategy after battle strategy. Aelia's input had both Rake and Rian highly impressed. When she spoke, Kristofer's attention came immediately. When a suggestion was made, she would study the map.

At one point, she even pushed Kristofer's hand out of the way and said, "Keep the war ships at bay until the third day. The Southern Army has more bodies than any of the others. If those ships arrive unexpectedly, it will boost the Northern, Eastern, and Western morale, and the men will fight against the South even harder."

"Clever girl," Rake said, having no idea the effect his nearness had on her.

Once they settled on a plan Kristofer was satisfied with, and after he had sworn them all to secrecy, he stood.

"I will depart. Aelia, come with me."

She took his outstretched hand and followed him out

of the tent, into the night. He pulled her behind him for a minute. Turning to look at her, he saw her swallow back tears.

"Do not cry, love. It is only for a little while."

"I cannot do this, Kristofer. Take me back with you!"

"I cannot. You'll be safe with my sister. Rian and Rake will cause you no ill-feelings."

Elora and Rian stepped out of the tent, and Kristofer turned to look at them. Even in the darkness, his vision was perfect. He could see everything as clearly as if the sun shone bright in the sky. But for Aelia, the light illuminating from the tent behind them was a blessing.

"What if you fall?" she whispered.

"If that should happen, Raum will find you. He will take you someplace safe. The East will founder if Kayne wins this war."

He brushed her tears away with his thumb, then leaned down and kissed her.

"I love you, Aelia. Remember that."

Nodding, she wrapped her arms around his neck and hugged him tight.

"You still owe me a new dress."

"Then I must survive so that I might fulfill my promise to you."

"I'll hold you to it." She pulled herself away from him and walked back to Rian and Elora.

He came up behind her, and Elora reached out and hugged him.

"We will survive this, and we will go home," she whispered.

Elora stepped back and took hold of Rian's arm for comfort and support.

"Take Aelia back with you," Kristofer said. "Kayne will certainly use her against me if the opportunity arises." To

Rian, he said, "Keep her safe."

Rian gave a curt nod. Kristofer grabbed a hold of the saddle horn and pulled himself onto Asen.

"The moment Aelia is settled, return," Kristofer told Raum. "There is much to do."

Raum nodded and mounted his horse. Aelia hurried to Kristofer's side, and he leaned over, cupping her face. Elora watched them with fascination. Kristofer brought his forehead to Aelia's, and they stayed like that for a moment.

"Please be careful," Aelia whispered.

Nodding, Kristofer kissed her. "Listen to Rian. Do not leave the castle."

"I promise."

Nodding again, Kristofer straightened. As he turned his horse and rode away, Aelia felt a sense of loss she had long forgotten.

Elora, Rian, Abignale, and Rake mounted their horses, and Raum leaned down to pull Aelia up in front of him.

—␣—

The trip back to the East was quiet, each member of the group lost in his or her own thoughts. As the Eastern castle came into view, Aelia was reminded of the first time she saw it—when Rian had taken her.

Inside the castle, Rake left them at the doors, and Raum and Aelia followed Elora and Rian to a room very close to Elora's.

"This will be yours, Aelia. You shouldn't need for anything."

"Thank you, Elora." Aelia then turned to face Raum, with sadness in her eyes. "You must go back now."

"We will win this war, Aelia. Have hope." Raum hugged her tight, then turned to face Rian. "It will be an honor to fight alongside you. Kristofer always told me to never engage you in battle. Now I know why."

Rian chuckled. "Even in these bizarre circumstances, it is good to know we have friends in all four corners. Be well, Raum."

Raum bowed low to Elora and Rian, and after casting one last look at Aelia, he walked out.

"Supper will be served soon," Elora said. "I will send a bath. I do not believe my clothing will fit you, but I will find something suitable and have it sent."

Aelia nodded, throat tight. Elora and Rian closed the door behind them, and true to her word, a bath and a beautiful golden gown were sent up shortly after. Without fear this time, Aelia bathed and dressed. Sitting on her bed, she looked around her room. A royal-blue rug, so thick that her feet felt like they walked on a cloud, shrouded the stone floor. The four-poster bed had white sheer curtains pulled back with a thin blue rope that matched the rug. A fireplace stood to the left, with logs piled nearby. A large bay window was to the right of the bed, and dark-blue pillows lined the sill, where Aelia could sit and look out. Beside the window was a small table with two beautifully carved wooden chairs.

Admiring the room, Aelia stood to look out the window. She could see for miles. The Manat River that divided the East from the rest of the territories snaked through the greenery. Aelia took a seat on top of the blue cushions and stared outside, wondering what Kristofer was doing.

A knock on her door caused her to jump. Elora walked in, informing her that supper would be served soon.

Aelia rose to follow her out of the room and into the dining hall. Rake sat at the head of the table, beside his beautiful raven-haired wife. Abignale sat on their right, and Rian and Elora to their left. Aelia sat demurely beside Elora. As the food was served, Aelia had to fight back the nausea that threatened to overwhelm her. Elora, sensing her unease, leaned to whisper into her ear.

"Eat. It will make you feel better."

Her plate was filled for her, and Aelia took Elora's advice. She ate silently, keeping her gaze fixed on her plate. Unable to eat much, she was surprised when a variety of sweets were brought out. With a small amount of amusement, she watched Elora reach eagerly for a syrupy apple.

Rian noticed the half-smile that crept onto her face.

"What amuses you, Aelia?"

Surprised at being called upon, she met his gaze.

"Nothing of importance," she replied.

"Still, I would know," he said.

"It is Elora," she said.

The room grew quiet, and Elora turned to look at her.

"What of me?" She returned Aelia's smile.

"Your brother has a taste for sweets also. The apple reminded me of it."

Elora laughed. "He always has. Will you tell us of him?"

Aelia tensed. The question made her uncomfortable, especially as she watched the Easterners lean forward with eagerness.

"I do not want war strategies," Elora said, "and I understand that our situation is uncomfortable and causes you great unease. But you are amongst friends now. I only wish to know what my brother is like. We have been separated for over ten years."

"Nor did we ever think he would settle down with a woman," Rian said. "I'd like to know how you tamed him."

Aelia laughed at this, and the tension faded away.

"I would hardly say Kristofer is tame." She stared at Elora's apple. "There is a bread that we make in the South. It is coated with syrup from maple trees that Kristofer personally has shipped from the North. Half the time, it is all I ever see him eat."

"He still eats that?" Rian raised his brow in surprise.

"You know of it?" Aelia said.

"Yes." Rian nodded. "Because of Kristofer, my father often brought me to the North when I was young. We were the same age, and both training to rule. I daresay we got into more trouble than was necessary, but I cannot tell you how often Kristofer tapped trees for that syrup. It was definitely not my favorite activity."

Rian's words brought laughter to the table.

"I remember it, too," Elora said. "He and I have always had a fancy for sweets." As if to give credit to her words, she took a bite of the apple.

"Elora tells me it is Kristofer who rules the South?"

Rake's voice caused Aelia's smile to falter, but she nodded against her feelings.

"Our people adore him. When he is unavailable, Raum rules in his place."

"So the South has become his home," Elora said, and Aelia's nod confirmed it. "Will he rule there if Kayne dies?"

"He hasn't told me." Aelia shrugged. "I know he has no wish to be king, but I do not know what he plans after this war is over."

"In that aspect, he has little choice," Rake said.

Aelia could not control the animosity on her face as she looked at him. Wishing she was home, she sighed and turned her gaze toward the desserts on the table.

"I've never shared Elora's fondness for sweets," Rian said to her, noticing the dark look that crossed her face.

His voice drew Aelia's attention, and she smiled.

"Nor I," she said. "I do love berries, freshly picked. Or apples, as the season changes."

"You were picking berries when my men and I, ah... interrupted." Rian leaned back in the chair.

"Interrupted?" Aelia lifted a brow. "Aye, those bushes

only grow on that side of the castle. I assume they get more sunlight there. Raum was difficult to convince, too. I haven't seen that side of the castle since."

Her tone was light, and Elora marveled at her ease of handling the situation so pleasantly.

"Aelia, what is the South like?" Olibia said.

The question caught Aelia off guard. "In what sense?"

"In general," Olibia said. "I hear it is very warm."

"Oh, the summers are." Aelia thought of gathering flowers with Kristofer, and she felt her throat tighten. "I've never been North, but Kristofer has told me of the winters there," she looked at Rian, "and the snow in the mountains. I cannot imagine places so bitterly cold."

"The snow rises more than twenty feet," Elora said.

They spoke of the weather in the different territories for a few more minutes, before Elora declared that she and Aelia needed rest. Elora rose and looped her arm through Aelia's and dragged her out the door.

"Thank you," Aelia whispered, as they walked up the stairs.

"I imagine being alone with Kristofer for all these years didn't warrant social gatherings," Elora said.

"Truer words were never spoken." Aelia smiled. "He never lets me out of the castle unless I beg, and it usually turns into an argument."

"And did you lose all the time?" Elora delighted in hearing about her brother.

"I won the last time, and then Rian took me. Truly, that was beyond my imagination. I finally got my way, and I wished I hadn't!"

As they arrived at Aelia's room, she turned to Elora and beckoned her in.

"How can you forgive him so easily?" Aelia said. "He would have killed you. You heard his confession."

Elora sighed and took a seat at the foot of the bed.

"When Kristofer left, it was beyond my comprehension. He and I were so close, Aelia. Inseparable, really. And I knew him. I knew he wouldn't do something like this unless there was a good reason. Rian, too, was inconsolable, but his anguish turned to anger. And as rumors of Kristofer's brutality grew, Rian lost all hope. I knew...I just knew that Kristofer wasn't gone, even when he captured me."

"Weren't you afraid? When Rian took me, I was beside myself."

Aelia sat down next to her, and they turned to face each other.

"I was terrified," Elora said. "You know my brother better than all of us. He was cold, determined, angry. But he showed kindness, and at times was more gentle than the situation called for. His men, they attacked me, and he was beside himself with anger. If he did not care for me, why did he care about that? It was so terribly confusing. Don't misunderstand me, I fought him, but I could never gain the upper hand."

"No one ever gains the upper hand against Kristofer. I rarely see that side of him, though." Aelia lifted a thin shoulder in a shrug.

"Even Rian was shocked at his gentleness toward you when he rescued you from here. We talked of it for a while." Elora laughed. "He must love you."

Aelia's smile faded fast, and Elora frowned.

"I..." Aelia cleared her throat and bit her lip. "I am fairly certain I am with child."

Elora gasped and threw her arms around Aelia in a tight hug.

"What incredible news. Are you not happy?"

Aelia's hand went to her still flat stomach. "I am sick with worry that Kristofer won't survive this. We are not married, Elora. Without Kristofer to protect us, I just don't know..."

She choked out a sob.

"Rian and I will keep you and the baby safe. Rian is angry still. Do not forget that there is years and years of misery and anger between him and Kristofer. I do think he loves my brother, though, and you needn't worry about anything concerning this child."

Aelia sighed in relief and hugged Elora. "Please keep it between us. Kristofer does not know, either."

"You have not told him?" Elora sounded surprised.

"I would have, if circumstances were different. He told me weeks ago that I would be traveling here and without him. With him going back South, and me in the East...I never found the right moment. He has so much to deal with that I hated to add to the stress of it. And then at the midway point, after hearing his story..."

"Did you know?" Elora said.

"I suspected. The more time he and I spent together, the less likely it seemed that he would betray those he loved. I didn't know it was his father that was involved, but I never thought he would willingly betray you."

"It's not in his nature," Elora said. "I must admit, I am so relieved to have him again. To know that he still cares. I just hope the past can stay in the past."

"We'll get through it. Even now, I find Rian easier to be around. Before, when he took me, I found him terrifying."

Elora laughed at this. "I imagine he can be. Same as Kristofer. Rian and I were raised together. My parents took care of him when his family died. And when my parents died, he was there for me."

"Kristofer told me that you and he would soon marry?" Aelia said.

"Aye, he asked after he rescued me from the South. But the constant ongoings with the war, and now preparing for the battle...a wedding seems..."

"I understand. After this war is over…"

"Yes." Elora smiled at Aelia. "I am glad that you're here. Kristofer will kill Kayne, I know it. And he will rise as king."

Aelia swallowed hard. If Kristofer were king, where would that leave her?

Oblivious to the change that had come over Aelia's face, Elora smiled to herself. She had her brother back, and he still loved her. All the unanswered years were at an end, and she felt peaceful.

"Where is your family now?" Elora said.

"Dead."

Aelia's tone brought a quick end to the conversation, and Elora shook her head out of sadness.

"So much has been lost," Elora said, "but there is a light at the end of our long road now. I'll leave you to rest. We will talk more tomorrow."

She stood up and left the room, quietly shutting the door behind her.

CHAPTER 23

In the following weeks, the people spent countless hours preparing for battle. Weapons were made in excess, meat was salted and smoked, and the excitement for the impending end of the war raced through the people.

Aelia and Elora spent a lot time together when Elora was free. Zemirah's troops came in like thunder, and when she was not working with Rake and Rian, she, too, joined Elora and Aelia.

One such afternoon, Aelia came upon Zemirah and Elora training in the courtyard. Aelia watched, mesmerized as the two women crossed blades. Zemirah's skill with weapons was now widely known, and men came from all over the city to learn new tactics.

Rian came up behind Aelia and watched the duel.

"They are incredible," he said. "I have never seen a woman so skilled with a blade."

"Nor have I," Aelia replied.

The past few weeks with Rian eased her tension and fear concerning him. She found his company comforting, and she delighted in hearing Kristofer's childhood stories—from which, he had many.

"I'd like to learn," Aelia said to him.

"Kristofer never taught you how to use a sword?" Rian said.

Her laughter had him looking down at her in confusion.

"No, he was adamant about keeping me away from them."

Rian looked her up and down and shook his head.

"I do not think a sword would be appropriate for you. They are heavy, and it takes years of practice. A bow would be better suited for you."

"Will you teach me?" she said, eagerness in her voice.

Rian nodded. "Come."

She followed him over to Zemirah and Elora, who paused their duel and looked at them.

"Aelia wishes to learn how to draw a bow."

Zemirah smiled encouragingly at the woman. She liked Aelia.

"I will teach you."

"Well, that was easy," Aelia said to Rian, and he chuckled.

He called a soldier over and ordered a bow and arrows brought. The man left and returned a short while later with the weapon.

"I suggest moving away from the soldiers," Elora said.

They walked to the side of the courtyard, and Rian dismissed the people that were there. When they were alone, Zemirah took the bow and shot an arrow against the wooden gate a hundred feet away. She then handed the bow to Aelia and showed her how to stand and nock an arrow.

"Now, try to shoot as close to my arrow as you can," Zemirah said.

Aelia released her arrow, and it hit so close to Zemirah's that the four of them stood staring at it for some time.

Elora said, "You have never used a bow before?"

"Never," Aelia said.

"Step back further," Rian told her. "Now hit between the two arrows."

There was less than a foot of space between the two, and when Aelia released her arrow again, it hit below the arrows that were there, but still centered.

"I think you've found your weapon." Elora smiled. "Keep practicing. You clearly have a talent for it. And do not tell my brother it was us who taught you!"

"I'm sure if we told him I picked up a bow and shot accurately the first time, he'd not believe it," Aelia said.

They practiced every day from there on out. Aelia excelled and enjoyed learning. She missed Kristofer, but knowing she would see him soon got her through her days. By now, she was certain of her pregnancy, and kept it a secret from everyone but Elora. After dinner every evening, Elora and Aelia would retire to their rooms and talk late into the night, occasionally joined by Zemirah and Olibia.

On the night before they were to leave for battle, Elora knocked on Aelia's door.

"Supper is almost ready," she murmured.

Aelia looked down at her hands and shook her head.

"I am not hungry," she said.

They shared a look of unease before Elora said, "Let us go. It'll take our minds off of tomorrow."

Nodding, Aelia stood, and they walked to the dining hall. Rake and Olibia were already there, but Rian had yet to arrive. Zemirah came to join them, and after a few minutes, Rian came in, looking tired.

The group was docile, nervous, and hardly anyone ate. When the sweets were brought out, it was Aelia who broke the silence.

"Is it always so before a battle?" She took a slice of milk cake off a silver plate.

Elora eyed her with amusement. She noticed in the last few weeks that Aelia's fondness for sweets was beginning to rival her own.

"Some battles, yes," Rian replied. "This battle will be bloody, and a lot of these men will not return home."

"Some will," came a deep voice from behind.

Aelia froze, hardly daring to believe it. Everyone at the table turned their head just as Aelia rose from her chair. Kristofer stood, leaning in the doorway, grinning at her.

"What are you doing here?" She threw her arms around his neck, instantly at ease and relieved.

He picked her up and embraced her tight.

"I could not ride into battle without seeing you again," he whispered, so only she could hear.

"It is dangerous for you to be here." She cupped his face and kissed him, oblivious to the chuckles coming from behind them.

He gave her a warm look before turning to the table.

"Raum knows I am here," he said. "If anyone asks, Elora requested a meeting in pursuit of settling matters outside of battle."

"Why would I do such a thing, brother?"

"Only a woman would care to settle matters without bloodshed," Rake said, eyeing Kristofer with caution.

A nod from Kristofer confirmed it, and Elora shrugged, helping herself to slice of cake.

"Kristofer, Aelia has reminded us of your love of desserts." Elora held up the cake. "You've arrived just in time."

"I would greatly like to know," Rake said, "how in fiery depths of hell you walk in and out of this castle without recognition. Not to mention, you never told us how you knew of the secret tunnels when you came back for Aelia."

Kristofer sat down, at ease, next to his sister, and took the plate she offered.

He replied, "No one notices that which is in plain sight, Rake. I merely followed the servants around. They know every possible outlet."

"You were in the castle?" Rake asked, wide-eyed.

"The entire time," Kristofer said. "I arrived here a few days after she did."

Abignale snickered, and Elora laughed.

"Why did you wait so long?" she said.

"I could not get to Aelia in the dungeon. Not without killing the entire platoon of guards you have stationed down there. The noise would have brought forth more men, and so on. It never occurred to me you would leave her down there for as long as you did."

"It was most definitely the highlight of my time in this castle." Aelia took a bite of cake.

"Indeed," Kristofer muttered. "Mine, too."

Rian had the decency to look ashamed, but Rake rolled his eyes.

"If anyone could handle what was done, it was you," Rake said. "My guards still talk of it." He waved a hand dismissively.

"It is a relief to know that I sustain the gossip of the torture chambers." Kristofer looked around the table and asked Elora, "Where are those apples?"

"How can you think of food on a night like this?" Aelia said.

Kristofer shrugged. "I will not worry over things I cannot control."

Aelia ran a hand over his arm, and he turned to her.

"Are they treating you well, love?"

Aelia's laughter eased the worry he had felt over it. It was partly why he had come.

"Are we treating her well?" Rian muttered. "I daresay she has become the best archer in the East."

Kristofer looked taken aback.

"You train to fight?" he said, his earlier amusement gone, replaced by a scowl.

Aelia gave him an irritated look. "No. Rian exaggerates. Everyone thought it was odd that I had no experience with any type of weapon. Rian suggested a bow, and it turns out that I am exceptionally good at it."

She smiled, and Kristofer relaxed.

"I'd very much like to see that," he muttered.

She smiled again. "I'll teach you."

Elora and Rian exchanged a happy look. It was almost as if the last ten years did not happen.

Rian leaned over and kissed Elora on the cheek. Kristofer watched the ongoings between them with a sense of deep satisfaction. He hoped that eventually, Rian would let go of his animosity. But if not, he knew his sister would be safe and loved with him.

Feeling immensely peaceful, Kristofer leaned back in his chair and studied the group. There was a sense of unease which was undoubtably due to the impending battle. But aside from that, he realized that Elora had been fine all these years. Especially with Rian at her side.

Kristofer took a bite of the cake Elora offered, before turning his attention to Abignale.

"There is a matter of higher importance we must discuss." Taking a deep breath, Kristofer studied the old man. "Kayne will not ride out until the third day. You need to understand that my men fight to kill, as yours should also. Thousands will perish, and there is nothing to be done about it. So," he looked at Elora, "fretting about it is useless."

"Will we know when he arrives?" Olibia said.

"Most assuredly." Kristofer told Abignale, "Part of the reason I'm here is because I need access to whatever you have. I assume you've put something together for me?"

"I have it ready," Abignale said. "I will bring it to you."

The click of the door closing signaled Abignale's departure. Undeterred by the uncomfortable air in the room, Kristofer waited patiently until Abignale arrived a few minutes later. The old man handed him a small, dark-blue pouch.

"This contains a poison that will surely weaken him. Coat

your blade in it before attacking. Do not touch it yourself. Do you have an archer you can rely on?"

"Raum."

"Coat his arrows also. Make sure he takes careful aim."

"Understood." Kristofer held the pouch on his lap, fingering the draw string absentmindedly.

Elora stood up and kissed Kristofer on the cheek.

"Tomorrow," she whispered.

Rian followed her out, and as Rake and Olibia rose to leave, Rake turned to Kristofer.

"Our differences are many, and a lot of the past cannot be undone. But I will help you in any way I can."

Kristofer inclined his head at Rake and watched them walk out. Before Abignale left, Kristofer called to him.

"Was it you who helped Raum when I was in the dungeon? He said there was inside help."

"Yes," Abignale said. "Although, a matter we must keep between us." With a wink, he closed the door behind him.

Aelia stood up and took Kristofer's hand.

"How long do you have?" she said.

"A few hours." He took her into his arms.

She kissed him, and together they walked to her room.

Rake must have dismissed the servants so that they might spend the night with their loved ones, for there was no one roaming the corridors. Aelia brought Kristofer upstairs, and he eyed her room with appreciation.

He stretched out on the bed as she closed the door.

"Tell me of your time here," he said.

Sitting at his side, she thought for a moment.

"Elora has become a wonderful friend. Rian isn't nearly as frightening as I thought. When there is time, Zemirah and I practice with the bow. She is incredible with almost every weapon. It is as pleasant as can be assumed with the impending battle upon us."

"What of Rake?" Kristofer said.

"We do not necessarily bother with one another. The only time I see him is in the dining hall. Other than that, I avoid him entirely." She drew her legs underneath her and turned to face him. "I miss home, and I miss you."

"The battle will be over soon, love. It will be decided either way."

"And what will you do, Kristofer? Assuming we all survive. Will you take the South under you rule?" Aelia placed a hand on his chest. "Rian said that the South will not follow anyone else."

Kristofer grimaced. Rian was right, but he wasn't sure if he cared.

"I have not yet thought that far. I don't wish to rule, Aelia."

"So you have said. But it is still our home."

"We will talk of that later," he said.

Aelia sighed and flung her hair over her shoulder. Kristofer studied her, and realizing something was off, nudged her chin up.

"There is something different about you."

Aelia was not ready to tell him about the baby.

"There is not." She shrugged. "It is just a trying time."

"You lie." He pushed himself up. "What is it?" His voice held a hint of apprehension.

Her mind racing, Aelia tried to come up with something to tell him. And then it occurred to her—what if he dies and she never gets the chance to tell him? It would not be right for him not to know. What if he was angry about it? What if he didn't want the child?

Kristofer watched the play of emotions across her face.

"Whatever it is, Aelia, tell me," he said in a gentle tone.

"There is something, Kristofer," she mumbled, keeping

her gaze averted. "I don't know how to say it, and I fear your response."

Kristofer felt his pulse quicken. "Has someone harmed you?"

"No. I..." She bit her lip hard. "I am with child," she whispered.

Kristofer was so surprised that he was at a loss for words. His silence made her nervous.

"I would have waited to tell you until after the battle, but what if..."

She looked up at him as he stared at her without saying a word, and her throat tightened. She stood up, wanting to put space between them, and walked to the window.

Kristofer watched her move away from him. He saw her place her hand on her stomach as she stared out into the night.

A child. A grin spread across his face as he sat there. It was unexpected, but the more he thought about it, the more surprised he was that it hadn't happened sooner. He and Aelia had been together for years. The timing couldn't be worse, but maybe it could...

If he was free from Kayne, he could have a family. Determined to see his plan through, he rose and walked over to Aelia. Wrapped an arm around her waist and pulled her against him.

"Why are you crying?" he said.

"I want this baby," she whispered. "If you don't, I...I won't stay. I'll leave."

"Leave?" He shook his head. "I don't think so, Aelia."

Before he could say anything else, Aelia pulled away from his arms and took a step back.

"I will!" she snapped. "I won't stay to have my child raised by a father who doesn't want him."

"Not want him? Where do you come up with this? I want

him more than anything, Aelia. Almost as much as I want his mother."

His smile confirmed his words for her, and she buried her face in her hands.

Kneeling in front of her, Kristofer took her hands in his.

"Why would you think I'd not want our child? And why did you not tell me sooner?"

Sniffing, Aelia wiped her face and sat down on the window ledge.

"I was not certain until a few weeks ago. I suspected, but I did not want to be mistaken. And the timing. He'll be illegitimate, and it worries me."

"He will not be illegitimate, Aelia. You give me hope, love. I will bring Kayne down, and I will claim this baby. I will marry you."

Shocked, she met his gaze. "You will?"

His laughter annoyed her.

"Why do you always question my affection for you? I love you, Aelia. Of course I will marry you."

"But we are not on the same plane, Kristofer! You are a king, whether or not you want the title. I have no noble blood."

"Which makes you all the more appealing. Regardless of where we end up, you will marry me, whether you want to or not."

Her eyebrows shot up at this. "You cannot force someone to marry you!"

"I can," he continued, his temper rising. "Especially when evidence of my paternity is etched into every line of your figure."

"And if I don't want to marry you?" she snapped, causing him to laugh.

"But you do, love. Who else will argue with me over everything? No other woman will drive me nearly as insane, and that kind of life seems dull and uninteresting."

She felt her anger melt away, and she, too, started laughing.

"All right then," she said. "But I would like a better proposal."

Still kneeling in front of her, Kristofer let his hand graze her cheek.

"Marry me when this war is over?" he said.

"Well, if you insist."

Her gaze met his, and his answering chuckle gave her immense relief.

"I love you, Kristofer. Make sure you come home."

"I'll come home."

CHAPTER 24

A elia woke up alone and ran down the stairs. It was a dreary, rainy day—an indication of the sorrow that would follow a bloody fight.

The army had many, many days of riding in order to reach the rolling hills of Dungar. Elora and Rian were at the stables, their horses saddled, and Aelia threw her arms around Elora.

"Be careful," she cried.

Elora, too choked up to speak, nodded and mounted her horse.

Aelia hugged Rian tight and kissed his cheek.

"Take care of yourself, Rian."

"We will send word to you, Aelia. Keep yourself safe."

She watched them leave with a heavy heart. The city was unusually quiet, and with a sinking feeling of dread, she made her way back inside.

The ground was muddied with blood. Limbs and bodies were strewn everywhere, and the sounds of dying men rang in Elora's ears. The clash of metal against metal filled the hills, and no matter which direction she turned, more and more enemy soldiers were there to replace those she had just cut down.

Rian fought alongside her, killing everyone in his path. Abignale and Rake were nearby, fighting and waiting. It was the third day of the battle, and each of them apprehensively anticipated Kayne's arrival. In the distance, Elora could see her brother on top of his huge black horse, slashing anyone who came near him. He was so lethal, so frightening, that for a moment Elora had to wonder if they were truly on the same side.

She ducked her head as a stream of arrows sailed passed her, raising her shield and catching four. Rian leaned down and ripped a pike out of dead soldier's chest. Taking aim, he threw the weapon and watched as it as it brought down a Red Soldier, before deflecting a blow from another enemy. Out of the air, Abignale grabbed an arrow aimed at his throat, and with a single, fluid motion, nocked it and took careful aim. A trail of bodies littered his path.

Rian and Elora rode toward Rake, watching as he swung his sword above his head and brought it down upon an enemy's helm, cleaving the man's head in two. It was still dark, but the crimson flow of blood shined bright all around them. Elora was sure she could taste it. Her nose was filled with the metallic smell.

With a growl, Rian parried to the right, his back against hers as ten or more soldiers surrounded them. Rake leapt off of his horse, pausing for just a moment to catch his breath, before aiding Rian and Elora against so many.

The sun was just beginning to crest the horizon, and Elora felt a change in the air. The hair on the back of her neck stood up, and she knew Rian felt it, too, for he looked at her just as a lone rider came over the hills. Elora recognized him immediately and gasped.

Kayne sat on top of a massive beige horse. The beast was intricately decorated in the colors of the South, and just as frightening as the man who rode him. Whether Elora imagined it or not, she couldn't be sure, but the horse's eyes gleamed red in the dawn light. The monster turned his head, and she wondered if anyone else had seen it.

Kristofer looked around, and upon seeing Kayne, bowed his head as Kayne rode up beside him.

"We win this battle, Lord," Kristofer said. "Their troops cannot hold up much longer. Their cavalry falls like flies."

Kayne's laughter boomed throughout the hills. Soldiers from each side turned to see where the sound was coming from. Those nearest covered their ears. His presence made the men nervous.

Raum rode forward and paused in front of Kayne and Kristofer. He bowed his head to acknowledge them.

"My lords."

Kayne turned to look down at the man, to study him. He had seen him once before, outside of Kristofer's chambers. He was the soldier who had rescued Kristofer from the East.

Raum turned his full attention to Kristofer. "Another army approaches from the direction of the Great Sea."

"What?" Kristofer said, astounded. "Who are they?"

"Their skin is the color of ebony," Raum said. "I do not know who they are."

Kristofer turned to look at Kayne. "Would you care to join me, sire?" he said, maniacally.

Kayne laughed again, and Raum winced at the sound.

"Let us kill them." Kayne sneered, handing Kristofer a flask.

He guzzled down every last drop and licked the blood off of his lips. As the feeling of power coursed through him, he shook his head to try to clear it. Warmth seeped into his body, and his earlier exhaustion was replaced by unlimited energy.

Kristofer flung the flask to the ground, then clenched his fists and grinned. Kayne laughed again, and they rode off toward the sea.

Elora, Rian, Abignale, and Rake looked at each other. It

was the plan to keep Zemirah's army at bay until the third day. Riding in from the East, Zemirah's army would attack, and Kristofer and Kayne would ride head first against them. Elora and Rian were to follow behind Rake and Abignale. Once they were away from the Southern soldiers, Kristofer would attack Kayne.

"It is time," Rian whispered.

He and Elora advanced through the fighting soldiers, slicing through the armor and shields that got in their way. They mounted their horses and circled around to the other side, meeting Zemirah's army from behind. After riding to the front line, Elora and Rian met with Zemirah, who sat on her horse, holding a crimson flail. Beside her stood Kwame, holding a massive battle axe. The weapon seemed too big, too heavy, for any one man to wield himself. Yet Kwame swung it with ease. Their dark cheeks were smeared with red war paint.

Zemirah barred her teeth, snow-white against her skin, at the sight of Kayne. She waited, like the others, their gazes locked on Kristofer.

It was now or never. Kristofer closed his eyes, his thoughts on Aelia and his child.

He glanced at his sister and grinned as he withdrew his sword and swung it at Kayne, who raised his arm, blocking the blow with his gauntlet.

He stared at Kristofer, stunned. "You betray me now?" he hissed.

It didn't take long for his surprise to turn to anger. And hatred.

Zemirah's army attacked the Red Soldiers, and Kayne glared at Kristofer.

"I will kill you for this."

Kristofer responded with another slash of his sword as Kayne drew his weapon. The clash of their blades was so forceful that it reverberated off the hills, and sparks flew off of the metal. Kayne flipped off of his horse, and Kristofer jumped in front of him, bringing the battle between them to the ground. The soldiers nearby, after realizing Kristofer had turned against Kayne, stopped fighting completely.

Elora, Rian, and Zemirah watched Kristofer, marveling at the speed and skill between the two men. All around them, soldiers paused on both sides to watch the fight. The only sound that could now be heard was from their swords.

Elora watched Kayne's sword tear across Kristofer's side, downing him. Knowing he would heal quickly, she released her breath.

They moved so swiftly that, at times, both men were just a blur.

The sun rose higher into the sky, rupturing the darkness and illuminating the raging battle below. Kristofer leaned backward, his head almost touching the ground as he avoided Kayne's blade. Then he withdrew a dagger from his boot and threw it at Kayne. It missed him and embedded itself in Kayne's horse's neck. The animal reared, and Kayne turned, giving Kristofer a chance to bring his sword down hard upon Kayne's arm. The poison that coated his blade drew a thick, unyielding wound down the length of his arm.

Now that Kayne bled, Raum released a steady stream of arrows at him. Only one found its mark, and buried itself deep within Kayne's thigh. Hissing in agony, he tore the arrow from his leg and threw it at Kristofer, who deflected it with the side of his weapon.

"What is this?" Kayne snarled, as blood dripped down his leg.

Neither realized that the fighting had stopped and all eyes were upon them.

"You cannot live forever, Kayne," Kristofer said.

"All this time?" Kayne said.

Their fighting paused as the two men stared at each other.

"I trusted you. I gave you everything."

Kristofer nodded and raised his sword just in time to block another intense blow. As the battle raged on, Kristofer sustained more and more wounds, and he began to realize the pain didn't fade as quickly.

A nasty cut across his chest oozed warm blood that ran down to his stomach, and every time he lifted his arm, he felt fresh blood spurt from the wound. Realizing he had moments to end it, Kristofer looked at Rian just as Kayne embedded his sword into Kristofer's stomach. Blood seeped from his mouth as Kayne withdrew the sword. Kristofer fell back, and Elora cried out.

Rian slowly got off of his horse and faced Kayne.

"If he could not defeat me, you certainly can't," Kayne hissed.

"Then I will die trying," Rian said.

Elora came up beside him, and together, she and Rian attacked Kayne.

Raum, seeing Kristofer fall, nocked another arrow and shot it at Kayne's back. It landed between his shoulder blades and threw him forward. Rian stabbed him before he could recover, and Elora jammed her sword into his side. The poison was taking effect, but it seemed to only slow him down slightly.

Raum sent another arrow flying, hitting him in the lower back. Kayne arched in pain, but raised his sword quickly to deflect Elora's attack.

Kristofer slowly pulled himself to his feet, one hand pressed against his stomach, where blood seeped from between his fingers. The other gripped his sword, and he stood in front of Rian and Elora.

"You cannot win this," Kayne snarled. "You will bleed out."

"It does not matter now," Kristofer said.

Raum's next arrow caught Kayne in the neck. He went to pull the arrow from his throat, but Abignale raised his bow and shot three arrows in succession, each one hitting a different part of his body. The force of it distracted Kayne, and Kristofer grasped his sword with both hands. He raised it and with all of his might, brought the blade down against the back of Kayne's neck, severing his head from his body.

As Kayne fell headless onto the grass, Kristofer's legs gave out and he collapsed. Raum ran over just in time to hear Rian order Kayne's body burned, but his brown eyes were glued to Kristofer's lifeless form.

Rian knelt beside Kristofer, two fingers pressed against his throat.

"The war is over!" Rian called. "Kayne has fallen." He turned to Elora, who stood frozen behind him. "Kristofer is still alive. Where is Abignale? Abignale!"

The old man hurried forth, clutching a pouch, and he knelt down beside Rian. Carefully, he cut away Kristofer's tunic to examine his wounds, while Rake and Zemirah leaned over his shoulder.

"I have brought herbs that might help him," Abignale said. "But his wounds are many, and they are deep. We need to get him back to the East."

Raum crouched beside Kristofer, his voice full of worry.

"Will he survive?"

Abignale studied Kristofer for a long while, before responding.

"I do not know," he said, finally.

"What can I do?" Raum asked. "The pyre is built. Kayne's body is burning as we speak."

"Rian, bring me my pack," Abignale said.

Rian hastened to the old man's horse and returned a moment later with it. Abignale set the pack beside himself and withdrew a small stone mortar and pestle, and began mixing a red herb with water to make a thick paste. Once he was through mixing, he covered Kristofer's wounds in them before wrapping his chest and stomach with the white cloth.

To Rian, he said, "Take his horse and bring him back East. I can create medicines there that might help. Here, I only have so much. Ride as fast as you can. We will follow."

Rian hesitated, and Abignale said, "If anyone seeks to attack him, only you can defend him."

Elora gave him a pleading look. "Rian, please? He did all that he said he would. He never betrayed us."

The urgency and desperation in her voice was more than he could bear. He nodded and mounted Asen with caution, unsure of the large beast, and Raum and Abignale handed Kristofer to him. The horse, sensing his master's bleak condition, turned and bolted.

"Raum, stay here and see to the wounded," Elora said. "My general, Brilor, and his men will accommodate you. When you have matters settled, return to us." She watched Rian disappear into the hills.

"As you wish." Raum bowed.

After casting a long look in Rian's direction, Raum and Brilor plodded through the bodies of fallen soldiers.

Elora called Ferox and got on her horse. Rake and Abignale mounted their steeds and followed, leaving the bloodbath and carnage behind.

CHAPTER 25

Aelia sat by the window, as she had for the past four days. The weeks passed with no word, and she worried herself sick over those she loved.

Fearing the worst, she rested her head against the window and looked out. The sun cast pink and orange rays across the blue sky, and she watched it set with a heavy heart.

The commotion she heard jerked her from her window, and she flew down the stairs.

"What is it?" she said to a nearby servant, who startled at Aelia's tone.

"Lord Rian returns."

"Well, where is he?"

"Aelia!"

Rian's voice made her whirl around. And upon seeing him, she threw her arms around him.

"What happened? Where is everyone else? Kristofer?" Her heart pounded in her chest.

"They are all right," Rian whispered, returning her embrace. "But...Kristofer is not."

Aelia gasped. "Where is he?"

Rian's face had Aelia near hysterics.

"He is in my chambers. Wait! Aelia! Wait!"

He tried to grab her, but she ran up the stairs. And after seeing a servant exiting a door on the left, carrying a bloody heap of linen, she shoved the door open.

Kristofer was lying on the bed. He was pale, and his eyes were closed. Around his chest and stomach were snow-white bandages.

Swallowing hard, she walked over to the bed and placed her hand upon his chest. She could feel his heart beating, and she sighed in relief.

Rian closed the door behind him and walked to her side.

"Abignale's herbs stopped the bleeding, but..."

But what? What could he say to Aelia to ease her suffering? How could he comfort her when the man she loved lay dying?

"Tell me what happened," she whispered, eyes filling.

She placed her hand on Kristofer's face while Rian replayed the battle that had raged on between Kristofer and Kayne, over and over in his head. The sword that slid into Kristofer's belly...

His feelings toward Kristofer were a confusing mixture of hate and anger, and a love for the friendship they used to share. Was he really who he said he was?

He had to be, Rian reasoned with himself. He killed Kayne...

"Rian?" said Aelia.

In a voice tight with unsorted emotion, he said, "I do not believe that, in any years past or future, there will ever be a battle like there was between him and Kayne." He shook his head as the memories assailed him. "It was the most intense fight I have ever witnessed, but he killed Kayne before he fell. Kayne is dead, Aelia."

She took his hand in hers and brought it to her cheek.

"Will Kristopher survive? Will he be all right?" She turned to looked up at Rian.

"Abignale does not know. His wounds are many, and he is not responding to any stimulation."

"I will stay with him, Rian. You must be exhausted." She turned back to Kristofer.

Rian nodded. "Elora, Rake, and Abignale will return shortly. They were not far behind me."

He cast one more look at Kristofer, before turning and leaving.

Aelia sat next to him, not entirely sure where to put her hands. Unsure of how long she sat there, she watched the sun rise into the sky, and still she did not leave his side. Even when Abignale came in, followed by Elora, she refused to leave.

Abignale leaned over Kristofer and shook his head.

"He's not healing at all," he told Elora.

"What does that mean?" Elora said, visibly upset.

"If his body doesn't mend on its own, he will die." Abignale stepped back and looked at Kristofer in dismay.

"How long has he been like this?" Aelia choked.

"It's been two weeks now," Elora said, her voice weak.

Aelia stayed by Kristofer's side for two days more. His body did not heal, and his breathing grew shallow.

Finally, Rian came in and gripped Aelia by the arm to drag her out, despite her protests.

"You need to rest. Sitting with him won't help matters."

"If it were Elora in there, would you leave?" she snapped.

"No. But still, Aelia. Take a bereavement."

Sighing, Aelia followed Rian down to the dining hall, where Elora sat in silence. Her elbow rested on the arm of the chair. Her face rested in her hand. Aelia sat next to her and covered Elora's hand with her own.

Elora gave her a weak smile. "To lose him now, when I've only just gotten him back, seems so unfair," she murmured. "Abignale said he will not survive the night."

Aelia felt a pain deep within her so intense that she was sure she'd die. She was beyond tears. A life without Kristofer was not one she was willing to partake in.

Placing a hand on her stomach, she thought of the child

he would never meet. There has to be answer!

All of a sudden, it came to her. She leapt to her feet and turned to a startled Elora.

"Where is the blade Kristofer gave you?"

"The ruby dagger? In my chambers. Why?"

Abignale stood up quickly. "Why didn't we think of it sooner?" He gasped. "Elora, fetch it quickly. Bring it to Kristofer's room!"

Rian and Elora looked at each other with bewilderment, but Aelia and Abignale were already out the door. Elora arrived a few minutes later, carrying the dagger. Aelia took it carefully and looked at Abignale.

"How do we get it out?" she whispered, handing him the knife.

Rian said, "Kayne's blood is in the ruby! Elora, it would be the only reason he'd ask you to keep a hold of it."

"Do not raise your hopes yet," Abignale said.

But Elora took the dagger from him. She popped the gem out with Abignale's knife, and held it to the light. While turning it over carefully, she found a tiny hole plugged with sap.

"It is here."

She took the jewel to the flames, held the ruby over the fire with a stick until the sap melted, and turned it to let the sap flow out.

Abignale leaned over Kristofer and opened his mouth while Elora poured a single drop of red down his throat. They stood back, watching breathlessly.

When nothing happened, Aelia sat down on the bed and buried her face in her hands. Elora turned toward Rian, and he put a comforting arm around her shoulders.

But Abignale waited. He saw the color come back to Kristofer's cheeks, and he noticed his breath grew stronger. His wounds began knitting themselves back together.

Kristofer opened his eyes and saw Abignale staring at him. He heard Aelia's soft cries, and saw his sister's face buried in Rian's chest.

"The battlefield was more pleasant than this," he said, with a weak voice.

Abignale bellowed a laugh, and Aelia gasped.

"You're all right!" she cried.

Afraid of hurting him, she didn't know if she should hug him or not.

Elora jumped on him first. And once Aelia realized she would not break him, she threw her arms around him. With an arm around each woman, he hugged them tight.

Elora pulled back, and her hands grazed his face.

"Do you feel all right?" Abignale said, from the side.

"A little hungover," Kristofer said. "But I'll be all right." He looked around the room, and his gaze rested on Rian. "There is room," he muttered, as Aelia and Elora fussed over him.

He pushed himself up slowly, which was difficult to do with both women on top of him.

Rian felt himself grin, realizing that he was relieved Kristofer was awake.

"I'll sacrifice my comfortability this once," he said, from his place at the foot of the bed.

Their gazes met, and Kristofer saw the anger still there. What he saw bothered him, and he realized that he wanted Rian's forgiveness. He wanted his friendship.

"I couldn't have done it without you," Kristofer whispered.

Rian saw the plea and the regret in his eyes. But for him, it wasn't enough. It would never be enough. He was relieved that Kristofer would survive, but their time apart had left a shadow looming over Rian's head, and he wondered whether or not his family, his brothers, would still be alive had Kristofer not turned on them.

With a nod, he acknowledged Kristofer.

Abignale stepped forward, knowing the internal struggle faced by both men.

"Kristofer, I daresay your story will become legend."

Kristofer laughed. "History will exaggerate, I'm sure. How long has it been?"

Two weeks," Elora replied. "Abignale told us you would not survive the night."

"Two weeks?" Kristofer said. "The dagger..."

"We didn't think of it," Elora muttered sheepishly, and Kristofer gave her a disgruntled look. "It is Aelia to whom you owe your life."

"You'd be quite dead if it were left upon our shoulders." Abignale gave her a look of fondness.

Aelia shrugged. "You had promises to keep."

"A marriage?" Kristofer grinned, causing Elora and Rian to raise their brows.

"I was thinking, a new dress."

"You are impossible." After pushing himself up further, Kristofer swung his legs over the edge of the bed and stood up.

"You should rest," Elora said.

"I've been resting for days."

"He's hungry," Aelia said, as if he were a child.

"I will fetch Rake and Olibia," said Abignale. "They'll want to know of your, ah...improved condition." He walked out of the room.

"I'll have food brought," Aelia said.

At Kristofer's nod, she followed Abignale.

Elora hugged her brother again. "We survived the war."

"I told you we would." He returned her affectionate gaze.

She cupped his face, and her smile faltered.

"Are you all right, brother?"

"I'll be fine, Elora. There is still much to do."

"We'll go. There is always tomorrow." She kissed his cheek.

Rian inclined his head to Kristofer, but his hesitation was clear. Kristofer returned the gesture and watched them leave.

Closing his eyes, he sighed. It was over. Almost a decade of his life gone. It was impossible for him to grasp the concept.

He could put the past behind him, he was sure of it. He had the future to look forward to—the freedom to marry Aelia and raise their child in peace. But there was a new concern that grew in his mind as he sat there. He was king now. There would be no dispute from any territorial leader. But he didn't want the crown.

He walked over to the window and looked out. In the last ten years, he had, essentially, become a slave to Kayne. With him out of the way, Kristofer wanted freedom. He was sure the crown he would be offered would come with a price he was not willing to pay.

He heard the door open, and turned to find Aelia walking to him. She wrapped her arms around his waist, and he held her tight against him.

"What ails you, Kristofer?" She sat on the edge of the bed. "If you are worried over the crown, push the matter from your mind for tonight. The problem will still be there in the morning."

"That is exceptionally true." He turned to her.

A knock sounded on the door. The servants entered, carrying several trays of hot food and a platter loaded with honeyed apples. They set everything down, bowed, and left without a word.

Kristofer moved to the table and scarfed the food down. Aelia leaned back against the pillows, suddenly exhausted, and watched him, feeling peaceful.

When he finally came to her, and laid down beside her, she rested her head on his shoulder, and they slept through the night and most of the next day.

CHAPTER 26

When Kristofer awoke, he was alone. Famished, he went to the table and finished the food that was still there from the night before.

Not relishing the idea of facing anyone just yet, he called for a servant and ordered a bath brought. And once it arrived, he thew his clothes on the floor and stepped into the hot water, resting his head on the edge of the tub. Hearing his door open, he turned his head to find Aelia standing there. She held a pile of clean clothes, and walked over to the bed to set them down before turning her attention to him.

"How do you feel?" she said.

"Should I not be asking you that?"

"I am well. Better, actually, then I have ever been. It is you I am worried about."

"There is a lot on my mind," Kristofer said. "Physically, I will be fine."

He held a hand out to her and gave her a small smile as she knelt down beside the tub.

"Oh!" Aelia said, as if she had suddenly remembered something.

She rose and opened a drawer to pull a bar of soap from it.

"Olibia had this soap made. It is wonderful."

He took it and stared at the small bar in his hand.

"Are those flowers?"

"Yes! Lilac. Here." Aelia took the soap from him and kneeled.

After lathering her hands, she ran them across his back and his chest, moving slowly toward his stomach. His body was healed, but his mind still caused him grief. She rubbed his shoulders, hoping to ease some of the tension from them.

When they finally left the confinement of the bedroom, it was nearly supper time. Servants bowed low when Kristofer passed them, but he hardly noticed anything except for Aelia. It was the first time in eight years that he was free to be with her.

He knew danger still lurked in the shadows. Kayne's followers would no doubt rally at some point. But for now she was safe, and he had no obligations to anyone other than to himself.

Aelia led him to the dining hall, where his sister smiled warmly at him, and Rake inclined his head with respect, shocking everyone in the room.

After seating himself beside Aelia, Kristofer had a servant fill a goblet with wine as the food was brought out.

"Have you decided on anything?" Rake asked him.

"Concerning the crown?" Kristofer said with bitterness. "Of which territory, Rake?"

Aware that the question would be put to him sooner rather than later, it still aggravated him.

"The North, South, and West are all under your control," Rian said.

Kristofer gave him a dark look. "The West is yours, Rian. You can go home and rebuild, with Elora at your side."

"And the North and the South?" Elora said.

Kristofer knew this conversation would happen, and still he was ill-prepared for it.

Aelia placed her hand on his leg to comfort him, knowing the internal struggle he faced.

Shaking his head in response to his sister, Kristofer leaned back in his chair.

Aelia said, "The South will uprise beyond imagining if either Rake or Rian try to gain control of it. You know this."

"Raum can control the South," Kristofer said.

"They need a king, Kristofer," Rake said. "It is in your blood to rule, and the South is your home now. You would have been king of the North had you not planned to assassinate Kay—"

"But I did plan an assassination, Rake!" Kristofer roared, slamming his hand on the table.

Elora jumped at his sudden outburst.

"For ten years, I watched those I love—my family, my own blood—die on my orders. I've seen innocent people slaughtered. I sacrificed my own sister for the cause. I will not take the Southern crown. Find another pawn."

"Why give up your birthright?" Rian said, his tone gentle, nullifying Kristofer's anger.

He watched Kristofer grimace, and the sudden realization of Kristofer's adamant refusal of the crown became clear to him. Kristofer wanted freedom, and he feared ruling would bind him all the more tightly.

Abignale took a sip of wine. His movement caught Kristofer's attention, and he turned his sky-blue eyes toward the old man.

"Have you nothing to say, Abignale?" Kristofer said.

Abignale set his cup down. "I do not think you should take the crown."

Surprise registered on everyone's face.

"If not he, then who?" Rake said.

"Kristofer has served this nation better, I daresay, than anyone ever has or will," Abignale said. "I'm not sure many could have sustained such a deception or given up a decade of their life just to kill Kayne." He turned his attention to

Kristofer. "Take Aelia and begin your life with her. It is clearly what you want. But first, I ask that you journey with me."

Kristofer raised a brow. "Where to?"

"Do you remember the story of the Last Great Battle?"

"Every child knows of it," Elora said. "It is a fable."

"It is not a fable, but a true story." Abignale never took his gaze off of Kristofer. "In the story, after the battle was won, the people met at the midway point, all of them, to settle their differences, find redemption. I want you to come with me to the midway point."

Annoyed, Kristofer stared at him in disbelief.

"For what purpose? You think the people from all four territories will congregate in the center of the nation because of an old story?"

"Yes, I do," Abignale said.

Kristofer pinched the bridge of his nose and leaned back in the chair.

"All right, Abignale. As you wish."

And so it was settled. The next day, nearly three weeks since the war had ended, Aelia and Kristofer mounted Asen, with Rian and Elora behind them, and Abignale, Rake, and Olibia beside them. No one spoke during the trip. Aelia rested against Kristofer, whose fiery temper put off everyone but her.

Elora and Rian grimaced at the destruction that was done to the land. In many parts of the country, the war had taken its toll. Houses were burned to the ground, and entire villages were deserted. It wasn't just the East, either. All the territories had suffered heavy losses. It would take a great deal to rebuild, but it was doable.

The journey took a couple weeks, and Kristofer was surprised to see the amount of people that had indeed made the trek to the center of the nation. People of every age had journey to find solace, to provide comfort, to start anew. As the post came into view, marking the center of the territories, Kristofer helped Aelia off the horse and turned to Abignale.

"Tell me why we have come here?"

Abignale held a hand out to silence him, and they made their way through the thousands of people. Somewhere in the middle of the throng of people stood a stone platform with three massive steps leading to its stage. In its center was a tall iron post marking the boundary where all four territories touched—the very center of the nation.

Abignale said, "Step up, Kristofer. I want you to see something."

Annoyed, he walked up the three stone steps and placed a hand on the post, remembering the first time he had seen it—on one of the many journeys he had taken with his father. Aelia, Rian, Elora, Rake, and Olibia stood at the foot of the stone steps and watched as a silence fell over the crowd.

"It is Kristofer!" came a voice.

"Yes! It is he!"

"Look! Kristofer!"

Before long, a cacophony of his name resounded throughout the land, and he turned startled eyes to stare at Aelia. She smiled, but to him the sound was deafening.

Holding a hand up to silence the crowd, he was even more bewildered to find every single person bowing before him. After turning again, to face Abignale, he watched the old man bend at the waist, bowing low—the truest sign of respect, for Abignale had never bowed before anyone.

Elora, Rake, and Olibia followed, and Kristofer's gaze came to rest on Rian. They stared at one another for a moment. It was there in Rian's eyes—his anger, his hatred, but also his respect. There was still a profound love, no matter how deeply it was buried, and Rian knelt before him.

Aelia watched the display of emotion across his face. Leaning forward, she started to bow, but Kristofer's hand on her chin gave her pause.

"You will never bow before me, Aelia," he whispered.

The cheers were loud and long as he kissed her.

"You are king, Kristofer," she said into his ear. "What will you do?"

He turned again to study the thousands of people that had congregated. For him, it was confusing...the thousands of people that screamed his name.

He looked from them to his sister, to Rian, and then to the others.

"Let us go home, Aelia." He stepped off the platform and faced Rian. "I could not have done it without you." With that, he bowed low before Rian. "You are, in the truest sense, a king. Your family would be proud." He rose.

Rian swallowed and gave Kristofer a long, hard look. In a gesture filled with emotion, Rian nodded, unable to speak.

Kristofer said, "I am sorry for what has happened. Hurting you and Elora was never what I wanted."

Rian nodded. "I know."

With the past behind them, Kristofer took Aelia's hand and walked through the throngs of people. After mounting his horse, Kristofer turned once again to look at the people who came to honor him, before leaning down and pulling Aelia in front of him. Once she was settled, he turned to the rest of his group.

"Let us go back East. We can settle everything there."

He waited for acknowledgment, and once everyone conceded, they rode back to the Eastern Kingdom, giving Kristofer time to think. Even though the journey took some time, nothing was discussed until they were seated in the dining hall, which had, by unspoken agreement, become the new meeting room.

―⁓―

Abignale situated himself directly across the table from Kristofer and met his gaze with a stern look.

"So have you made your decision?"

"Aye." Breathing deeply, Kristofer said, "I will take the Southern crown."

Rake grinned and clapped him on the shoulder.

"There are matters that must be addressed before we leave," Kristofer continued. "For one, there is no one to rule the North. Elora, this is your domain."

"I have thought of this, brother." She turned to Rian. "How do you want to handle this, my love?"

Before Rian could answer, Kristofer leaned forward.

"The North and West are currently under my control. The North's condition is not at all bad. The people bowed before me easily. It is my birthplace. The West, not so much. They fought me long and hard, and I took them down. You'll need to go West to rebuild. You can rule the North from there until something else is established."

Rian grimaced. "How bad is it?"

"Bad," Kristofer replied.

"Then...we will go there, Elora."

She nodded and looked up. "The North will bow before you, Kristofer. You would have no problem establishing your reign."

"No," Kristofer said. "The North is no longer my home, and I have no desire to go there. Aelia and I will be married here, if it can be arranged. Then we will head South. I will lend support to the territories. Especially the West. Our coffers are full in the South, and rebuilding will be easy enough with the extra silver."

Rian nodded. "Then it is settled."

"Where is Raum?" Kristofer said. "I have not seen him since the battle."

"I sent him and Brilor to settle the damages done during

the fight," Elora said. "He should return soon."

Kristofer nodded and stood. "Olibia, how quickly can you arrange for a wedding?"

She looked up, surprised. "I imagine I can arrange for one in under a month's time. Why the need for haste?"

Kristofer looked at Aelia, and she nodded.

"Haste is a necessity at this time," he replied. "The South will need a queen. The political dispute over Aelia's lack of royal blood will be easier to handle with the least amount of time passed. The South knows her well. Unless either Rian or Rake have an issue with it, the South will not care."

"Of course not," Rake said, startling Aelia. "She has more than proven herself, and the people will feel more comfortable with a queen they know."

"Queen..." Aelia murmured, as if realizing it for the first time.

Elora smiled. "A sister to rule with sounds wonderful. Usually, we are outnumbered by men."

Aelia smiled, but it did not touch her eyes. Feeling overwhelmed by the prospect, she stood.

"I'm feeling faint," she told them, and Kristofer looked at her with concern. "I will retire."

"I'll be with you shortly." Kristofer watched her leave the room.

"The prospect of that kind of responsibility is daunting for her," Abignale said.

"If I must rule, then so must she," Kristofer said. "It will be fine. Olibia, I will send Aelia to you tomorrow to prepare for the wedding."

"All right." Olibia frowned. But as she thought about it, her eyes lit up and she laughed. "Could it be?"

Knowing Aelia had given her consent, Kristofer smiled and nodded.

"Yes, Aelia is with child."

Rake laughed and stood to clasp Kristofer's arm.

"A father and a king. No wonder you fought so adamantly against the crown. That is a lot."

"Perhaps..." Olibia said. "Perhaps a double wedding?"

She looked at Elora, who in turn looked at Rian.

"You two have waited a long time," Olivia continued. "Go to the West with a wife, Rian. Especially one as loved as she. It will boost morale."

Elora shook her head. "No. I will not infringe on Aelia's wedding day."

"Aelia will not feel so, Elora," said Kristofer. "If anything, it will ease her transition."

"Aye," Rian said. "I've waited too long."

Olibia beamed with excitement. "This will be wonderful! With so much to do, I must go." She turned to Rake.

He nodded, and she left the room, grabbing Elora's hand in the process and dragging her out.

"When Raum returns, I must speak with him immediately." Kristofer sighed. "I will go talk to Aelia."

Knowing her mood, he was not looking forward to the conversation they would have.

After leaving Abignale, Rake, and Rian, Kristofer made his way to her chambers and found her sitting next to the window, looking out.

"It is not so daunting a prospect as you think, love." Kristofer kneeled beside her.

She kept her gaze fixed on the green hills beyond the castle walls.

"I find it daunting," she replied. "Did you not find being king overwhelming?"

"Not for the same reasons you do."

Aelia turned to glare at him. "You said that political unrest might follow because I have no royal blood."

"There might be a small group that won't like it, but it is

not their decision, Aelia. You carry my child within you. You have political experience, and I will guide you. Where else did you see this going?"

"When you said you did not wish to rule, I thought we might retire to the country, from where I came."

He nodded in understanding. "It was an option, but—"

"I understand your position, and that it takes precedence. I just want time to process it all."

"I can give you a small amount of time. Olibia is planning a wedding, not only for us, but for Elora and Rian, too."

Surprise registered across her beautiful face. "A double wedding?"

"Will it bother you?"

"No! Actually, I like the idea of not having to face it alone."

He laughed. "Is marriage to me such an unbearable thought?"

"Certainly! It is not every day that a king weds a farmer's daughter. You should consider yourself fortunate."

He threw his head back and laughed. "I do, my love." He glanced at the door to make sure it was closed, then sat down beside her. "There is something else I wish to talk to you about, but it must stay between us for the moment."

Her smile faded quickly, and she nodded.

"You know that the North is without a ruler, for Elora will follow Rian to the West, where they are most needed at this time."

Aelia nodded again, and he continued.

"When Dagr set fire to Rian's brothers' room, only one of the boys died."

Aelia gasped. "Does Rian know?"

"He does not. I kept it a secret because I feared for his brother's life. If I survived the war, Raum had orders to bring him here. I believe that is what is keeping him."

"Where did you hide him?" Aelia said, wide-eyed.

"I made arrangements to bring him South after his castle fell under Southern control. He stayed with a farmer. It is a long story, but I did not say anything to Rian in case something happened to him before we could get him here. When Raum arrives, I'd like you to stay with him while I find the words to tell Rian."

"You truly are remarkable, Kristofer. What is his name?"

"Ander. Although, he assumed a new name for fear of his life."

"I will help you any way I can. Rian deserves his brother back."

CHAPTER 27

More than three weeks later, Raum entered the castle. He looked tired and travel-worn, and he was in desperate need of a bath and something to eat.

After being escorted by a guard to the dining hall, Raum waited to be announced. Upon seeing Kristofer, he bowed low.

"How did you fare?" Kristofer rose to his feet. "Did all go well?"

"Aye, Lord. *Everyone* is well."

"Eat. What of the bodies?"

"A mass funeral pyre was built for bodies not claimed. Women who wanted their husbands home made arrangements, if possible. Other than the blood-soaked ground, no evidence of the battle exists."

"Excellent news," Elora said. "Brilor?"

A dark look crossed Raum's face. "He'll be back shortly, Lady."

Aelia laughed. "Did you two not see eye to eye?"

"On very little." He turned to Kristofer. "Everything is done. You would be pleased. If you're agreeable, I require rest, and then I'd like to head back to the South."

Aelia's eyes sparkled with playfulness. "And not stay for the wedding?"

Raum paused with a leg of duck halfway to his mouth.

"The wed—" Laughing, he looked at Kristofer. "You'll marry?"

"The South requires a queen, does it not?"

Raum's smile faded as he stared at Kristofer.

"You will take the crown?"

At Kristofer's answering nod, Raum looked exuberant.

"It will be my honor to continue serving you."

Elora studied Raum's handsome face, wondering at his unyielding loyalty toward her brother. It surprised her when Kristofer, Raum, and Aelia stood up and announced their departure. Keeping a hand on the small of Aelia's back, Kristofer led her and Raum out of the dining hall.

"Is he here?" Kristofer whispered.

"Aye," Raum said. "I told the guard to give him a room near yours. I will bring you to him."

Kristofer nodded, and he and Aelia followed Raum up the stairs. Down a long corridor lit with torches, Raum pushed open a door not far from Kristofer's chambers. A tall, dark haired man turned around quickly. He was cloaked completely in black. He wore a black cape buttoned at the throat, with the hood hanging down his back. Black boots came halfway up his calves, and when Aelia saw his face, she gasped. He was startlingly similar in appearance to his older brother—handsome, dark, tall. His hair was jet black, like his clothes. He had a long, straight nose and a wide mouth. The only difference Aelia saw were his dark-brown eyes. Rian's eyes were a deep blue.

Upon seeing Kristofer, Ander bowed, and Aelia shut the door behind them.

"You have survived," Kristofer said.

"Because of you, Lord." Ander's voice was deep and rich, and his mannerisms were similar to Rian's.

Kristofer studied him for a moment. "You have grown."

"Eight years is a long time, Lord. Much has changed." With eagerness, Ander said, "My brother?"

Kristofer hesitated. "Ander, I have not yet told Rian about

you. He believes you to be dead, along with your brother Arius. I've kept you a secret to protect you all these years. I will send Rian to you after I've spoken with him."

Ander nodded, but the disappointment on his face was great.

"I ask that you stay in this room for now," Kristofer said. "If you need anything, Aelia will accommodate you."

He turned to her, and she took a step forward

"Thank you," Ander said. "But I have no desires other than to see Rian. I will wait."

"As you wish."

Kristofer turned, and Aelia and Raum followed him out. The door closed quietly behind them.

"Raum, take my quarters and rest," Kristofer said.

Raum bowed before departing, and Aelia sent a servant to him.

Distracted, Kristofer turned to Aelia. "I will talk to Rian now. Wait for me in your chambers."

While making his way to Rian's room, he tried to find the words to tell Rian that his brother was alive. He was hesitant and nervous, worried that Rian's anger and hatred would double when he realized that Kristofer had kept Ander hidden for so long. He dwelled on it until he found himself standing outside Rian's door. He knocked, and Rian's voice sounded from inside.

"Enter!"

After opening the door, he found his sister and Rian sitting on the floor, next to the fireplace.

"What is it?" Rian said in a sharp tone, unaccustomed to the look he found on Kristofer's face.

"Elora, I need to speak with Rian privately."

Her eyebrows drew together in a frown, but she nodded, then rose to her feet and shut the door quietly behind her. Kristofer inhaled deeply and took a seat on the edge of Rian's chair. Rian raised a dark, questioning brow.

"I do not know how to say this, or how to make my actions sound justifiable. But know that what I did, I did for the years of friendship between us before I joined the South."

"You look stricken." Rian stood.

With his arms crossed over his chest, he leaned against the wall, watching Kristofer.

"It is about your family and what really happened the night we raided the Western castle."

Rian inhaled sharply, and a dark look crossed his face. His dark-blue eyes met Kristofer's light ones and held his gaze.

"Our orders from Kayne were to bring you, Rian, unharmed to the South. You were the heir to the throne, and viable. Kayne left no specific instruction, other than that. Dagr, at the time, was a general, and I merely a soldier. He outranked me, and I had little choice but to follow his orders. When the gates were stormed, it was he who met your father's blade, and they fought. In the end, Dagr won, and he killed your mother shortly after. Once I was inside the gates, I heard screaming coming from the twins' room. I could see smoke billowing out of the window, and I knew Dagr had set fire to their bed chambers. With all my father had drilled into me to prepare for my role as Kayne's right hand, I was still ill-prepared to face you and your family."

"I don't understand where you are heading with this, Kristofer. Come out and say it," Rian growled.

Kristofer grimaced at his tone. "I told you that I found the boys dead in their room, but it was not so—"

"If you are here, to tell me that you killed my brothers," Rian snarled, "speak not another word. For it will destroy any camaraderie."

"I did not kill your brothers," Kristofer said, and Rian's face relaxed somewhat. "Arius was dead when I arrived, but Ander was not..." He rose to his feet. "Do you see what I'm saying?"

"I don't," Rian said, more calmly now.

"Ander is alive, Rian."

He watched the shock register on Rian's face, and then confusion.

"He is not dead?"

"He is not."

At a loss for words, Rian walked over to the table and sat down on a chair.

"Where is he?"

"I took him from the room that night and replaced his body with a dead soldier's. I had him don the Red Uniform and literally ride out with us. His height was to his advantage, and with the grime and blood I had him smear on his face, his disguise was deceiving. I knew of a farmer near the Southern border whose wife and son were killed the summer before in a raid by Rake's men. His boy was similar in age to Ander, and I thought if luck were upon me, he would take Ander in and raise him as his own. His name was changed, and a false identity that we came up with on the road was given to the farmer. He raised Ander as his own. Raum was told of it when he returned from here after our meeting at the midway point. I sent him to bring Ander back, which is why he was gone for as long as he was."

"But Raum returned tonight?" Rian frowned.

"With Ander. Your brother is in the castle."

Rian's throat tightened, and he looked down at the stone floor while he processed this bit of news.

"Take me to him."

"I will. But remember, Rian, he has been gone for over eight years, and the man that raised him, he loves."

"Take me to him." Rian rose to his feet.

Thinking it could have gone worse, Kristofer led Rian to Ander's room and opened the door again. Rian pushed past him and stopped dead in his tracks when he came face to face with his brother. Each man stared at the other until Rian moved closer.

"It is true," he whispered, turning to Kristofer, who nodded in response. "Ander?"

"Rian." Ander said his name so quietly, it was barely audible.

Rian grabbed his shoulders and embraced him tight.

"I thought you were dead," Rian choked out.

He took ahold of Ander's shoulders again, and pushed him away to look at him.

"Why did you keep this from me?" Rian turned back to Kristofer.

He stepped inside the room and shut the door behind him.

To Ander, Rian said, "Why did you never seek me out?"

Ander looked at Kristofer, unsure of what to say.

"I told him he was not to go near you." Kristofer closed his eyes at the memories.

Rian struggled to understand. "I would have kept him safe."

"You could not have kept him safe from me," Kristofer said. "If Kayne knew a Western prince had survived, he would have had me go after him. I saved him once. I could not risk doing it again. He would have died, and most likely, at my hand. I explained all of this in some detail to Ander, and I made him swear upon his brother's grave that he would not betray my standing. He was the only one who knew the truth."

"But even after? It's been weeks since the battle." Rian lowered his hands from Ander's shoulders and stepped back.

"After I left Ander at that farm, I had no further contact with him until today. I did not know if he survived or not, and I did not wish to tell you about him, only to take him away again. Forgive me, Rian? It was the only way I knew how to save him, and I did it for you."

"Forgive you?" Rian turned to Ander, who looked him straight in the eye.

"What he says is true, Rian. And for his sake, I never betrayed our confidences. I owe him my life."

"I will leave you two to talk." Kristofer reached for the doorknob.

"Kristofer," Rian called.

They looked at each other for a moment, before Rian said, "Thank you."

Kristofer closed the door and leaned against the wall for a moment, sighing in relief. He walked back to Aelia's quarters and found her seated near the window, where he walked over to her and sat down. She placed her arms around him and pulled him to her.

"How did Rian and his brother fare?"

"They are together now. Rian was stunned, to say the least."

"And you? Where do you stand now?" Aelia ran her fingers through Kristofer's hair.

"Beside you and this baby."

"The baby is a boy."

Kristofer pulled away and gave her a skeptical look. "How can you be certain?"

Aelia placed his hand on her stomach and covered it with her own.

"Because he grows within me. It is a boy. Mark my words."

"I believe you," Kristofer said. "To have a son..."

He shook his head in disbelief at the turn of events in his life.

"Have you any more surprises in store for us?" Aelia said. "Ander was quite unexpected. Then again, so was your killing Kayne." She started laughing. "You do nothing by the book, do you?"

Kristofer gave her a devilish grin. "What fun would that be?"

CHAPTER 28

Kristofer and Rake leaned over rolls of parchment in the drawing room. Unable to come to an agreeable solution on how best to handle the destruction in the West, Rake swore loudly.

"Where is Rian?" he said. "Should he not be present for discussions on the affairs of his own territory?"

"He will be here shortly." Kristofer turned back to the parchment and ran a finger over the map. "I cannot go into the West until Rian has regimented his control. The Westerners will vie for my head."

Rake snorted in amusement. "You pillaged the castle, destroyed their territory, and killed half of them."

"Those people would not cave. Adamant they were about following Rian."

"If anyone could break their spirit, it was you," Rake said.

Kristofer shrugged. "War does not show you who is right, only who is left."

Sighing, he took a step back from the table and raised a goblet of wine to his lips. After a couple sips, he set it down.

"Let us leave this matter until Rian can frequent these meetings," he said.

"I'd still like to know where he is," Rake said. "I haven't seen him since last evening."

Kristofer shrugged and headed from the room. He always hated political meetings, for they never seemed to end.

Eager to get out of the castle, he went in search of Aelia. Not finding her in her chambers, he looked for her for over an hour, before becoming uncomfortable with her disappearance.

He found Elora descending the stairs, and stopped her.

"Where is Aelia?"

"I have not seen her, brother. I've only just come from Rian's quarters."

"How does he fare?"

"They are both well. I imagine they'll join us for supper." Elora flashed him a brilliant smile, and stood on her tippy toes to kiss him on the cheek. "You still astound me to this day. Care to join me for a walk outdoors? After so long inside, the castle becomes..."

"Enclosed?" Kristofer said.

"Precisely."

She looped her arm through his, and they descended the rest of the stairs and headed outside. The weather was warm for the East. The sun shone brightly, with not a cloud in the sky. The courtyard was filled with people, and everyone they passed bowed low before them. They left the tall gates and made their way to the fields outside the castle wall.

"There is Aelia." Elora pointed.

Kristofer found her leaving the barn, and called for her. Exasperated, he reached for her.

"I've been looking for you."

Aelia raised a brow at him and gestured to the barn.

"I've been here. Come look!"

Elora and Kristofer exchanged a look, but he knew what would keep Aelia inside a barn on such a fine day. Sure enough, she led them to the back of the barn, behind the stables, to find a mother dog nursing her puppies.

"Aren't they sweet?" she said, eyes glowing.

Elora laughed and knelt down to stroke the mother's head.

"I do believe the last time you found infant animals, it did not end well." Raum's voice sounded from behind them.

Aelia ignored him. "Perhaps I could keep one?" She looked at Kristofer. "They are too young to leave their mother just yet, but in a few weeks..." She looked hopeful.

"Why do I have this feeling that the Southern castle will soon be taken over by stray animals?" Raum said to Kristofer.

"*That* will not happen," Kristofer said.

Aelia turned around to glare at him.

"Do not look at me like that, Aelia. He laughed. "Come." He held his hand down to her and helped her to her feet.

Elora said, "I think I would like one, also. Rian will be much easier to convince." She laughed.

Kristofer looked at the women before turning his gaze to Raum.

"Raum, Rake holds morning meetings. We are discussing the state of each territory and what needs to be done to bring each back to its former glory. I want you to attend them."

Raum inclined his head at the order. "As you wish."

Raum offered his arm to Aelia, and she wrapped her hands around it as he escorted her out of the barn. Kristofer took his sister's arm, and together, the four of them strolled and admired the beauty of the day. Elora, feeling contented, tightened her grip on her brother's arm.

"You look happy, Elora," he said.

"I am." She looked up at him. "And I believe, so is Rian."

She nodded to Kristofer's left, and he turned to see Rian and Ander walking toward them. They stopped in front of Kristofer, and Ander smiled warmly at him. Aelia studied them, wondering what their parents looked like. Rian caught her eye and grinned, and she returned the look with a smile of her own.

"It is good that you've finally left the confinement of your chambers," Kristofer said to Rian. "Rake is looking for you."

"No doubt, to drill into me the destruction of the West." Rian sighed.

"That is precisely it. Our meeting this morning was entirely too much fun," Kristofer said. "And there are some things we need to discuss concerning it when our company is less enthralling." He looked at his sister and Aelia.

"I daresay the West would like to see you hang," Aelia said in a cheerful tone, and took a seat on the grass.

Raum laughed loudly. "Aelia, always politically correct."

Elora chuckled. "We can overcome the unrest in the West. Especially with Ander alive and well. His life alone will diminish much of the hatred toward you, Kristofer."

Ander sat down, and Aelia watched him absentmindedly finger the grass.

"That is true," Rian said. "Especially when the story gets out. Ander, we," he gestured to Kristofer, Raum, and himself, "have business to attend to with Rake. Come, if you wish."

"No." Ander waved a hand in the air. "I have no desire to discuss the affairs of the state just yet. I will meet you in the dining hall for supper."

Kristofer crouched next to Aelia and kissed her.

"I love you," he whispered to her.

"And I, you," she whispered back.

He stood and saw Rian place his hands on Elora's waist. She wrapped her hand around his neck and kissed him, then whispered something in his ear.

"I do not care, Elora," came his response. "Why is that a secret?"

Elora glanced at Aelia with a grin, and Aelia's eyebrows shot up.

"Kristofer!" She rose to her feet.

Raum understood first and burst out laughing.

"Give her a puppy, Kristofer," he said.

"By the gods," Kristofer muttered. "You had to bring it up again, Elora?"

Aelia said, "If you don't—"

"What will you do, love?"

"I will raise hell, I swear it. Rian does not care. Why do you?"

"I don't," Kristofer said.

She gave him a disgruntled look.

"Why do you always seek to irritate me?" Aelia sat back down on the grass.

"Because you rise, so beautifully, to the occasion."

Ander laughed. "Are they always like this?" he asked his brother.

"Always," Rian said. "Kristofer enjoys practical jokes, and unfortunately for his soon to be wife, he likes setting her temper on fire." He looked at his brother with fondness. "Don't think much of it. Aelia is well-suited on delivering her own torments."

"Speaking of," Aelia said. "Elora, I have a favor to ask of you."

"Oh no, you will not drag me into these games of yours. Have you any idea what my brother and Rian used to do to me?" She shook her head, "I daresay Kristofer has not changed much."

"I have not yet heard these stories," Aelia said with delight.

Kristofer and Rian exchanged a look.

"Rian, we are not so old that we could not replicate the past."

Rian glanced at Elora, but before she could move away from him, he tightened his grip on her waist.

"Agreed," he said. "But now there are two women."

"Aye, but one of them will fight back." Kristofer grinned.

Aelia ignored them. "What did they do to you?"

Elora cringed and tried to pull Rian's hands off of her.

"Suffice it to say that their behavior drove me to learn how to sword fight," she replied.

Raum and Ander laughed so hard that tears sprang to their eyes. Rian turned around, his shoulders shaking with the force of his mirth, and Kristofer laughed until his sides hurt.

"Don't you men have matters to attend to?" Elora said.

Still laughing, the three of them left Ander with the women and headed back into the castle. Shaking her head, Elora sat down beside Aelia.

"Will you not attend the meetings?" Ander asked Elora.

"Not these. It is mostly your territory that my brother destroyed. Rian needs to decide how to handle it. And realistically, it is his home foremost. Kristofer can offer suggestions on the matter, but I cannot. I have only been to the West when I was much younger, and I don't know the area well enough to contribute any insight." She gave him a long, quizzical look. "What of you, Ander? How do you fare?"

The look he gave her was so much like Rian's that Elora smiled.

"I knew that this day would eventually come," he replied. "It seems as if I'm as ill-prepared for it now as I was eight years ago." He cleared his throat and smiled weakly. "I know everything will fall into place."

A servant came running forward and bowed awkwardly.

"My queen!" she said to Elora. "Your brother has sent me to fetch you. He and the other lords request your presence."

Sighing, Elora nodded at the woman and rose to her feet.

"I thought you said you could be of no help?" Aelia said.

"If Rian, Kristofer, and Rake are calling for me, then the discussion is on the Northern territories. Kristofer has no need to discuss the South. I will see you both at supper."

The two of them watched Elora walk back to the castle before Aelia turned her full attention to Rian's brother. He stared off absentmindedly into the woods, and Aelia noticed a nervous clench of his jaw.

"You seem so distracted, Ander. What is the cause?"

He shrugged and ran long fingers through his midnight hair.

"Is it the man who raised you?" she said. "Do you miss him? You can speak freely with me. I will keep our conversations between us."

Ander glanced at her before returning his attention to the grass.

"I miss him greatly. I miss my wife even more."

Aelia inhaled sharply, and he met her gaze. Wide green eyes stared at him.

"You've married?"

Ander nodded. His voice lowered with regret and pain.

"My brother does not know. You cannot tell him just yet."

"It is not my place, Ander. I will not say a word. What is she like?"

"Syeira." He said her name with longing. "She is magnificent. And furious at me for hiding who I really am all these years."

Aelia leaned forward with curiosity. "Have you any children?"

"I have a son, Cas. Cassander. In his second year of life."

"And you never told your wife the truth?" Aelia said. "Why?"

"Aside from Kristofer, no one knew I was alive. I feared that if word got out, I would become a target, and through me, those I love. Arius died in my arms, and I had no desire to lose anyone else. By the time I met Syeira, I had lived with the secret so long that to speak of it was almost unnatural. I love her, Aelia, and our son. I just haven't found the words to explain to Rian."

"Send for her, Ander. She and your child will be safe. Kristofer has men near the South-Eastern border. Escorts can be arranged."

He nodded, already knowing this. "She was furious with me, and I don't blame her. Rian wishes me to go West, and without Syeira, I cannot make any decision."

Aelia reached over and placed a hand on his arm.

"Rian loves Elora" she said. "He will understand."

"He does, doesn't he?"

Aelia laughed and nodded. "There was a time where Rian and I were bitter enemies."

Ander glanced at her in surprise, from under dark brows.

"Then, I would have told you to run," she said. "But now that I know him better, I think Rian will be happy that you are happy. You are not a king. You have more freedom to marry whom you choose. Tell him and let the matter ease from your mind."

Ander was silent for a long time before he finally nodded. "I will tell him tonight."

Nodding, Aelia drew her legs underneath her.

"Tell me about the man who raised you."

Ander smiled, his brow softened. "His name is Terric. I was traumatized over Arius' death, and when Kristofer brought me to him, he told Terric that my family had been slaughtered, and that I needed a home. Terric never questioned any of it. He took me in and treated me as his own. Taught me to work the land, and our home was secluded. For a long time, it was just him and me. When Syeira came along, Terric encouraged our marriage. He wanted a grandchild, and we gave him one."

"Did he know who you are?" Aelia said.

Ander shrugged. "I think he always suspected. Why would

Kristofer, of all men, bring a random child to him otherwise? But he never asked about my family, and I never brought it up. I lived with all of these secrets for so long, and now I feel like I've been thrust into a world I no longer belong in. Rian will not want me married to a commoner."

"That matters little," Aelia said. "The deed is done, and your son stands to inherit. I am nothing more than a farmer's daughter."

This bit of news shocked Ander. "You are not of noble blood?"

Aelia shook her head. "Not at all. Kristofer found me after my family was killed, and brought me to the White Castle. From there, the story can explain itself." She smiled. "Do not despair. I think you give Rian little credit concerning the situation."

"I will speak with him tonight," Ander repeated. "Thank you, Aelia."

Ander stood and offered a hand to her. They walked back to the castle, but Ander begged an excuse and left Aelia at the door, where she met Olibia and Elora. Olibia took her arm and insisted they begin planning for the wedding. Aelia looked behind her, but Ander had disappeared.

CHAPTER 29

O libia brought Aelia and Elora to her bed chambers, where she explained that a huge feast was to take place at the end of the month. A stout older woman was waiting patiently to measure Aelia and Elora for new gowns.

Aelia found this extremely nerve racking, and her unease showed. Once the maid left, Aelia turned to Olibia and Elora.

Her voice lowered in anguish as she confessed, "I have no dowry."

Elora smiled. "My brother certainly knows this, and does not care."

"But it is inappropriate," Aelia said. "It was different when he was a general. But now..."

Olibia sat down beside her. "Is this what has been weighing on your mind? That you are not good enough for a king?"

At Aelia's answering nod, Olibia continued.

"You are the best part of Kristofer. He told me he would not have survived his time with Kayne had it not been for you. You are his redemption, and the child you carry is more than enough for him."

"You truly believe that?"

"Yes," Elora and Olibia answered in unison.

"Now push the matter from your mind," Olibia said.

Fumbling with the clasp on a trunk, she glanced at Elora as she pulled a length of silk from inside.

"What is it, Elora?"

Elora hesitated, feeling foolish.

"There is something," she mumbled, blushing.

"Well, what is it?" Aelia said.

Elora giggled. "I am nervous."

Aelia raised her brows, and Olibia smiled.

"Wedding jitters," Olibia said. "I, too, was very nervous."

"Were you?" Elora bit her lip. "'Tis normal, then?"

At Olibia's nod, Elora relaxed somewhat. They spoke quietly to each other, but Aelia stopped listening, as this, above all else, made her feel terrible. She knew Kristofer didn't mind, and in truth, Rake's soldiers stole from her what should have rightly belonged to her husband.

She closed her eyes against the memories, and placing a hand on her stomach, stood quickly, eager to get out of the room and away from Olibia and Elora.

Startled, Elora stood with her.

"What is it, Aelia?"

"Nothing. I...I am not feeling well."

Claiming it was the pregnancy, Aelia left and made her way back to her chambers and laid down, where she fell asleep. When she awoke, the sun was low on the Western horizon. Realizing she had slept the entire day away, she pushed herself up and splashed cool water on her face from the basin on the table. After putting her hair over her shoulder, she pulled free the ribbon that bound the braid and raked her fingers through it.

Her thoughts returned to her conversation with Elora and Olibia, and she felt unease grow within the pit of her stomach. Wishing that she was home in her own chambers, she wondered why she was so bothered by it. So lost in her thoughts was she, that she did not hear the door open.

"I came earlier, but you were sleeping."

Aelia jumped at the sound of Kristofer's voice.

"Elora said you were not feeling well?"

"I am all right."

Kristofer didn't look convinced. "What is the matter, Aelia?"

"I cannot marry you!" she blurted out.

Kristofer leaned against the wall and folded his arms across his chest.

"And why not?"

He had wondered if Aelia would panic about their impending marriage. She had said before that what she had pictured was a country home. In truth, she cared little for jewelry or gowns. She wore simple dresses, kept her hair braided, as was the way of a woman born and raised in the country.

Kristofer found her lack of finery even more appealing. There was no other woman on earth as beautiful or elegant as she. There was an innocence about her that was never lost, even after the destruction of her village, her life. Her mind was as sharp as his—from the war strategies they discussed together, to the books she read aloud. Aelia was his other half.

She shrugged, unable to express herself with words. He walked over to her, but she moved away from him and sat down on the bed. He stood by the window, giving her the space he knew she needed.

"Let us walk," he said.

"Yes...all right"

He took her hand, and together, they walked outdoors. The fresh air made Aelia feel better, and Kristofer let her lead the way. He found himself in the stables, where Asen neighed with excitement. He opened the stable door and ran his hand over the horse's side. Asen trotted out, and Kristofer slipped the mouthpiece over his head before mounting him. Using his legs to steady himself, he leaned over and slipped one arm around Aelia's waist and lifted her in front of him.

She leaned against him, and Asen, excited to be near his master, trotted out of the stables. Kristofer directed him out into the fields, and after bringing Asen to a slow trot, leaned down.

"Tell me what is troubling you," he whispered.

Aelia turned her head to glance up at him, and saw the concern etched into his face.

"It's ridiculous," she muttered.

"All the same. Talk to me."

Aelia hesitated before everything came tumbling out.

"Olibia is planning the wedding, and today, Elora and I went to her chambers to discuss preparations. Elora mentioned that she was nervous about the wedding. I don't understand why exactly, but it made me feel terrible. Sometimes it is so hard to forget those soldiers that attacked me. You are king, and I feel...I feel like I'm not enough. You've done so much, and I've done nothing."

It was strange for Kristofer to hear Aelia's declaration. For him, she was everything. She was his solace, his redemption.

"Aelia," he whispered in her ear. "You are more than enough."

She turned to look at him. "I feel like I have nothing to offer you."

"You offer me a child! We are all ashamed of the past, for some reason or another. What was done to you was—is—reprehensible. But you are the most important thing in my life."

He nudged her chin up, but she jerked from his touch. After pulling on the reigns to bring Asen to a halt, Kristofer took hold of Aelia's arms and turned her around to face him.

"I've never told you this, but I decided once to give up," he said. "Kayne and his atrocities became entirely too much for me to bear. I decided to ride home and forfeit the entire plan. That morning, Raum came to me with news of pillages nearby, and he and I rode to assess the damage. That was the day I found you. Once I saw you sitting beside that grave, I could not desert. I knew as soon as I saw you that you were for me. And if I gave up then, what would become of you and those like you? You are the reason I stayed in the South and carried out my father's plan. You, Aelia, are the reason we won this war. If you do not feel worthy now, I don't know what else I can say to convince you. I have loved you from the moment I saw you."

For a moment, Aelia was speechless. "You wanted to desert?"

"I would have, the day I found you. I was alone. My sister and Rian at least had one another. But I was in a strange territory, and the years of the brutality I had witnessed had mostly undone me. You held me together. You do not give yourself enough credit. Noble blood only goes so far. We have both bled mercilessly for this war. Let us, from here on, put it behind us."

Feeling as though a huge weight had been lifted off her shoulders, she wrapped her arms around him.

"All right," she said.

Kristofer let Asen guide them back to the stables, and Aelia got down and peeked in on the dog and her puppies.

"Which are you taking?" Kristofer said, from behind her.

"I think the mother." Aelia sat beside the dog.

Kristofer sat down beside her, and Aelia picked up a puppy and placed it on his lap.

Kristofer couldn't help the smile he felt on his face as the puppy squirmed on his lap.

"They are hard not to love," Aelia said.

He picked the puppy up and examined it. "I would say these are part wolf, Aelia."

"Raum was of the same opinion. Come, we will be late for supper."

Kristofer placed the puppy beside its mother and followed Aelia out of the stable.

"Are you feeling better now?" he said, before they entered the castle.

"Yes, much." She stopped to kiss him.

The guard standing outside the door opened it for them and bowed as they entered. To the left, they found Rian and Ander descending the stairs. Aelia gave Ander a questioning look, and he nodded.

"Kristofer," Rian said, as they reached the bottom. "Ander and I must speak with you."

Ander said, "It's all right, Rian. Aelia knows."

Rian raised a brow and looked at Aelia questioningly.

"Knows what?" Kristofer said.

"I will leave you here to talk," Aelia said.

But before she could dart to the dining hall, Kristofer snaked his arm around her waist.

"I'm sorry, Aelia." Ander gave her a small smile. "I thought for sure you would have told Kristofer."

"You thought for sure she would tell Kristofer what?" he said in a tone Aelia had last heard during the war.

"My brother has married," Rian said, "and he wishes his wife and son to be brought here. Their home is near the South-Eastern border, and I ask that your men escort his family here."

Kristofer's face was unreadable. "I will send a man out first thing in the morning. Ander, take Aelia to supper. Rian and I will be along shortly."

Ander's hesitation made Kristofer laugh.

"Allow me to diffuse your brother's anger."

"You knew of this?" Rian fumed.

"I did not," Kristofer said. "Ander, Aelia. Go."

Ander took ahold of Aelia's arm and led her away from his brother and Kristofer.

Once they were out of earshot, Kristofer returned his full attention to Rian.

"Why are you even surprised?" he said.

"Why are you not? He has married a commoner and—"

"And what?" Kristofer growled. "Has a child with her? His situation and mine are not so different."

Rian held a hand up. "I meant no disrespect."

"It is why you are still standing," Kristofer barked. "Ander was a child who watched men butcher his family. He was not brought up the way you were. You were a man when you took control of the army. He was a boy, and was raised not as a prince, but as a farmer's son. He is your brother, Rian. Instead of sending a man out, let us ride out with Ander to meet these people. You owe the man Ander's well-being, and you have a nephew. Let us find out where they stand."

Rian stared at the floor, deep in thought, for a long time.

Finally, he said, "All right."

"Do not alienate him, Rian. His marriage to this girl cannot be undone. If he chooses to stay where he was raised, and you fight him, you will lose him all over again."

Rian crossed his arms over his chest and contemplated this.

With a sigh, he said, "You're right. He's not a boy anymore. I will talk to him again."

Kristofer nodded, and together, he and Rian made their way to the dining hall.

Rake was talking to Ander, and when he saw Kristofer, he said, "Kristofer! Rian! Aelia has just introduced us to Ander, who has beguiled us with the tale of his rather remarkable rescue."

"It was indeed a dangerous endeavor," Kristofer said. "But I'm glad to see how well it played out. As it turns out,

Ander has a wife and child near the border. Ander, with your consent, Rian and I would like to ride out there with you to meet your family."

Ander nearly lost the sip of wine in his mouth.

"That would indeed be wonderful!"

"Kristofer, allow me to go," Aelia said. "It—"

"No—"

"I think Aelia should accompany you." Elora looked at Rian. "Ander's wife is no doubt in shock. Were it me, I would feel betrayed and angry."

"She does," Ander said.

"A women," Elora continued, "especially Aelia, will no doubt bring her great comfort and allow for an easier transition. Allow her to go, brother."

"I have no qualms with it," Rian said.

Ander agreed with a nod. "Please? If it will help, let her come, Kristofer."

"All right." Kristofer raised his hands in defeat. "We'll ride out first thing tomorrow."

Before the sun rose, Kristofer, Rian, and Ander had their horses saddled and ready. Aelia joined them just as the first rays of light were creeping through the eastern sky. After pulling her in front of him, for Kristofer was adamantly against giving Aelia her own horse, they rode toward the Southern border. It would be a two-day journey, with only one night of camping. Aelia was thrilled to be out of the castle and back into nature.

When they made camp that evening, before the sun set, Rian built a fire and Kristofer nocked an arrow, but Aelia held her hand out.

"Allow me." She grinned. "I wonder if I could hit a moving target."

Kristofer handed her the bow, and she took careful aim at a wild turkey that hid in between the long grasses of the prairie. She released the arrow and hit the bird in the eye, killing it instantly.

Rian laughed at the shocked look on Kristofer's face.

"I told you she has become very accurate with a bow."

"I am impressed, love." Kristofer went to retrieve the bird.

He plucked and cleaned the turkey, and while it roasted, Aelia leaned between Kristofer's legs as Ander and Rian reminisced about the times before the war.

"Why does Elora hate it so when you talk of your visits North, Rian?" Aelia said.

Kristofer's deep laugh rumbled through her.

"Because they all but tortured her." Ander grinned. "I do remember a party of sorts." He looked at Rian. "Arius and I were allowed to accompany you to the North. Elora had dressed in this exquisite gown, and she was just leaving her chambers when Kristofer threw a bucket of cold water over her head."

Rian and Kristofer howled with laughter.

"I had forgotten about that!" Kristofer said, through his mirth.

"You did that?" Aelia gasped. "How cruel!"

"We were children, Aelia!" Rian said, coming to Kristofer's defense. "Elora was younger and weaker, and it was all fun."

"She did not fight back? I would have used every resource to make you both pay." Aelia laughed because they were.

"I have no doubt," Kristofer said. "I do believe you have gotten the best of me more than once."

"Somebody had to," Aelia said.

"You have literally met your match, Kristofer," said Rian. "Be careful, Aelia. Throwing water at Elora was the least of Kristofer's games."

"There were the snakes," Kristofer said.

Aelia gasped. "You didn't!"

"He did." Rian laughed again. "To this day, she loathes snakes.

"Do not give me all the credit, Rian. You were right there beside me, pitching in."

"You?" Aelia said in surprise. "Kristofer, I could see. But you?"

"Who do you think held Elora while I was busy throwing snakes at her?" Kristofer said.

"That is terrible! Rian! I am ashamed of you," Aelia said, feigning alarm.

"It cannot be that bad." Rian turned the spit the turkey roasted on. "She agreed to marry me, did she not?"

"You're welcome." Kristofer grinned.

"You had nothing to do with it," Rian said.

"I believe I did. Remember when I so casually strolled into your camp and stole her from you?"

"*Casually strolled*?" Rian said. "You attacked on horseback and killed everyone in sight."

"Matter of opinion," Kristofer said. "We had several charming weeks together, riding back to the South. She told me about her concerns, and I do believe I alleviated many of them."

"Of course you did," Rian said.

"This will go on for hours," Ander said to Aelia. "They did this, even as children."

Rian shoved Ander. "How is it you remember? You could barely walk!"

"I remember! I was not so little," Ander said, exasperated. "The West was attacked two years into the war, yes?" Ander calculated in his head for a moment. "I was ten when the war started, and I remember you and Kristofer quite well from about five years and upward. In which case, I have five years of stories, Aelia. What do you wish to know?"

Aelia and Kristofer laughed, and Rian scowled.

"I cannot wait to hear them." Aelia leaned forward.

"I can," Kristofer said. "Let us eat before Ander makes us sound a lot worse than we were."

Using a knife he pulled from his hip belt, Rian pulled the bird off the fire and waited for it to cool enough so that he could handle cutting into it. Once they had satiated their hunger, they went to sleep.

CHAPTER 30

The closer they got to Ander's home, the more eager he was to get there. As they crested the top of the hill, Ander pointed to a herd of cattle grazing.

"Those are ours," he said. "We are here."

A large stone cottage came into view. Smoke billowed from the chimney, and Ander looked at it longingly for a moment, before he urged his horse forward. Aelia turned to look at Kristofer, and he nudged Asen forward, Rian right beside them.

At the sound of approaching horses, the door opened and an old man stepped out, shielding his eyes from the sun. Ander dismounted and walked slowly to him. Staying on the horses, Kristofer, Aelia, and Rian watched the scene before them. The old man placed his hands on Ander's face and pulled him in, embracing him tight.

Ander returned the hug and held him for a long while.

"Forgive me," he whispered. "I could not tell you."

"It does not matter," Terric said. "You are my son, and I love you."

Ander's eyes shone bright, and he felt his throat tighten. Swallowing hard, he turned to the riders still upon the horses.

"Rian, Kristofer, and Aelia...my father, Terric."

The introduction startled Rian, but he hid it well beneath a mask of passiveness.

He dismounted, and Terric bowed.

"Do not bow before me, Terric. Were it not for you, my brother would be long dead."

Straightening, Terric eyed Rian with respect.

To Kristofer, he said, "We meet again, Lord."

Kristofer dismounted, "I was pleased to find Ander in better condition than what I left him in."

"He has been a light in my life." Noting Aelia, Terric bowed. "Lady."

Kristofer turned and helped Aelia off Asen.

Keeping an arm around Ander's shoulders, Terric said, "Please, come inside. I fear it is not much, but it is home."

Ander paused with hesitation Terric had rarely seen.

"Where is Syeira?"

Terric sighed, and Ander felt every fiber of his body tense.

"She took Cas for a walk. She is beside herself, Ander. We were not expecting you so soon, but it is good that you are here."

"You've never called me Ander before."

"It is who you are, son. Syeira will understand, but your soldier dropped a heavy load upon her shoulders, and neither of us were fully prepared for it. She will return soon. Come inside."

Rian turned to give Kristofer a disgruntled look.

"I told Raum to proceed cautiously." Kristofer shrugged.

They followed Terric inside to find a cozy, well-kept home. The smell of roasting meat filled the air. A fireplace stood to the side of the living area on the left, and to the right was a large dining area, where a hand-carved table and chairs stood invitingly. A bowl of fresh fruit sat on top of the table.

Ander was so tense that Aelia placed her hand on his back and gave him a small smile.

"It's all right," she whispered so only he would hear.

"My wife..."

Aelia gave him a sympathetic look.

"Ander," Terric called. "Sit down. This will sort itself out, and all will be well. Do not conjure up woe."

Ander nodded and sat down at the table. Rian sat next to him and clasped a hand on his shoulder.

The house reminded Aelia of the home she grew up in, and she looked around with happiness in her heart.

"This brings back such memories, Kristofer," she said. "It is so like my home. It even smells the same."

"You grew up on a farm, Lady?"

Aelia nodded. "My family is from closer to the center of the South. A village called—"

"Apollis?" Terric said.

"Yes. You know it?"

"Yes, I was very distraught to learn of the village's fate."

"The experience was something else entirely." Looking at Terric, she said, "Would it be all right if I walked around? I'd love to see the animals."

"Of course, several calves were born in the last couple days, by the pasture you rode in from."

Delighted, Aelia looked at Kristofer. Knowing he'd never let her out alone, she beamed when he agreed to accompany her.

Ander sat beside his brother, who looked around the room with curiosity. He knew Kristofer and Aelia had left to give them some privacy. Terric sat down across the table from them and looked at Ander.

"Have you decided what you'll do?" Terric asked Ander.

"No." He glanced at Rian. "I am lost on this, Father."

Rian stood abruptly. "Ander, I'll leave you and Terric to talk."

Ander winced at his brother's retreating back.

"He does not like that you call me Father." Terric smiled. "I imagine it is just as hard for him as it is for you."

"Why do you say that?" Ander said.

"He is the king, Ander. He believed you to be dead, his family gone. To have you back, with no recognition of your former self, is—"

Ander scoffed. "I know who I am."

"Do you? Are you a prince? Or a farmer's son?"

Ander rested his head in his hands. "I am a father and a husband. That much, I know."

Terric looked at him with sympathy. "You are all of these things."

Ander's voice lowered in anguish. "But I cannot be your son and a prince!"

"Why can you not? What do you want?"

"I don't want to lose you or Rian. But I have made my life here with you and Syeira. I don't want to leave this behind."

"Syeira will be home soon. I think speaking with her will prove extremely beneficial for you."

Sighing, Ander nodded as Terric rose.

"Let us find your brother and your friends. We will sort all of this out."

Together, they found Rian and Kristofer watching Aelia play with a calf in one of the fields. Ander and Terric walked up to them and leaned on the wooden fence next to them.

"Where is the bull?" Ander said, causing Kristofer to turn quickly.

"He is in the other pasture," Terric said, watching Kristofer's reaction with amusement. "She is a farm girl. She would know."

"She *is* a farm girl." Ander looked to Kristofer. "You are marrying her, are you not?"

"I am," Kristofer said, without taking his eyes off of her.

Catching Ander's meaning, Kristofer turned to him.

"It is possible, Ander. This farm is under my jurisdiction. If you choose to stay, you'll see no judgement from me or Aelia. But do not forget your birthright."

345

Rian kept his face impassive. He knew it was a decision Ander would have to make on his own, without his interference.

Aelia walked over to them.

"Will we have cows now?" Kristofer said, amused.

Aelia shot him a disgruntled look. "It may not be a bad idea."

Rian let a bark of laughter. "I am glad Elora and I are going West. Your kingdom will be overrun with animals, Kristofer."

"It certainly seems that way." Kristofer opened the gate so Aelia could walk through it.

Ander laughed and turned his back to the fence to lean against it.

"It is so peaceful here!" Aelia said.

As she leaned against Kristofer, he wrapped his arms around her and kissed the top of her head.

Rian turned to his brother. "It is beautiful here, Ander. No wonder you are so fond of the country."

Ander smiled at his brother, but his smile faded quickly.

"Syeira," he whispered, pushing himself off the fence.

They all turned toward Ander's gaze to find a tall, dark-haired woman holding a child's hand. She wore a simple blue cotton dress with a white apron tied to the front. Her dark hair hung to her hips. Almond eyes stared out from underneath dark brows and long lashes. High cheek bones gave her an exotic look.

Seeing Ander, she froze and stared at him.

"Papa!" A small version of Ander came running up to him as fast as his little legs would carry him.

"Cas!" Ander knelt down and caught the boy in his arms.

"Papa!" Cas said again, and rested his head on his father's shoulder. "Look!" Cas held up a wooden carved sheep and delightedly showed his father.

"Did you carve that by yourself?" Ander said, with a

serious face, through Cas's squeals of laughter.

The little boy shook his head, and Ander glanced nervously at his wife.

Syeira made no move toward her husband, but took in the group of people he had arrived with, having no idea who they were.

"So you have returned," she said, her voice cold.

"Syeira." Ander handed Cas to Terric and walked toward her, but she backed away.

"Do not." She covered her mouth with her hand, and Ander heard a sob escape from her throat.

"You must talk with me. Allow me to explain."

"To fill my ears with more lies? So you can leave again? No, Jase." A pause filled the air, followed by a pained whisper. "That is not even your real name." She shook her head. "You will not do this to me and Cas. Go if you are going."

"Let me explain, please?" His voice was laced with pain.

Rian and Kristofer exchanged looks, and Kristofer took Aelia by the hand. They walked away, and Terric followed, holding Cas close.

CHAPTER 31

Ander watched them leave before returning his attention to his angry wife.

"Let us go inside," he said.

For a moment, Syeira looked as if she would argue, but she turned on her heel and Ander followed her into the house, closing the door behind him.

"Listen to me," he said calmly, but she whirled around.

"Will you take Cas from me?" She choked back a sob.

"I...what? Why would I?"

"Will he not stand to inherit? Your blood flows through his veins. I cannot lose my son."

"Syeira, I would never!" He was stunned that she had even brought it up. "I have no wish to break our family apart."

"Don't you? Why did you lie to me? Even after Cas was born?" She cried then.

Sitting down on a chair, she buried her face in her hands.

"I had to," he said. "I did it to keep you safe."

"From?"

"Kristofer." He sighed.

"I don't understand." Syeira wiped her cheeks with the palm of her hand. "I thought he saved you?"

"He did, Syeira. It is a very long, complicated story." Ander sighed.

"Well, we have time. No more lies...Ander."

He winced at the sound of his own name.

Kneeling in front of his wife, he told her everything. He told her how Kristofer had rescued him and brought him to the farm. He stressed the need for secrecy concerning Kristofer's standing in Kayne's army, and how fatal it would be should word get out that a Western prince had survived. Ander was determined to make Syeira see it from his point, and from Kristofer's.

"If I had betrayed Kristofer, and word of my survival leaked out, Kayne would have sent Kristofer after me and those I love. I am no match for him. No one is. To this day, he is more powerful than any man, but he is a good man. I was a child, Syeira, and I had no wish to die in a Southern torture chamber at twelve years old. And then all those years passed, and the lies became my life, and to speak of them felt...unnatural. When I met you, I was no prince. I love you, Syeira, and I love Cas. I want you with me. I had to go with Raum. Rian is still my brother, and I...I had to go..."

When Raum had come for him, Ander felt, with equal measure, excitement, guilt, and fear. Throughout the years, whenever possible, he sought news of the war and whether the Western king was alive and well. Always, he felt immense relief to find out Rian was still fighting, and with Elora at his side.

"Kristofer wouldn't torture a child," Syeira said.

Ander placed his hands on hers, but she did not pull away this time.

"Kristofer made it clear that if I betrayed him and Kayne found out, that he would come after me and I would die in a most unpleasant manner. I was twelve years old, and I had just witnessed my family...Arius...my brother...he choked to death in my arms. I watched him choke on smoke because our bed chambers were on fire. I couldn't breathe, either. I don't know why he died and I didn't. But my home was burning, and the person I was closest to died horribly in front of me. Royalty or not, I was a child and I was terrified."

Having never heard this story, and even though it was vague, Syeira couldn't imagine what her husband must have gone through. She reached forward and cupped his face.

"Why did you not confide in me?"

"Because I loved you. I would have told you when the war was over if Kayne lost. I had planned on it, but I never got the chance. Kristofer sent for me almost immediately, and in the two weeks that followed the end of the battle, I could never find the right moment."

Syeira was silent for a long time.

"I understand why you are angry, Syeira. But can you not find it in your heart to forgive me? I swear I did not lie to hurt you."

"I know," she said. "I'm sorry. I was in shock, and I was terrified that you would take Cas away from me."

"I would never take him away from you. It is the furthest thought from my mind."

Syeira met his gaze easily now, and nodded.

"When the soldier came for you, he said that Cas was a prince and of royal blood. I thought you and Rian would take him and leave me here. I was more frightened than angry."

"My brother would never separate a child from his mother. Come, meet him. You will like him. And Aelia, Kristofer's woman, came to help you adjust. Kristofer is king, not even a prince, and Aelia is a commoner. Although, I daresay not to call her such in front of him."

"Kristofer will take the Southern crown?" Syeira said.

They had survived the war with minimal grievances, and she was heartened to hear the news.

"Aye," Ander replied.

"What will you choose?"

"I don't know, Syeira. But whatever it is, I need to know that you and Cas will be there beside me. Imagine your fear that I would take Cas from you. I have the same fear that I will lose you both."

She heard the anguish in his voice, and it broke her heart.

"No." She shook her head, realizing for the first time, what she would do. "Cas and I will go wherever you go."

The weight that had been sitting on Ander's shoulders the last week lifted suddenly, and he pulled Syeira to him. His throat tightened for a moment, until he kissed her.

"We will sort it out," she whispered.

"Father said the same thing." Ander smiled. "Come. Come and meet my brother. Cas looks just like him."

Syeira rose nervously and smoothed out her dress. Leaving the house, she wrapped her arm around Ander's, and feeling peaceful—although, a little nervous—for the first time since Raum had arrived for her husband, she followed him toward his friends. As they walked, Syeira informed him that her horse had finally borne a colt. A male that could be broken for Cas to ride when he was a bit older.

He laughed. "I thought the horse would never give birth."

"I believe you said the same thing about me."

Ander grinned at her. "Perhaps we should give Cas a sibling to play with."

"I think our son would like that."

The scene they came upon surprised Syeira. She found her son sitting on a grass knoll, where a beautiful woman was tickling him. His excited laughter reached her and tamed some of the unease she felt.

Standing behind the woman was Terric, who was deep in conversation with two men. The darker one was undoubtably Rian, as he was a mirror image of his younger brother. To his right stood a tall, blond man with a powerful air around him. She looked nervously at her husband, and he smiled encouragingly at her, but Kristofer's presence frightened her. She had heard stories of his feats, and word of his betrayal of

Kayne had reached even her secluded farm.

"That is Kristofer?" she whispered. "Why did he come here?"

"You have no need to fear him, Syeira. He is here because our home is inside his territory. He may not have, but Aelia wanted to come. I think she is thrilled that there is a woman involved, like her, of no nobility. Kristofer rarely lets her out of his sight, anyway. Either way, he would have been here."

Seeing Ander, Aelia rose to her feet, and following her gaze, Kristofer and Rian turned. Ander walked up to them, his wife clutching his arm.

Rian said, "It is a pleasure to meet you, sister. Ander has spoke of your beauty, but his description pales in comparison to seeing you before me."

Blushing at the praise, Syeira went to bow, but Kristofer caught her arm before she could.

"You are royalty now. Others will bow before you."

The shocked look on her face made Aelia laugh.

"You will get used to it," she said.

Unsure of what to say, or who to say it to, Syeira glanced at Ander. But Rian broke the silence again by picking up Cas.

"It is one thing to learn I have a nephew. But another thing entirely to meet him. He is a remarkable child."

"He is." Syeira smiled. "And evidently, looks just like your family."

Rian laughed, completely beguiled by the boy.

"He looks like our mother. Our father wasn't nearly so dark." Rian looked affectionately at his brother.

Kristofer nodded in agreement. "She would have loved him, Ander. Nor would she have cared where his roots lie."

Syeira looked surprised. "Wouldn't she?"

"No," Rian said. "Kristofer speaks the truth. She would have loved a grandson. Royal blood means nothing in the face of family. Welcome to ours, Syeira."

Ander placed an arm around her shoulders.

"Thank you, brother," he said.

Syeira took a deep breath and released it slowly, then smiled at Rian.

"Aelia." She looked at the other woman. "Would you like to walk? I daresay the men have much to discuss."

"Yes," Aelia said, eager to know her. "I would like that."

Kristofer looked as if he was about to argue, but Rian stepped in.

"Kristofer, nothing can happen."

"The West—"

"Would not dare attack with me standing right here."

Syeira looked at her son with worry. "Are we in danger?"

"No." Rian glared at Kristofer.

Aelia sighed. "We will not go far."

She looped her arm around Syeira's and pulled her away before Kristofer could say anything else.

"You are entirely too protective." Rian shook his head.

"The last time I let my guard down, you kidnapped her and dragged her across the country."

"I have no desire to do so again. Therefore, you have nothing to worry about," Rian grinned. "Now leave the women be. We have a lot to discuss." He looked at Cas, sitting happy in his arms. "It is never too early to teach the boy political accuracy."

Aelia and Syeira walked arm in arm.

"It is a lot to grasp," Aelia said. "I assume you and Ander sorted through your differences?"

Syeira nodded. "Yes. I believe this was the worst week of my life. I'm glad it's over."

"I understand." Aelia sighed, looking at the pastures. "I grew up on a farm so similar to this, it makes my heart ache."

"Ander mentioned such. Where is your family?"

"Eastern soldiers slaughtered them." Having no desire to

talk about that, Aelia said, "Kristofer and I will be married at the end of the month."

"But he is a king?"

"And I am a commoner?" Aelia raised her brows, amused.

"I meant no disrespect," Syeira said.

"None was taken. It is true. I have no royal blood. But he loves me, anyway. It is something you and I have in common, and I am ever so happy."

Syeira felt her eyes fill.

"I know it feels like your life has been turned upside down," Aelia said. "But Ander loves you. It is, after all, why we are here."

Syeira glanced behind her to where the group of men were small figures on the crest of the hill.

"What is Rian like?" she said. "I fear my husband will want to go to the Western territory."

Aelia followed her gaze. "Rian is kind and compassionate. I don't know much about him as a king but Kristofer once said that as a ruler, there would be no one better."

Syeira nodded and leaned against the wooden fencing that overlooked the horses.

"You fear leaving here?" Aelia said.

"Yes. This is my home. And I know my husband. He will go with his brother. It is where his duties lie."

"Did you tell him this, Syeira?"

"No.

"Ander does not yet know himself what he will do," Aelia said.

"I am telling you what he will do. He will go with Rian, and until he realizes it, I can offer him no guidance."

"Will you go with him?" Aelia said.

"Yes."

"Then know that you have a friend, and you are not alone."

Syeira smiled warmly at Aelia. "Thank you. It brings me great comfort to hear it." She turned toward the house. "Let us head back. Cas will be awaiting his supper."

Aelia and Syeira walked back to the house in silence, each admiring the farm and pastures, each for different reasons. Aelia was reminded of her home, and Syeira wondered if she would ever see it again.

Syeira pushed open the door to find the men congregated around the table, deep in conversation. None of them noticed the women, and Aelia and Syeira exchanged a look.

"But the North..." Rian was saying.

"It would take years before—" Kristofer began.

"And five rulers to accommodate him!" Rian snarled.

Ander put his head in his hands, and Terric placed his hands on his shoulders.

"I am not opposed to the idea," Ander said. "But there are other things to consider. Rian, be reasonable."

"What else would you have me do?" Rian said. "It makes perfect sense. With Kristofer ruling both the North and the South—"

"As an adult with years of training behind me!" Kristofer slammed his hand down. "Twelve years is not nearly enough time—"

He stopped speaking because he noticed Aelia and Syeira standing by the door. Rian, Terric, and Ander followed Kristofer's gaze.

"Where is Cas?" Syeira said.

Rian moved aside to show Syeira that her little boy was seated beside him, playing with a wooden carved cow and horse.

"And you are shouting in front of him?" she said in a sharp tone.

The men had the decency to look abashed.

She pushed past them and picked Cas up to bring him

over to the fireplace, where she ladled stew into a bowl. After taking Cas outdoors, she seated herself in the grass while the food cooled.

"What is the matter?" Aelia said, from where she stood by the door.

Kristofer straightened. "Rian wishes Ander to take control of the North."

Aelia turned surprised eyes to Rian and then Ander.

"Not right away!" Rian said. "In years, perhaps. When it can be arranged."

"But you can rule both territories efficiently, can you not?" Aelia asked Kristofer.

"It is not an ideal situation, but it can be done."

"Until such other efficiencies arise," Rian said.

"Ander, I thought you were heading West?" Aelia said.

"I have not made up my mind either way, Aelia. They need a ruler, and it seems that my brother forgets I was raised as a farmer for the last eight years."

"And for twelve years before that, you were raised as a prince," Kristofer said. "It is not an abhorrent idea for you to take on the North. But you are young and without proper guidance, and the North will not survive."

"Why not send Elora?" Ander snapped. "She is clearly fit to rule."

Aelia saw a muscle twitch in Kristofer's jaw. His expression went from calm to angry in the blink of an eye.

"Easy, Ander," Terric said, for he, too, noticed Kristofer's reaction.

"Kristofer," Rian said.

"Forgive me, Kristofer," said Ander. "I meant no disrespect. The entire situation is overwhelming, and all in less than a couple weeks."

Turning to Rian, Kristofer growled, "This was your idea. You handle it how you see fit."

He stormed out of the house and slammed the door behind him. Aelia stood rooted to her spot.

"Why is he so angry?" she said.

Rian sighed. "Kristofer has little desire to rule two territories. But because the South did not suffer overly much in response to the war, he can focus his attention on the North. I cannot spare Elora when the West is in such dire need of repair. Kristofer has agreed to control the North from the South until we can come up with something else, and I suggested Ander. He does not think it is a good idea."

"Neither do I." Aelia walked over to the table and took a seat across from Rian. "For Ander to take control of a nation, with Syeira and Cas alongside him—"

Rian said, "We have been over this, Aelia—"

"Let me finish! Leave Kristofer as ruler of the North. The people will be happy to serve him. And merely name Ander regent."

"Why?" Ander said.

"Ander, regardless of your time here," Aelia said, "you are of noble blood and fit to rule a nation, especially with Kristofer to guide you. The problem arises, I believe, from you coming back from the dead after eight years, and with a wife and child. Am I correct?"

"Yes," Rian said.

"The North, which is not your birthplace to begin with, will know of your story soon enough. Dying at twelve as a prince will earn you no respect. But if Kristofer maintains the crown there and you rule under him...well, it just might work."

"We'll put the matter to Kristofer," Rian said. "Will you call him in?"

Aelia nodded and went to find him. She returned a few minutes later, with him at her side.

"Tell him of your idea," Rian said.

Kristofer sat down and listened intently while Aelia filled him in.

"A regent," Kristofer said, once Aelia was through. "I've thought of this. But I still foresee issues."

"There will always be issues." Rian sighed. "War was easier than this."

"For you," Kristofer muttered. "Let us set this aside for tonight. If need be, we can return back to the East with Ander. Rake and Olibia will be of some use, too."

Terric stood and offered stew to the party in his dining room.

"Syeira made a loaf of bread just this morning," he said.

"Thank you, Terric." Aelia accepted a bowl.

She seemed to always be hungry these days.

As they ate, Syeira came back in, holding Cas.

"I will put him to bed and join you."

"I'll do it." Ander rose.

He held his hands out toward his son, and Cas leaned forward, wrapping his little arms around his father's neck. As they walked up the stairs, Syeira watched them go, before returning her attention to the rest of them. Sitting down where Ander was, she studied the people before her.

Aelia and Kristofer sat beside one another, laughing, her hand on his arm. Rian was more reserved, less comfortable. Probably because of the circumstances—thinking his brother was dead, only to find out he was very much alive. What joy he must be feeling, clouded by, what she was sure was confusion.

Terric, like her, studied those around him. They both noticed that Kristofer and Rian were heavily armed. Swords hung from both their hips, and each man had a dagger strapped to the their belt. A bow and a quiver of arrows leaned against the wall. The weapons made Syeira uncomfortable.

Kristofer noticed Syeira eyeing the bow with disdain.

"Our weapons cause you unease, Syeira?"

Startled at being jerked from her thoughts, Syeira pulled her gaze from the bow to Kristofer.

"Yes," she replied. "Why are you both so heavily armed if the territories are under control and the war is over?"

"Because there is still unrest in each territory," Rian said. "There was, and always will be, the need for defense. Your location, as secluded as this is, kept you safe, as most of the battles were fought in more densely populated areas. It is probably why Kristofer brought Ander here to begin with. No one would recognize him."

"But he looks so much like you," Syeira said. "How could he go unnoticed all of these years?"

"It is the location, Syeira," Kristofer said. "Did you have any idea what Rian looked like? Aside from descriptions you may have heard."

"No," she said.

The cleverness of Kristofer's deception concerning her husband was beginning to dawn on her.

"You I have seen," she said, "although only from afar. I do not believe I would have recognized you in any other situation."

"Because this is my territory, but I have not been to this part of the country since I left Ander here. Unless you traveled closer to the White City, you would not have seen me."

"I grew up closer to the city," Syeira said. "My father and Terric have known each other for a long time. My father visited the farm one year, and brought me with him. It is how I met Ander."

"That was why he brought you." Terric laughed. "I told your father about Ander, and he was determined that you meet him."

"Good thing that he did," Ander said, as he came down the stairs. "Cas is sleeping peacefully," he said to his wife.

He stood behind her and placed his hands on her shoulders. She turned her head to smile at him, and he returned it warmly.

"It is so beautiful out," Syeira said to him. "Will you not build a fire for us?"

"If you wish it," Ander said.

Her answering nod made him move to the doorway.

"We often have fires at night, once Cas falls asleep," Syeira said.

"That sounds wonderful." Aelia turned to Kristofer. "How long will we stay?"

"Until Ander decides on a course of action. We'll need a direction, one way or another." He looked at Ander, who stood by the door. "Which is not to say to rush your decision. Take the time you need. Any decision made in haste will not end well. Besides, I enjoy the tranquility."

Aelia nodded in agreement, and they followed Ander outside. The back of the stone cottage had a large dugout with rocks placed around it in a perfect circle. Beside it sat a stack of firewood.

"Terric and I tried to build one the night before last, with little success." Syeira laughed.

"In my old age, my hands do not work as well as they once did." He rubbed his knuckles.

It was meant lightly, but Ander frowned. "How can I leave you alone here?"

"Son, we will go where you go," Terric said. "Whether you choose to stay here or follow your birthright."

"But this is your home." Ander dumped the load of wood in his arms near the pit.

"Our home is with you, Ander," Syeira said. "The only

issue here is to figure out what to do with all the animals."

"I have a potential solution to that." Kristofer sat down next to Aelia.

"What is it?" Syeira said.

"As royalty, you will not need for silver or a home," Kristofer replied. "There are many people who are displaced. Their lives ruined because of the war. Livestock, given to them freely, will provide for an easier life, and the animals will be well-tended to because they are the means of survival. If you wish to go down that road, Rian and I can certainly help in that aspect."

"That would indeed be a relief," Terric said. "See, Ander. Everything falls into place, one way or another. If you are worried about me, don't be. I wish to live out my final years with my family, my grandchildren."

Realizing he had been holding his breath, Ander let it out with a *whoosh*. Relief washed over him knowing Terric would stay with him either way.

Squatting beside the pit, he grabbed two stones and lit the dried grass he had thrown under the wood. Before long, a fire blazed before them. They stayed there, watching the flames burn lower and lower, before retiring for the night.

CHAPTER 32

The next day, over breakfast, Syeira mentioned that the nearby villages were congregating for a festival a few miles south of the farm. It was something that was done every year. And every year, Syeira went.

"Honestly, I had forgotten about it," she said, "with what was going on with Ander. Aelia, let us go. It is barely an hour ride. It will be fun. Although, I'm sure not nearly as extravagant as the ones in the city. And with the war, there have not been many merchants. But perhaps now, since it's over, there will be vendors from all over."

Ander grimaced at the prospect of facing the people he had known for the last eight years.

"Ander, I think it would be wise of you to go," Rian said. "Word of your true identity has probably already leaked out. With Kristofer and I there, it will confirm the rumors and allocate for an easier transition."

"So we will go?" Aelia clapped her hands with excitement.

"According to Rian." Kristofer lifted a brow.

Having no desire to spend the day at a fair, he was even less eager to argue with Aelia over it.

Within the hour, the horses were saddled, and Kristofer picked up the bow and situated it over his shoulder. As they reached the fairgrounds, Kristofer and Aelia dismounted as Asen began pawing the ground. Kristofer felt the hair raise on the back of his neck, and he looked at Rian, who felt it too. A young boy came over to take the horses, but Kristofer shook his head.

"Do not tether him," he said, and the boy paled at his sharp tone.

"What is it?" Aelia asked.

He shook his head, taking her hand.

Leaning close to Rian, he said, so only he could hear, "Keep Syeira near you. Something is wrong here."

Rian nodded. "I feel it, too."

Aelia pulled Kristofer along, admiring every merchants' wares. As she looked around, people stopped and stared at him. They reacted even more strongly when Rian appeared at his side.

"They have noticed us," Rian said.

Ander, keeping his gaze fixed on his wife and Aelia while they admired shawls, leaned close to his brother.

"Something is off. We should leave."

He watched Kristofer and Rian's hands move to the hilt of their sword. Without offering an explanation, Kristofer took Aelia's hand.

"Take Syeira and head back to Asen. Ride until you get to the farm."

"Syeira, come," Ander said. "Let's go back to the horses."

Before they took more than a few steps, Syeira was torn away from Ander by a man wearing a grisly mask. Hearing her scream, Rian and Kristofer turned quickly, drawing their swords. Ander grabbed a knife and threw the blade, catching the man in his thigh. He howled in agony, and Syeira ran to her husband.

In seconds, Kristofer, Rian, Ander, and the women were surrounded by eight men. The masks they wore distorted their mouths, creating a deranged O. It took Kristofer a moment to realize that the masks were made from the skins of others. They wore a dead faces.

"These are Kayne's followers," Kristofer snarled. "Show no mercy."

"You betrayed us," one of them hissed.

Kristofer smiled, a murderous gleam in his eye.

"Who leads you?" he said. "Come fight me."

When no one stepped forward, Kristofer focused his attention on their eyes, seeing where they looked for guidance. Twice, he noticed their gazes darting to his left.

With a savage cry, the group of masked men attacked them. A short, fierce battle raged on, separating Aelia and Syeira from the men. They ran, trying to put as much distance between themselves and the masked monsters.

"Get to the horses!" Aelia cried, grabbing a hold of Syeira's hand.

Together, they ran out the way they had come in. They reached the horses, and Aelia looked around for Asen. What she saw made her heart leap into her throat. A masked man was walking slowly over to her and Syeira. A gleaming sword was clutched in his hand.

"Run," Aelia whispered.

She turned, but felt a strong, unyielding arm wrap around her waist. Before she could cry out, his hand covered her mouth. A second masked man had come from behind the stables.

"I've got the woman," Aelia heard her captor say.

The other man raised his arm and hit Syeira across the face, knocking her back. She fell and did not get up. Aelia let out a strangled cry as Asen came galloping up and reared, kicking the soldier in the chest, killing him instantly.

Holding Aelia tight, the one soldier threw his sword at Asen, where it sunk deep into the animal's chest.

"No," Aelia whispered, tears blurring her vision.

Trying desperately to fight her attacker off, she couldn't take her eyes off the fallen horse or Syeira's unconscious body. He dragged her behind the stable and untethered a brown steed. Pulling Aelia up in front of him, he kept a firm hold on her while he kicked the horse into a run.

Hysterical and terrified, Aelia fought for all she was worth, finally causing the man to pull on the reigns. The horse stopped, and from a pouch on his side, he pulled a long rope and proceeded to tie Aelia's hands tightly together. Once he was through, and Aelia was immobilized, he kicked the horse again, urging it to go as fast as possible.

Kristofer, Rian, and Ander stood in a circle. The bodies of Kayne's fallen soldiers lay at their feet. After turning and not seeing the women, Rian grabbed Kristofer's shoulder.

"Where is Aelia and Syeira!"

Kristofer and Ander whirled around.

"The horses." Kristofer ran to the stable.

What he saw made his heart pound. Ander ran to Syeira and pulled her into his arms. A bloody nose and a bruised cheek were the worst of her injuries. Knowing that she was all right, Kristofer knelt next to Asen, confirming that he was dead. Anger surged through him.

"Rian, bring them home. I'm going after Aelia."

"Alone?" Ander said.

Kristofer studied the tracks left by Aelia's abductor.

"It is one rider."

Grabbing a horse from the stable, he leapt into the saddle and urged the animal to follow the rider's tracks. It did not take long for Kristofer to catch up. A horse carrying one rider was much faster than a horse bearing two people.

After pulling an arrow out of the quiver across his back, he nocked it and released it at the rider, where it landed between his shoulder blades. His lifeless body slid off the horse, and Aelia screamed. She was unable to grab the reigns because of her tied hands, and the horse kept running.

Kristofer brought his horse side by side to Aelia, and

leaned over to grab the reigns, and pulled. The horses stopped beside each other, and using his sword, Kristofer slashed through the rope that bound her hands. She collapsed into his arms, and he pulled her onto his horse, where she cried.

"I'm sorry, Kristofer." She sobbed. "Asen—"

"It's all right, Aelia. I know."

He held her tight, feeling as if a knife had stabbed him in the gut. Asen was no more. He'd had that horse for more than six years. To lose him now, after the battles and the war were over, seemed so unfair.

Insatiable anger surged through Kristofer, and he reeled the horse around. After galloping back to the stables, Kristofer dismounted to find a group of people, hunched over the body of his horse and the masked man. Keeping hold of Aelia, he pushed through the crowd and ripped the mask off. There was nothing spectacular or memorable about the face that lifelessly stared back.

He felt a hand on his shoulder, and turned to find Rian standing beside Ander and Syeira.

"We can bring Asen's body back," Rian said.

Nodding, Kristofer got to his feet.

"Find me a horse," he said to no one in particular.

One was quickly brought forth, while Rian made arrangements to have some of the villagers bring Asen back to the farm.

The ride there was quiet. Kristofer's dark mood left little room for any discussion.

When they reached the house, Terric came out with a smiling toddler. Seeing the distraught look on everyone's faces had little effect on Cas, but Terric was instantly sober.

"What has happened?"

Ander and Syeira went inside to explain the horrific events of the day. Rian saw to the horses, and Aelia went with him, leaving Kristofer alone. She pulled the saddle off the new horse and handed it to Rian, who took it wordlessly. He hung it up on a nail in the barn before turning to her and reaching for her hand. He lifted her arm carefully, looking at the red welts on her wrists. While his thumb grazed over the marks, anger coursed through him.

"What happened?" he said.

The unmistakable look of despair crossed over her face as she told Rian what she'd witnessed. She paused when she came to the part where Asen killed the masked man and then died for his efforts. A tear crept down her cheek.

"Kristofer is devastated over Asen's death," she said.

"I imagine." Rian sighed. "Let us go back to the house. Kristofer will return when he is ready."

It was well over an hour before Kristofer came back. Aelia and Syeira were sitting on the floor, playing with Cas, while Ander, Rian, and Terric watched in silence. When the door opened, Aelia stood up and walked over to Kristofer, who took a seat at the table. She sat down beside him and took his hand in hers. He grazed his fingers over the marks on her wrist, and she saw a muscle twitch in his jaw.

"How do you want to handle this?" Rian said.

Kristofer took a while to answer.

He finally lifted his gaze and looked at Ander. "I know I told you to take your time making your decision. You can still have the time you need, but I want you to take your family and go back East."

"So soon?" Syeira gasped.

"You can have tomorrow," Kristofer said, without feeling. "When the sun rises the day after, I want you all ready to leave."

Ander and Terric exchanged a look.

"It's not enough time, Kristofer," Ander said.

"I will leave tonight and head back to my city, where I will assemble an army."

Aelia gasped, but Kristofer ignored her. Rian looked shocked.

"You are angry, and you are not thinking this through." Rian sat down. "Kristofer, be reasonable."

"I have thought this through," Kristofer growled. "It is true. I am extremely displeased over Asen's death. He was a fine war horse, and he will be impossible to replace. But the bigger issue I see is that Kayne's supporters are rallying in this area. They will be difficult to bring down. I cannot have all of you here when a battle is imminent. Rian, take them back and keep them safe. My army will take very little time to prepare, and we can put a stop to this before it gets out of control."

"Kayne's supporters will be all over the nation, Kristofer," Rian said.

"All the more reason to crack down on them here and now. Aelia is a target. She's a means to get to me, and they are angry over my betrayal of Kayne."

"But they cannot defeat you," Aelia said. "Especially not with an army behind you."

Kristofer met her gaze. "No, they cannot defeat me. But they will take down what I love, as you saw today. Your body would have been strewn across the four quadrants, Aelia. This is a serious matter, and it needs to be rectified. I agreed to take the crown, and it is upon my honor to ensure this threat is alleviated."

Syeira, unable to bear the thought of leaving her home, got up and went outdoors. Ander watched her go, but Terric followed her out, leaving Cas with his father.

Rian stood, grinning as an idea came to him. He leaned forward, arms braced against the table to support his weight, and chuckled. With his amusement came Kristofer and Ander's immediate attention.

Kristofer raised a brow. "What could possibly amuse you?"

"Those who followed Kayne...there must be hundreds of them, yes?"

"More, I'd wager," Kristofer said.

Aelia reached over and placed her hand on his arm again, and he gave her a weak smile.

"This war is personal for them," Rian said. "They against you. Let us make it personal against them. I will bring Aelia and Syeira, Terric, and the child back to Rake's kingdom. I'll lead my army, and we'll have Ander lead Elora's. Let us fight side by side, Kristofer. Three armies will desiccate Kayne's followers."

"Even so," Aelia said, "you don't need that kind of force. They are not so many that thousands and thousands of soldiers must march upon them."

"This is true, love," Kristofer said, then all of a sudden laughed. "Rian, that is clever." He turned to Aelia. "The West despises me because I, essentially, destroyed their territory. If Rian leads the Western Army, and I lead the Southern, side by side, a lot of that animosity may diminish for a mutual cause. Kayne's supporters count on the West rebelling against me, which, even with Rian, is a possibility. That alone would mean that my men would have to defend themselves against the West, regardless of my personal affiliation with Rian. Do you understand?"

"I believe so." Aelia nodded. "If you do this, then the West and the South may avoid a war?"

"Precisely," Rian said. "Maybe some good will come out of today, after all."

"Let us hope," Kristofer muttered, then looked at Ander and studied him for a moment. "Can you do this?"

"I am not that well-versed in sword fighting."

"But you are excellent with a bow," Rian said.

Ander grimaced. "To bring meat to the table."

"You've never taken a life," Kristofer said.

"No," Ander replied. "And I won't. The two of you killed Kayne's men today. I can injure without remorse. But I cannot, in good conscious, kill."

Rian clenched his jaw, but Kristofer shrugged.

"It is of no consequence," he said. "My sister can lead her army. Your involvement would have merely been an introduction to the people. The West and the South can still join forces." He turned and whispered, "Rian, will you and Aelia give us a moment?"

Aelia stood and gave Rian a devilish grin. "I believe there are some baby lambs that need a feeding."

"Well, let us go warm some milk," Rian said, with mock enthusiasm.

Kristofer chuckled and watched them leave, before returning his attention to Ander.

"Sit." He gestured to the chair beside him.

Once Ander was seated, Kristofer inhaled deeply.

"Ander...I understand your lack of desire for the crown. Whether as prince or king, it matters little. However you choose to look at it, royal blood still flows through your veins."

Ander glared at Kristofer, but said nothing.

"You cannot give up your monarchial claim. I believe you know this, and I think that is what is holding you back. I wouldn't have broached the subject so soon. I would have given you some weeks. But in light of today's events, your decision is here on this table. You must choose now. Your son's life is at stake. Your life as farmer is over. The war is over—"

"But there are still very real threats," Ander said.

"Precisely! There are none fit to rule, other than what you see here. Rian, myself, my sister, and Rake. Other than that, Ander, you are all we have. I did not rescue you all those years past for you to abdicate your claim to the throne. I saved you so that if Rian fell, there would still be a chance for another king to rally against the South."

Ander met Kristofer's gaze. "I have thought of all of this already, Kristofer. What kind of king would I be having no background in governing?"

"You have twelve years of training. You have me and your brother. My sister will help you. We will guide you. You can rule underneath me until you feel comfortable. Your family will follow you. You will not lose here."

"I am young," Ander said.

"You are two years older than Rian was when he inherited not only a nation, but an entire army that he had to lead into war."

Ander sighed. "I am not my brother. How can I hold the lives of thousands of people in my hands? How can I reassure them? How can I lead them when I myself require leadership?"

"You are not looking at this in the proper context. We rule this land, Ander. All of us. You will not be alone any more than I or Rian are alone."

"Rian has Elora!" Ander's tone rose out of frustration. "She alone is fit to rule. And you have Aelia."

"Aelia has no political background," Kristofer said.

Ander looked startled. "But she offers advice, and she is beside you with your decisions."

"Of course she offers advice. And it is sound. She has no royal blood nor nobility of any kind. Aelia is a farmer's daughter who was nearly destroyed by the war. Her family was brutalized, and she barely survived. Where you come from does not matter. The only true value of life is what you choose to do with the time allotted to you."

"Aelia is so poised and regal," Ander said. I mean no disrespect, Kristofer, but how can you marry outside of your station? Won't that rally anti-supporters?"

"Of course it will. Not everyone at the same time will be happy. But what do I care? I am ruler of the South, with a massive army behind me. Let them say what they will of Aelia and me. You are in the same position with your wife. Nobody will care about her lack of royal blood if you and she prove yourselves. It is what Aelia has done, and I daresay it was far more difficult for her in Southern court than it ever will be for you in the North. Many of my military strategies, I have run by Aelia and have taken a great many of her advices under consideration. Some of which have been implemented. There will never be a good king without a good queen behind him, and you will have that, Ander."

Ander glared at Kristofer. "So you give me no choice?"

Kristofer looked at him calmly. "You have choices. Make the right one."

With that, he took his leave, going in search of Aelia and Rian. He found them over a hill, where Aelia was sitting with a baby lamb on her lap. It was eagerly drinking milk from a bottle she held.

Rian, sensing someone behind him, turned.

"I do not think you should leave tonight, Kristofer. Leave in the morning."

Kristofer nodded. He sighed and shook his head in disbelief at the day's events.

"I'm sorry about Asen," said Rian. "I know you were fond of your horse."

Kristofer had nothing to say. He watched Aelia pull the bottle out of the lamb's mouth and make her way over to them, with the baby lamb following behind her.

"Kristofer..." Pushing open the gate, she stood before him and placed her hands on his waist.

His hands rested on her shoulders, and he looked at her with skepticism.

"What is it, Aelia?"

"You are going back to the South tonight, and—"

"I'll leave in the morning," he said.

"Oh." She hesitated. "Well, that is even better. Please take me back with you?"

Kristofer looked at her in surprise. "Why?"

Rian raised a brow.

"I want to go home," she replied. "The war is over, and your army is there. It is safe! Please?"

Both men looked at her as she pleaded with Kristofer with wide eyes.

"Please?" she begged.

When he would have spoken she cut him off.

"I will stay in the castle," she spoke quickly, eager to convince him. "You can station your guards where you see fit, and I won't fight you on it. I don't want to go back to Rake's kingdom. I will do anything, please?"

Kristofer glanced at Rian, who shrugged with equal confusion. Wanting to give them a moment, Rian pushed himself off the fence and walked away.

Kristofer nudged her chin up, his eyes searching hers.

"Why are you suddenly so adamant against going East?"

Aelia bit her lip. "It is not sudden. I've never wanted to be there, but I understood your reasoning before the battle. And afterward, you needed to recover, and you were with me. But I cannot bear the thought of being there without you. Every time Rake's soldiers pass me, I wonder if it...if...if it was he who..." She struggled for words. "Please? I just want to go home."

"Why did you not come to me sooner?" Kristofer said.

"Why would I? You have matters to attend to. But this is an opportunity to go home, and I want to go."

"All right," he said.

Aelia was taken aback. "Really?"

"If that is what you want, I see no reason why not to

accommodate you. We'll leave in the morning."

Relief washed over Aelia so strongly that she leaned against the fence for support.

Kristofer leaned against the fence and looked out into the fields, deep in thought.

"Perhaps..." He turned to Aelia. "Let us find Rian. I think it would be better if, instead of going East, Ander and Rian rode South."

"For what purpose? Won't the people disapprove of Rian?"

Kristofer shook his head. "Not in any great magnitude. Do not forget that Rian lifted his sword in defense of my life against Kayne. If Rian had not joined in, along with the others who helped, I would not be here. Kayne was not popular. His death is of no great loss to the people."

"You'll also need a good horse," Aelia said.

Kristofer grimaced.

"I know how much you loved Asen," she said. "Do you want to talk about it?"

"Not particularly," Kristofer muttered. "I will take a temporary steed until I can find a colt I can break from infancy. I'll train a horse myself."

"Ander mentioned a horse breeder not far from here," she said. "Perhaps on the way home, we can stop there."

"The sooner the better," Kristofer said. "Let us find Rian and Ander."

They went in search of the brothers, only to find them deep in conversation with Syeira and Terric. Cas was busy entertaining himself with a pile of dirt and his wooden toys. As Kristofer walked over to them, Syeira eyed him warily.

"Do not look at me like that, Syeira," Kristofer said, his voice soft. "I do not ask you to leave here because I'd like to see you all suffer in a different territory. If Kayne's followers are here, then they are all over. We must dispatch a messenger informing Elora and Rake that they have struck, and to prepare to ride."

"Why dispatch a messenger when we ride there in less than two days?" Rian said.

Kristofer grinned. "Ride South with me. Have Elora and Rake meet us with their armies. Syeira, Terric, and the child will be safe in my kingdom. It is much closer than us riding back East and then riding South."

Kristofer looked at him, waiting for his response. Rian thought for a few minutes, before nodding in agreement.

It did make sense. The Western, Eastern, and Northern armies were all situated in the East. With Elora and Rake to lead them, they could merge those armies with the Southern Army, creating an impenetrable force of strength that could destroy any threat.

"You can announce an alliance with me and the West," Rian said. "Most of your soldiers saw us fight together against Kayne. That will alleviate one problem. What of Elora? Will she be received honorably?"

"She is my sister. She will be treated as such."

"But you tried to have her publicly executed, and it was not so long ago."

"Different times will call for different measures. If we all align ourselves as allies right away, Elora, you, myself, and Rake can undoubtably rule together, peacefully. I'd also like to take down the anti-cross border law. Many people have family and friends in different territories. Let them reconcile."

"I was going to suggest that," Rian said. "I'm fine with this plan. Ander?"

He turned to his brother, who nodded.

"If you think it is best." Ander wrapped his arm around Syeira's waist.

"Also, Ander, I would like you to train with me or your

brother concerning sword fighting. Rian said you know how to fight. It is just a matter of remembering technique."

"That is correct." Ander took a deep breath and looked at his brother, and then at Kristofer. "Kristofer, concerning our conversation earlier..."

Kristofer gave a curt nod and waited for him to finish.

"I will do as you say. Also, before I—"

"Do you wish to go West before you go North?" Kristofer said.

Surprised, Ander nodded. "Yes. I would like to spend a couple of months there."

"That is fine," Kristofer said. "I figured you would." Thinking of Aelia's words, he said, "Ander, Aelia told me you know of a horse breeder?"

"Yes. They are friends of ours. Maybe a league past where we were today."

"We'll stop there tomorrow." Kristofer cringed at the thought of riding another horse.

"I made arrangements for the villagers to bring Asen here," Rian said. "We will find you another horse, Kristofer. Perhaps it would be easier to begin searching where you found him."

Kristofer laughed. "I did not find him. Aelia did. Nor was it under the best of circumstances," He eyed her.

Aelia grinned sheepishly at him, but she noticed movement behind him and frowned.

"Kristofer, look." She pointed.

"That is a very large group." Rian tensed.

Kristofer eyed them with apprehension.

"It is not an angry mob," he said. "They seem peaceful."

"It is still a lot of people," Rian said. "What do they want?"

"Let us find out," Kristofer replied. "Aelia, stay here with Syeira. If blood is drawn for whatever reason, take Cas and hide."

Aelia nodded while Kristofer and Rian went to address the crowd of people. They watched as a man stepped forward and began speaking to them. A minute later, the man bowed, and Kristofer and Rian returned.

"They've brought Asen's body here," Kristofer said. "And they've come to pledge their loyalty to me as the Southern king. Apparently, our behavior toward those rebels did not go unnoticed, and they wanted to thank us personally for our services."

Syeira and Aelia exchanged a look of relief. Aelia took hold of Kristofer's hand and pulled him toward the people.

"Let us put Asen to rest," she said. "I will personally take it upon myself to find you another horse, my love."

Kristofer raised a brow. "Do not dare."

She ignored him and smiled, pulling him along.

The people took it upon themselves to build a large pyre. Kristofer's horse was laid in a wagon, and they pulled his body off of it and laid it onto the pyre. The wood was lit, and Kristofer stood back silently and watched the flames burn higher and higher.

"It's hard to believe I won't ride him home tomorrow," he said to Aelia. "It's also shocking to think I'm this upset over a horse." He smiled lightly.

Aelia gave him a weak but reassuring smile. She, too, loved Asen, and he died defending her. A tear crept down her cheek.

As the flames burnt low, the crowd of people left one by one. Kristofer and Rian watched them go as Aelia and Syeira, holding Cas, went inside.

"The people do seem to adore you," Ander said to Kristofer.

"It is the price received for keeping them fed throughout the war."

Rian looked at his brother and grinned. "Compassion goes a long way, Ander. Your people are anxious to love you. All you need to do is provide reasons."

Ander nodded. "I will strive for it." He returned Rian's smile. "Syeira is struggling with the departure. I will be with her tonight."

Rian clapped Kristofer on the shoulder before following his brother inside.

Kristofer stayed by the fire for a long time, watching the flames die completely, until all that was left were dancing orange embers.

"Kristofer?"

Aelia's voice carried through the night air, and he turned around.

"Come inside. The hour grows late."

"I have no desire to go in." He returned his gaze to the remnants of Asen's pyre.

Aelia came up behind him and wrapped her arms around his waist. Tomorrow, they would ride for the castle. Ride for home. Aelia could scarcely wait, after being gone for so long.

The weather was warm, and the castle would be even warmer. The strawberries would be ready. She was eager for tomorrow.

CHAPTER 33

The sun's rays rose like long arms to greet the surface of the earth. Pink and orange streaked across the morning sky. The warmth of the breeze blew Aelia's hair from her shoulder, and she smiled at the day, happy to be going home. Kristofer saddled one of Terric's horses as he watched Aelia lean against the fencing, gazing at the horizon. Rian and Ander were on the other side of the stable, laughing as they packed Cas's bag onto a spare horse.

Syeira walked in, her dark hair falling in waves down her back. She met Kristofer's gaze and gave him a warm smile, which he returned before setting his sights back on the task. Once the saddle bags were packed and everyone was mounted on a horse, they rode away from the farm. Syeira rode her mare while Cas sat in front of his father on a chestnut stallion. As the miles passed, Ander and Syeira lost themselves in conversation. To Kristofer and Rian, it was obvious they were upset.

Finally Ander turned to his brother. "Along the crest of the next hill are friends. This family I grew up with. It is they we will ask to take care of the animals we left behind."

Heart pounding, Ander glanced at the pond they use to swim in as children. He and Syeira were swimming just a few weeks ago with Avram and his wife, Calla. After Kristofer left Ander in the South, Terric had introduced Avram and Ander. They were the same age, and quickly became friends. Terric knew Ander needed someone he could relate to, and in some small way, Ander equated Avram with Arius.

As the cottage came into view, Syeira smiled encouragingly at her husband. He handed Cas to his mother and dismounted. A young woman in the late stages of her pregnancy was carrying a basket filled with corn. At the sound of the approaching horses, she looked up, shielding her eyes from the sun.

Seeing Ander walking toward her, she froze and darted her gaze around. Unsure of what to do, she bowed awkwardly, her pregnancy making it almost impossible.

"Ja-uhm-lord," she stuttered.

Ander turned to his brother for help, but it was Syeira who gave Cas to Rian and walked up to them.

"Calla." Syeira threw her arms around the woman's neck.

Calla hesitated before returning the hug eagerly. When they pulled apart, Ander saw tears in Syeira's eyes, which she wiped away quickly.

"Where is Avram?" she said.

"In the hay field," Calla replied. Unsure of how to act, she looked nervously at the rest of the group. "He's been there since dawn. He should be returning any moment."

As if on cue, a man rounded the side of the house and came face to face with Ander. He was tall, almost as tall as Ander, with strawberry blond hair and a blond beard streaked with red. His cotton shirt was soaked, and beads of sweat dripped off his forehead. His gaze locked with Ander's, and for a moment no one said anything.

Kristofer watched the ongoings with amusement, even smiling when Aelia craned her neck to get a better look. Finally, the man bowed before taking a step back. The uncomfortable silence grew until Cas uttered a cry of delight and demanded to be put down. He ran to Avram, who hesitated as the child pawed at his legs.

"He is still your godson," Ander said, his tone stiff.

With that, Avram bent over and lifted Cas into his arms. Cas squirmed and pointed to Calla's stomach.

"Baby!"

Kristofer's laughter diffused the situation. He climbed off of his horse and made his way to stand before Avram and Calla.

"By the Gods..." Avram whispered. "Kristofer."

Calla gasped as they bowed. Amused, Kristofer waited for Rian to come up beside him.

"My brother, Rian." Ander looked at him, and Rian clapped him on the shoulder.

"Forgive us," Avram said. "This is most unexpected. Please, come inside."

Calla led Ander and Syeira inside as Aelia hopped off the horse before Kristofer could assist her.

Terric embraced Avram. "Do not judge him too harshly. He did what he had to do to survive."

With a nod, Avram said, "I will be in in a moment."

Once everyone was seated, Calla busied herself by offering freshly baked bread smeared with honey, to which Cas was only too eager to accept. Seating himself on Terric's lap, the little boy licked the honey off of the bread while Calla took a seat on a rocking chair beside Syeira.

After splashing water on his face and arms, Avram came in, his gaze never leaving Ander.

"What can we do for you?" he said with respect.

He watched his wife and Syeira look at one another. Syeira looked distraught, and Calla ran her fingers through her friends hair. Syeira smiled weakly and reached to clasp Calla's hand.

Kristofer replied, "Ander's identity is no longer a secret. Especially after the events of yesterday. As a prince, his duties now lie elsewhere. I imagine this is uncomfortable for everyone. But most of all, for Ander. His farm will need tending. The animals most of all, until other arrangements can be made. I will send men here once I return to my city."

With a frown, Avram said, "You wish us to tend to your livestock?"

Ander nodded.

"Of course!" Avram said, sounding surprised, almost relieved.

Syeira stood quickly, covering her mouth, and ran from the room. Feeling a tremendous sense of guilt, Ander sighed.

"Calla," Avram said. "Go speak with her."

Calla stood slowly, hand upon her stomach, and left the room. Avram watched her leave, before turning his attention to Ander again.

"Solan and Stefan will help. Do not worry about the farm. We will see to it."

Ander nodded gratefully, but Rian saw the struggle he faced.

"I know I have no right to ask this, but where will you go from here, Ja-lord?" Avram caught himself and cleared his throat. "Will Calla lose Syeira?"

Unsure of what to say, and realizing that neither Rian or Kristofer would help him here, Ander walked to the window and looked out. He saw Syeira, her face buried in her hands, and Calla hugging her out of comfort.

"Lords," Ander turned to his brother and Kristofer, "I need time alone with Avram."

Rian nodded.

Aelia turned her head to glance at the window. Seeing Ander and Avram hug their wives, she felt a sense of sadness for them. She remembered the loss she felt after her family died—the friends she never saw again. If not for Kristofer, she wasn't sure how she would have survived. As it was, it took the better part of a year for her to trust him, but he was patient with her.

She reached for his hand and squeezed it.

Terric set Cas down on the floor and watched as the child helped himself to another piece of honey bread.

"This must be hard for you," the old man said to Rian.

Rian looked up in surprise. "What makes you say that?"

"I see the way you look at your brother. You love him, and yet he struggles terribly over all of this. You feel guilty."

Rian snorted and stood.

Kristofer rose beside him. "You could not have protected him all those years ago, Rian. You would have died if you had been there."

"Probably. The twins dying haunted me more than any other part of the war. More than you leaving. More than my parents dying. Even more than my kingdom falling into Southern hands. That I could not protect the boys was the most unbearable thought. And then to find out Ander lives! To see him and hold him again..." With a sigh, he looked out the window. "I know Ander loves me, but he is not the brother I lost—""

"He will be far better," Kristofer said. "Far more compassionate and understanding, having lived as he has. He is young still, and he has lost as much as you. Perhaps more so, for you escaped witnessing Arius's death. He watched his brother die, his home burn. It is not so that he grew up here, but that he rode away from all he knew, dressed like the men that killed his family. He would not have been the same boy you knew, even if you got to him the next day. Give him your love, Rian. He will come out of this far better. Nor does he need to lose those he loves. It is unorthodox, aye. But if these people mean so much to him, there is no reason why he must separate himself from them entirely."

"But the distance..." Aeila said.

"We do not know what they discuss outside," Kristofer said. "If Ander and Syeira entrusted the well-being of their son to Calla and Avram, then it is obvious that they are family. Let Ander come up with a solution. He will."

Rian pinched the bridge of his nose as he watched Ander cup Syeira's face. He could see, even at the distance, how distraught his sister-in-law was. He could see the tears and how her shoulders shook with the force of her emotion.

Terric leaned forward to wipe a crumb off Cas's little face. Smiling at the boy who looked so much like his father, Terric picked him up and placed him on his lap. Cas yawned and rubbed his eyes.

Terric kept his gaze focused on his grandson, smiling again when he leaned back and rested his head against his shoulder. Terric thought about the first few months after his wife and son were killed—the anguish, the despair, and the hopelessness he felt. Those feelings diminished the day Ander came into his life. A child as troubled as he was, gave Terric something to strive for. He was determined to help Ander through the trauma he held onto—the family he knew Ander had lost.

Terric shifted Cas to a more comfortable position. "When Kristofer brought Ander to me, he did not talk to me for months. Loud noise would cause him to jump out of fear, and he woke in the night, calling out. He often called your name, Rian. And it was this that made me suspect who he was. His pain mirrored my own. And then one night, after months and months, after I thought all was hopeless, he came outside and watched as I built a fire in the backyard. I asked him if he wanted to learn how to build one. 'I can build one,' he said. It was the first time he spoke to me, and from there he began to trust me. I never asked him where he came from, for I felt that if he wanted me to know, that he would share. He has come so far...so far." He turned his head and watched them through the window for a moment. "He will make an excellent king."

Hours later, Ander came back inside. He took a seat in the wooden rocking chair closest to Rian.

"Avram and a few others will tend to the farm so that needn't be an issue we must contend with." He sighed and rubbed a hand over his face. To Rian, he said, "I told Syeira we would return here as often as we could. She and Calla have been together since infancy."

Syeira, Calla, and Avram came back in. No trace of Syeira's tears remained, other than slightly red eyes.

To Syeira, Rian said, "My brother tells me you will return here often?"

Apprehension crossed Syeira's face, and she nodded with a glance to her husband.

"I will make sure it happens, Syeira," Rian said.

Shock registered on Ander's face as he turned to face Rian. Before he could utter a word, Syeira flung her arms around Rian's neck and began crying all over again.

Kristofer said, "I understand that this is your home, Syeira. And neither Rian nor myself wish to see you so unhappy. I believe, between my sister, Rian, and myself, that you can return as often as you wish."

Calla let out a cry of delight, and even Avram smiled.

"The hour grows late. Will you sup with us?" Avram asked Ander.

Ander hesitated before Kristofer accepted the offer.

"Your hospitality is appreciated."

Syeira, Calla, and Aelia, went into the kitchen to prepare food. The men sat in the living room, talking. Avram spoke of Ander's time in the South, regaling Rian with tales of his upbringing.

They ate outside as Cas ran around, and Rian watched much of Ander's tension disappear.

As the sun began to set in the western sky, Kristofer caught Rian's eye. With a grin, Kristofer's hand went to the hilt of his sword.

Rian smirked. "No one can match your blade, Kristofer."

"No one can match yours," Kristofer replied, the grin still etched upon his handsome face.

"Arius and I used to love this," Ander said to Syeira. "Kristofer taught Rian how to sword fight, and then they would often duel after supper."

Rian stood slowly and faced Kristofer. Their swords met with such force that it echoed over the hills. Avram watched with fascination as each man parried blow after blow. Rian raised his sword over his head and caught Kristofer's blade before it could slice through his back.

Horrified, Syeira said, "Is this not dangerous?"

"They will not hurt one another." Aelia smiled. "I have often watched Kristofer train with his men. Although, I do not think any of his soldiers were as skilled with a sword as Rian is."

Cas, who was sleeping peacefully in his mother's arms, did not so much as stir from the clangs of metal against metal. Rian wrapped his sword arm around Kristofer's and pulled him close.

"I don't believe you're fighting at your full potential!" Kristofer shoved him back, laughing, and lowered his weapon.

Rian flashed a wicked grin.

"You've learned new techniques." Kristofer sheathed his blade.

"A few things over the years."

With a grin, Rian and Kristofer sat down as the sun cast red and golden rays across the sky.

CHAPTER 34

I t did not take long to pack up their saddle bags. It was the parting that delayed them and took hours. Tearful goodbyes, long hugs, and promises to return took the better part of the morning.

Kristofer dispatched one of the locals to the East, ensuring all haste was made, and that his letter would be placed in no one's hands except Elora's or Rake's.

Ander led them to the horse breeder, but Kristofer was dissatisfied with the animals.

As they made their way to the Southern Kingdom, people came out of their homes to bow or to offer food. Kristofer declined for want of reaching the castle sooner. It would take the better part of several weeks to reach the White City, and none of them were as eager as Aelia to be home. With every mile that passed, she grew more excited. If she were not so focused on reaching the White Gates, Aelia would have enjoyed the journey.

With Kristofer behind her, she could hear his laughter. He bantered with Rian, and even went so far as to conjure up new ideas on how best to torment his sister.

Syeira was more subdued, but she did her best to appear happy for her husband's sake. Ander worried that the trek would take a great toll on Terric, but the old man seemed to be enjoying himself immensely.

"It makes me feel young again, son!" he would say every

time Ander asked how he was feeling.

Cas needed more frequent stops. He needed to run and release energy, but the longer Aelia spent with the child, the more she grew to love him. His endearing ways and wooden toys provided entertainment, and when they would camp for the night, Ander would take out a piece of wood and begin carving another animal. Cas delighted in watching his father, and his excitement provided a light air.

On the morning of the sixteenth day, Aelia began to recognize sights. It would still be another week or so worth of travel but her excitement grew by the day. Nine days later Kristofer announced that they would be home by sunset.

"We will be home before the sun sets," Kristofer said in her ear.

As the towers rose into view, Aelia breathed a sigh of relief. The drawbridge was lowered, and the soldiers rushed about. Cries of, "Kristofer is home!" sounded in every direction. They rode through the courtyard and found themselves safely inside.

Syeira looked around in awe at the tapestries that hung on the wall, and the rugs made of wool. Vases of flowers every few feet added a pleasant, inviting smell. Servants bustled about, eager to accommodate, and Syeira was given a maid.

Her and Ander's chambers were readied in a short time, and a stout woman, her hair pulled back into a tight bun at the nape of her neck, eagerly escorted them to their room.

Rian, exhausted, followed two servants to his quarters, while Aelia raced up the stairs to her room. Kristofer closed the door quietly as Aelia threw herself down on her bed. Her happy, contented face made him smile, and before long, a steaming bath and plenty of food was brought.

Aelia sank into the tub after choosing a rose oil to add to the water. She washed her hair—a hard task, for its length and thickness made it so. Once she was done, the water was dumped and clean water was added so Kristofer could bathe.

After dressing in a simple blue dress, Aelia propped a pillow underneath her and laid on her stomach, watching Kristofer.

"It is so nice to be home," she said. "But I wonder what will you do with all of Kayne's concoctions?"

Kristofer leaned his head against the rim of the tub.

"I've spoken with Abignale. He will come here and sort through everything. I imagine the rest will be destroyed."

"And how do you feel to be home?" Aelia said.

Kristofer lifted his head to look at her, before resting it back on the rim of the tub. He was silent for a long while, staring absentmindedly at the tapestry on the wall. Aelia waited for him to speak, her brows drawn together in confusion at his silence.

Finally, "I feel trapped, Aelia. Chained. As if I were still in Rake's torture chamber."

Aelia pushed herself up. "Why? You do not wish to be king?"

He shook his head and stood. Water glistened on his body as he grabbed a towel and dried his face before wrapping it around his waist. He stepped out of the water and took a seat on the chair beside the table.

Aelia ventured with caution. "I understand you wish for your freedom, but what could be more liberating than destroying Kayne and taking the crown? The world bends to your whim, Kristofer. There is no one more powerful or more skilled than you. You are cherished by every man, woman, and child you come in contact with. You have Elora and Rian back. You will be a father. What more do you seek?"

It had been weighing on him for quite some time, and he was loath to share it with Aelia for fear of what she would think. Would she think him weak? A coward? Would she be angry? Hurt?

Gently, as if talking to an injured child, she said, "Talk to me, my love."

Aelia watched a muscle twitch in his jaw. In a voice tense with control, he stood and paced.

"When Rian and Abignale defeated me, I fought well. Do not think I did not. I had accepted my defeat and my death as easily as one accepting the weather. I looked forward to death, if at the time I could die, which, I believed I could with enough blood loss. I welcomed the pain because I knew it would be over soon. I was weak." Sorrow laced his handsome features, and he turned his back to her. "I made arrangements for Raum to keep you safe, but inevitably, Aelia, I would have left you, and I was eager for it. I wanted it over."

She nodded and found herself smiling. "That is what makes you human, Kristofer. It is what separates you from an abomination like Kayne. It is not a weakness that you indulged, but a life hardly worth living. You lost your home, your family, your friends." She stood to wrap her thin arms around his waist, her cheek resting against his back. "And whereas you had me, Raum, and your men even, I imagine losing your sister and Rian, especially now that I see how you are with them, would be an unbearable torture."

He unlocked her arms and turned to face her.

"How awful it must have been." She again took a seat on the edge of the bed. "And my sympathies are for your struggle, but—"

He waved his hand. "But I was born to privilege."

"You were born to kill Kayne. And you have fulfilled your duty. If you told Rian and Elora what you have told me, they would not, I assure you, think less of you. If you believe that wishing for death after Kayne and Rake tortured you, after you lost all that you did, would make you a weak ruler, you are stupid." She shrugged with the simplicity of her statement.

"You, more than anyone else, need to put the war behind you. I will help you in any way that I can, but do not forget that you have what you lost—Rian and Elora. They would do anything for you."

"You do not think less of me for it?" he said.

Compassion filled her eyes, and with a shake of her head and a light smile, she patted the bed beside her. Once he seated himself, she pushed him on his back and leaned over, her hair creating a curtain around him.

"I wanted desperately to die after my home was destroyed," she said. "Even after you brought me here. I did not want it. I did not want you. But look now how things have turned out. I can assure you Rian has faltered during the war in some way. Elora, too." She shrugged again. "Maybe, perhaps, Abignale has not, but he's the only one. And he's had many years to perfect the art of not wishing for death."

Kristofer felt a grin spreading across his face, which turned into long-winded laughter. Aelia laid her wet head on his shoulder, her finger traced the hard lines of his chest.

"I'm so proud of you," she said. "Never feel less than what you are."

She felt him nod.

"You know, Aelia, I do believe you'll make a fine queen."

"Of course I will!" She lifted her head and kissed him.

A kiss he returned with ardor, for at that moment, there was only her.

CHAPTER 35

I t was over two months later when Elora arrived in the South with her army. Kristofer had men posted on the tallest tower, and they notified him of the approaching army. While her soldiers made camp on the outskirts of the city, she ran into the castle and into Rian's arms.

"It took you long enough," Kristofer said.

Elora looked around the magnificence of the rooms, remembering her first time in the castle.

"Have you any idea, dear brother, how much work is involved in assembling an army in a matter of weeks? I thought it could not be done. Your messenger arrived a few weeks after you sent him. I've had barely a month to ensure my army was at its full potential. Not to mention, Rian's army is marching here as we speak. Rake and Olibia should be here in the next day or two."

"No other woman could handle two armies, Elora," Kristofer said. "It must be because you're my sister."

Aelia hugged Elora tight and rolled her eyes at the men. She had been watching Kristofer improve dramatically in the last weeks. His hesitation disappeared entirely, and if it was possible, their conversation seemed to have brought them even closer together.

Kristofer grinned at his sister, and Rian shoved him playfully, his arm still around Elora's shoulders.

"Elora, ignore your brother. He is uncontrollable at times. Meet my sister-in-law, Syeira."

Elora turned, one arm still around Rian's waist, to study the woman before her. Syeira bowed her head before Elora as Ander came up beside her.

"Syeira." Elora released Rian and hugged the woman tight. "It is wonderful to meet you."

"The honor is mine," Syeira whispered.

Ander put his arm around her shoulders and smiled warmly at Elora.

The doors opened again, and Raum came in, pulling his scabbard over his head. Seeing the group in front of him gave him pause, and he bowed quickly.

Kristofer laughed. "A sight you never thought you'd see in the South?"

Raum stared at him for a moment. "A sight I never thought I'd see anywhere. It is good to be home."

Kristofer grinned and clasped his forearm. "Settle yourself, then return to hall. We are most eager to hear of what you learned."

Raum grimaced. "It was not all good, Lord."

"And a few minutes of waiting won't turn the tides in either direction."

With a nod of his head, Raum departed. And after a bath and food, he returned to the meeting room and leaned over the long wooden table. Kristofer's map lay open, and Raum jabbed a finger in a southernmost region—a village called Rall.

"This, Lord, is where Kayne's supporters are congregating."

Kristofer examined the map. "I've had trouble with those villages before. Those in the deep South are superstitious. They have strange customs. An uprising there led me away when Aelia was taken."

Elora and Rian studied the map.

"That wasn't so long ago, brother." With her finger, she traced the village further down to waves of blue. "Rall is a coastal area?"

Raum nodded. "Aye, the sea is an outlet if you're willing to go deeper into the South. It is uncharted, and there is underpass of rock two hundred miles long that leads to the coast. Entire ships and thousands of men have entered that pass and were never seen again."

"You lost men in the deep South?" Rian raised a brow.

"Nay," Kristofer murmured, his gaze never leaving the map. "I've never sent my army through that pass for that very reason. Thanos lost eighty of his best war ships when Kayne became a threat. My father could not coach me on much concerning this area, as no one has any insight on it. These people keep to themselves, and their ways are strange. What I do know comes from traveling there, but I've never seen any indication of groups supporting Kayne—"

"They wouldn't have hid from you at the time, would they?" Aelia said. "You were closest to Kayne. Would they not have rallied to join you?"

"Probably not," Rian said. "If they are as ritualistic with their customs as Kristofer says, they would not leave the area or make themselves known until the need arose. Kristofer killing Kayne brought them out of their seclusion. They will fan out, I'm sure, and wreak havoc in all four territories."

"And that is precisely what we must avoid," Kristofer said. "Elora's army is already here. Rake and Rian's will be here any day. If Rake attacks from the Eastern side, and I lead my army straight on, Rian and Elora can attack from the Western point. Assuming, of course, they have not left the area."

Raum shook his head and took a seat beside Aelia.

"They have not," he said. "The attack at the fair was due to Ander. They wanted to kill him off before he became a greater threat. I do not think they realized you and Rian were already there. It was a fatal mistake on their part. They will be much more cautious now."

Elora watched Syeira swallow hard and glance at her husband. Her nervousness was not lost upon Kristofer either.

"If it consoles you at all, Syeira," he said, "they care more for my head than Ander's. He will not be a target, so long as I am around."

"How reassuring, brother," Elora snapped.

"It is the truth, Elora," Rian said. "Kristofer will undoubtably be their target. I believe Rall might be Kayne's birthplace. It is my guess that he has blood relatives there, and it is they who are so angry."

Kristofer nodded his agreement. "Well, we cannot solve all of this in one day. I believe the idea to march from all three sides is a good one. We'll need to strategize, but it does not have to be done at this moment. We still need Rake, and I daresay Abignale would be an asset. Elora, you must be tired. Retire. We will continue this later."

Elora shook her head. "I'm all right, Kristofer. If we are through here, I do wish to explore the castle. Last time I was here, I did not see much of it."

Kristofer threw her a disgruntled look, and she gave him a sweet smile.

Aelia leaned over and whispered something to Elora, who nodded vigorously.

"Syeira, come with us," Elora stood. "We will walk!"

The women departed, and Kristofer looked at Rian and Ander.

"Aelia plans something." He grinned. "Rian, we still have a few good years left."

Rian laughed. "Shall we show Elora just how young we can be?"

Ander got up. "I want no part of this."

With that, he took his leave, and Kristofer and Rian followed him out. Ander took the stairwell to his chambers, but Rian and Kristofer headed out onto the balcony that overlooked the back of the castle. The moment they did this, a sheet of water rained down from above, soaking them both. Through Aelia's peels of laughter, Kristofer looked at Rian, and they both bolted back inside.

Elora held her sides as she doubled over laughing.

"I believe any retaliation I receive will be worth it!"

"Is that so, little sister?" Kristofer stood behind them with his arms folded, just as Rian came from the other side.

"How did you get here so fast?" Elora gasped.

But the sight of them dripping wet incited another bout of laughter. Syeira, too, joined in, and Rian grinned at her.

"Syeira is the one who dumped the water!" Elora cried, as Rian advanced on her.

"Aye," Syeira said. "But I believe I hear my son calling me!"

She dodged Rian and ran up the stairs to find Ander. Their games lightened her mood and made her feel as if she belonged.

"Aelia, my love, what have you to say?" Kristofer took a step toward her.

"Why, tis all Elora's idea. Surely you would not think I would do something such as this." She gestured to their wet clothes.

With a smile, she stood her ground as Kristofer walked over to her. She leaned against the balcony behind her until he stood an inch from her. Taking the pie that she hid from him on the ledge, she threw it and it hit him right in the face.

Rian and Elora roared with laughter as Kristofer grabbed her. He held her tight and rubbed his cheek against hers.

"Kris—" Through her laughter, she could not form a coherent sentence. "I will...stop it! I will be all sticky!"

"You'll be sticky!" Kristofer cried in disbelief.

Using his forearm, he wiped the remains of the pie off of his face.

Elora shrieked as Rian locked his arms around her. Rian whispered something only she could hear, and Kristofer grinned as her amused look turned to horror.

"You would not dare!"

Whatever he said to her was lost upon them as she grabbed his arm, and using an elbow, caught him unaware in the stomach. Placing a foot on the balcony, she kicked off using Rian's shoulders as a hold and flipped nimbly over him, landing on her feet. With a grin at Rian's shocked face, she ran away.

"Well, she certainly is your sister," Rian said before racing after her.

"I want to learn to do that," Aelia whined, using the hem of her gown to clean the pie off of her face.

Kristofer laughed. "I feel bad for my sister. Rian will no doubt come up with some way to get her back."

As they walked to their chambers, Aelia said, "I thought you were the mastermind behind these childish games."

"Oh, aye. But Rian has certainly come up with excellent retributions, all of which were to torture my sister."

The weeks passed. The armies arrived, and Rake and Olibia settled in, both seeming to love the heat of the South. For Kristofer, the time was laden with laughter and practical jokes. The threat of the deep South was still there, but he had his family. Aelia's thickening waist was a constant reminder of the child they would soon meet.

It was over supper on a day riddled with practical jokes that even Ander and Syeira had joined in for, that Kristofer brought up the topic of marriage.

"As events in the deep South continue to negate our plans in the East," he said, "I believe a wedding here would be just as beneficial."

Rake and Olibia nodded in agreement.

Rake said, "Eradicate Kayne's followers and wed thereafter. We will march upon them in a week's time. It shouldn't take more than another week to destroy them."

Aelia smiled warmly at Elora.

"I cannot plan a wedding," Elora said.

"We can!" said Syeira.

Olibia nodded with eagerness. "'Tis true. Elora, worry not about it. We will make preparations while you march your armies into the deep South."

And so it was settled as Rake, Kristofer, Rian, Ander, and Elora all prepared for battle. Ander's hesitation required constant reminding and reassuring, but with his brother and their friends behind him, his fear disappeared, replaced by a determination to sanctify the nation.

As they rode into the deep South, unified and as one, to eradicate any remnants of Kayne and his followers, the uneasiness of the soldiers from the different territories began to lift. There was hostility that was quickly rectified by both Kristofer and Rian, but overall, the territories united.

It was as Rake said—it took hours to destroy Kayne's followers. Kristofer ordered the armies to show no mercy against them, and none was shown. The fight was quick, and with so many against Kayne's followers, it was not much of a battle. Once the last enemy had fallen, Kristofer ordered their bodies burned. The armies pulled out and marched home. It was that simple.

As the White Castle came into view, Kristofer felt a rush of relief to be home. With Kayne's followers destroyed, he felt as though the war was really over. There was no lurking danger that he could surmise. He felt a sense of freedom that he had not felt since before his father started training him.

As the drawbridge was lowered, he and Elora, Rian, Rake, and Ander rode into the courtyard. The doors opened, and Aelia ran out to greet him. He wrapped his arm around her waist and he kissed her hard. Her eyes sparkled with happiness, and when he set her down, she hugged Rian and Elora.

Ander got off his horse as his wife threw herself into his arms. They made their way inside and found Cas racing toward his father, who swept him up. Syeira, who adamantly refused a nursemaid, smiled as Terric made his way toward them. Rian watched Ander set his son down to hug the man who had raised him. They parted at the doors, each heading toward their chambers.

Aelia's hand never left Kristofer's arm. "I know you are tired, my love, but I have something to show you."

She smiled at his quizzical look, but no matter how much he prodded her, she would not answer his questions. She led him outside, where they walked to an enclosed pasture behind the stables. Kristofer peered over her head as she stopped near the gate of the fence. A young black horse was trotting nervously in the pen, and she felt his hands come to rest on her shoulders.

"He looks just like Asen," Kristofer said.

Aelia smiled. "He was sired by Asen."

Kristofer drew his brows together in confusion, and he opened the gate to step inside. The horse watched him with apprehension, but Kristofer was patient, and soon enough, the animal nuzzled his hand.

"How can you be sure?" he replied.

Aelia closed the gate behind her and inched toward them.

"While you were away," she said, "one of the men outside of the city brought him here as a gift. A thank you of sorts for all that you did. He claims that Asen visited his black mare on more than one occasion, and having heard of Asen's death, he thought you might want his son. I couldn't very well say no. Do you like him?"

At a temporary loss for words, Kristofer nodded slowly.

"He is magnificent, my love."

CHAPTER 36

T he weeks passed peacefully. The castle was filled with laughter and excitement. The wedding plans were finalized, and Abignale arrived not only to bestow the blessing of marriage upon Kristofer and Aelia and Rian and Elora, but to sort through Kayne's contrivances. He worked from sunup to sundown, meeting them at the dining table once he completed his itinerary for the day.

The day of the wedding was finally upon them. Aelia and Elora stood in Aelia's chambers as Olibia and four handmaids added finishing touches to the gowns and their hair. Elora's nervousness came out in small gestures: a hand pressed against her stomach, smoothing the skirt of her dress, pacing, wringing her hands together.

Aelia finally took pity on her and grabbed her hands.

"Be still, Elora! You are making me nervous."

Elora smiled and took a seat as the door opened and Syeira stepped inside. With a huge smile, she sat down between Aelia and Elora, placing a hand on each of theirs.

"All is ready," Syeira said. "And Zemirah has traveled here to attend the wedding. She asked me to tell you that she sent her people home, and would join them soon after the ceremony."

"Wonderful!" Elora said.

She knew that Zemirah was eager to return to her country and rebuild. It was meaningful, and a gesture of everlasting friendship, that the woman stayed behind to offer her support.

Aelia smiled. She liked Zemirah.

She stood, brushing a strand of long hair off her shoulder. She had left it down, knowing Kristofer preferred her hair like that, and added a crown of white and yellow flowers she fashioned together herself. Both women wore white gowns. Aelia's fanned out slightly, hiding her thickening waist, while Elora's pleated down the length of her long legs. A golden crown was placed on Elora's head as she stood to follow Syeira and Aelia out of the room.

The ceremony was held in the gardens outside of the castle. More than half of the nation had journeyed South. People could be seen for miles in either direction outside of the castle walls. As the doors to the garden were opened by two guards who bowed, Aelia and Elora saw Kristofer and Rian waiting at the end of a path of petals. Each man saw only the woman he would marry.

Abignale stood, smiling in front of Rian and Kristofer, each of whom held their hands out. Aelia couldn't help but smile at Kristofer's grin.

As Abignale bestowed the marriage blessings upon them, Kristofer was certain that his life was finally complete. The ten years he spent serving Kayne were over. He had won, and he had Aelia at his side.

As Abignale finished bestowing the blessings, each man placed a jeweled bracelet on their wife's wrist. With the ceremony complete, they turned to face those before them: Ander and Syeira, Cas and Terric, Raum and Brilor. And in the back, sitting quietly, was Zemirah.

It was the beginning of a new world.

ABOUT THE AUTHOR

Dominique Churchill lives in a small Upstate New York town, with her two children. She has a Science degree, but her true passion has always been writing. An avid book lover, Dominique enjoys the calm and quiet of the country, where she can read and write peacefully.

When she was younger, Dominique lived in India for three years. She continues to enjoy traveling, camping and kayaking.

Connect with and follow Dominique:
Twitter: @DSChurchill4
Facebook: dom.churchill.5
Bookbub: bookbub.com/profile/2967683603